PRAISE FOR KENNEDY RYAN

"Ryan is a powerhouse of a writer."　　　　　　　*—USA Today*

"Ryan is a fantastic storyteller and superb writer."　　　—NPR

"Ryan creates characters who are deeply relatable, so compelling and lushly drawn that they feel like old friends."　　　　*—BookPage*

Before I Let Go

Book of the Month selection

NPR Best Books of the Year

Entertainment Weekly Best Romances of the Year

Washington Post 10 Best Romances of the Year

Women's Health Best Books of the Year

Publishers Weekly Best Romance Books of the Year

"Real. Raw. Magnificent!"
　　　　　　—Colleen Hoover, #1 *New York Times* bestselling author

"A knockout."　　　　　　　　*—Publishers Weekly*, starred review

"I am a sucker for high-stakes, once-in-a-lifetime soulmate love—and *Before I Let Go* hits every spot! Yasmen and Josiah's story is emotional, raw, real, *grown-up*, and it perfectly crystallizes the idea that real, lasting love is an imperfect journey of patience. Forgiveness. Healing. And, of course, wildly hot, steamy sex! Kennedy Ryan has gifted us with yet another addictively delicious read."
　　　　　　—Tia Williams, *New York Times* bestselling author

"Kennedy Ryan pours her whole soul into everything she writes, and it makes for books that are heart-searing, sensual, and life affirming. We are lucky to be living in a world where she writes."

—Emily Henry, #1 *New York Times* bestselling author

"Ryan always manages to ring her heavy stories with an aura of hope and a propulsive narrative that makes them impossible to put down. Grade: A."

—*Entertainment Weekly*

"Breathtaking, gut-wrenching, viscerally romantic. I want to curl up and live in this book."

—Talia Hibbert, *New York Times* bestselling author

"The most raw, poignant, and romantic journey of healing I've read in a long time. Kennedy Ryan has a fan for life."

—Ali Hazelwood, *New York Times* bestselling author

"A gorgeously poignant story of healing, family, and love. Kennedy Ryan is a true artist."

—Helen Hoang, *New York Times* bestselling author

THIS
COULD
BE US

Also by Kennedy Ryan

The Skyland Series

Before I Let Go

The Bennett Series

When You Are Mine
Loving You Always
Be Mine Forever
Until I'm Yours

All the King's Men Series

The Kingmaker
The Rebel King
Queen Move

The Hoops Series

Long Shot
Block Shot
Hook Shot

The Soul Series

My Soul to Keep
Down to My Soul
Refrain

The Grip Series

Flow
Grip
Still

Forbidden Hollywood

Reel

THIS COULD BE US

KENNEDY RYAN

FOREVER

New York   Boston

Copyright © 2024 by Kennedy Ryan
Reading group guide copyright © 2024 by Kennedy Ryan and Hachette Book Group, Inc.

Cover art by Natasha Cunningham. Cover copyright © 2024 by Hachette Book Group, Inc.

Forever
Hachette Book Group
1290 Avenue of the Americas, New York, NY 10104
read-forever.com
twitter.com/readforeverpub

First Edition: March 2024

Forever is an imprint of Grand Central Publishing. The Forever name and logo are trademarks of Hachette Book Group, Inc.

The publisher is not responsible for websites (or their content) that are not owned by the publisher.

Forever books may be purchased in bulk for business, educational, or promotional use. For information, please contact your local bookseller or the Hachette Book Group Special Markets Department at special.markets@hbgusa.com.

Library of Congress Cataloging-in-Publication Data
Names: Ryan, Kennedy, author.
Title: This could be us / Kennedy Ryan.
Description: First edition. | New York: Forever, 2024. | Series: Skyland
Identifiers: LCCN 2023046022 | ISBN 9781538706824 (trade paperback) |
    ISBN 9781538768785 | ISBN 9781538706848 (ebook)
Subjects: LCGFT: Romance fiction. | Novels.
Classification: LCC PS3618.Y33544 T55 2024 | DDC 813/.6—dc23/eng/20231003
LC record available at https://lccn.loc.gov/2023046022

ISBNs: 978-1-5387-0682-4 (trade paperback), 978-1-5387-0684-8 (ebook), 978-1-5387-6878-5 (Barnes & Noble special edition), 978-1-5387-6743-6 (library hardcover edition)

Printed in the United States of America

CW

10 9 8 7 6 5 4

*To those of us who never quite fit into the spaces
they made for us. May we find our people.
May we make our way. May we find our home.*

AUTHOR'S NOTE

There are parts of this story I've been writing for the last twenty years. More accurately, there are aspects of *This Could Be Us* I've been *living* for the last twenty years, since the day my son was diagnosed with autism. He is a mold-breaker. A one-of-a-kind supernova who manages to convey so much compassion and kindness and curiosity even without many words. He's a big guy, over six feet tall now, and everywhere he goes they call him "gentle giant." LOL. He doesn't talk much, but he *speaks*. His life speaks, and I wanted to depict a character navigating the world in my pages of fiction the way he does every day. When they call autism a spectrum, they ain't lying. It's everything from my son, who requires intense supervision and has very high support needs, to someone who may have a lot more independence and appear pretty typical from the outside. Those folks have unique challenges of their own. Both "ends" of the spectrum and everything in between deserve respect and dignity.

Can I be honest for a second? I can? Good. It took me a long time to write about autism because I was concerned that I would get things "wrong." I've written a lot of stories that weren't my lived experience, always with interviews and research and sensitivity readers. But this, my lived experience as a parent and someone who loves an autistic person, kinda intimidated me. The last thing I wanted to do was misrepresent or inadvertently harm the community that has embraced my family and my son so beautifully his entire life. But as I started thinking about Soledad's story and her passion for *her* children, I knew these two boys you are about to meet in *This Could Be Us* would play a pivotal role, so it was time.

For this story, I interviewed several autistic people and parents, hoping to capture a broad range of experiences. There's no way everyone will see themselves exactly as they are, but my hope is that many will feel resonance—will feel seen, cared for, respected, and hopeful.

Many things in the autism community become "hotly debated." Even how those on the spectrum should be addressed. Specifically, someone "having autism" versus "being autistic." I have chosen to use "autistic" for this story, and I respect those who choose otherwise. I also reference level 1 and level 3 as clinical classifications. There are some who don't embrace that language and some who do. I reference it in the story merely as part of their formal diagnoses. If you are autistic or a loved one of someone who is, we are all navigating the tough parts and, hopefully, celebrating the terrific moments when they come. However it looks for you, however you are managing, I extend you grace and wish you the very best.

I hope I've written the twin boys in this story with the same compassion I always want to see extended to my son. I hope you love them as I do.

As you begin this story, I want to mention that there is discussion of a parent's death, in the past, off the page, and of cancer. Please take care of yourself as you read.:-)

"There are years that ask questions and years that answer."
—Zora Neale Hurston,
Their Eyes Were Watching God

PROLOGUE

JUDAH

'm sure I loved her once.

And she loved me.

I remember the fluttery emotions early on, the quick-burn passion, the commitment that felt like it was anchored in cement. It became something that required little thought or feeling. What had once been a groove carved between our hearts settled with dismal comfort into a rut. Seated across from Tremaine now as we "mediate" the end of our marriage, looking into her eyes, I only see the remains of that love—mutual affection and respect.

We failed each other epically. Not through cruelty or infidelity, but through neglect. The idea we had of a love that would last forever, it's a casualty of hardship and indifference. This should hurt more. I should be more disappointed that my marriage is over, but instead there is a sense of relief that almost overwhelms me. A breath that has been lodged behind my ribs, maybe for years—I released it when Tremaine finally asked for the divorce. What should have felt like a slice through me instead felt like a sigh.

Yeah, this should hurt more, but it doesn't. So all I can think about now is the end and the new beginning, whatever that means for her, me, and our twin boys, Adam and Aaron.

"Custody," says Kimberly, the child specialist, glancing up from the small stack of papers on the coffee table in our living room. "We need to create the parenting plan."

"Right," Tremaine agrees, uncharacteristic uncertainty in her eyes. A small frown knits the smooth brown skin between her brows. Her hair, in two-strand twists, billows around her face like a weeping willow, softening the keen features. "I don't know how much they understand."

"Adam gets it," I say. "He's been asking about divorce nonstop. He told me today it derives from the Latin *divortere*, which means separation. He can't always wrap his emotions around things, so he leans more on facts."

"Wonder where he got that from?" Tremaine asks with a wry smile.

Tremaine used to joke that the diagnoses for our twin boys might not be autism. Maybe they're just *mine* because they share so many traits with me. I admit I may not have a formal diagnosis, but the more we've learned about autism over the last decade, the more of myself I've seen and understood.

"In my meeting with the boys," Kimberly continues, "it did seem that Adam grasped what was happening. Aaron...I'm not so sure."

Both boys are on the spectrum, but they present differently. Aaron doesn't have much expressive language and is classified as level 3, which simply indicates the intensity of support he needs. Many tend to underestimate him, to overlook him, because he doesn't often speak. Adam, classified as level 1, is less "observably" autistic than Aaron to others, so people often assume he needs less support than he actually does. Because he's so bright in the ways in which we often measure intelligence, people may offer him fewer accommodations or expect things he has trouble giving. Some people still speak in terms of more or less severe, but it's all autism. Just different needs that evolve, and we meet them as best we can.

We don't compare Aaron and Adam, but try to meet each of them where he is with whatever he needs. They started at basically the same place, but along the way their paths diverged—Adam making more gains faster and Aaron lagging behind, still gaining, but less and more slowly.

"Aaron may not talk a lot," I say. "But his receptive language—what he understands—is much higher."

"Most of the time he just doesn't care to let you know he understands what you're saying." A smile dents dimples in Tremaine's cheeks. "That boy. There's a whole world in his head he keeps to himself."

"I did sense that," Kimberly says. "Regardless of how much they understand, this is a huge transition. It would be for most, but especially for kids who need routine and predictability as much as Aaron and Adam do, for kids with autism."

She pauses, looking between us.

"I'm sorry," she says. "I should have checked. Do the boys like to be referred to as 'autistic' or 'with autism' or..."

"'Autistic' is fine," Tremaine replies. "We appreciate you asking."

"Just wanted to make sure. Different families prefer different things." Kimberly closes the file on the coffee table. "We'll have to handle this transition with care."

"Tremaine and I want to do anything we can to ease their way," I offer.

"That's what this whole process is for, right?" Tremaine sends me a quick look, as if to confirm we are on the same page. I nod and reach over to squeeze her hand where it is clenched on her knee.

We've both made sacrifices, each of us working from home or not at all early on when the boys kept getting kicked out of daycare centers or we had to assume their education ourselves. Adam, so bright he eventually placed in gifted classes, struggled with potty training even at seven years old. He has poor interoception—meaning his body can't always sense what's happening inside it. He had trouble telling when he needed to go, and by the time he realized how close he was, it would be too late. Interoception is a complex concept even for some adults to grasp, and kids definitely didn't understand. They teased him badly. Adam felt so much shame when he had accidents at school and begged us to let him learn from home. Tremaine delayed law school and worked at night, staying home with the boys during the day, while

I took the evenings. One year I freelanced, pursuing forensic accounting cases that allowed me to work remotely, squeezing in the boys' lessons while Tremaine busted her ass at the firm.

"We've decided the boys will stay here with Tremaine during the week and me on the weekends," I say.

"Yeah," Tremaine weighs in. "Them being in one place all week is more stabilizing for their schedule at school."

"We'll split the commute, doctor appointments, therapy, et cetera as evenly as possible," I say. "But they'll spend most of their time here in the house, where they feel most comfortable."

"Have you told the boys yet?" Kimberly asks.

"Not yet. We wanted to see what you thought first," Tremaine says. "Aaron responds better to visual aids, so we'll create a schedule for when they'll be with each of us to help him understand."

"Sounds like a great plan." Kimberly claps once. "No time like the present. Why don't we call them downstairs and see what the boys think?"

Tremaine stands and crosses over to the stairs. Even at home wearing casual clothes, she's elegant and commanding, like she could persuade any jury or judge. "I'll go get them."

Ours is what they call a "collaborative divorce." It's as amicable as you'd expect when two people who respect each other deeply, and used to be in love, agree their kids are the only things they still have in common.

"I'm glad we have you," I tell Kimberly. "And thanks for coming to us."

Kimberly typically meets clients in her office, but she made an exception tonight considering Adam's been having a rough time lately. Just when we think we've found a solution to reduce the seizures associated with his tuberous sclerosis, they come back with force.

"No problem." She reaches for the glass of water on the coffee table and takes a quick sip. "We love seeing parents put their kids first in situations like this."

The boys come bounding down the stairs. They're identical and so different. Both have my eyes and facial shape, but their smile is all Tremaine. Their hair is a little coarser than mine. Their skin a little lighter. Adam glances from Kimberly to me, his expression curious. Aaron doesn't look at anyone but sits down on the couch, an assistive communication device cradled in his lap. It took us a long time to get him using it, but now he carries it everywhere. Severe apraxia limits the words he can *speak*, but the device with its images and voice approximations exponentially increases what he can *say*.

"Boys," Kimberly starts, looking between Aaron and Adam, "remember what we talked about last time? That you'll have two houses soon? And your mom will live in one, and your dad will live in the other?"

"Divorce from *divortere*," Adam says immediately. "*Di* means apart and *verte* means different ways. Mom and Dad are going different ways."

"That's right," I say carefully. "You'll stay in this house with your mom. My house will still be here in Skyland. Just a few blocks away. You'll be there on weekends, but I'll see you during the week too."

"Do you understand what we're saying, Aaron?" Tremaine asks, her brows furrowing.

He doesn't respond but starts scrolling through images and picture cards we've collected and loaded into his device over the years.

"It may take a little more time," Kimberly offers, watching Aaron work with his device. "He may not—"

She stops midsentence when Aaron wordlessly sets the communication device in her lap. She glances down, a frown forming on her face. "I'm not sure…"

"Let me see." I extend my hand to accept the device and glance at what he pulled up to show her.

It's a candid shot Tremaine took of us a few years ago. Both boys have often had trouble sleeping. During one of Aaron's big growth spurts, he barely seemed to sleep at all. Sometimes I'd read to him, hoping it would help when the melatonin didn't. In this photo, I had fallen asleep right there with him, *Goodnight Moon* open on the bed between us.

I look up now to find him watching me intently. Eye contact can be difficult for both boys. They often gather information through quick, flitting glances and through other senses—exploring the world more deeply with touch and sound and taste. Sometimes they connect by simply sitting close or even holding my hand. But right now, Aaron's holding my *stare*. His eyes bore into mine, conveying a silent message I pray I'll understand. It's a window opening into his mind, a world I don't always have easy access to.

"Son, I don't..." I falter, not wanting to admit I don't understand what he's telling me. When he tries like this, I don't want to let him down. I wish like hell I knew exactly what he's trying to say. Does he want to make sure I'll still read to him once I move out?

He takes the tablet, fingers flying across the surface, pulling a few words into a short sentence. His reading skills are almost as limited as his speech. Something about words on the page never seems to click for him. Reading has been like the tide, coming, then receding. Progressing, then regressing. He'll gain words and then they'll slip from his mind before he can truly own them, but simple phrases he can manage. He hits three buttons, and a digitized voice emerges from the device's speakers.

"Stay. With. Me."

He doesn't have the filter most would by twelve years old, the one where he feels awkward voicing his preference for one parent over the other. That is one of the blessings with this kid. You get what you get. There is no guile, no deception, no dissembling.

He wants to stay with me, or rather he wants me to stay *here*.

Somewhere along the way, Tremaine and I became co-caregivers, glorified roommates and even the best of friends. We may not have passion anymore, but we have that bond, and we know each other too well. I hazard a glance at my soon-to-be ex-wife. She's a magnificent mother, a warrior or a nurturer as needed. To hear Aaron express a preference for me to stay here could hurt. She meets my eyes squarely, a half smile quirking one corner of her mouth even as she blinks back tears.

"We should have seen this coming," she says with a shrug and a swift swipe under her eyes. "You're his person, Judah. If he has you and Adam, the world falls into place. I know he loves me. Don't worry. We'll just flip it. Five days with you. Two days with me. You stay here and I'll take the new house. That will be the easier transition for him. And we know Adam wants to be wherever Aaron is."

"Are you sure?" I ask, still concerned that this stings more than she's revealing.

"Are *you* sure?" Tremaine chuckles. "You know we'll split all the responsibilities as evenly as possible. I'll see them every day, but they'll spend most of the time under your roof."

Aaron spoke. Every word out of that kid is like gold to me, even when it comes from a voice box. There's nothing I won't do to make this transition better for our boys.

"Yeah." I nod, unable to look away from Aaron and Adam, my heart split into two identical parts. "I'm sure."

PART I

"The longer I live, the more deeply I learn that love—whether we call it friendship or family or romance—is the work of mirroring and magnifying each other's light."

—James Baldwin, *Nothing Personal*

CHAPTER ONE

SOLEDAD

Three Years Later

T onight is really important, Sol."

I glance up from my jewelry tray to stare at my husband's back as he strides into our walk-in closet.

"It's a company Christmas party," I reply dryly. "Not a board meeting."

"May as well be," Edward mutters, knotting the tie his mother gave him last Christmas.

God, I hate that tie. It's plagued with red oversized polka dots that closely resemble drops of blood.

"Delores Callahan will be there," he continues, a warning in the tone and the look he aims over his shoulder at me. "Let's not have a repeat of last time."

"The woman asked." I grimace, remembering the last conversation I had with the daughter of CalPot's CEO.

"Pretty sure she didn't expect a Yelp review of our own product. Much less a scathing one."

"It was not scathing." I cross our bedroom to join him in the closet and flip through his ties, which I've organized by color. "It was honest. I told her the new pan only accommodates three average-size chicken breasts, and I'd love it even more if I could cook four at a time."

"And the heat thing?" Irritation pinches the corners of his green eyes.

I shrug, plucking an embroidered Armani tie from the red section.

"Well, it *doesn't* heat evenly. I practically have to turn the thing every few minutes just to get the meat cooked all the way through. They're one of the biggest cookware companies around. Aren't pans kinda supposed to be their thing?"

"Just saying I already have Cross up my ass. I don't need Delores Callahan after me too."

"Cross is the new accountant?"

"Director of accounting, yeah."

I stand in front of him and brush his fingers aside, tugging the awful tie loose and tossing it to the floor. "Not this tie, babe. Trust me."

"If you say so."

"I do say so." I knot the preferred tie. "Besides, this one matches the red dress *you* asked me to wear tonight."

"I love that dress on you."

"I like the gold better."

"The gold shows too much. It's a Christmas party, not a strip show. I'm not giving Cross room to criticize *anything* tonight. I don't want to draw attention to us. I'm telling you, Sol. That guy has been after me ever since the day he showed up at CalPot."

"Hasn't he only been there six months? Maybe he's still settling in."

"It's been a year." Edward scowls. "A year of him watching me like a hawk and sniffing around my department all the time."

"Let him look. You don't have anything to hide."

The expression that crosses Edward's face is not so much a frown as a . . . twitch. Some tiny disruption in the symmetry of his handsome features, gone almost before it could be detected. Except we've been married sixteen years, together for eighteen. I make it my business to detect everything concerning my husband and our three girls. I practically know when this man loses an eyelash, I'm so attuned to his moods and emotions. Or at least I usually am. Lately he's been harder to decipher and predict.

"Yeah, well," he says. "I don't need some geeky bean counter riding me."

I rise up on my toes to press my lips to his ear.

"I've got an idea." I grab the hand hanging limply at his side and place it on the naked curve of my butt in the skimpy thong I hoped he would have noticed by now. "Instead of thinking so much about Cross riding you, think about how *I'll* ride you when we get home."

He swallows, and that twitch happens again. Here and gone like a tumbleweed blowing across his face before I can catch it. He drops his hand from me and walks deeper into our closet, approaching his shelves of custom-made shoes.

"Damn, Sol," he says, his tone cool. "I tell you I'm stressed at work, and you go straight to sex."

I stiffen and force myself to reply evenly. "I didn't mean to offend your delicate sensibilities, but when you haven't fucked your wife in nearly two months, she tends to bring it up every once in a while."

"It hasn't been two months."

"It has."

"If you're that horny," he says, turning to glower at me, "you have a battery-operated solution in your bedside table."

"Oh, believe me, it's been earning its keep." I practically stomp over to my side of the closet. "And if you thought you'd make me feel ashamed with that snide comment, sorry to disappoint you. I have needs, and I'm not embarrassed by how I meet them when *you* won't."

Something has fundamentally shifted in our marriage the last two years. Every couple experiences slumps, ruts. We are no exception, but it's more than that. I've felt Edward slipping away from this marriage, from this family. I've tried everything to stop it, but my arms feel emptier, our bed feels colder, every day. I can't hold off a landslide by myself, and lately Edward seems content to watch it all fall down.

I turn away from the row of designer dresses to find his hard stare. "I love sex, Edward. I always have. You used to like it too."

"Can we not do this right now?" His words are graveled with irritation. "I have enough on my plate without having to think about satisfying my sex-starved wife."

"That's unfair. Why are you trying to make me feel bad for wanting to save our sex life? To revive this marriage? I understand if—"

"You don't understand a damn thing."

"I understand if," I resume, carefully laying out my next words, "you're having trouble in that area. Sometimes as men age—"

"I'm forty, Sol," he fires back. "Not eighty. You ever think maybe the problem isn't with me, but with you?"

"What do you mean?"

"Women's bodies change."

"I'm in the best shape of my life." I hear the note of defensiveness creeping into my voice and start again. "I do yoga and Pilates a few times a week. If anything, I'm trying *not* to lose this."

I grab my generous ass. A gift from my *abuela*, it ain't going anywhere anytime soon. It is time-tested and exercise-resistant, and I like it that way.

"I don't mean the outside." He reaches for his suit jacket. "You *have* pushed out three kids. Things get loose down there. What's that thing women do to tighten up? Vaginal rejuvenation or whatever? Maybe that's where you start reviving our sex life."

It's a sucker punch that knocks the breath out of me. I go still, my hand hovering over the red dress. I can't believe he said that, and with such deliberate aim.

"*Your* three kids," I reply, making sure the wobble I feel inside doesn't make my voice waver. "I pushed out *your* three daughters. They literally had to stitch my vagina back together after the last one. Until you've known the pain of a third-degree tear, don't complain to me about my loose pussy. Go to this party by your damn self."

I stride out of the closet and into the bedroom, snatching my robe from the bench at the foot of our bed. Slipping my arms through the sleeves, I sit, bracing my hands on the bench to hide their shaking.

When did Edward turn cruel? He wasn't always like this. Maybe I was so fooled by his brightness, by the beauty of him, that I overlooked this ugly underside. He was ambitious, yes, and sometimes careless, but something is rotting inside him now. It's only lately I've smelled the stench.

He walks back into the bedroom in bare feet and with measured steps. The look he angles at me from under his brows is careful, calculating. I know this man. He needs me on his arm tonight at this party and is wondering what he should say to get me there.

He squats in front of me, taking my hands in his. "Look, I shouldn't have said—"

"No, but you did." I hold his gaze, not softening mine even though he *appears* contrite.

"I'm sorry," he says. "You know I've been under so much pressure at the office—"

"That can't be your excuse for everything, Edward. For being home less with me and the girls. For working all the time. For saying your assistant's name in your sleep."

His head snaps up. "I explained about that. Nothing's going on between Amber and me. We've been working so hard on these projects that I—"

"Dream about her?" I cock my head to the side, snatching my hands away from him to fold my arms across my chest.

"No, I . . ." He shakes his head, his contrition and patience wearing thin. "We don't have time to rehash this. Not right now. It only happened a couple of times. God, are you holding me responsible for my subconscious? I told you it was nothing. Can we just go?"

He reaches for my hands again, looking at me with pleading eyes.

"Sol, baby, I need you."

I stand, glaring down at him, still not ready to release my indignation. "Then act like it."

I leave him there and head back into the closet, flick through the clothes until I find what I'm looking for. The one-shouldered gold dress I wanted to wear shimmers among the blacks, grays, and other more muted colors. I've never worn it, but I remember how it cuts low over my breasts and rides high up my legs. Letting the robe fall to the floor,

I wrench the dress from the hanger and yank it over my head, showing little consideration for the delicate material.

"I thought we agreed on the red," Edward says with a frown.

"You like the red dress so much?" I shove my feet into the five-inch stilettos I coveted online for months before breaking down and buying. "You wear it."

I leave the room in a flounce of gold and fury, taking the stairs at a breakneck pace, slowing when I realize I could literally break my neck in these heels.

"Wow, Mom." My daughter Lupe whistles from the bottom of the stairs. "You look great."

"Thank you, honey." I pause to kiss her cheek. At fifteen, she already stands a few inches above me, but the heels give me a slight advantage. "I have a feeling I'll regret these shoes, though."

"There's still time to change."

"And waste all this glam?" I kick up one heel and force myself to smile even though I'm still seething from the confrontation with Edward. "No way. Looking this good might be worth losing my pinkie toe at the end of the night. Beauty is pain sometimes."

"I'll remember that for prom."

My smile drops and I slap my forehead. "Ugh. Can we not talk about prom right now? I'm not ready."

"You've got plenty of time to adjust. Maybe no one will ask me."

My daughter is so pretty she gets stopped on the street by modeling scouts. We both know someone will muster the courage to ask her, but I'm not ready for her to grow up. Next will be college, and I'll probably have to get several cats and a dog to survive that.

"Make sure your sisters do their homework," I say, diverting the conversation. I was already furious. Why add melancholy to the emotional mix before we even arrive at this party?

The thud of Edward's footsteps descending the stairs revives my anger, slipping a rod down my back. When his hand curls around my hip, I barely resist the urge to slap it away.

"We'll be home late, baby girl," he tells Lupe. "Call if you need anything."

"Okay, Daddy." She flicks a look between us, a slight frown knitting her brows.

My three girls are my greatest joy. Lupe looks the least like me with the red hair she inherited from my father, Edward's green eyes, and her own pale-gold skin, but her temperament is the most like mine. Overachieving. Naturally nurturing and deeply intuitive. If there's a ripple in the water, she feels it. A tsunami is happening between her parents, and I think she senses the tension in me. With a conscious effort to relax my muscles, I pull away from Edward and head for the garage.

"Love you, Lupe," I call over my shoulder, not waiting to see if Edward follows. "Watch your sisters, and don't wait up."

The thirty-minute drive to Brett Callahan's house is quiet and frosted with tension. Neither of us breaks the brittle silence. The first time we attended one of these holiday parties at the CEO's sprawling mansion a few years ago, Edward had just started at CalPot. We barely concealed our awe, elbowing each other and trying not to gape at the ostentatious surroundings.

"I'll get us one of these someday, Sol," he vowed, eyeing the high ceilings and priceless art decorating the walls.

I laughed it off because, though we live a comfortable life, in many ways a privileged life in Skyland, one of Atlanta's most desirable in-town communities, we'll probably never have a place like that. Brett Callahan's palatial home is practically an estate north of Atlanta. I always find myself squirming when we come this far north of the city, places that less than half a century ago didn't welcome people who looked like me.

I pull down the visor to check my makeup. My skin glows cinnamon gold in the mirror light, which emphasizes subtle hollows under my cheekbones, my glossed lips, my favorite set of false lashes, and the hair, pressed tonight from its usual springy curls into a silky fall around my shoulders.

Edward shows his license to the security officer at the gate and passes

through. He pushes out a long breath when we pull into the large cir-
cular driveway.

"I can't believe you wore that dress." He frowns over at me in the
passenger seat, the length of my leg exposed by the high slit.

"There's nothing wrong with it." I smooth the silky material over
my knees. "I don't understand why you're so uptight about tonight and
this Cross guy."

"I know it doesn't make sense." Edward reaches across to grab my
hand and turns to me as the valet hired for the night approaches. "But
trust me when I say Cross is not our friend. Just stay off his radar. Can
you do that for me, Sol?"

He strokes the back of my hand, and my heart softens a little at
the first sign of tenderness he's shown me in days. Maybe I am under-
estimating the pressure he's under. This Cross guy must be a real ogre
to get my usually unflappable husband this flustered.

"I said I can. I will." I squeeze his hand, catching his stare and smiling. "And I promise not to tell Delores Callahan her nonstick coating
starts flaking after only a few uses."

He huffs a short laugh, shakes his head, and opens the door to hand
over the keys.

Once inside, I note the few changes they've made to the decor since
I was here for last year's party. A new crystal light fixture. Slightly more
garish wallpaper in the foyer. New window treatments? I can't remember if they were this tacky before. To have all this money and so little
taste. Tragic, really.

"Edward, good to see you." Delores Callahan greets us before we
can join the party in the large room where everyone is mingling. Her
dark hair is tightly curled tonight, and she seems not quite at home in
a floral dress, her wonderful wide shoulders and forceful personality
pushing against the seams and straining the collar.

"Delores," Edward says, his smile stiff and his hand slightly tightening on my elbow. "Haven't seen you since the sales meeting weeks ago.
We've missed you around the office."

"Been up in Canada," Delores responds, her eyes gleaming with sharp intelligence as she watches my husband. "They're really buzzing up there about your White Glove program. Several of our customers say they hear great things and want in. Can't believe we didn't think of something like this before."

"You know me." Edward practically preens. "Always looking for ways to innovate."

I barely catch my eye roll and keep my smile fixed in place.

"Who'd have thought someone would pay that much just to feel like they're getting the VIP treatment?" Delores shakes her head, the grudging admiration clear on her face. "And the retreats? Stroke of genius."

I was skeptical when Edward first introduced the White Glove program for CalPot customers who purchased the most product and spent above a certain threshold. They would get special agents assigned to their accounts who were always available for questions and concerns, as well as expedited delivery and even retreats as a thank-you for their continued business. Seemed like a possible waste of money to me, but I was wrong. The program has thrived, and it earned Edward a huge bonus last year.

It's also why he says he and Amber have had to work so hard and so closely together.

"We're doing Cabo next," Edward says, reeling me back to their conversation. "That is, if Cross gets off my back."

"He's just doing his job," Delores says. "We're lucky to have him. Best at what he does."

"Which is what?" I ask, ignoring the quelling look Edward shoots me.

"Forensic accounting. Not exactly what we hired him for, but that's his background," Delores answers, casting a narrow-eyed glance at me. Not unfriendly, but like she's trying to remember something. "You're the wife, right?"

"Yes." I flash a saccharine-sweet smile and lean into Edward. "I also answer to my given name, which is Soledad."

Edward coughs and tugs my hand. "We better be getting into the party."

"Chicken breasts." Delores snaps her fingers and points to me. "You wanted a bigger pan."

I search for an answer that won't put Edward in an awkward position or upset him. "Well, I—"

"Our test group agreed," she says.

My half-formed apology dies. "They did?"

"They did." She nods, approximating a smile. "I kept thinking about that one lonely chicken breast sitting off to the side waiting because our pan was too small."

I flick a sidelong glance up at her, surprised to see the corner of her mouth twitching. I smother a giggle. "Oh, my gosh. That's hilarious. Are you serious?"

"Absolutely." She lifts borderline bushy brows that I'm itching to tweeze. "Well, not the part about the lonely chicken breast, but I did ask our designers about it. They polled a group of consumers who overwhelmingly agreed with you."

"Of course they did," Edward interjects, slipping an arm around my shoulder. "Sol's full of great ideas. I'm always telling her she should speak up more often."

I suppress a retort at his blatant lie and accompany him and Delores into the large room of tables loaded with food. The tantalizing scents draw a growl from my empty stomach even though, if tradition holds, the food won't be as good as it smells. We take our place in line for the buffet, and Edward touches my elbow to get my attention.

"Hey," he leans down to whisper. "I see Amber. I need to ask her something."

My body involuntarily tenses at the woman's name. He must feel my muscles turn rigid beneath his palm because he gives my arm a reassuring squeeze.

"I won't be long, but there was something we were closing right before I left the office. There's no room for error."

"Of course," I say stiffly, selecting a plate from the stack of china at the end of the table.

"Be right back."

He walks away, heading straight for the woman smiling at him from across the room. I've seen her name flash up on his phone and have even caught a glimpse of her young, pretty face and silvery blond hair on-screen during video conference calls, but this is the first time we've been in the same room. She oozes sensuality in the dress seemingly shellacked to her lithe figure. Judging by the appreciative smile on Edward's face, he's not concerned with *her* dress being too revealing or drawing undue attention. They leave the room, heads bent together conspiratorially. Holding my empty plate, I push down the persistent sense of unease.

"Are you in line?"

A woman I recognize as the wife of one of the department heads stands behind me, sliding an impatient look from the stack of plates to my immovable self.

"Oh, sorry!" I let her pass me in line for the buffet. As awful as the food usually tastes at these Christmas parties, I bet she won't be eager for long.

I'm scooping up green beans that look about as stiff and unseasoned as starched flannel when a movement at the door distracts me. A tall man stands a few feet away, filling the doorframe. He's handsome, with skin the color of burnt umber stretched over features constructed of steel and stone, but that's not what is so arresting. He's not *that* tall. Maybe an inch over six feet. He'd tower over my five four, but it's not his height that sets him apart either. It's the contrast between the utter stillness of his athletic frame and the energy he emits in waves, like there's a million thoughts swirling behind those dark eyes. There's something imposing about the set of his shoulders, the proud angle of his head, that gives the impression of looking down. Not exactly arrogantly, but literally looking down, like he watches from an aerial shot and is analyzing everyone and everything in minute detail. Those assessing eyes gleam beneath a bridge of a brow, the dark line dipped into a slight frown.

He stands there, seemingly at ease, with his hands thrust into the pockets of well-tailored pants. His gaze passes slowly over the occupants of the room, never pausing too long on any one thing or person. How would it feel to hold his full attention? To be the object of that stare, a gaze so sharp it could pin you to the wall? It's as if he's searching for someone he hasn't found. His survey reaches the buffet table, passing indifferently over us, but then swings back.

To me.

I wondered how it would feel to hold his full attention, and it's nothing like I thought. There's nothing cold about his intent stare. It heats with interest. I assumed you'd feel like an insect trapped beneath the cold glass of a microscope. Instead, my breath catches when he tilts his head and narrows his gaze on me, like I'm a particularly fascinating butterfly whose every detail he should take in before it flits away. I realize our eyes have been locked for seconds and look down, breathing easily for the first time since he entered the room. Trying to ignore the unreasonably frantic pounding of my heart, I reach for the serving fork and pierce an anemic drumstick.

"The chicken looks dry," a man remarks beside me.

I startle, trying not to gape at the guy who moved from the door to my side so fast.

"Oh, yeah." I drop my eyes to the unsavory meat on my plate and clear my throat. "Not too, um, appetizing."

I shuffle forward, training my stare on the back of the woman who was so eager to get to this bland food.

"I don't have room to talk," he continues, his voice washing over my shoulders and neck, the deep rumble raising long-forgotten goose bumps. "I'm not a chef myself, but I'm not catering this event, so I don't have to be."

"True." I release a laugh, not looking back even though I can *feel* his stare burning between my shoulder blades.

"Maybe it's better than it looks," he says, the faint sounds of him serving himself reaching me from behind.

"It's not." I even my voice out, irritated that I'm so disconcerted by a man doing nothing more than getting his food in the buffet line. "Pretty sure a Callahan cousin caters this party every year, so you'll soon be enjoying the sweet taste of nepotism."

"Explains a lot. You cook?"

"Uh, yeah."

"You any good at it?" he asks, amusement threading the question.

I pause and glance over my shoulder, allowing a small grin. "I'm actually really good at it."

"A confident woman." His smile melts at the corners as our eyes hold. "I like it."

I hastily turn back around and move forward with the line, scooping a lumpy mound of potatoes onto my plate.

"What's your favorite dish to make?" he asks.

I smile but don't risk facing him again. "*Carne guisada.*"

"Come again? I don't know what that is. *Carne* sounds like steak or beef."

"It is. It's a beef stew we make in Puerto Rico."

"You're from Puerto Rico?"

"I wasn't born there," I admit, "but my grandmother lived there, and we'd visit her during the summers. She taught me how to cook many things, but *carne guisada* is my favorite. It's the best comfort food. I make it for my family all the time."

The word "family" lands in the air, weighing it down a moment before he speaks. "What division do you work in? I've only been here a year, but I would have remembered seeing you."

At that I look over my shoulder and our glances tangle. My breath hovers between my lungs and my lips, trapped in my chest as he waits for my answer.

"I don't work here." I lick my lips and lower my eyes but force myself to look back up. "My husband does."

His expression turns inscrutable, but something, a distant cousin to disappointment, rises in his eyes before he crushes it.

"Your husband." He nods and turns his attention to the buffet, eschewing the green beans but transferring a conservative dollop of potatoes to his plate. "Lucky man."

I manage a wan smile and face forward, knowing it's best we end the conversation there but hating to leave. It's not just sex Edward has been stingy with lately. It's attention. Conversation. Interest. All the things I found unexpectedly in a few moments with a stranger, and it feels like the sun on my face after winter. So hard to turn away from that warmth when you've stood out in the cold.

The touch at my elbow makes me jump and almost drop my plate.

"Whoa," Edward says, chuckling and reaching to steady my hand. "You okay?"

"Yes, of course." I smile up at him and force my eyes not to stray to the quiet man behind him. My tiny prickle of guilt is unfounded, unreasonable.

"Great." Edward plucks a cherry tomato from the salad I don't even recall putting on my plate. "Sorry about that. Amber was working on something before we left the office and needed to update me."

"Sure," I answer absently, unable to even arouse my suspicion about Edward's assistant after the impact of my brief interaction with the stranger. "You getting a plate?"

"Yeah, I'll grab one." He turns, stopping and saying a little too loudly, "Cross, didn't notice you there."

I spin around, my wide stare pinging between my husband and the man he's complained about so much.

"*You're* Cross?" I blurt. "The geek?"

Horror creeps into the vat of silence following my words as I realize just how badly I've stepped in it.

"I mean..." I tighten my fingers around the edge of my plate and gulp. "I'm sorry. I didn't—"

"No need to apologize," Cross says, addressing my comment but never looking away from Edward. "I see my reputation has preceded me."

The two men stare at one another, hostility crackling in the air, though both their faces remain impassive. They couldn't be more different. My husband with his winter pallor, skin pale and lightly freckled. His wavy dark blond hair cut close and parted on the side. Edward has always been a charismatic charmer who draws people effortlessly. Cross, a few inches taller, broader, somehow projects a guardedness that makes him seem unapproachable, only that wasn't how I felt a few moments ago, before he knew who I was. Whom I was married to. A muscle twitches in the unyielding line of his jaw, and his eyes crinkle at the corners with an approximation of indolent amusement that doesn't match the flatness of his stare.

"My wife," Edward murmurs smoothly, placing his hand at my back and gently guiding me a little closer. "Soledad."

There is no thaw in the cold eyes that flick between my husband and me. "Nice to meet you, Mrs. Barnes," he says, the formality such a contrast to the easy warmth between us before.

"Nice to meet you too, Mr. Cross." I glance up to meet his eyes briefly.

"Judah," he replies, his gaze softening a fraction.

"I'm sorry," I say. "What?"

"My name is Judah. Judah Cross."

I offer a smile that feels like wax hardening on my face. "I've heard a lot about . . ." I let the words peter out because he probably knows that everything I've heard about him from Edward has been an insult.

"Let's go sit down," Edward says, clamping his fingers around my wrist, probably harder than he realizes because it makes me wince. I bite back a gasp but send a glare from his fingers tightened painfully around me up to his face. His hand falls away, and he rubs the sore spot on my wrist. "Sorry, babe, but we need to find our seats and eat. I'm starving."

He guides us forward. I don't look back, but I am supremely

conscious of Cross...Judah...behind us. Before Edward has even finished loading his plate, I break away and stride swiftly toward the tables across the room, sit down without checking the place cards to see if it's the right spot. Even conscious of Edward's coworkers around us, I can't wipe the scowl from my face.

"What's your problem?" Edward mutters in a low voice for my ears only, smiling at a coworker across the table. "You're the one who made me look like a fool in front of the very man I told you has been on my case. I should be the angry one."

"You left me alone to skulk off with Amber," I say hotly, stabbing the drumstick with a fork.

"I did not skulk off. I told you exactly where I was going and that I had something I had to address with my assistant. Judging by the way I saw Cross looking at you, I should be the one who's suspicious."

My hand freezes, suspending the fork between my plate and my mouth. "What do you mean?"

"He couldn't take his eyes off your ass." Edward smirks. "Didn't know he had it in him. He's always such a cold fish."

The way his eyes held mine. The warm smile that slipped behind a cloud when Edward came. Judah hadn't seemed cold to me. Focused. Intent. Imperturbable. Yes.

But cold?

When I recall the few moments we shared in the buffet line, my cheeks heat, but I shiver.

"It's that skimpy dress," Edward says around a mouthful of green beans.

"What?" I force myself to focus on his words.

"If you had worn the red dress I liked, you wouldn't be cold now."

Glancing down at my bare arm, I see the telltale goose bumps and clear my throat. "I'm not cold."

"Well, I'm not gonna complain, because of the way Cross was looking at you in that dress." He chuckles and reaches for a glass of wine from the table. "And then to realize you're *my* wife. Priceless."

The self-satisfied expression on his face steals what little is left of my appetite. I push my plate away and stand. He stares up at me, an unspoken question on his face.

"Bathroom." I toss the linen napkin over my barely touched plate of tasteless food. "I'll be right back."

I leave the room, relief slumping my shoulders as soon as I'm out of view. A long hall stretches before me, which, if I remember correctly, leads to a powder room. Once inside, I stare at my reflection.

The way Cross was looking at you.

Edward's words ring in my head. What did Judah see when he looked at me? I assess the woman in the mirror, turning this way and that to view myself in the gold dress from every angle. Not bad for a mother of three.

Rejuvenation, my ass.

Even though I see Edward's hurtful comment for what it is, a tiny sliver of doubt pricks my heart. I've spent my whole adult life with one man. Slept with one man for nearly two decades. He wasn't my first, but he's been my last, and I've been his. And now I have to *beg* him to fuck me?

Would anyone else even want me? Maybe I'm... maybe I'm not...

I draw in a marshaling breath and fluff the hair around my shoulders. I will have my midlife breakdown just like every other self-respecting woman in Skyland—in the privacy of my home, with a good wine to drown my doubts, without fear of public humiliation.

I leave the bathroom and stand still in the hall, dreading returning to the table and to the fake smiles and sharp asides Edward and I have been exchanging all night. Hell, all week. A giggle somewhere close echoes in the hall. Curious, I follow the sound, cautiously poking my head around the corner. Amber stands in an alcove, almost hidden. A man with dark hair has his arms wrapped around her, one hand on her ass. She giggles up at him but catches sight of me over his shoulder.

"Mrs. Barnes!" she squeaks, jumping guiltily away from the man.

"Sorry." I raise my hands as if in self-defense. "I was looking for the powder room and started wandering."

"Yeah. Of—of course," she stutters, her eyes zipping from me to the guy. "This is my...cousin Gerald."

Cousin? What, in the backwoods? With that hand on her ass? I'd hate to see *that* family reunion. Incest much?

He turns to face me, a phony smile pasted on his face.

"Gerald works in IT," Amber rushes on. "Right, Gerald?"

Gerald nods. "Right."

"Oh, that's great," I murmur. "Well, it was nice finally meeting you, Amber. Edward says you're invaluable."

"Thank you." Her eyes flick away from me and then back. "He's a great boss."

"Well, I'll let you get back to..." Get back to what? Groping your relative? "I better get back. See you later."

I think I'm as happy to get away from them as they are for me to leave. I've put it off as long as I can. If I don't get back soon, Edward will come searching for me. Each step down the corridor becomes more agonizing, a sharp pain assaulting my pinkie toe and heel.

"I knew these shoes would be the death of me," I mutter, reaching down to take off one stiletto and then the other. I hook the heels over my hand, even if for just a few steps before I have to put them back on. "Beauty is not worth this much pain. I'd kill for an orthopedic shoe right about now."

I'm stepping cautiously with my bare feet on the slick marble floor when a sound from a room up ahead stops me.

Clack clack clack.

I approach, pausing before the ajar door and peeking in to find a library. Books line the shelves, and the smell of expensive cigars mingles with that of the lemon polish that must be making the hardwood gleam beneath a patterned Persian rug.

A boy, maybe fourteen or fifteen years old, sits in one of two armchairs flanking a table holding a lamp and four Rubik's Cubes. Wearing headphones, he holds another cube, seemingly oblivious to my presence. I'm about to leave when he glances up, meeting my eyes for the briefest moment before looking away, fingers flying. I freeze, unsure why that stare, as brief as it was, felt familiar. He pauses long enough to slide one of the cubes forward on the table before resuming the swift motions of his hands. I'm not sure, but I believe that was an invitation.

I step farther into the room, crossing over to take the other seat and pick up the cube he offered. Edward's left me waiting enough lately. He'll be fine for a few more minutes on his own or with his pretty assistant to keep him company.

"It's been a long time since I did one of these," I say, laughing a little as I settle in and tentatively turn the bottom row. "What's your name?"

It's silent in the room for a few moments, and I start to think he won't answer, that he can't hear me with the headphones on, but then he replies, "Aaron."

"Hi, Aaron. I'm Soledad." I cross my bare feet at the ankles and turn the cube a few more times, dismayed when after several minutes I'm nowhere close to getting a side all one color. Meanwhile, Aaron places a finished cube down and picks up another without missing a beat.

"Wow," I say, thoroughly impressed. "You're really good at this."

He doesn't thank me or acknowledge the compliment, but keeps turning, twisting, lining up blocks into solid walls of color. It might appear odd to someone watching from the outside—me sitting with a young teenage boy I don't know in silence, the only sounds in the room the *clack clack clack* of our Rubik's Cubes. His movements swift and efficient. Mine slower and less sure. He's finishing another cube when the door opens wider. Judah Cross stands there, leaning one shoulder against the doorjamb. My fingers falter.

"I see he recruited you," Judah says without preamble, walking forward.

"I don't know if *recruited* is the right word." I turn the bottom row, taking my eyes off my cube long enough to smile at him. "He's going so fast."

"You're supposed to be racing," Judah says, a bit of humor in his eyes and the slight curve of his full lips.

"Oh." I stop and laugh, setting the cube down on the table. "Then I give up. I could never beat you, Aaron."

"He told you his name?" Judah raises his brows.

"Yeah. Was he not supposed to because I'm a stranger or something?"

"Nah." Judah shakes his head and comes closer, picking up one of the cubes. "He just sometimes doesn't feel like talking. Isn't that right, bud?"

Aaron doesn't answer but flicks his father a cursory glance before refocusing on the cube.

"The only person who comes close to giving him a run for his money," Judah says, "is my other son, his twin brother, Adam."

"Wow, that's..." I break off, my eyes widening. "You have twins?"

"Yup."

"Is your, um, wife here tonight?" The question doesn't come easily. Being attracted to a married man when you are a married woman makes things awkward that way.

"Adam's with her." He studies me before speaking again. "She has them most weekends. We're divorced. Aaron sometimes just wants to stay in his room at my place. My ex was doing something he didn't want to do. Thus..."

He doesn't finish the thought, but nods to his son, who is completing yet another cube and picking up a new one.

"You're terrific at that, Aaron," I say, observing his supreme focus and the flying fingers.

My middle daughter, Inez, was a lunch bunch buddy for an autistic kid at her school. I guess hanging out with neurotypical students was supposed to help with socialization. I think Aaron may have autism, though I could be wrong.

"Did you finish your chicken?" I tease Judah lightly.

"Uh, kind of." He cracks a small smile. "I ate as much as I could bear."

"Told you." I pluck restlessly at the ruffle along my hemline. "Look, I'm sorry about what I said earlier."

"You mean calling me a geek?" He flicks a glance up at me, his expression slightly amused instead of annoyed. "But I am. I've always been. I crunch numbers for a living. I'm used to it."

I shift in my seat uncomfortably, recalling all the other unflattering descriptions Edward has applied to "Cross in accounting" over the last year. "Well, I still feel bad."

"Why? It's your husband who doesn't like me. It's fine. I don't like him either."

We stare at each other in the awkward silence following his assertion. Awkward for me at least. He seems completely comfortable insulting my husband to my face. I'm still formulating an appropriate response and realizing there isn't one when Judah startles me with a touch.

It's a soft brush of long, strong fingers across my wrist. A dark bruise is already forming a small shackle where Edward gripped me too tightly. I draw a sharp breath and snatch my arm away like his light touch was fire.

"Sorry," he says, frowning. "Does it hurt?"

"No, it's . . . it's nothing, really. I bruise easily. Always have."

"Always?" he asks, the frown deepening.

"Not always like he *always* bruises me," I say with a nervous laugh. "He never . . . He doesn't do that. He just wasn't thinking."

"That tracks," Judah replies with a sardonic twist to his mouth.

I bite my lip and look away, unable to hold that steady stare.

"Here you are," Edward says from the door. His tone is amicable, but I know him too well not to detect the irritation in the glance he flicks from me to Judah. "It's time to go, Sol."

"Oh." I stand and smooth my dress down, pausing as I recall Edward's claim that Judah was ogling me, staring at my ass. He's not staring at my ass now, though. He's staring at my wrist, his cold eyes shifting from the bruise to Edward. His lips settle into a firm line, and he walks over, picking up two of the Rubik's Cubes. He tugs Aaron's sleeve and mouths, "Let's go." Aaron removes his headphones, places them in a case he retrieves from the floor by his feet, stuffs the cubes in a backpack, and stands.

Father and son face each other, and I realize why Aaron looked so familiar. Their profiles are carved from the same mountain, the lines of their cheeks and jaws edged in granite. Aaron is a handsome boy and must look a lot like Judah did at his age.

"Aaron, are you going to tell Mrs. Barnes goodbye?" Judah asks, nodding toward me.

Aaron looks up at me, a frown pinching his dark brows. "Soledad," he says, surprising me.

"That's right." A smile breaks out on my face like I've won something. Maybe I have. Connecting with Aaron for those few minutes when maybe people usually don't get that privilege feels like a prize. "You can call me Soledad. It was so nice meeting you, Aaron."

He doesn't respond but walks toward the door.

Judah's mouth tips into a half smile. "Guess that's my cue. It was nice meeting you, Soledad."

His gaze ices over when he looks at Edward. "See you Monday, Barnes."

And with that, he follows his son from the room.

"See what I mean?" Edward demands as soon as we're alone. "I told you he's an asshole."

I recall a warm smile that felt like the sun on a January morning. Sincere amusement creasing the corners of dark, watchful eyes. Gentle fingers touching the shadow of my husband's careless strength.

"Yeah," I agree, grabbing my stilettos from the floor. "I see exactly what you mean."

CHAPTER TWO

SOLEDAD

"Coach wants me at the gym at five tomorrow morning," Lottie says, piercing a cucumber in her salad and bringing it to her lips. "Can you take me, Mom?"

"Of course."

Yester-me may regret encouraging my youngest daughter's interest in gymnastics. How could I have known she'd be so darn good at it? Or that it would be so expensive? Baby girl better bring home the gold one day, as much as this "hobby" is costing me in coin and sleep. "We'll go straight to school from there."

"So how will I get to school?" Inez asks with a frown, her dark eyes pinging between her sister and me. "Daddy leaves so early for work."

"I'll come back to scoop you up while Lottie's practicing. Here, hon," I say, passing a platter of perfectly marinated steak (if I do say so myself) to Edward. "We'll drive by the gym to grab Lot, and I'll drop you both off at Harrington."

"God, I'm glad I don't go to that elitist school anymore," Lupe drawls.

"Yeah. You're soooo cool all up in APS," Inez says, rolling her eyes. "While me and Lottie, poor things, have to attend one of the top schools in the state, with an Olympic-size swimming pool, world-class facilities, and restaurant-quality food in our dining hall. Public school rocks, huh?"

"We make the sacrifice," Lottie pipes up. "Every time I play water polo, an angel gets her wings."

I smother a laugh behind my fist and scoop up some risotto, which for once turned out perfectly fluffy.

"Well, I'd trade all that to be in a school that's even vaguely diverse," Lupe fires back. "Harrington's the Twiwhite Zone."

"You got that from Deja." Inez rolls her eyes.

"Of course I did," Lupe says, a pleased smile on her face. "She's my best friend."

I love that my daughter is best friends with the daughter of one of *my* best friends, Yasmen Wade, and have never regretted allowing Lupe to leave private school when Deja did. Lupe may look more like Edward than my other two daughters, who took a deep dive into the African American and Puerto Rican end of my gene pool, but her fist *stays* in the air for the culture.

It used to bother me when people assumed that with my textured corkscrew curls and darker skin, I was Lupe's nanny. I look around the table, seeing my mother and *her* mother in Inez and Lottie, with their hair and skin and eyes so like ours. With all the ethnicities and cultures running through my blood and Edward's, we played genetic roulette and won big-time. All our girls are beautiful exactly as they are, and I always make sure they know it.

When my two sisters, Lola and Nayeli, and I would visit our *abuela* for the summer, she used to tell us about the colorism she'd witnessed in the old days on the island.

"First time *my mami* met *her* husband's mother," Abuela said, quickly crossing herself, "may she rest in peace, she threw away Mami's cup after she drank the coffee. White Puerto Rican. Black Puerto Rican."

My *abuela* assessed us three girls with omniscient eyes—me and Nayeli lighter and with silkier hair than our half sister, Lola. "All the same," she used to say. "You love each other, take care of each other all the same, eh?"

"All the same," we always repeated, giggling a little at the ridiculousness of it because it never occurred to us that we were anything *but* all the same. To us, Lola wasn't our half anything. She was our whole heart, and we were hers. Everyone knew my mother's kids stuck together. You messed with one of Catelaya's girls, you messed with them all.

Now, parenting this beautiful palette of daughters, I know too well the rest of the world doesn't always love the same. I appreciate my *abuela* and *mami* always making sure we understood. I can create that same unconditional love here in my home for Lupe, Inez, and Lottie.

"I would help getting them to school," Edward says, slicing into his steak, "but I need to go in extra early tomorrow. Amber and I have a huge presentation to the board in a few days."

My spine straightens involuntarily. Amber's name may always be triggering for me. A side effect of lying awake beside your husband while he says another woman's name in his sleep.

"Seems like you and Amber have had lots of overtime lately," I say, keeping my tone neutral.

"Yeah, thanks to that Judah Cross." Edward saws at the tender meat so hard his plate scrapes across the table. "Asshole making my life hell poking into things that don't concern him."

"Edward," I say, glancing at Lottie. "Language."

"I know the word *asshole*," Lottie assures me, steak sauce ringing her mouth. "Coach said it last week."

"Well, we don't say it," I tell her. "And neither should he in front of you."

I make a mental note to talk to Coach Krisensky. He can cuss at his own kids, but not mine.

"I shouldn't have said it," Edward admits, taking a deep gulp of his wine. "That man is just always up my—"

"More vinaigrette for your salad, hon?" I cut in, saving him from himself and more profanity at the table.

He has the decency to look chagrined but shakes his head no. "Sorry. He just pisses me off."

Lottie looks at me, eyes round like she caught her father in another oops because we don't say "piss off" either. At least my eleven-year-old doesn't yet. I wish I could hold on to every scrap of her innocence, but I know how fleeting this phase is and how fast it goes. I complain sometimes about all the practices, the carpool, the laundry, the meals—all the work and chaos that come with raising three active girls—but Lord help me when it's over. A quiet house feels like a blessing now, but I know one day, when they're gone, it might feel like a curse.

"Why's Judah Cross such a jerk?" Inez, the classic daddy's girl, asks with a scowl.

"He's not," I say before I can catch myself.

In the absolute silence that follows my ill-advised comment, I take in my family's reaction, ranging from confusion to doubt to—and this one's Edward—rage.

"I mean..." I clear my throat. "I know at work the two of you bump heads, honey, but at the Christmas party he—"

"You meet this guy for ten minutes at my Christmas party," Edward snaps, shoving his plate away. "You feel flattered because he watches your ass all night, then take his side even though he makes my life at work a fucking nightmare? That's just great, Sol. Thanks a lot."

Waves of shock reverberate over the table, all three girls watching us with wide, worried eyes.

"He was not—" I break off, refusing to air this in front of our children. "Let's just drop it."

"Yeah." He pushes away from the table and to his feet. "Consider it dropped."

"You didn't finish your dinner," I protest feebly, clenching my fists in my lap.

He stops beside my chair, looking down at me with a sneer. "I lost my appetite." He makes quick strides to exit the dining room. "I'm going out back for a while."

"Out back" is his man cave. When we bought this house, there was a small storage shed in the backyard. Edward said he'd make it his retreat for when the estrogen of four women in the house got to be too much. He found the furniture, chose the paint and carpet, the gargantuan plasma TV. And, of course, installed his "priceless" collection of Boston Celtics paraphernalia.

I stand and follow him, telling the girls, "I'll be right back."

I catch him in the foyer and take his arm.

"What the hell was that?" I demand with low-voiced outrage. "How dare you speak to me that way in front of our children? How dare you speak to me that way *at all*? Are you really so angry with Judah that you lose control like that?"

"Did I lie? You think I didn't see the way he watched you? He wanted you."

"Is that why you deigned to fuck me that night when we got home? Because the villain of the story in your head wanted me? Is that the only way you can get it up these days? The villain Viagra must have worn off because you haven't been back since."

He reaches out and grabs me by the arms, gripping so tightly I wince.

"Don't push me, Sol," he growls. "You have no idea what I'm dealing with. You wouldn't take his side if you knew."

"Let go," I grit out. "You're hurting me."

His hands fall away immediately, and he runs his fingers through his hair, disheveling the neat blond cap.

"I don't know what's gotten into you lately," I say, rubbing my arms, "but you need to—"

The chime of the doorbell cuts into the tirade I had all queued up for him.

"Literally saved by the bell," he says. "The last thing I want to hear is you lecturing me on..."

He opens the door and trails off. We both take in the small group of people gathered on our porch. Their jackets read *FBI*. A knot forms in my stomach, and even though I don't know what they're doing here, it can't be good.

"Edward Barnes," says the man standing in the front, flashing his badge. "You're under arrest."

CHAPTER THREE

SOLEDAD

There's a hurricane tearing through my house.

"You're making a mistake!" Edward shouts, straining against the cuffs around his wrists, his face mottled with rage.

"What's going on?" I ask, splitting my question between Edward and the stranger who barged in with an army of ants crawling all over my house.

"It's that motherfucker Cross," Edward says, panic taking his voice higher. "I told you he was after me. I'd bet my life he's behind this. It's all a misunderstanding."

"Officer," I say, turning on the man who first presented himself at the door and seems to be in charge. "You can't just come in here and tear our house apart and arrest my husband. Do you have a warrant?"

"Agent," he corrects. "Agent Spivey, and yes, ma'am."

He holds up a document that must be at least twenty pages, flips to the end, and points to the signature at the bottom. "Search warrant, and also a warrant for Mr. Barnes's arrest."

"It's a load of bullshit," Edward interrupts tersely. "That's what it is."

"Embezzlement," Agent Spivey inserts, looking at Edward. "Your husband knows exactly why we're here and what we're looking for."

On the page Agent Spivey holds up, words like *affidavit, search, seizure, investigation, subpoenaed bank records, forfeiture* swim like fish in an ocean of ink and confusion.

"Edward?" His name trembles on my lips because I'm so deeply afraid he *does* know what this is about. His out-of-character behavior. The late hours. All the "projects" he's been working on lately that were never such a huge part of his job before. Could it all add up to this?

"Dammit!"

The curse comes from an agent struggling to catch my prized Cristina Córdova ceramic in the foyer as he flips my rug.

"If you're not planning to pay for that when it breaks," I snap, "I suggest you be more careful."

Agent Spivey glances from the shamefaced agent to me. "We actually do pay to replace anything we break," he says. "I know this is a lot, but we're just doing our job."

A group of agents stride to Edward's office, where others are already rummaging through his desk and pulling paintings off the walls.

"Call Brunson," Edward says as they march him toward the door. "Tell him I've been set up and I need him right away."

The reality of calling our friend who is a lawyer to get Edward out of *jail* hits me like a semi, and I can't breathe. Dumbly I take in the scene unfolding. Of Edward being hustled down our steps. Of my hydrangea bush being trampled by some careless agent checking the exterior of our house. Of our neighbors stepping out into their front yards, pulling curtains back, some standing boldly on the porch with folded arms and judgmental faces, gawking in the early-evening glow of streetlamps. I step onto the porch and blink at the tears standing in my eyes, not falling by sheer force of will.

"This is a mistake," Edward screams as they walk him across our perfectly manicured front yard, I think as much for the benefit of the onlookers as to reassure me. His eyes are wild when they meet mine, and I've never felt less assured, less safe in my life.

A sob from behind me draws my eyes to all three girls huddled at the front door, faces thunderstruck, watching their father be dragged away. Watching agents swarm our house searching for God knows what.

"Girls," I say, fighting the panic crawling up my throat and threatening to strangle me. "Get inside."

"Daddy!" Inez screams, the word torn from her throat as she shoves past me and down the porch steps. She throws her arms around Edward's middle, though he can't hug her back with his hands cuffed behind him. She burrows into his chest, tear-streaked face buried in his shirt, her small frame shaking with sobs. I rush across the yard, picking my way through the agents encircling my husband and daughter.

"Hey, it's okay, sweetie." Edward bends to hold Inez's tearful gaze. "It's a big misunderstanding. I'll be home in no time."

I meet Edward's eyes over her tousled curls, and I have no idea if we can believe the words coming out of his mouth. There's too much smoke for there to be *no* fire at all, and watching my daughter come apart, watching our *lives* fall apart, I'm afraid we'll all get burned.

An agent prods him toward the car waiting at the curb.

"Sol!" Edward yells, ducking his head when the agent nudges him into the back seat. "Call Brunson."

"Okay." I nod, feeling the weight of every eye in the cul-de-sac bearing down on us. "I will."

The door slams, and Edward drops his head to the seat, not looking back when the car pulls out of our driveway.

"Come on, baby," I whisper to Inez, my eyes fixed on the disappearing taillights. "Let's go back inside. We'll talk to your dad soon."

We cross the yard, Inez clinging to my arm. Lottie and Lupe stand on the top step, tears streaking their faces. My heart pinches at their chorus of sniffles and sobs, and I shuffle them inside, slamming the door on the wave of curiosity and censure rising over our cul-de-sac. Herding them back past the marauding agents, through the dining room, and into the kitchen, I close the door behind us, blocking out the mayhem in our home and sealing us in this space where, for just a second, the madness can't reach us.

"What did Dad do?" Lupe asks, her voice hushed.

"He didn't do anything," Inez says, her tearful words pebbled with anger. "You heard him. Judah Cross set him up."

"Honey, we don't know that." I run a shaking hand over my hair, letting it slip from the haphazard pony I threw it in while making dinner. It feels like years ago that my greatest concern was whether the risotto had cooked long enough.

"Are you defending Judah Cross?" Inez's face scrunches with adolescent indignation. "God, Mom. How could you?"

I slam my hand on the counter, the palm making a loud *whack* that jerks all three sets of startled eyes to my face.

"Don't." The word comes out quiet and flat. "I don't have time for your histrionics, Inez. You know I support your father completely. We aren't sure what's going on yet, and while we figure it out, please don't make this any harder than it already is."

A tear slips down Inez's cheek, and she presses her lips together, sniffing and nodding.

"Look at me." I tip her chin up and meet her eyes, the hard lines of my mouth softening, on the verge of shaking. "It's gonna be okay. *We're* gonna be okay."

"But Daddy," Lottie sobs, her slim shoulders shaking. "They're taking him to jail."

"Hey." I cup her wet cheek and look at the three of them one by one. "I'm not saying this won't be hard. I don't know what's happening either, but there's one thing I do know."

I wait for them to quiet their sniffles and give me their full attention.

"I will take care of you."

I pull the three of them close to me in a tangle of limbs and hair and tears. "You are my life, and I will take care of you. We *will* be all right. I promise you that."

By the time the agents finish their search and ask me a bunch of questions I have no answers for, I've called the lawyer and persuaded the girls to go up to their rooms for the night. Needless to say, no school tomorrow. And Coach Krisensky can shove that five a.m. practice up his vaulting horse.

I'm on the stair landing when I hear three hushed voices coming from Lupe's room. I can't make out what they're saying, but their words are interspersed with *shhh*es and tears. I hesitate, torn between going in to comfort them and letting them be there for each other. I spent the last hour plying them with thin reassurances I'm not even sure I believe. It melts my heart a little that they're together in one room. It's what my sisters and I would have done. Hell, what we *did* do anytime something scared us or left us unsure.

I decide to leave them be for now and head down the stairs to survey the damage—displaced couch cushions, dirt from my plants carelessly strewn through the hall, and broken glass from fallen picture frames. Under normal circumstances, there's no way I could go to bed with my house this trashed, but in the wake of adrenaline and fear, a bone-deep weariness takes up residence. All the possibilities bow my shoulders and strap themselves around my ankles like weights. I'm dragging myself up the stairs to pull the covers over my head and try to prepare for whatever tomorrow holds when the doorbell rings.

"I can't." I shake my head and pull my hair off my neck. "I can't take one more thing."

But I walk to the door and peer through the glass panes, half expecting Agent Spivey to be standing on my porch with another search warrant because there is some tiny corner of my life they forgot to upend.

It's not the agent.

It's my best friends.

I wrench the door open, so glad to see Yasmen and Hendrix illuminated under the porch light, worry etched into their faces.

"Yas," I choke out. "Hen."

They cross the threshold, pulling me into a them-scented hug that shatters the last of my composure. The tears come in a deluge that scalds my cheeks and leaves my throat raw from sobs.

"Hey, hey, honey." Yasmen pushes the tangled hair back from my face. "It's gonna be okay. Come in here and sit."

I force one leg in front of the other until I reach the couch and collapse, letting my head fall back so I can stare up at the coffered ceiling I was so particular about when we were designing. I had to have

Calacatta marble for the counters. Viking oven. Bifold doors leading to the patio. None of it seems important now because we could lose everything, and the only things that matter are my girls.

"This son of a bitch done fucked up," Hendrix says, flopping into an armchair. "I knew it was only a matter of time."

"Hen," Yasmen chides, dark eyes wide and curly Afro moving with a quick shake of her head. "We don't have the full picture."

"Oh, I do." Hendrix's bold features—high cheekbones, slashing dark brows, and full lips—twist with disdain. "He done fucked up, but even I, who have never been this man's biggest fan, didn't think it would be of these here epic proportions. The FBI? Shiiiiiit."

"How do you know it was the FBI?" I ask, sitting up. "Wait. I'm so glad you're here, but how did you know to come? I was gonna call you in the morning."

"It, um . . ." Yasmen runs her palms over the legs of her black jogging suit. "It's already all over Skyland, Sol. I'm sorry. You know if somebody sneezes at night, Deidre from the bookstore is dropping off a box of Kleenex in the morning."

"Well, and it *was* kinda on the news," Hendrix adds, a subdued frown sitting ill at ease on her face.

"The . . . who . . . what . . ." I lean forward, resting my elbows on my knees. "Did you say on the news?"

"CalPot is one of the biggest employers in the state," Hendrix points out. "Six million dollars may not bankrupt them, but it's still a lot of money to—"

"Six million dollars?" I squawk, bouncing an incredulous look between them. "What six million dollars?"

"On the news," Yasmen says, reaching over to squeeze my hand. "They said Edward is accused of embezzling upward of six million dollars from the company."

"That's ridiculous." I launch myself from the couch to pace in front of the fireplace. "I mean, I get it. He's not your favorite, but you know he's not capable of something like this, right? There has to be a mistake."

What if Edward goes to prison? We've been at odds lately, but he's still my husband. Fear for him, for the girls and me, strangles a sob in my throat. I'm spinning in some alternate universe with zero gravity. If even half of this is true, then my husband is not who I thought he was. Then the father of my children is a liar. A criminal.

Untrustworthy.

Irresponsible.

Reckless.

And how could I not know? Nearly twenty years with him, and how could I not know?

Each question hammers at my temples. I need answers. I reach for the remote and aim it toward the television, only to have it snatched from my hands.

"No, ma'am." Hendrix hides the remote behind her back. "Not tonight. We told you the highlights. It's late. Tomorrow's gonna be a bitch. You should get some rest."

My phone rings, and my heart pounds when I see Brunson's number.

"It's the lawyer," I tell them, accepting the call. "Brunson, oh, my God. What's going on?"

"Sol," he says, sounding as tired as I feel. "Sorry I didn't call sooner. I've been trying to detangle this mess."

"When is he coming home? What exactly are they charging him with? What's this about six million dollars? What the hell is going on?"

"Okay, one thing at a time. They'll have an arraignment, if not tomorrow, then the next day, to set bail. *If* we can get bail. The prosecution will try to say Edward's a flight risk."

"A flight risk? Like he'd leave the country? He wouldn't run."

There's a small silence on the other end before Brunson goes on. "As far as the charge, it's embezzlement. And yes, they are saying it's in the neighborhood of six million dollars, so it's a felony."

My knees give out, and I sink to the ottoman in the center of the room.

"I don't...I don't understand. From CalPot? CalPot is accusing him of this?"

"Yeah, apparently some guy they hired, this new director of accounting, used to be a hotshot forensic accountant. He's the one who found it. Or presumably. Of course, Edward denies it."

Judah Cross. My teeth grind together. He did this to my family, and I let a little attention and conversation distract me from the threat he could prove to be. Edward tried to warn me.

"So is it too late for Edward to get his call or whatever?"

"What do you mean?" Brunson asks, confusion in his voice. "He did make his call."

"But he didn't...I haven't heard from him."

The silence on the other end thickens with speculation and maybe understanding. Instead of using his one call to phone home and reassure his wife, tell his family what the hell was going on, Edward called someone else. Someone who is *not* his lawyer.

I close my eyes, futilely trying to block out the crushing reality of my circumstances. When I open my eyes again, bracing for the next blow, Yasmen and Hendrix are sweeping up the dirt and glass, righting the cushions. Fresh tears prickle my eyes. I don't know what is going on with Edward, and he apparently didn't see fit to call and tell me. Everything with him feels like shaky ground right now, but some things I can count on. My daughters and my friends.

"We have a big day tomorrow," Brunson finally says, his voice kind, compassionate. God, maybe even pitying. "Get some rest and we'll attack in the morning."

"Yeah." I split a wobbly smile between my two best friends, who send me a smile in return. "In the morning."

CHAPTER FOUR

SOLEDAD

Mom, we're outta milk!" Lupe calls from the kitchen.

It's the first thing I've heard from her all day. She's been quiet in her room. Lottie climbed into bed with me in the middle of the night, like when she was younger and had a bad dream. Last night was a nightmare, and even as she tossed in her sleep, she was obviously shaken. Inez still hasn't emerged. My tentative knock was met with a grunt and a sniffle, even though when I cracked the door open, she feigned sleep, huddling deeper under the covers. I get that. I want to hide, too, but that's a luxury I don't have.

I scribble *milk* on the pink pad in front of me on the dining room table, the practical task of making a grocery list temporarily distracting me from the disaster of our life. I know there are digital notes, apps and things for lists now, but there's something grounding about pen to paper, seeing my handwriting that looks so much like my mother's on the page. She used to pin a scrap of paper—electric bill, junk mail, whatever—to the fridge, and my sisters and I would add grocery items we needed as we walked by.

Lola always wanted junk food. Twizzlers, Little Debbie Fudge Rounds, Doritos.

Nayeli was all about the health even then. Grapes, cucumbers, plantains.

Me, I loved to bake. Vanilla extract, semisweet chocolate chips, a tub of Duncan Hines icing.

The urge to bake, to *make* something tickles my brain. Warms my heart. I know my girls' favorite ooey-gooey brownies won't make all this shit with Edward disappear, but they're something they love. Something familiar that will give us, even if only for the few moments the taste touches our tongues, something to enjoy. I add cocoa, eggs, and vanilla to my list and start my Instacart order.

I woke up to a few news trucks parked outside. I cannot believe this is happening, but CalPot, despite its small pans and sometimes-flaky nonstick coating, *is* one of the premier cookware brands in the nation. One of its top executives embezzling six million dollars? Definitely newsworthy. With those buzzards circling overhead outside, I'm not leaving this house. Like Edward, we're prisoners.

Still no word from him. All I know is that the arraignment isn't today, and that was courtesy of Brunson. Is Edward okay? Being treated well? Chief among my questions: What the hell is going on, and what has he done to put us in this situation? Anger *at* him, worry *for* him slosh anxiety in my belly, and I pace over to inspect the contents of the refrigerator.

I don't usually let supplies get so low, but post-Christmas, things have been really hectic for the girls, and I've gotten pulled into committees at Harrington for several things, including a book drive to raise money for the charitable causes the school supports.

As the daughter of two librarians, I've always found books a solace. With each child, each new responsibility, each new level of adulting, my reading seems to have suffered a little more. For birthdays and holidays we received whatever we'd asked for, but my parents also included a book, prettily tied with ribbon.

A familiar ache nicks my heart. I miss my folks. My dad, a ginger with freckles and a gangly frame, couldn't have been more different from Mami's first love, Lola's father, Brayden, but he was what she needed, and I know she loved him. Lola now lives in the South Carolina house where we grew up, but when we cleaned out Mami's room after the funeral, I found a few scraps of timeworn, faded paper tucked into a shoebox at the back of my mother's closet. Poetry she'd written for Bray. About him.

Your skin is summer night and your kiss is all I want.

That line is burned into my brain. At the time, I tried to imagine Edward writing something like that to me, or even me writing something like that about him.

I couldn't.

Edward.

Shit.

This walk through memories makes me miss Mami, which happens all the time even though she has been gone for years. I still pick up the phone to call her when something good happens. And for the bad things too. I started dialing our old home number last night, only to remember Mami's gone.

But my sisters are still here.

I fire off a group text so I can catch them up.

Me: Hey! I need to tell you both something. It's important. Can we FaceTime?

Lola: Is it bad? What happened?

Nayeli: Lemme put the babies down.

My little sister, Nayeli, had six kids in eleven years. She went through a heavily Catholic phase and decided to "trust the Lord" to give them His will. Needless to say, she now has an IUD. Lola says she may have kids one day, but maybe not the traditional way. Since her "bi awakening," she's not sure when or if she'll want the dick again.

"What's popping, Sol?" my older sister, Lola, asks, her eyes sharp on my face and her brows dipped into a frown. She jokes that her claim to fame is that she's the most "undiluted" of us. Mami being African American and Puerto Rican and Bray being African American, Lola's darker complexion is hued with rich red undertones. Her hair, usually puffed into a luxuriant textured mass around her head, is tamed today into straight backs with baby hairs teased out at the edges.

She's gorgeous and she knows it.

"Hey, *mijas*!" Nayeli waves, holding a suckling infant to her breast with one arm and propping up her phone with the other. A long braid slinks over one shoulder, and she squints at us from behind her glasses, looking more like Mami than any of us. "I miss you."

"Miss you guys too," I say. It's only as I see their dear faces that I realize how much.

"We can kiki later," Lola laughs. "I love you. I miss you. Yada yada yada. The Boricua High Council is in session. What's this about, Sol?"

"Yeah, well, um." I take a deep breath and force it out. "It all started last night at dinner."

I launch into an explanation of what happened, watching shock ripple over their faces. Hearing it all out loud makes me realize just how outrageous my situation has become.

"What does Edward say?" Lola demands.

"He says it's a misunderstanding." I scribble Lupe, Inez, and Lottie's names in the corner of my notepad. "And that he's being set up."

"By who?" Nayeli asks supersoft because my niece in her arms is doing the slow blink of soon-to-be sleep. "Who does he say would do such a thing?"

"He says it's CalPot's director of accounting," I tell them. "Judah Cross."

"And why exactly does Edward believe the director of accounting would set him up to take the fall for six million dollars being embezzled?" Skepticism sharpens Lola's words. "Better yet, why does he think we'd believe it?"

"Lola, don't leap to judge," Nayeli says. "Have you talked to him at all since he was arrested, Sol?"

"No. He hasn't called. I don't...I have no idea what's going on. The lawyer says he'll call today." My voice cracks, but I clear my throat. "I know it sounds ridiculous, Lola. I get it, but I'm not ready to even consider that Edward actually did it. That he would put our family in a situation like this. That I've been living all these years with a man who's capable of doing this. That I've had his children and—"

"Okay," Lola cuts in firmly. "All aboard the hysterics train. I need you to get off at the next stop. I didn't mean to upset you. I'm a cynic. You know that. Edward has never given you reason to believe he'd do this, so we'll just wait and see how it plays out."

"I wish I could get away," Nayeli sighs, patting Angela's little back. "I'd be on the next plane."

"No, I'll be fine," I rush to assure them. "Yasmen and Hendrix were here last night. They'll come back today."

"The new semester just started for me here," Lola says. "And you know middle schoolers are the worst. Just look at Inez."

I smother a chuckle because Inez is truly entering that *piece of work* phase of adolescence. It looms ahead like an oncoming train.

"Don't talk about your niece that way," I chide unconvincingly. "She's actually a lot like you at that age."

"Then you truly *are* in for a ride," Lola says ruefully. "Remember the shit I put Mami through?"

When Lola entered her teens, she and Mami clashed so much, she lived with our *abuela* on the island for a year, then spent that summer with Bray's mother in South Carolina. We actually joined her there because we missed being together so badly. To this day I still call Bray's mother Grammy.

"It all worked out," Nayeli says. "You were only gone for a year, and Inez isn't that bad, is she?"

"Not yet," I sigh. "She's such a daddy's girl. I hope this doesn't traumatize her too badly. She hasn't come out of her room all day."

"I'll drive down soon," Lola says.

"I wish I was closer," Nayeli adds. "Don't get me wrong. We love

LA, but I hate being this far away. Plus I've been fruitful and multiplied so much, I may not get to leave the state until this one is four years old."

We all laugh, and I'm glad I called them. I needed this. Even though they aren't physically here, that safety net of love and acceptance we made for each other as girls, it still holds. It still catches me.

"I'm gonna go. We need food," I tell them. "Let me finish my Instacart order. I'm not leaving this house today. All of Skyland is buzzing about Edward, and I don't want the stares or the questions at the checkout line."

I don't even bother telling them about the news trucks parked outside. That would only make them feel worse for not being able to get to me right now.

"Boricua High Council adjourned," Lola says. "Love yous."

"Love yous," Nayeli echoes.

"Love yous," I say, swallowing the burn in my throat. These few minutes almost made me forgot how bad things are.

I pull my laptop across the dining room table to complete my order before checkout. Except it doesn't check out.

"What do you mean, 'payment not accepted'?" I mutter, frowning at the screen. My card is the saved payment method, and I've used it several times, so I know I didn't enter the information wrong. Maybe the card is expired and I didn't realize it. I reach for my purse, but my cell rings, distracting me. I answer, still eyeing the cart of grocery items on my laptop screen.

The contact is Harrington.

Probably someone calling to see why the girls are out of school today.

"Hello," I answer.

"Soledad, hi," Dr. Morgan, Harrington's headmistress, replies. "How are you?"

"Dr. Morgan, as you've probably heard," I say with a small, humorless laugh, "things aren't great, but we're trying to get it all sorted out."

"Yes, it's very unfortunate. Please let us know if we can help."

"Thank you. If you're calling about the girls being absent, I just thought it might be better—"

"No," she interrupts softly. "I figured as much. I'm calling because we processed tuition today."

"Oh...okay."

"I know Inez and Lottie's tuition is on autopay."

"Right."

"The payment didn't go through."

It's quiet enough on the phone to hear a gnat fart, as Grammy used to say.

"I don't..." I glance at my laptop and the declined total for groceries. "Oh, God."

"Soledad, it's fine," Dr. Morgan says soothingly. "Of course, I don't usually personally call families when a payment doesn't clear, but you're one of the most involved, dedicated parents we have. You're an asset to our school community. A blessing, really."

"Thank you," I mumble through numb lips.

"And of course, I understand these are...extenuating circumstances you find yourself in."

"Extenuating, yeah. Um, Dr. Morgan, I'm getting a call I need to take. Can we talk later?"

"Of course. I know you have a lot—"

"Right, bye."

I hang up before she can mete out more sympathy while suppressing her rabid curiosity. It will be all over Skyland by the close of business that I'm broke. I spend the next hour on the phone with my bank, whisper-screaming so I don't alarm the girls. They're so sorry. The FBI has frozen our assets, which is why none of my credit cards work. And am I aware our accounts are involved in an active investigation regarding stolen funds?

"Aware?" I snap. "My husband is sitting in a cell as we speak and I don't even have money to buy groceries, so yeah. I'm aware."

"We can't buy groceries?" Lupe asks from the dining room's arched entrance, eyes wide and startled.

Lupe and I consider each other in horrified silence. She's horrified we don't have money for food. I'm horrified that she knows.

"I have to go," I tell the unhelpful customer service rep.

"There's a survey about your experience today if you—"

I hang up and toss my cell onto the table.

"Don't tell your sisters. I don't want them worried. I didn't want *you* worried."

"But what are we gonna do? Can we get on food stamps?"

The statement is so out of left field, a laugh erupts from me.

"Oh, honey." I wave her over. "Come here."

I pull her onto my lap. Talk about ridiculous, she's now a few inches taller than I am, but she's still my baby. She snuggles into me and tucks her head in the crook of my neck.

"We are gonna be okay," I say, not sure if I'm convincing her or myself. "Promise. How about some lunch, huh?"

The aroma of food and our insistent nudging coaxes Inez to finally leave her room and join us. I'm so glad to see signs of life, I don't even complain when they bring their phones to the table. Inez plays *Animal Crossing*. Lottie sticks her headphones in and bobs to whatever song is playing. Lupe scrolls across social media. Foot pulled up to rest on the stool, she absently bites her sandwich every few swipes of her screen.

"Oh, my God." Her eyes go rounder, fixed on her phone. "Did Daddy steal six million dollars?"

"What?" I ask, snapping my head up.

"Somebody posted it on Facebook." She bounces a glance between me and the screen. "There's all these comments about how he deserves what's coming to him and—"

"Gimme." I hold out my hand, nodding to the phone. "We're not reading that."

"But, Mom," Inez says. "Why are they saying—"

"Give me your phones." I slide the fruit bowl to the middle of the counter. "All of you put 'em in here till we finish lunch."

"Seriously?" Inez groans, but drops her phone between a banana and an apple.

Lottie and Lupe follow suit.

"Has Dad called?" Lupe demands. "Do we know—"

"No and no to whatever you were gonna ask," I say, walking the fruit bowl into the dining room and placing it on the table. "I haven't talked to your father yet. He'll call as soon as he can. The lawyer says the arraignment should be tomorrow. That's all I know as of now."

I'm on my way back to the kitchen when an unknown number flashes on my phone with a text.

Soledad, we need to talk.

It could be a reporter. A few have called the house line today.

Me: Who is this?

Unknown Caller: Judah Cross.

I pause by the counter, pressing the phone to my chest in case my daughters see me chatting with public enemy number one.

"Don't touch that fruit bowl," I admonish, speed walking down the hall to the powder room and dialing the number. "Be right back."

I close the door and take a seat on the closed toilet.

"How did you get this number?" I hiss into the phone.

"Employee records," Judah replies, his deep voice clear and calm. "You're in Edward's."

"What do you want?"

"Like I said, we need to talk."

"Then talk."

"I'd prefer in person."

"Well, I can't leave my house, thanks to you."

The silence following my biting words lengthens.

"If you think this is my fault," he replies after a few moments, "we have more to discuss than I thought we did. I'm around the corner. I saw the news trucks out front. How should we do this?"

"You could come through the back, but I..." The girls' muted conversation reaches me from the kitchen. "I don't want my daughters to see you. There's a shed behind the house. I'll leave the back gate unlocked. Meet me in there."

"See you in five."

He disconnects, and I walk swiftly back to the kitchen.

"Hey, I'm going out to Daddy's shed for a bit," I tell them, keeping my face as straight as possible. "I need to look for something. Be right back."

"Mom," Inez says. "Do we have to go to school tomorrow?"

I pause on my way out and turn to assess the three of them. "Do you want to?"

Lupe's gaze wanders to the dining room table, where the outside world is still wedged into the fruit bowl. "I have a history test, but I can make it up. I guess... I guess one more day won't hurt."

"I want to get back to the gym," Lottie says. "But we can call Coach, right? Think he'll understand?"

"I know he will," I say. "Inez? What do you want to do?"

"I don't want to hear them all lying about Dad," she says, her mouth set into a mutinous line. "We don't have anything to be ashamed of. It's all a big misunderstanding. We didn't do anything wrong, and neither did Daddy."

I don't address that because Edward hasn't given me the ammunition to answer honestly or with any confidence.

"One more day, then," I tell them. "We'll let this die down, and I'm sure we'll hear from your father by then with some answers."

I start for the back door, calling over my shoulder, "Finish your lunch."

I want to curl up under my duvet and sleep until this shit is figured out and I can get my life back, but curiosity and more than a little anger propel me to meet Judah at the shed out back. Once I've unlocked the fence, I slip into Edward's domain. It's been semiransacked. The agents didn't leave it a complete mess, but apparently they searched hard for something. I have no idea what they may have found.

I straighten up some of the mess they left behind, pausing to study Edward's most prized possession. A signed Larry Bird jersey. It hangs on the wall behind the couch, framed and under glass. Lola teased me when I first brought Edward home to meet my family.

"Not only is he a gringo," she said, "but a Celtics fan? The fuck outta here. At least you coulda married a cool white guy."

I slide my hands into the pockets of my jeans and find the pink grocery list wadded up, useless until I can figure out how to buy food. I always keep a little cash stashed upstairs, a legacy of a grandmother who didn't trust banks. My *abuela* used to hide money in socks, boxes, mattresses. I'm not that bad, but there is enough cash to at least get food until our accounts are unfrozen, once I'm ready to brave the outside world.

If our accounts are unfrozen. I have no idea when that might be. I have no idea about a lot of things, and the uncertainty hangs over me like a guillotine.

Tossing the list onto Edward's pool table, I prop my butt on the edge, waiting for the man who started this storm.

The door creaks open and Judah pokes his head inside. I forgot how handsome he is, his features arranged into striking sharp angles and blunt edges. Even in dark jeans, a sweatshirt, and some J's, he's impressive.

I fold my arms across my chest in what I recognize is a defensive posture, but I can't help it. I *feel* defensive. I don't know if Edward's animosity toward Judah is completely justified, but I do know he has something to do with how my life has been destroyed.

"I gotta give it to you," I say, not even bothering to round the edges of my harsh words. "You got some nerve coming to my house when you're the man who put my family in this situation."

"Let's be very clear." He watches me intently. "I'm not the man who put your family in this situation. Your husband did that, but I am the man who wants to get you out of it. I'm taking a risk just coming to talk to you about this. If I didn't want to help, I wouldn't even try."

I frown, processing his words. "How can you help? Why are you here?"

"To encourage you to cooperate with the FBI any way you can. Tell them everything you know."

"I don't know anything. They asked me a lot of questions last night, and I told them the truth. I can't help them. And why would I help them prosecute my husband?"

"Because in cases like these, the spouse is always a suspect. Who benefits more from Edward stealing this much money than you? They'll be watching to see if you access the offshore accounts or try to run to the summer house or—"

"Offshore accounts?" My head spins and, trembling, I rest one hand on the pool table for support. "The hell? What summer house? I have no idea what any of this is about."

"You may not," Judah says grimly. "But Edward does."

Every time I think I might see just a bit of the sky, another set of storm clouds rolls in. A house and accounts I've never heard about? I don't want to believe it, but a tug in my gut gives me pause, feeds my rage that I even have to sort this shit. All because of two men. One of them is behind bars and one of them stands in front of me right now.

"You actually think Edward stole six million dollars?" I ask.

"No." Before I have time to allow myself any relief, he goes on. "It's actually five million, eight hundred thousand, four hundred forty-four dollars and thirty-three cents. At least that's how much I've been able to trace. There's probably more."

"You can't know—"

"I'm a forensic accountant. A damn good one, so yes, I can know."

"And how exactly do you think Edward stole all that money?"

"The White Glove program. He was invoicing customers more for their annual fees than he was recording in CalPot's books."

My heartbeat stutters. "I don't...I don't understand." I link my hands behind my head to keep them from trembling. "How is that even possible?"

"So many cases of embezzlement happen because a company trusts one person too much and gives them too much leeway. Edward had too much autonomy and very little oversight. That was a red flag for me before I even met him. And after I met him..."

He lifts his brows and allows a mocking tilt to his lips. "Let's just say meeting him only increased my suspicion."

"Why?"

"He's arrogant, entitled, and thinks, mistakenly I might add, that his shit doesn't stink. He doesn't have the competence to back up his confidence. Guys like that often look for shortcuts to excel since they don't have the actual work ethic to achieve. It's the here-and-there kind of theft employees often get away with for a long time. Some never get caught. In addition to the surplus Edward collected from annual fees, he also held those retreats twice a year. When I dug into the expenses, they were higher than they should have been. I checked with hotels and airlines and several vendors to find original receipts, which showed a pattern of them charging us less than we paid. Edward had complete control, and the amounts were sometimes so small most wouldn't even notice."

"But you're not most, huh?" I don't know if my words are accusing or admiring.

"You asked how I thought Edward pulled it off and I'm telling you."

I run a weary hand over my face, glancing through the window to our back lawn with the firepit and bright green grass that have earned us yard of the month more than once. "I...I need to talk to my husband. I need to hear from him. To...I just need to talk to him."

"He hasn't called?" Judah asks with a frown.

"Well, he's a little busy fighting for his life. I'm sure he'll get around to it as soon as he's all done with that."

Judah levels an exasperated look at me. "I didn't make this up out of thin air. The evidence is there. We just need more of it. I don't actually give a fuck what happens to Edward because he deserves these consequences. I'm here because you and your daughters don't."

Our eyes lock, and that same breathless, dizzy feeling assaults me, the one I couldn't seem to escape at the Christmas party.

"I promise this is the first I've heard about any of this." Frustrated anger makes my voice shake, and I steady myself before going on. "I can't help them. Hell, I can barely help myself right now."

He sends me a frown, his eyes alert. "What does that mean?"

"Our assets have been frozen. My kids' tuition payment bounced. None of my cards work." I pick up the wadded pink slip of paper and hold it out like it's evidence. "I can't even buy groceries."

"I knew your accounts were frozen. That's by court order," he says, confusion settling on his face. "Pretty standard, but the court should also assign a trustee to your family to help cover some basic needs, like food. Especially in situations involving kids, the court tries to avoid traumatizing them as much as possible."

"Oh, yeah, because it wasn't traumatizing at all seeing their father dragged off in cuffs," I snap. "And I haven't heard anything about a trustee or food."

"It can take a few days to get it all sorted. Your lawyer hasn't told you this stuff?"

"You mean Edward's lawyer," I scoff, nearly choking on my reply. "I've heard very little from him and not at all from..."

I let that thought die, not wanting to admit how in the dark I am. How in the dark Edward has *kept* me. I drop the list back on the table and turn my back on Judah, holding on to my composure with slippery hands. I cover my face for just a few seconds, determined not to cry in front of this man.

"Hey." He touches my shoulder and I jerk, startled by his gentleness. "Look at me."

I slowly turn, hoping my nose isn't red like it usually gets when I'm on the verge of crying. His eyes drop immediately to my nose.

Damn. It's red. I just know it.

"It's going to be okay," he says.

"Oh, I'm not falling for that." I let out a caustic laugh. "That's the line I've been feeding the girls all day, and I have absolutely no idea how it *will* be okay."

"You're telling them things will work out, and you have no idea how, but you'll do everything in your power to make sure they'll be taken care of. It's called parenting." He pauses, squeezing my shoulder. "Or friendship."

"You mean us?" I snort a laugh of disbelief. "Friends? I don't see how."

"Allies, then. You help me, and I'll help you."

"How can I help you?"

"You may know something you don't realize you know. Remember something strange. Anything. If that happens, let the FBI know as soon as possible." He picks up the eight ball from the pool table, testing its weight before rolling it to knock noisily against the others. "Look, I can't get your assets unfrozen. They're pressuring Edward to show them where the money is. I'm not sure it'll work."

"Why do you say that?"

"Because he's a selfish asshole. I know he's your husband, but don't count on him, Soledad. Not when your future is at stake. You need to look out for you and your daughters. You think of something that could help this case, then it could help *you*. Go to the FBI with it immediately."

"Why are you doing this?"

His eyes scan my face, tracing each feature carefully, but he says nothing. Finally he turns on his heel and heads for the door.

"Let the FBI know if you think of anything," he says over his shoulder before closing the door behind him.

I draw in a shaky breath and replay our conversation, letting my gaze wander over Edward's retreat stuffed with his toys and prized possessions. Offshore accounts? Summer house? I need answers. I go back into the house to check on the girls and then call Brunson.

"I was going to talk to you about the trustee today," Brunson answers when I ask about assistance for basic expenses. "It's in process. How'd you know about that?"

I open my mouth to recount the conversation with Judah, but something gives me pause.

I'm taking a risk just coming to talk to you about this.

I have no reason to protect Judah Cross, but if he did take a risk coming to warn me, people aren't exactly lining up to help us right now. I know we can't be friends. I'm not sure we can be allies, but I do believe he can be useful.

"Read it somewhere online," I mumble. "I still haven't heard from Edward. Why not?"

"They've been questioning him all day, but he'll call as soon as he can and explain everything. Bail's gonna be sky-high," Brunson warns.

"This is a nightmare. He's innocent so he'll get out of this, right?"

I say it even though I'm not even sure I can quite believe it myself anymore. I have to keep saying it until I know it's a lie. It's a thinning thread of sanity, the only thing that's connecting this hellish alternative universe to the life I occupied just twenty-four hours ago.

Brunson is quiet for a few moments. For too long if the answer is a simple yes. "I'll let Edward explain," he finally says.

The doorbell rings, and I pray it's not a reporter or a "friendly" neighbor just checking on us.

"Someone's at the door," I tell him. "I'll talk to you later."

Through the glass panes, I see a young woman on the porch with several bags at her feet. I open the door and poke just my head out, peering behind her to check for any sign of the news trucks. Thankfully, they've all left.

"Can I help you?" I ask, taking in all the bags.

"You ordered groceries?" she asks.

"Uh, no."

"You're not Soledad Barnes?" She hands me a receipt. "This isn't your stuff?"

I scan the receipt, my mouth dropping open in shock to read every item from my list.

"How...I didn't..." I glance up to see her looking over her shoulder at the car idling on the curb. "Let me grab my purse."

"Already tipped." She jerks her thumb toward the waiting car. "I gotta go for my next delivery. Bye."

There must be ten bags on the porch.

"Girls," I call, a real smile breaking out on my face. "Come help me with the groceries."

Once all the food is put away, I walk back out to Edward's man cave and check the pool table where I left my pink list.

It's gone. This had to be Judah. I don't know if I can trust him or how much of what Edward has said about him might be true, but I know he sent food, and I appreciate it.

Caring father? Villain? Ally? I'm not sure what to make of the enigma that is Judah Cross, but I know in this moment that whatever his motivation, he was kind. I pull my phone out to text.

Me: Thank you for the groceries. You didn't have to do it.

Judah: I told you I want to help. Try to remember anything that might be connected to the case. That's how you'll help yourself.

CHAPTER FIVE

JUDAH

My lungs are on fire and my legs are linguine, but you wouldn't know that from the even pace I maintain for the last half mile of our morning run. We pass the Skyland fire station, and I nod to a couple of the volunteers I recognize. Tremaine and I took the boys around the community and introduced them to as many first responders as possible. There are too many horror stories of cops unwittingly mistreating a disabled person because they didn't know or understand. In some cases it's not ignorance but cruel mistreatment from someone in a position of power. I can't control everything, but we prepare and equip our boys the best we can. They both wear medical ID bracelets in case of emergencies, but it is especially important for Aaron to be easily identifiable, with so many barriers and limitations on his communication. Add that to the fact that our boys are young Black men in an affluent neighborhood, and I'm not taking chances.

"Great job, guys," I tell Aaron and Adam, who both bend and place their hands on their knees, chests heaving. "But you let your old man beat you again."

"Water," Adam pants. He stumbles up the steps to our house and into the kitchen. After wrenching the refrigerator open, he grabs one of the glass bottles of water we keep stocked and chugs it down in one gulp.

I slide the tray that holds their prescriptions and supplements across the counter. Both of them pop the pills and chase them with a full glass of water without complaint. I take it for granted sometimes now, how easily those pills go down, but it used to be a fight or sleight of hand slipping meds into ice cream or applesauce. It's taken a lot of work to get them as far as they've come, and there is still so much ahead, as their transition into adulthood is closer than I can really wrap my head around.

Aaron slots his bottle into the dishwasher.

"Shower," he says, and turns to walk upstairs.

Some words are crystal clear, and others are approximations that only those who know him can decipher. He and Adam were developing speech typically until about age two, when they both stopped talking. It was kind of eerie for them to both go quiet like that, and we assumed one was mimicking the other's behaviors. When we got their autism diagnoses, it made sense. I didn't hear Adam speak for another two years, and then one day all these words came tumbling out of him. For Aaron it took longer, and when his expressive language did return, it was much less.

"Can we skip tomorrow morning?" Adam asks, hope lighting up his sweaty face.

"Maybe we can skip a day this weekend," I bargain. "You know you do better when we run."

The boys take medication for various reasons. Adam mainly for his seizures and mood management. Aaron for mood, too, and to reduce self-injurious behavior like banging his head and chin with his fist. The meds do their work, but our occupational therapist recommended running. It's great input for their joints and may help decrease sense-seeking behaviors. I'm a man who loves data, and I can't prove that running works, but I do recognize patterns. Their toughest days tend to be the ones when we don't run in the mornings. On this journey I've learned to lean into anything that makes shit better.

"Go shower," I tell Adam. "Your mom will be here soon. You can grab breakfast after and take it with you if necessary."

"Okay." He turns toward the stairs.

"You done?" I ask with a pointed glance from the bottle to the dishwasher.

"Sorry," he says sheepishly, loading the bottle before taking off to get ready.

I'm downing a handful of vitamins and my green juice when Tremaine calls.

"Hey." I start up the stairs and enter my bedroom. "What's up?"

"Any chance you can take Adam to school?"

I glance at my Apple Watch. Aaron's school, designed for kids on the spectrum, is near my office. Harrington, the private school Adam started in January, is near Tremaine's, so we split the commute.

"What's up?" I ask with a frown while I flick through the suits in my closet.

"You remember Mrs. Martin?"

"One of the parents you're helping?" Tremaine advocates for and lends her legal expertise to so many disabled people and their families, but I think I remember this one. "Tall lady? Daughter's in middle school?"

"That's her." Tremaine releases a heavy sigh. "She has an emergency IEP meeting. She believes they may have restrained Maya, and there's a bunch of red flags waving. I wanna be there to help if I can."

"Do what you gotta do. I got you." I strip off my sodden T-shirt and jogging pants. "I'll take the boys."

"You sure you can?" she asks, even though the relief is evident in her voice.

"Yeah, if you let me go now," I say, teasing a little.

"I'll owe you big-time. Come over for dinner next week and I'll repay you in your favorite currency. Food."

"First of all, my favorite currency is actual currency. And second of all, how you gonna repay me using your new husband's skills? I already know Kent'll be cooking dinner."

"What can I say?" she laughs. "I hit the jackpot the second time around."

"That really hurt." I shake my head and chuckle. "Are you implying I wasn't everything you dreamed of when we were married?"

A small silence builds on the other end of the line, and I wonder if I misread the situation. I miss a lot of social cues. I thought we were joking, but maybe I was wrong.

"Look, Tremaine, I—"

"You were, you know," she says softly. "Everything I dreamed of. You were fine as hell. Smart as a whip. Great dad. Fantastic in bed… at first."

"Well, this took a turn." I reach to start the shower. "We've gone from your unending gratitude to a one-star rating on my sexual prowess."

"You know what I mean," she chuckles. "I used to think we got so caught up in everything the boys needed that we neglected what *we* needed from each other, but I think it was more fundamental than that."

"Did you mention an emergency? Needing to go? You can imagine how eager I am to end this conversation, right?"

"I just think we never had that kind of love," she persists, her words void of sting.

I stand still, caught off guard by her honesty, by her voicing something I suspected long before we filed for divorce.

"You and Kent have that kind of love?" I query, genuinely wondering. "It won't hurt me if you say yes."

"That's how I know you and I never had it, because if we had, it *would* hurt. Yes, Kent and I have it. I hope one day you do too."

"I doubt I'll try the marriage thing again. I may not be capable of what you're talking about."

"Oh, you are. No one loves their boys as deeply as you do who isn't capable of it elsewhere. If anything, I think you'd love too much, too hard if you ever find the person who makes you feel that."

"For someone who needs to go," I answer by *not* answering, "you sure have a lot to say this morning."

"Now that's the evasive, emotionally avoidant man I know and love."

For some reason—or more accurately for no reason—Soledad Barnes comes to mind. I barely know the woman, but I can't stop thinking about her. And that's not just since news broke about Edward's lying ass. I've thought of her often since that Christmas party. When I first saw her, it felt like someone hit me in the solar plexus. Kicked me in the throat. I didn't even realize I was staring until she turned away. I've lived like a monk since the divorce. Between my work and my boys, there hasn't been time for much else. No one has really caught my interest.

Until Soledad.

And just as I mustered the nerve to brush off my game and at least talk to her, I discovered she's married to the man I was already in the process of bringing down. I blow out a heavy breath, determined to forget what stirred in me at the Christmas party and again yesterday afternoon. She's married to an asshole, yes, but she's *married.*

Besides, I've got my own shit to deal with. I don't need to be any more entrenched in the drama of this embezzlement than I already am. She thinks not accessing her bank account is bad. She has no idea how bad it's about to get. CalPot won't care that she and her daughters are a casualty of their war with Edward.

But I do.

"You can psychoanalyze me later," I tell Tremaine. "Let me get in this shower since my commute just doubled."

"Sorry! I'll make it up to you."

"Hmmm. I may have to cash in on that favor. A lot of shit popping off at work. I might be asking you to take up my slack some over the next few weeks."

"Is it that embezzlement case?"

"Yeah. It's a mess, and of course, your boy is left holding the mop."

"I saw it on the news. I know that guy's wife vaguely, at least by sight. She's at Harrington all the time, but her daughters are younger than Adam."

I stop by the shower, naked and needing to get off the phone, but unable to shake the image of Soledad two days ago, trying to hide the trembling of her hands from me, blinking so her tears wouldn't fall, lines of worry etched around the vulnerable curves of her mouth.

"I better go," Tremaine says, pulling me back into the conversation. "Thanks again."

By the time the three of us are all showered and changed, have eaten, and are out the door, I'm cutting it really close. Harrington's out of the way. Aaron will probably be late for school, and I may be late for my first meeting.

"Will Ms. Coleman still be picking me up?" Adam asks from the passenger seat while we wait in Harrington's drop-off line. A thread of anxiety runs through his voice, which is just starting to deepen now that he's turned fifteen. He thrives on predictability, in some ways even more than Aaron. Sometimes the slightest change in his routine can trigger a meltdown. It doesn't happen as often as it did when he was younger, but I still want to reassure him so his whole day isn't wrecked.

"Ms. Coleman will pick you up," I say, holding up my index finger. "She'll take you to your social group after school." I hold up another finger to count off the second step. "And then she'll take you home and cook dinner." I hold up a third finger.

He nods and releases a slow breath through his nose. "Okay."

Ms. Coleman is a godsend. She started as a respite worker to offer Tremaine and me some occasional relief, but she's so much more than that now. Practically a part of our family.

"You got your stuff?" I ask.

His "stuff," as he likes to call it, is a collection of fidget toys and stress balls he carries in his backpack. Both boys keep their tools of choice close at hand to help them manage.

"Got 'em," he says, patting the backpack in his lap and grinning.

"Okay." I reach over and cup his head. "Love you. Have a good day."

He hops out and strides determinedly toward the building, not looking left or right. My mom says I walked just like that when I was his age. I wasn't supersocial as a kid. Hell, I'm still not the friendliest guy. I haven't expanded much beyond the same small circle of friends I made in high school and college. It's hard for me to trust new people.

We're waiting for the line to move forward, and two girls climb out of a silver Range Rover a few cars ahead. Both have long dark hair and lightly tanned skin. One is a little taller than the other. When they're almost at the school entrance, one of them turns back toward the car, her face puckered into a frown like she's trying to understand or hear. The driver's-side door flies open, and a woman jumps out carrying a backpack and runs it to the older girl.

It's a jolt seeing Soledad in a place I didn't expect to. Tremaine did say she sometimes sees her here at Harrington, but I didn't anticipate seeing her today. She's wearing slim-fitting jeans that hug her curvy figure. Small breasts, narrow waist flaring into thicker hips and butt. Oversized sunglasses hide her eyes. She smiles tightly at the teacher monitoring the carpool line but rushes back to her car. Harrington is north of Skyland, but the embezzlement case has made Atlanta news. I'm sure everyone knows, and it's probably a challenge for her even showing her face here today.

She's stronger than she looks. I bet many underestimate her.

I won't make that mistake.

CHAPTER SIX

SOLEDAD

How are the girls doing?"

Edward sounds as casual as if he's calling from the office, not from a federal prison. I sit on the edge of our bed and squeeze the phone hard since his neck isn't within choking distance.

"How do you think they're doing, Edward?" I press my lips together to stymie a stream of vitriol. "They watched the FBI tear their home apart and drag their father off to jail."

"I know." He breathes heavily on the other end. "I miss them. I miss you. You should be able to visit in the next few days."

"I don't want to visit. I want you to come home."

He pauses, and when he speaks his words are meted out with slow care. "I'm not sure when that can happen, Sol."

"Brunson did say they'll set bail really high. I don't know what we can do since they've frozen our accounts."

"What the hell?"

"I tried to buy groceries and couldn't even do that."

"You need food? Cash? Call my mom. She'll wire you money."

My mother-in-law and I have never been close.

"We're okay for now," I tell him. "I got food and have a little cash on hand at the house for emergencies, and Brunson says we'll be assigned a court trustee soon to help with some basics."

I decide not to mention that the food came courtesy of the man who essentially put him in jail.

"Right. Brunson did mention that," Edward says, his voice dipping lower. "So there's something we need to discuss."

"You mean like what the hell is going on?" I'm deceptively calm. He's kept me in the dark while speculation has run rampant in the news.

"Has the FBI questioned you?" he asks.

"Yeah. A lot. When they were at the house."

"What did you tell them? What'd you say?"

"I didn't have anything *to* say. I don't know anything. Edward, what the fuck?"

"The less you know, the better."

"You really think I'm going to accept that?" I huff an outraged breath. "Tell me what's going on right now."

"I can't. I need you to trust me."

"You say that to me? That I should trust you when I can't even access our accounts and our credit cards are shut down? From what I hear, that's just the first wave. They'll come for the house next. Our cars. CalPot wants their money."

"They should ask their wonder kid Cross where it is since he seems to have all the answers," he says, bitterness making his words hard. "All I can tell you is that I'm securing our future."

"Edward," I whisper. "They mentioned offshore accounts and a summer house. What have you done?"

"Nothing they can prove."

He did it. He really did it. Oh, my God.

The world as I knew it falls apart yet again, bits of his lies and deceptions flying around my head, projectile, sharp, cutting at everything I believed about life, about our past. About our future. Dread gathers in my belly and slithers up my throat while the silence elongates between us. I'm rendered speechless by his arrogance, by his recklessness. I don't know if he's done everything Judah accused him of, but he's done something. Until this moment I had held out hope that it was the misunderstanding he had claimed, that they had the wrong guy. But Edward's evasiveness, his refusal to assert his innocence, confirms a horrible suspicion that's been lurking in the back of my mind since the FBI showed up on our front porch.

"Even if I'm prosecuted," he finally says, filling the terrible quiet, "Brunson predicts I'll do eighteen months, two years at most in some low-security spot. And when I get out—"

"Shouldn't you be looking for ways to not get *in*? Instead of calculating how little time you'll do?"

"Sol, listen to me." He lowers his voice again. "When I get out, we'll be set for life."

"Oh, my God, Edward." I lean forward, dropping my forehead into my hand and closing my eyes, trying to block out the awful truth he essentially just confessed. "Of all the stupid—"

"You say that to me? When I did this for you? For us? For our girls?"

"Don't lie to me." My head snaps up and I glare at the bedroom peppered with reminders of him. His watch on the bedside table. The shoes he discarded as carelessly as he handled this situation. "You can lie to yourself, but I don't buy your bullshit, Edward. And for the girls? Don't . . . just don't."

I cut myself off, packing down the rage and resentment to let in a deep breath I hope will clear my rioting thoughts.

"What do you expect us to do for two years while you're languishing in this minimum-security facility you have all picked out? Lottie and Inez's tuition check bounced. They'll take our cars. They'll leverage anything they can to pressure you to give them their money."

"I thought about that. You and the girls could go live with Mom."

"In Boston?" I shriek. "You want me to uproot our daughters, move them from schools and friends they love, leave the house we took years to make feel like a home, to live in Boston? A place they've rarely ever even visited?"

"Whose fault is it they've so rarely visited? They barely know my mother."

"Your mother favors Lupe over Inez and Lottie because she looks white."

"What the hell, Sol? How could you even think that?"

"It's true. You just don't want to admit it. They would pick up on it, if they haven't already. I've spent their whole lives building them up and making sure they knew we loved them all equally. I won't risk your mother undoing that in a year with her biases."

"She's from an earlier generation. Cut her some slack."

"An earlier generation? We're not talking about not knowing how to FaceTime. It's racism."

"I can't believe you're making this harder for me right now. I ask you to do this one thing."

"Really? When this *one thing* is covering up stealing six million dollars? You expected my cooperation?" Sitting on the bed, I dig my nails into the mattress, wishing it were his flesh. "The hell you did."

"Be very careful," he says, lacing his words with warning. "If you lose your head, you could ruin years of planning. If you just do everything I tell you, you'll be back to designer bags and diamond facials in no time."

"Is that what you think I do with my days? Shop and get facials?"

"I know you don't work. I do that, so if you could just let me do my job and take care of you and the girls the way I see fit, we'll be fine."

"You don't think what I do is work? Cleaning, cooking, organizing, driving, taking care of our children. All tasks people pay to have done for them. Is it not a job because I do it for my family? Did you think all these years you were the only one working just because you left the house every morning?"

"Oh, God, Sol. I don't have time for this feminist bullshit tirade. I know you have some things you do to stay busy, but I'm talking—"

"*To stay busy?* There aren't enough hours in the day for all I do, and you think I'm looking for ways to 'stay busy'? Was I staying busy when I worked at the hotel's front desk during the day and cleaned rooms at night, seven months pregnant, so you could focus on your MBA? Was that just staying busy?"

"That's ancient history. Focus. We need to deal with now."

So it's *we* when he needs something and all about him every other minute of the day.

"I have to go," I say abruptly, not sure I can take another minute of his bullshit and disrespect.

"Where are you going? I still have some time."

"Sorry. I have shopping and extravagant lunches scheduled before picking your daughters up from school."

"Dammit, Sol, this is no time to get self-righteous. I'm trying to speak as plainly as I can."

"The time to speak plainly was before you did this stupid shit and expected me to fall in line. To be your accessory." I rub the back of my neck, where tension has been building for the last two days. "Look, whatever. I'll check with Brunson to see if we are any closer to getting you out of there. Not for you, Edward, but for the girls. They want you home. We'll deal with what happens once this goes to trial."

"I won't..." He clears his throat. "I won't be making bail."

"They haven't put a lien on the house yet. I can try to—"

"There won't be any bail," he says as if it's an admission.

"Edward, let me try to—"

"They've deemed me a flight risk, Sol. No bail."

"Why would they think that? How—"

"I didn't want to tell you unless it became necessary because I knew you wouldn't understand, but they found out about a plane ticket I purchased."

"Plane ticket?" I ask with the still quiet that occurs before an explosion. The ground slides beneath my feet. The world tips and I don't know when my life will be upright again. "What the hell are you talking about?"

"I knew Cross was closing in on me. I panicked and bought a plane ticket, just as an insurance policy in case I needed to get out of the country to a place they couldn't reach me."

"And leave me and your children here with no money, no house, no car, and the FBI considering *me* a suspect?"

"I never planned to use it," he says in a defensive rush. "I just needed an escape route if it became necessary."

"And where were you *not* planning to go, exactly?"

"Bali. They don't have an extradition treaty with the US."

"Wow. You had it all planned out, down to sending us to live with your mother, who can't stand me."

"Just lay low and don't ruin this. We'll come out richer than you can imagine if you just hold down what you know and leave what you don't know alone. You and the girls mean everything to me."

"Right. That's why you bought *one* ticket to Bali that I didn't even know about. I can tell how desperate you were to spend your remaining days with your family."

"I love you," he says, desperation leaking through his composure. "I did this for you."

"Bullshit." If I have to listen to one more word out of his lying mouth, I might fight my way through this phone and down his throat. "I gotta go."

"Remember what I said," he adds hurriedly. "Don't tell them anything. Let this play out."

I hang up without saying goodbye and flop back on the bed. Closing my eyes, I replay the call, fighting the urge to scream. There's a little time before I have to get the girls from school. A little time here alone, where I don't have to pretend everything is fine or that it's all going to work out.

I used some of the cash I had on hand to get gas. I have the groceries Judah sent. Dr. Morgan has given me a little grace to figure out Lottie and Inez's tuition, but the FBI will be back, and it will start applying more pressure the longer it takes to find the money Edward stole.

I need to be cautious, but I want to be bold. I want to be honest, but lying seems to be the thing that will protect us. I'm tossed in every direction and going nowhere. Hot tears leak from my eyes and slide into my hairline.

I miss Mami.

It's not a constant ache anymore, the grief, the immeasurable loss of someone who is absolutely irreplaceable. Mami passed a few years after my father, and the compounded devastation was almost unbearable. Necessity compelled me to keep going. My daughters needed me. My husband needed me, though he seems to have forgotten that I played any significant role in his success. My mother was never Edward's biggest fan, but when I got pregnant soon after I graduated from Cornell and we decided to marry, my parents supported the decision. She never spoke against him, but I would catch her watching him sometimes with a wariness usually reserved for strangers. I didn't ask her then what she saw. Maybe I was afraid of the answer. Afraid the path I had chosen was the wrong one. That *he* was the wrong one.

"Mami, what do I do?" I whisper to the empty room.

There is no audible answer, of course, but a thought does occur to me, and I have to wonder if it's a mystical nudge she managed from the other side. When Mami died, my sisters and I each took a few of her things we wanted for ourselves. I force myself to stand and walk into the closet. At the very back, in a cubby at the top, sits an old chest. Not too large and more than a little worn, it appears incongruous among my Hermès bags and shiny stilettos. I grab my step stool and reach up to pull the chest down.

I can't hear Mami's voice, but when I open this small chest of her things, I feel closer to her. It smells faintly of the Egyptian musk she used to wear from the beauty supply store. It was cheap, but I'd trade all my pricey fragrances just to hold her close now and bury my face in the crook of her neck. Let her stroke my hair and dry my tears.

But she's not here, so I settle the chest on my closet floor and kneel, reverently opening it. Inside are treasures I haven't looked at in years. Not because I'd forgotten they were here, but because it is bittersweet, the ache of missing her and the comfort of having her things.

The first is an old, dog-eared copy of bell hooks's *All About Love.* I flip through the pages of the book, which is more than twenty years old, and note Mami's annotations, little colorful flags poking from the pages, her highlights, like neon mile markers, and her neat hand-writing in the margins, sloping in and out of English and Spanish.

Mami's favorite *pilón* is also in the chest. I watched her use the mor-tar and pestle to mash garlic and peppers for her *sofrito*. I pull it out and set it on the floor so I can take it back down with me to the kitchen.

One of her journals is here, though there's still a stack of them in the garage at the house where we grew up. I hesitated to read this after I saw the poetry she wrote to Bray, feeling like an intruder on a part of Mami's life she had kept for herself.

All loves aren't created equal. Some spring from the earth and wrap around and twine through our souls like vines. Some are plants that start with tiny seeds in your heart and blossom over time, nurtured by years and commitment. Bray was Mami's vine, a tall, handsome giant of a man. Abuela used to joke that Bray swept Mami off her feet. My father caught her when she fell. Bray wasn't a good husband, but he was a terrific father, so he was always in Lola's life. Always in *our* lives.

Once he dropped Lola off after a weekend visit, and I caught him with Mami in the kitchen. My sweet mother, who lingered after work to flip through the library's new arrivals and loved the smell of books. Who knit in the evenings, glasses sliding down her nose while she watched Pat and Vanna on *Wheel of Fortune*. When I walked into the kitchen, she was clutching Bray like he was air and she was suffocat-ing. His hands were everywhere. On her ass, in her hair, which had tumbled down her back, loosened from the neat knot she always kept rolled at her nape. Her glasses lay forgotten on the floor. They made desperate, starved, craving sounds, and I understood that this was not what she had with my father. I stepped back, afraid they'd see, but I stayed at the door.

"I can't," I heard her whisper, tears in her voice. "Bray, we have to stop. Jason."

My father's name in the middle of all that passion was like a shot ringing out in a quiet forest. Bray didn't come inside our house after that. Lola would instead bounce down the steps to his car, but sometimes I'd catch him looking, longing.

He attended my father's funeral, and I believe he respected him. That he'd stayed away out of respect not only for Mami, but also for my dad. But once Mami was a widow, Bray couldn't stay away. With us girls all gone from the house to pursue college and life, they started up again. My *abuela* would tut and shake her head, muttering about the power of the *polla*, but it was more than that. When Mami was diagnosed with cervical cancer, Bray never left her side. And when she passed away, at the funeral he wept unashamedly. I never knew if it was just for her passing or for the years they'd missed because when he'd met the love of his life, he hadn't been ready for her.

I still don't crack the journal open even now. Maybe one day I'll work up the nerve.

There is also a ticket to a Lisa Lisa and Cult Jam concert. She was our freestyle queen. I can still hear Mami belting "All Cried Out" and "I Wonder If I Take You Home" while she cooked *arroz con gandules* for dinner.

Next is a folded cloth. I take it out and unfurl it, my heart singing with pride to see the first Puerto Rican flag, that of the Grito de Lares, a symbol of rebellion against colonization. A battle cry for independence.

Finally, at the bottom of the chest, beneath a threadbare cardigan, lies the prized possession of kitchens in my family for years. A machete with a mother-of-pearl handle and surprisingly sharp blade. Women of my family have used this to cut back brush when seeking fruit and vegetables. It has split coconuts and sliced through pork shoulders. It goes back three generations, and the weight of it in my hands somehow connects to the weight in my heart, threads it through my soul like the eye of a needle. I feel these items stitching me together in a way I can't explain but appreciate.

The respite from anxiety these things, *her things*, bring is short-lived. My phone buzzes in the bedroom. I blow out a short breath, stand, and carefully replace the chest in its cubby. When I walk back out to the bedroom, my phone is lit up with a text message.

Lottie: Don't forget I need to be at the gym by 3:30 today. Coach wants to go over the new routine before next week's meet.

Me: I got you. See you at carpool.

Lottie: And can you bring string cheese? I'll be starving!

It's ironic that Edward believes I have so much leisure time when it usually feels like my life revolves around my family and this house, both of which I love so much. But when is it time for me?

"Certainly not now," I mutter, grabbing my purse and a sweatshirt to slide over my head as I run down the steps and to the garage.

CHAPTER SEVEN

JUDAH

"A ny update on the situation with Barnes?" Brett Callahan asks, fixing his eyes on me from the other end of the boardroom.

"He's still in custody and not talking," I tell the room full of directors since our CEO obviously assumes I should know. "I remain in close communication and cooperation with the Feds, but we're pretty hands-off at this point, unless they need something clarified or to follow up with more questions. I did convey I suspected that coward had planned a way to run. The FBI followed that thought and discovered the ticket to Bali. He's been deemed a flight risk. No bail."

"The audacity of that motherfucker," Delores Callahan spits from the other end of the table. "After all this company has done for him. Are they any closer to recovering our money?"

"The FBI is following every lead," I report with a frown. "It's harder to trace than I would expect, especially some of the offshore accounts in countries that won't cooperate because of privacy laws. Some of the trails lead to shell companies and some just vanish. It's actually pretty elaborate and complex."

"We need him to talk," Brett says. "They froze his money, right? Get the Feds to apply pressure everywhere we can. Make his family feel it."

My teeth grind with the effort it takes not to yell that it won't make a difference. It will only hurt Soledad and her daughters, not Edward.

"That's out of our hands at this point," I say. "They have frozen the accounts by court order, but there's not much more we can do as a company to exert pressure."

"You're not going soft on us, are you, Cross?" Brett booms, a crooked grin slicing across his face. "You're usually the hard-ass of the bunch."

"I just don't think we should waste energy and time coming up with things that won't get us what we want," I assert. "Edward Barnes is a selfish asshole counting on a short sentence for a white-collar crime, after which he'll go dig up the money he's buried in accounts all over the world. At this point all we can do is assist the FBI's investigation however we can."

"We do control the family's health-care benefits," says Dick, one of the department heads, who more than lives up to his name. "That is one of the few places we can still exert pressure."

Keeping my face expressionless, I grip my pen so tightly, it may start bleeding ink all over the conference room table.

"Maybe that pretty wife of his'll buckle when she can't pay for a sick kid or send them to that fancy private school," Dick continues.

"Does it matter that she's pretty?" Delores asks with raised brows, and, if I'm not mistaken, a touch of affront. "Sometimes I think I'm the only thing standing between this company and a sexual harass-ment suit."

"I don't care if she looks like the bottom of my fucking shoe," Brett thunders, his good-natured smile replaced with a scowl on his florid face. "I want my money, and if squeezing Soledad Barnes gets it, then you damn well better squeeze, Judah. Dick's angle on medical benefits may have some merit."

The hell it does.

I stay silent but glance up at the CalPot CEO to at least acknowledge I've heard him. I'm the most logical, *ruthless when I need to be* son of a bitch in this room, and while I don't think pressuring Soledad will yield any real results, I understand that is the smart play. But I can't let them make it. I will find a way to stop them from making it. It's irrational, this desire to shield her—to protect her from the fallout of

Edward's actions. What if my gut is wrong? What if she *does* know more than she's letting on? Am I, the man who has always been impervious to distractions, being blinded by luxurious dark, amber-streaked curls, a pouty mouth the color of grenadine, and an ass that...

I blow out a long breath, forcing myself to refocus on the meeting I'm supposedly leading. "I believe if Soledad thinks of anything or finds something that will help us, will help her and her daughters," I say, "that she'll share it."

"Maybe I should talk to her," Dick drawls, his smile slipping into a leer.

"No," I say, the word clipped and my unwavering stare flinty. "You won't."

I had a hard time not looking at Soledad in that gold dress at the Christmas party, but Dick didn't even try. With his wife right beside him, he shamelessly ogled Soledad. The fuck he's going to her house to "talk to her."

"What I mean," I continue, evening out my voice, "is that we should have little to no contact with Edward's family right now."

"Says who?" Dick demands.

"Says the FBI," I shoot back. "One wrong word or interaction between us and them could jeopardize this case."

Which makes the risk I took warning her all the more foolhardy, not to mention out of character. I hope that decision to go to her house doesn't bite me in the ass.

"You seem to have taken a special interest in Mrs. Barnes, Cross," Dick sneers.

"I have a special interest in getting our money back." I look around the table at the ten or so directors and department heads, taking time to hold each person's gaze. "If you recall, no one in this company knew there was a problem until I told you there was. If you've trusted my instincts to get us this far, trust me now."

I glance down at the printed stack of evidence I've been collecting for months. "I don't believe he did this alone. Someone smarter helped, but working with someone smart doesn't make you smart. I'm counting on Edward to have done the stupid thing somewhere along the way. When we find that, we'll crack this case open."

"We better," Brett says, standing and signaling the end of the meeting. "I want him to pay, and I want our money back. I don't care who we have to squash to make that happen."

He strides from the room, his assistant, Willa, tripping to keep up with him. I take some time gathering my things—the iPad and the burgeoning file folder—even though my instinct is to rush back to the office and reexamine every piece of evidence immediately. I want to convey a sense of calm despite feeling the same urgency Brett does. Maybe more. The longer this goes on, the worse it will get for Soledad. I don't even want to analyze why that matters to me so much. I've never been swayed by a woman's looks.

And that's not it.

You could miss how much more there is to Soledad, but I've seen her strength and her fortitude and her humor and sacrificial love for her children. I recognize that because it's why Tremaine and I rearranged our lives, our dreams, our goals to do whatever was necessary for Aaron and Adam. Beyond her obvious assets, it is the way Soledad engaged with Aaron that most impressed me. He doesn't try to make it easy for others to connect. It's not a natural priority for him, so sometimes it takes someone who's willing to go the extra mile, to extend themselves even though, at first, it doesn't seem like you'll get much in the way of a response. When I walked in and saw them cubing together, recognized how much it meant to Aaron even if his expression didn't give it away, something lodged in my chest that I haven't been able to pull free since.

"Good work so far on this, Judah," Delores says, a portfolio tucked beneath her arm. "Keep at it."

"Thanks." I stand too. "We'll keep trying."

"Despite what my father seems to think," she laughs, her thick brows crinkling. "That's all we can do. And I appreciate you looking out for Soledad."

My head snaps up, a protest already on my lips. "I'm not looking out—"

"I'm not Dick, Judah. I don't think you have some ulterior motive. She's not the kind of person who would do this. She's too honest. Too forthright, almost to a fault." She chuckles and shakes her head. "You should have heard her criticizing our pans and telling me how to fix them."

"If I'm wrong about her," I answer, matching my steps to Delores's as we approach the conference room exit, "I'll eat my briefcase."

"If you're wrong"—Delores pauses, places her hand on my shoulder, and gives me a more sober look—"my father will eat *you* alive. He doesn't abide fools, and he hates being made to look like one. This has become personal for him, and he'll break Soledad if he has to."

I stiffen and glance from the hand on my shoulder to her serious expression. "I'm afraid I can't let him do that."

A smile inches onto her face and she nods.

"I was hoping that's what you would say."

CHAPTER EIGHT

SOLEDAD

Good news," Brunson says. "You can visit Edward."

"Oh, great." I know I don't sound enthusiastic, and after my conversation with Edward yesterday, I can't even find the energy to fake it.

"You can go as soon as today if you want."

"Thanks for letting me know." Adjusting my earbud so I can hear him better, I plate a waffle and set it in front of Lupe, who is seated at the kitchen counter.

"Um, visiting hours end at three o'clock," Brunson continues, a note of uncertainty entering his voice.

"Lottie has a gymnastics meet today." I nod to the pantry. "Inez, grab the syrup. Sorry, Brunson, we're having breakfast."

Inez returns with the syrup and hands it to Lottie, who drowns her waffle.

"All right," I warn Lottie, nodding to her loaded plate. "You're gonna feel that when you go flipping through the air. Slow down."

"Well, I know how eager you were to see him," Brunson ventures. "Sorry it took a few days. I'm sure he'd love to see you tomorrow if you can't make it today."

"Of course." I join the girls at the counter, slice into my own waffle, and pierce a chicken sausage link. "Sounds good."

"If you change your mind about today, just let me know and I'll get it set up. Let him know you're coming."

"Okay." I sip my orange juice. "Talk to you soon."

It's silent on the other end, and the lawyer's confusion reaches me over the phone. I went from desperate to see my husband to *I'll see him if I see him.*

"Look, Sol—"

My phone beeps and I glance at the screen, frowning when I see my doctor's name.

"Brunson, lemme call you back. This is my doctor's office."

"Everything okay?"

"I had my annual. Probably just confirming that things checked out. I'll talk to you later."

I catch the call and am surprised not to hear my doctor's nurse on the other end, but the physician herself.

"Dr. Claymont," I say. "Reaching out to me personally, and on a Saturday? What's next? House calls?"

I wait for her answering humor, but it doesn't come. We've been together a long time. She was fresh out of med school and we had just relocated to Atlanta when I first started seeing her more than fifteen years ago. I know her pretty well, and her easy humor is usually evident.

"Shelia?" I glance at the girls eating breakfast and allow a nervous laugh to slip out. "What's up?"

"Sol, I know it's unusual to call on a Saturday, and for me to call personally, but I wanted to talk to you about some results from your annual."

My belly knots with a familiar dread. I leave the kitchen and walk through the living room and out onto the front porch before answering.

"If it's cancer"—I force the words out and sit on the top step—"just spit it out. You know my mother—"

"It's not cancer."

"Oh, thank God." I slump, letting my back hit the hard edge of the porch steps.

"I know," she says, compassion tingeing her words. "You're fine. I mean . . . you don't have cancer."

"But I'm not fine?" A frown accompanies my brief laugh. "Just tell me what's wrong."

"You have chlamydia."

The silence swells and bursts in my ears, ending in a roar where all the sounds of the neighborhood—Mr. Calloway's dogs barking, the kids up the block squealing as their mom pulls them in a wagon, the airplane flying low, headed for Hartsfield—all come rushing back in.

"Oh, wow," I giggle. "Sorry. For a second I thought you said I have—"

"Chlamydia, yeah. You do, Sol. I'm... I'm sorry."

The humor burns to ashes on my lips, and for a few seconds I can't speak.

"It's not life-threatening," she continues, reassuming a strictly professional tone. "You probably didn't even know anything was wrong. You didn't report any symptoms when you were here earlier this week. It's curable. I've already ordered a round of antibiotics that you—"

"Wait a minute." I stand to pace our driveway. "There's a mistake. A mix-up with someone else's results or something. Shelia, you know that couldn't be. I've only been with..."

My husband.

I've only had sex with one person for the last two decades. Apparently Edward can't say the same.

Shelia's instructions about the medication, her telling me the prescription should be waiting at the pharmacy—very few of the details compute. I only absorb the pain of Edward's betrayal. It batters me from the inside, pounding the tender muscle in my chest again and again. The beating of my heart.

In a daze, I disconnect the call and drop to the front step with a thud, the winter air drying tears on my cheeks into stiff tracks. A pain so visceral it literally steals my breath spears right through me. My mind reels, replaying every moment since the day Edward and I met on campus, finding the thread that runs through good and hard years, through three delivery rooms and nearly two decades under the same roof, sharing the same bed. I'm tired of gripping that thread, searching for the moment things started to change. I only know they did; *he* did, and his deceit has unraveled our lives completely.

I've been so stupid. All the nights I wondered why he didn't want to sleep with me, and he was fucking someone else. The irony of me practically begging him to make love to me the night of the Christmas party. Now I understand his comments about vaginal rejuvenation weren't just simple cruelty. He was redirecting; distracting me from his duplicity by making me feel inadequate, deliberately planting seeds of insecurity so I focused on me and not on the shit he was up to. My paranoia that sprang from his odd behavior the last two years wasn't paranoia at all, but intuition. Instinct I was too afraid to follow to its natural conclusion.

It's not even the infection itself that makes me feel dirty. It's his betrayal. I feel stained not by what he has given me, but by what he has taken away. What he withheld from me when I held nothing back from him and gave everything to the life we promised we'd build together.

The hurt settles like sediment, sinking all the way to the bottom of me, and solidifies into rage. Not only has he put our financial security at risk, left the girls and me completely vulnerable, but he has violated me in the most egregious way. Not just breaking our vows, but defiling what was supposed to be sacred between our bodies and our hearts.

Or did he ever even see it that way? Was he ever the great guy I thought I married right out of college? The one who made me the envy of every girl in our class? When did he change into this monster who steals millions of dollars and has unprotected sex with other people? Or has he spent the last twenty years hiding behind a grotesque mask?

Only one way to find out. I dial Brunson and don't even wait for him to speak.

"Hey, I do want you to make sure I'm on Edward's visitors' list today after all."

"Okay. Did something change?"

"Yeah." I sniff and brush the last of my tears away. "Everything."

CHAPTER NINE

SOLEDAD

I rushed to get to the prison, and now I can't make myself move from the parking lot. Sitting here, staring at the building, I swallow the tide of emotion that keeps rising in my throat, threatening to flood my eyes. Edward doesn't get any more of my tears. He's not worthy.

I check my reflection in the rearview mirror. I'm wearing very little makeup, a simple sweater and jeans. The guidelines Brunson sent indicated modest clothing. I wish I could show up wearing sackcloth and ashes, mourning the death of my illusions, of my marriage, of the world as I knew it. I'm climbing out of my truck when I spot a blond woman exiting the prison. She looks familiar, and as she draws closer, I know exactly who she is.

"Oh, my God." I hop back into the Rover and dip down in my seat, pushing my head up just enough to see her unlock a black Porsche convertible.

Amber.

All my suspicions about her come rushing back. Actually they never left. I just filed them away because Edward always had an answer, and I could never catch him in a lie. He always had an excuse.

Until now.

There is no excuse he can offer this time because the proof of his infidelity, of his perfidy, I carry in my body.

I'm parked at the opposite end of the parking lot, so she doesn't see me. I lie flat in my seat for a few minutes, allowing time for her to leave.

I slowly raise my head to make sure her car is gone. Exhaling my fears, my uncertainties, my hurt, I breathe in indignation and resentment like noxious fumes that, instead of weakening me, make me stronger. Strong enough to get through this confrontation. As I store my purse in a locker and walk through the metal detector, I rehearse the wrongs Edward has done to me, to our family, nursing my rage. Keeping it barely checked and growling at the surface to unleash on my pathetic excuse for a husband.

Fortunately, when I enter the visitors' room, there aren't many people there. It's not a private space, but inmates and their visitors are spread out, and the conversations are low-voiced, for the most part. Edward stands from the cheap couch as soon as he sees me, arms outstretched. I stop a few feet shy of his touch and pour all my fury into the glare I send him. His arms drop slowly to his sides, a frown knitting between his dark blond brows.

"Soledad," he says, but it sounds more like a question, one he dares to pair with a small smile. "Glad you changed your mind. Brunson said you had to take Lottie to a meet but might make it tomorrow. I wasn't expecting you."

"Is that why Amber was rushing off?"

His smile petrifies, and I see the moment he realizes I've caught his ass. His eyes glint with calculation before he blanks his face.

"What do you mean? You saw Amber? Talked to her?"

I place my hands on my hips and stare up at him with lifted brows. "She is the one you're fucking, right? The one you got chlamydia from?"

He looks around furtively, embarrassment burning his face bright red. "Have you lost your mind? What the hell are you talking about?"

"Oh, I guess you're not showing symptoms yet either, or maybe you forgot you recently deigned to fuck your wife and could have passed it on to her. Your girlfriend isn't just *yours*, Edward. She's spreading her shit elsewhere, and thanks to you, it's spread to me."

He pulls in a long breath, the muscles along his jaw bunched. "The notion of me being unfaithful to you is ridiculous. If you have the clap, I'm asking who *you've* been with."

"Do you expect this to work?" I fold my arms across my chest and narrow my eyes, seeing him more clearly maybe than I ever have. "That you can bravado your way out of this? That you can flash your Whitestrips smile and I'll be so dazzled I'll forget you cheated on me?"

"Shut up," he hisses, glancing around. "We cannot have this conversation here. It's too dangerous."

"What was dangerous was you having unprotected sex with Amber and then fucking me."

"If you're going to make wild accusations, then I think you should leave."

"You're kicking me out?" I bark a laugh that is so close to sincere. "Of prison? Why? So you won't have to face the fact that your side piece has something on the side too?"

"She's not with him any—" He catches himself, but not before I grab another tiny piece of the puzzle confirming my suspicions. "If you insist on being loud and jeopardizing my case with a bunch of unfounded speculation, then yeah, you should leave. You need some time to cool off and think rationally."

"Oh, I'm real rational. So rational I've been thinking about all those late nights you spent with Amber at the office. Maybe you weren't just sleeping together. Maybe she's a part of your scheme."

A gate falls over Edward's face, and his lips thin so much they almost disappear. "You have no idea what you're talking about."

"Oh, but I do. Judah believes someone worked with you, that you're not smart enough to pull this off by yourself. And now that I think about it," I say, touching the tip of my finger to my chin, "he's right."

"You just couldn't wait to run to him, could you?" Edward asks, his words dripping with contempt. "Now do you believe he was after me?"

"Yes, and for good reason. You're a crook and a liar and a..." The sob catches me by surprise and I cover my mouth, refusing to give him that. "How could you, Edward? How could you do this to me?"

And I see it now. Beneath the charm, there's ice in his eyes, and I strain to remember the last time he looked at me with warmth. With care. How long has he been looking right through me? Not seeing the woman I've become? Did he ever love me? Is he even capable of it?

"What's the use of denying it now? You caught me." He holds up both hands like he's at gunpoint. "Guilty as charged. I found a younger woman, someone exciting and ambitious and smart. Maybe this is a blessing in disguise. You apparently aren't interested in riches beyond your wildest dreams and would only hold me back. When I get out of here, I'll divorce you and we can go our separate ways. You'll only have to see me on weekends when I take the girls."

I lunge at him, but stop short when I notice an officer with an alert expression watching us closely. I step closer to Edward, but not threateningly. I reach up and cup his neck, bringing his head down to my lips. He strains to pull away, but I won't let him go, sinking my nails into his flesh.

"If you think I'll let you have anything to do with my daughters," I hiss in his ear, "you really are delusional. If you're so tired of being the family man, don't be."

"Hey," the officer says, frowning and motioning for us to separate. "Step back."

I shove Edward away from me and curl my lips around the last promise I'll make to this man. "I won't shield them from who you really are, Edward. I won't lie for you. I'll tell them how you've stolen. That you're a thief and a liar. That you cheated on their mother."

I turn toward the visitors' room exit, immune to the stares our raised voices drew.

"You can't do this," Edward hurls at my back. "You have no money. They'll take the house. What do you have without me, Sol? You won't survive."

I look back over my shoulder and give him a smile that costs me everything but is worth the worry in his eyes.

"Watch me."

CHAPTER TEN

SOLEDAD

I pull into the garage, and my phone lights up with a text message. Several, actually, on my thread with Hendrix and Yasmen.

Hendrix: Are you okay, Sol? What's going on? I just dropped Lottie off at your house.

Me: I'm good. Thank you for taking her. Just got home myself. I owe you big time.

Yasmen: Are you gonna tell us what's going on?

My fingers hover over the keypad. More than once, my best friends have dragged Edward. Warned me he was hiding something. And I knew it, didn't I? On some level, I knew there were things he kept from me, but I never would have imagined him capable of this kind of criminal behavior or even cheating on me. Mumbling Amber's name in his sleep a few times was one thing, but actually sleeping with her? Unprotected? Passing an STI on to me?

I grip the steering wheel as shame washes over me. As much as I love my friends, I can't bring myself to admit how foolish I've been, not even to them. They would never say I told you so, but we all know they did, in one way or another. I didn't want to believe my perfect life slept on a bed of lies. I'm too tired, too embarrassed to reveal the massive scope of his embezzlement, his infidelity, the clap.

I stare at the little bag from the pharmacy that holds my prescription. I never got an STI in high school or college, and at almost forty years old I do? I'd laugh if my heart weren't broken so wide open. If I weren't so embarrassed.

> **Me:** It's a lot going on, but I'd prefer to talk about it tomorrow. Is that okay? It's late.

> **Yasmen:** Are you sure? Josiah's here with Kassim. Deja's at the movies. I can come.

> **Hendrix:** And my child-free, man-free ass can come, too. We'll be there. Just say the word.

> **Me:** Tomorrow is the word, okay? I'll tell you everything. Just don't ask me to do it now.

> **Yasmen:** I'm sorry, Sol. I truly am, honey.

And I know that she knows. Not the details, but that they were right. That Edward ain't shit, and that my life has been one massive falsehood after another.

> **Me:** Love you guys. Come over tomorrow for brunch. I'll make you a frittata and a Bloody Mary. You know I'm a stress cooker, and you can try to cheer me up.

> **Hendrix:** Heavy on the Bloody Mary. It's been a long week. ☺ Okay. We'll let it go tonight, but tomorrow, yo li'l ass is telling us everything.

> **Me:** Promise. Tomorrow. Love you.

I turn my phone off because I can't take their care anymore. It makes me want to cry how they love me no matter what, but my husband whom I've known half my life couldn't manage that. There aren't enough sonnets for friendship. Not enough songs for the kind of love not born of blood or body but of time and care. They are the ones we choose to laugh and cry and live with. When lovers come and go, friends are the ones who remain. We are each other's constants.

The girls are in the living room when I enter the house.

"Mommy, look!" Lottie hops up from the couch and shows me the ribbon pinned to her warm-up suit. "First place."

"Oh, sweetie."

I've never missed a meet. They're not all crucial, but I'm always there. I hate that I missed this one because I was chasing after their pathetic father, but it had to be done. And I meant what I said. I won't lie for him. I won't tell the girls he's a good man when he's a cheat and a criminal. We'll line up our therapists now for the possible daddy issues this may give them, but I will not protect him when he didn't protect us.

"How was Dad?" Inez asks, glancing up briefly from the game she's playing on her iPad. "When's he coming home?"

"He's fine." I drop my purse and pharmacy bag on the couch. "It may be awhile before we know when he'll get out. The lawyer's working on it."

Out.

Not *home*, because if I find a way to keep this house, he'll never live here again.

"But he will get out, right?" Lupe asks, setting her phone aside.

"Girls, I want to tell you something." I perch on the ottoman in the center of the room and look at them one by one. "Your father has made some bad choices. I can't get into the specifics right now, but he may have to pay for some of the things he's done."

"But he said it was Mr. Cross," Inez protests, her brow creasing into a frown. "That he got set up."

"No one has set him up," I say firmly. "I don't want to talk about the case too much yet because things are still developing. I just want you to understand that your father may not get out on bail yet. We'll deal with the rest as we go."

"But what are we gonna do?" Lottie asks, blinking rapidly, her sweet mouth pulled tight. "Daddy takes care of us."

"I'll take care of us," I tell her without hesitation. I don't know exactly how, but I will.

"But you don't have a job," Inez says.

It's like a knife to my heart. Edward has barely been around the last couple of years. He said it was increased workload. Now I know it was playing fast and loose with the company's money and his assistant. I've given my whole life to these three humans, to that man, to this home, to this family. And at least in this moment, it feels like my worth to them is measured by the paycheck I don't have.

"We're her job." Lupe pops Inez on the side of her head. "Mom, she didn't mean it that way."

"Mean what what way?" Inez's wide eyes fly to me. "I didn't mean to hurt your feelings, Mom. I was just saying—"

"It's all right, baby." I stand and bend to kiss her head and do the same to Lupe and Lottie. "I know what you meant. I'm gonna go upstairs for a bit, okay?"

"Mom," Lupe says with a worried frown that's too old for her face. "Are you sure you're—"

"I'm good." I muster a reassuring smile that I hope convinces her because it's the best I can do right now. "How about pizza for dinner?"

Their agreement is subdued compared to the usual enthusiasm, and I know my girls so well, I can practically see their thoughts floating over their heads. Kids are resilient. They're trying to go about business as usual, but their father is behind bars. The FBI is involved. They know this could change life as we know it, and they aren't sure what will happen.

That is one of the parts about being an adult that really sucks. You're the one who has to be sure or has to figure it out. My parents always figured it out. We didn't have a lot of money, but I don't remember worrying about it. I want my girls to have that. Not blissful ignorance. I knew things were hard sometimes, but I was always sure Mami and Dad would see us through.

Thoughts of my parents compel me to the closet when I reach my bedroom. I drag my step stool out and climb up to grab Mami's chest. Sitting on the floor and lifting the lid, I breathe her memory in and draw her close for comfort.

If she were alive, she would heap a stream of curses on Edward's name. She would threaten him with my aunt Silvana, who embraces the old ways and still practices Sanse. Mami always said none of that vodou stuff was real, but let somebody mess with us. She'd call Aunt Silvana back on the island so fast. A solitary tear coasts down my cheek and slips into the corner of my mouth. It's not salty. It's bittersweet with the remarkable years I had with my mother and the years I've had to live without her.

When we were a little older, she talked more about her life with Bray before my father. She told us he'd cheated on her once, and that was it.

"You accept a man shitting on you," she used to say, "he'll make himself at home. There's no three strikes. You use me, take me for granted, you prove you don't deserve to be in my life."

She would dust her hands together. "You're gone."

Her sassy sagacity teases the edges of my memory, reminding me of the truth. It's not that I failed Edward. Not that I wasn't sexy enough or didn't do enough. It's not my loose pussy, my almost-forty-year-old self, the fine lines creeping around my eyes. It's him. His sorry, no-character, vow-breaking ass. Men married to the most gorgeous women in the world still cheat.

Hello, *Lemonade*?

And yet this wave of *not enough* washes over me as I stare down at the chest through a scrim of tears. I lift the flag and press it to my face, letting the flag of the Grito de Lares absorb the dampness of my pain. This flag hung in my *abuela*'s house on her wall. It was a symbol of

righteous rebellion and a declaration of war in the name of independence. As I hold the flag, its pride, its anger, its fierceness blanket me.

How dare he?

How could he?

The hurt spreads so deep and so wide, it threatens to swallow me.
I'm drowning in it, but I reach for my rage, and like a lifeline it rescues
me. The machete glints at me like a wicked smile from beneath Mami's
journal. I push aside the leather-bound book and grab the knife. I hold
it flat across my palms, and my mouth waters for vengeance. For retri-
bution. If Edward were standing in front of me, I might chop his dick
off and hang his balls from my rearview mirror as souvenirs of how I
felled him. How I unmanned him.

But he's not here.

His things are.

The thought of destroying his expensive wardrobe and slicing up
all his handmade shoes hasn't even fully formed before I'm on my feet
with the machete, slicing off the arms of his Armani, tearing through
the back of his Marc Jacobs, and amputating the legs from his Gucci. I
take my knife to his shelves of shoes, dicing them like vegetables until
leather confetti litters my closet floor. I grab that tacky tie Edward's
mama gave him with the red polka dots and *chop chop chop* until it
bleeds all over the closet floor in a mound of ruined silk.

More.

Even taking in the destruction I've wrought, the beast in me hun-
gers for more, like Edward's entire wardrobe was merely the appetizer
and I'm starving for the main course. I rush down the stairs and tiptoe
past the living room so the girls won't see, and then I streak out to
the backyard. I stand there a moment, glaring at the structure where
Edward spent so much of his time. I stalk through the door and assess
the space Edward wanted for his "sanity" in a houseful of women.

"Motherfucker," I growl through gritted teeth, bringing the machete
down on his mahogany desk. It chops into the wood with a satisfying *thunk*. I raise the knife again and again and again in a blur of

blades, frenzied in my fury until I stand over it shoulders heaving, sweating.

Sobbing.

"Why are you crying?" I scream, tears running in rivulets down my hot cheeks. "You stupid bitch! For him? Dry your fucking tears."

The desk lies at my feet in a heap of broken wood, but it's not enough. I rush over to his pool table and use the machete to chop into the green felt. I can't do enough damage, so I pick up the balls and hurl them into the wall, leaving dents and holes. One flies on a wild trajectory to the window, shattering the glass.

Something about the shards of glass on the floor feels right. Feels like the way I am inside. Large, sharp pieces of myself on the floor beyond repair.

I need more glass.

My gaze falls on Edward's most prized possession, the signed, framed Larry Bird jersey. Destroying that would be like slicing his jugular vein. I charge toward it, leaping over the rubble of his desk and swinging my machete into the glass frame. It shatters, shards flying all around me. Heedless of the danger, I reach into the frame and yank out the jersey, spreading it on the floor and tearing into it with my knife. For three generations, the women of my family wielded this knife. The machete is not just a line of steel, but a lineage of it. I use it now to cut down the insecurities, the shame, the hurt that will eat me alive if I let them.

Finally spent, clothes soaked through with perspiration, throat raw from screams and sobs, hair tangled around my shoulders and down my back, I collapse on the floor and sit with my back to the wall, knees pulled up. During the adrenaline-fueled rampage, I didn't notice the pain, but as soon as I sit, I assess my throbbing hand with a shard of glass buried in the soft flesh of my palm. I jerk it out and toss it onto the shredded jersey at my side. Strips of Celtics-green cloth litter the floor, mixed with glass and wood and plaster. Grim satisfaction fills me at the ruined space Edward used to deem sacred.

I push to my feet, but a sliver of silver glinting in the debris gives me pause. Rolling my hand into the hem of my T-shirt to stop the flow of blood, I reach down to pick through the wood and find the silver. It's a tiny rectangle of metal attached somehow, maybe glued, to the collar of the Celtics jersey. Or what's left of it.

A flash drive.

I stare at it for long seconds, afraid to hope it holds any significance.

It could be nothing.

Or it could be exactly what I need.

CHAPTER ELEVEN

JUDAH

Where's my money, Cross?"

There's still no easy answer to Brett Callahan's question, no way to know how much Edward embezzled from the company or where most of that money is stashed. We need to strengthen our case, or this asshole could end up getting a slap on the wrist, and we *still* won't know where the money is.

"As you know, it's in the FBI's hands now, but based on the trail my team was able to establish," I answer, looking down the length of the table, "we've traced about three million and recovered about two million of that. Without account numbers and a reliable map of his transactions, I can't be sure."

"So your best estimate is that we have recovered maybe a third of what he's taken," Delores says. "But most likely less than that."

"I would say that's a fair assessment." I nod. "I still think we're missing something. Or rather *someone*."

"Are you saying you think another CalPot employee," Brett starts, his expression darkening, "is part of this? That we have a thief still on our payroll?"

"I can't say definitely," I admit. "It's an instinct."

"Your instincts have gotten us this far," Delores says. "I know you've got that fancy degree, but I think that gut of yours is the best thing you have going for you."

"It'll take more than my gut to get that money back." I lock my fingers behind my head. "We need a break."

Or a miracle.

"Fuck instinct," Dick says, seated across from me. "Have we put more pressure on the wife? Is everyone on this team taken by a pretty smile and a great ass? That's where we should be applying pressure. I'd bet my next paycheck Soledad's in on it."

"I'll take you up on that offer." I sit forward and rest my elbows on the conference room table, tenting my fingers and looking dead in his eyes. "Donation to my favorite cause?"

"What are you talking about?" Dick huffs a confused laugh.

"You said you'd bet your next paycheck that Soledad is involved in Edward's shit. I'm taking you up on it. When I figure this out, and Soledad didn't do anything wrong, you can donate your full paycheck to the cause of my choice. I know several charities who could use it."

"I didn't..." Red flares on Dick's cheeks. "I wasn't—"

"We all heard you," Delores weighs in. "You did say you bet your paycheck."

"It's a figure of speech," Dick says stiffly.

"It's someone's life," I counter, my calm tone belying the anger straining my composure. "Someone's children you're talking about. I take it all very seriously, including when you put your paycheck up to persuade this team to ruin Soledad Barnes without any substantial proof."

"It's that damn booty," Dick sighs, shaking his head.

"Enough," Brett snaps, looking between Dick and me with impatience. "There'll be no bet and there'll be no more pressure applied." He looks at me meaningfully. "For now. The longer this goes on, the colder that trail gets and the less likely we'll recover our money."

He rises, jerks his head for Willa to follow, and leaves the room.

I stand immediately in case Dick says some sideways shit to provoke me. He is not usually perceptive, but he somehow has tapped into something I hate to admit even to myself.

I have a soft spot for Soledad.

As much as I try to ruthlessly suppress my instinct to protect her, it won't stay down.

Delores stands at the door waiting. I keep walking past her, even when I see her open her mouth to speak.

"I have a meeting in ten minutes," I tell her, not pausing on the path to my office. "We can talk later."

If I have a soft spot for Soledad, so does she, and I don't need any help sympathizing with a woman who could very well be the missing link to crack this case open.

I round the corner to the suite that holds my office and come to a halt when I reach my assistant's desk. Sitting in the waiting room is the last person I expected to see.

"Soledad?" I ask, slowing my steps until I'm standing in front of her.

She looks up, her eyes liquid and dark, her face a landscape of lush lips and heavy lashes. The deep waves of her amber-streaked hair pile into a messy bun, soft curls escaping at the edges of her hairline and neck. Her slim-fitting jeans, ballet flats, silk T-shirt, and long camel-colored cashmere coat make her look delicate and expensive.

But there's desperation in the way she clutches her purse strap, in the wide eyes ringed with fear. Signs of strain peek out from beneath her carefully crafted composure.

"I told her you have a meeting in a few minutes," says my assistant, Perri, impatience in her tone and the press of her lips. "She insisted that—"

"It's okay, P," I tell her, not looking away, *unable* to look away from the sober expression on Soledad's face.

"I just need a few minutes," Soledad says, her voice hoarse and scraped over. "I won't take much of your time."

"I've been trying to tell you," Perri says. "He doesn't have a few minutes. He has a meeting. You can't just come in here and—"

"Cancel it." I swing a glance at Perri to shut her protests down. "The meeting. Cancel it."

I'm the only Black director at Callahan, the first to ever serve as director of accounting. As one of the few other Black employees on this floor, Perri is always careful to present herself professionally. Full face of makeup, stylish wardrobe with coordinating hijabs. Prompt, efficient, thorough. She takes pride not only in her position, but in mine. It makes her very protective.

Eyeing Soledad with some suspicion, she asks politely, "Could I get you something to drink, then? Water or tea? Soda?"

"No, but thank you." Soledad offers a small smile and stands, tipping her head back to meet my eyes. "I didn't mean to disrupt your day."

Perri sucks her teeth, and I catch her eye with a quelling glance.

"I just..." Soledad licks her lips and expels a short breath. "You said if I came across anything that might help to—"

"Of course," I cut in, eager to gain some much-needed ground on this case. "Let's talk."

I set my hand at the small of her back to guide her into my office, needing to get her away from possible prying eyes. She is slim and tight under my touch. A fresh scent wafts up to me. Shampoo? Perfume? She smells like flowers in full bloom under the sun. Fresh and alluring. I draw in a deep breath and play back Dick's words about being taken in by a pretty smile. That sobers me, and I drop my hand from her, nodding to one of the chairs in my office.

"Have a seat," I tell her, and perch on the edge of my desk.

"It was only after I got here," she says, sitting and glancing down to the hands clenched in her lap, "that I remembered you saying it was a risk for you to come see me. I guess it's a risk for me to come see you too, huh? I'm sorry. I should have..."

She grimaces, her throat bobbing with a deep swallow. "It's been a rough couple of days. I wasn't thinking clearly. I hope me coming here doesn't—"

"It's fine. Did you think of anything?"

"I may have found something, yeah." She opens her palm to reveal a small silver jump drive. It's only then I notice the white bandage on her other hand.

I reach for the bandaged hand and turn it over. "How'd this happen?"

She pulls away and lets the injured hand fall in her lap.

"It's nothing. Did you not notice what's in my *other* hand?" Amusement caresses her voice, and a small smile touches her full lips.

I reach for the jump drive, but she closes her hand and pulls it behind her back. "I think it has information you need, but there are things *I* need first."

I lift my brows and cross my arms over my chest.

"If that's evidence for the case, I can get the FBI to retrieve it."

"And I can conveniently forget we even had this conversation and lie very convincingly to anyone who asks me about it, but then neither of us would get what we want, would we?"

I can't help but smile. There's a shark under all those curls and cashmere.

"I like getting what I want," I tell her, hoping that didn't sound as suggestive as I think it did.

"So do I," she replies without missing a beat. "And what I want is to keep my house, my accounts unfrozen, my cards reactivated, and for this company to leave me and my girls alone."

"I want that too, believe it or not. I also want the six million dollars your husband stole. Do you think what's on that drive could help us both?"

She draws a shaky breath, pulls her hand out, and offers me the drive.

I reach for it, but she doesn't surrender it right away, holding on with the tips of her fingers.

"I need your assurance that I'll get the things I asked for. I need to keep the money that's in our accounts. I have a few months of savings to help us survive while I get on my feet. This isn't a gift, Judah. It's a negotiation."

"I can't make promises without knowing what's on it. Hell, I can't make promises at all, but at least let me see what you've got."

"I'm not a math genius like you, but even I can tell what's there could be crucial to the case."

I stare at the tiny drive in my hand for a second before rounding my desk and sitting down to slide it into the laptop. There are so many folders, all with numbers for file names. When I open the first file, it contains a series of figures I immediately recognize as account numbers and international transaction codes.

"Shit," I breathe, my pulse quickening as I click on file after file detailing transactions and laying out a clear trail to shell accounts, some of which I recognize from what I've been able to uncover on my own. "Soledad, do you have any idea what this is?"

She nods jerkily, drawing her bottom lip between her teeth and biting down. "I don't know what it all means, but I can tell it's damning."

"It blows the case wide open. It's basically a road map to places the money has been sent. Passwords, account numbers. Everything."

"Oh." She rapid-blinks, as if processing what I'm telling her. "Okay. So that's good, right?"

"For us, yeah." I need this information, but she's been taken advantage of enough. She should understand the implications of turning this over to me. "This strengthens the case against your husband significantly. I can't guarantee he won't get more time if we have this information than he would have if we didn't."

"I understand that, but we all make choices. Edward chose this scheme over our family." Her eyes are hard and diamond bright. "He'll serve the time for what he did, but my girls won't suffer. He's not taking us down with him. He doesn't get to ruin their lives."

"So you'll turn it over to the FBI?"

"I'm turning it over to you."

I stare at her and then at the on-screen evidence the Callahans need to condemn Edward and recover as much of their money as possible.

"Why?" I ask simply. "Why me?"

"I don't trust the FBI." Her laugh is harsh and hoarse. "I certainly can't trust the Callahans, but I can't do this by myself, so I have to trust someone. I choose you."

Shock rolls through me like thunder, and something else. Satisfaction? Pleasure? I'm pleased that she trusts me. I want to be worthy of it.

"No one knows this case better than you do," she goes on. "You have the inside track with the Callahans, and you've been the liaison with the FBI. No one is positioned better to advocate for my family and me.

I know it's not your job, but for some reason, I believe you will. Please don't make me regret this."

She glances down and toys with the edge of the bandage. "It's the proof you need, but it's also the proof *I* needed that the man I've been with nearly half my life doesn't exist."

Her composure is vellum, so sheer it barely hides her devastation.

"I'm sorry, Soledad."

"There's something else you should know," she goes on, not acknowledging my sympathy. "You said before that you thought Edward was working with someone. This could just be a woman scorned, but I think you should look at his assistant, Amber."

"What do you mean, 'a woman scorned'?" I ask, watching her closely.

"They're having an affair." She sniffs and swipes at a tear before it even falls.

"You're sure?"

"Oh yeah." Her smile is bitter, and she releases a harsh breath. "I'm very sure about that."

A man would have to be a fool to cheat on a woman like her, but we've already established that's exactly what Edward is.

"I'm sorry," I say again, though I realize how empty it must sound to her.

"Don't be." She clears her throat and tucks a stray curl behind her ear. "I know the truth now. That's all that matters."

Her pain, though she is deliberately dismissive of it, is evident in the tightness around her mouth. The knotted hands in her lap and the dark circles under her eyes that she didn't even try to conceal. It's obvious she isn't here to discuss her feelings but to handle her business. The least I can do is respect that and let her deal with the emotional toll later and in her own way.

"What makes you think Amber's involved?" I ask.

"Edward used working late as an excuse all the time over the last two years, but they did have a lot of meetings, and I would see her calling him all the time. I saw something at the Christmas party that hasn't added up, and it's got me thinking."

"What's that?"

"Amber's cousin Gerald works here in IT. I caught them in the hall at the Christmas party and they looked intimate. Not like relatives at all."

"Okay. Go on."

"If Gerald works in IT, he'd potentially have access to all kinds of data here at Callahan. Maybe Amber was fucking him too, and he was part of the scheme?"

My mind whirs with the information she just shared. Like one of Aaron's Rubik's Cubes, several possibilities start sliding and shifting until a scenario forms in my head that could actually make sense.

"This is fantastic." I look at the screen again and grin at Soledad. "Truly. I need to get my team on all of this so we can—"

"I want my drive back." She stretches her injured palm out, brows lifted, head cocked to the side. "You've seen what I have. Go to the board, the FBI, whoever, and get me what I need for my family. I'm not asking for much. Just that they leave us alone and confine their fight to Edward."

She didn't have to trust me with this, but she did. I'm not going to abuse that. Reluctantly, I remove the drive and place it back in her palm.

"I'll talk to them." I lean forward, catching and holding her eyes. "There is a lot of evidence there. I can't emphasize enough that it could add time to Edward's sentence."

"Don't tempt me with a good time," Soledad says, her laugh short and sharp. "Edward has proven he doesn't give a damn about me or his daughters' well-being. I'm paying him the same courtesy."

She stands, tucks the drive into a small purse, and heads for the door. Despite the worry and exhaustion on her face and in her eyes, she glows. Triumph, confidence, wisdom? I don't know what added this layer to her beauty, but it's new. There is a lot she has lost over the last few days, not the least of which is her marriage, but there is something that she's found. Without even knowing exactly what it is, I can see she plans to hold on to it.

CHAPTER TWELVE

SOLEDAD

"How the hell do you make a charcuterie this good when your life is falling apart?" Hendrix asks, spearing an olive from the wooden board on my coffee table.

"First of all," I reply, folding a slice of salami around a hunk of Gouda, "I could make this board in my sleep."

"Please make this board for me in your sleep," Yasmen mumbles around a mouthful of preserves. "My God, is this jelly stuff homemade?"

"That 'jelly stuff' would be my secret-recipe pear preserves," I tell her, scooping more of it onto her plate. "And getting back to my second point, my life is falling apart, yes, but not ruined." I grimace and sip my pinot grigio. "At least I hope not. Thank you, guys, for coming over to take my mind off all this for a bit."

"Are you kidding?" Hendrix cackles. "You went all Angela Bassett *Waiting to Exhale* on Edward's clothes and his man cave. We had to see the damage unhinged Soledad could do."

"It's pretty spectacular." Yasmen raises her wineglass in a toast. "To you, Sol. You did that. If Edward does manage to slither his way out of prison time, he won't have a stitch to cover his pasty ass, and you've taken all his toys away."

"My favorite is the Boston Celtics jersey." Hendrix pauses to sip, then giggle. "The irony of him hiding the drive there and you taking a machete to it. Girl, classic."

"It felt good in the moment," I say, sighing and scooping up a handful of almonds from the board. "But if I'd been thinking, I would have sold all his shit instead of destroying it. I'll need every spare penny. Plus now I have to clean it up."

"Get them girls out there helping you," Hendrix says. "It'll take no time."

"I hate for them to see just how enraged I was." I give a wry smile and shake my head. "I think it's the clap that pushed me over."

Their smiles dim when I mention the STI. I had to tell them, and their anger rose even higher than mine. I had to physically restrain Hendrix from setting Edward's golf clubs on fire in the cul-de-sac.

"I'm so glad he'll get what's coming to him," Hendrix says now. "And know what you'll be having while his lying, cheating ass is behind bars?"

"What?" I ask with a smile queued up because I know this will be good.

"A big ol' pan of peace cobbler!" Hendrix raises her wineglass and then downs every drop.

"I like that!" Yasmen scoops up some more preserves. "Sol, you should totally make a peace cobbler. I'd eat it."

"You eat everything," Hendrix laughs.

"Truth." Yasmen grins, popping some Gouda into her mouth.

"You know what I've really been thinking about doing?" I ask, not waiting for them to guess. "Clearing out Edward's newly demolished man cave and making it my space. My she shed. You know I love a good DIY. Maybe claiming that space will help me reclaim *myself*. I didn't even realize Edward was taking so much from me. I want all my power back."

"I love that idea," Yasmen says. "And I like you planning as if this house will remain yours, because it *will*. It's gonna work out. I feel it in my bones."

"So we're waiting on the accountant to confirm what CalPot wants to do?" Hendrix asks. "When will we know if they're gonna take the evidence in exchange for leaving you alone?"

"He thought it might be today." I take a long gulp of my drink. "I guess it's tonight now, so maybe tomorrow? Whatever he says, it only relieves the pressure temporarily. It unfreezes our accounts and whatever money is there. We actually sometimes make two mortgage payments at once, so I have a little cushion on the house. And the court-assigned trustee says until there's a conviction, they can help some with the house payments. All in the name of reducing the impact on the girls. But with Edward's job gone, I need to find steady income long term. I'll need a way to support us once Edward is behind bars."

"Oh, you have a lot of income, honey." Hendrix gestures to the charcuterie board and my living room. "Everything you cook, the house you decorate, the life hacks for cleaning, and all you know about domestic world domination *is* your income waiting to happen."

"Yeah, Sol." Yasmen licks preserves from the corner of her mouth. "Your business is right here under your roof. This life you've made for your family has been a labor of love. Why not start actually getting paid for it?"

"You know," I say, brushing crumbs from my jeans, "even when I was at Cornell getting my degree, I knew I wanted to be home someday—that when I started having kids, I wanted to stay home with them."

"Nothing wrong with that," Hendrix says. "But someone as driven as you, as ambitious as you, it surprises me that you didn't want more."

"More than what?" I ask, injecting the words with a slight challenge. "Giving shelter to the people you love most, making sure they are well fed, well adjusted, happy? Ready to navigate the world? That *has* been fulfilling to me."

I shrug and go on.

"I know neither of you are wired this way, but I always have been. We used to split the summers, my sisters and me, between my *abuela* in Puerto Rico and Lola's grandmother—Grammy we called her—in South Carolina. Grammy told us that back in the day in Greenville, it was illegal for Black women to stay at home."

"What do you mean, illegal?" Hendrix frowns.

"They passed an ordinance requiring Black women to work. During the First World War, Black soldiers would send money home to their families. For some of their wives, it meant they didn't have to work outside the home for the first time."

"What was wrong with that?" Yasmen asks, sitting up, leaning forward.

"When white women in town asked them to clean their houses and look after their kids, they didn't need the money and refused." I laugh, shaking my head. "They couldn't stand that, though, so they literally passed an ordinance requiring the 'negresses' to work outside the home, giving them back their nannies and domestics."

It's quiet for a few moments as we all sit with the injustice of that and nibble from our charcuterie board. We've come a long way.

"Other women have always been allowed to stay home," I say. "To make their homes and their families their life's work. Not us. When Grammy told us that, it struck a chord in me. It was like 1918, and we were still being denied even the privilege of saying no to working for someone else. I've always known I didn't want to work for anybody but myself."

"Then work for yourself," Hendrix says with a shrug. "You need the money now and you've got the seeds of an empire right here. Get your UGC, your GRWM, and that AMA. Put all the letters on all the platforms to work."

"I don't even know what any of those letters mean," I laugh.

"She's right, Sol," Yasmen says. "You know I was skeptical about Deja being a natural-hair influencer, but even I can see that if she wants to make a living doing it, she could. We're in a unique time right now. Where you can get paid to wash your face and make your coffee and share all the life hacks you've cultivated over the years running your home like an enterprise."

"*Make* it an enterprise," Hendrix urges. "We've talked before about you becoming an influencer, a content creator. Brands reach out all the time asking my clients to do posts and ads on their socials. I might be able to connect you with a few for a little boost to begin. Given what I've seen, you could grow fast."

Hendrix manages talent, including several popular reality TV housewives, so she knows of what she speaks.

"While you think about that, we're low on vino." Yasmen hoists her empty glass and starts to get up. "We need reinforcements."

"No, sit." I wave her back to her seat on the floor and stand. "It's still my house for now. Lemme enjoy it while I can."

"That's not funny," Hendrix says. "It's gonna work out and you're keeping your house, but while you're up, could you also restock the olives?"

I roll my eyes and smile all the way to the kitchen. I'm glad I told them the full story of Edward's betrayal. Going through this is bad enough. Going through it alone? I can't even imagine.

I'm headed back to the living room with a fresh bottle of wine and Hendrix's olives when the doorbell rings. Through the large glass doors, I see Judah Cross standing on the front porch. The warm light carves out shadows beneath his high cheekbones and melts the dark chocolate of his eyes.

"Oh!" I open the door and step aside for him to come in. "Sorry. I wasn't expecting anyone."

Yasmen and Hendrix's laughter drifts to the foyer.

"I mean, my friends stopped by." I smile, tipping my head toward the living room. "But I wasn't expecting anyone *else*."

The foyer is spacious, but as soon as he steps inside, the walls seem closer, the air—scarce. It's ridiculous that the future of my family is in the balance, and I'm having to remind myself not to stare at his lips. There is some major compartmentalizing happening. Potential financial ruin over here. Blistering attraction off to the side. It's a feeling I've been fighting since the moment we locked eyes at the Christmas party. It wasn't appropriate then, and it isn't now.

"I'm sorry I wasn't able to come sooner," Judah says. "I'm sure you must be anxious to know what CalPot decided."

"It has crossed my mind a time or two hundred since our meeting, yeah. Only my life in the balance."

"I know, but the board had to weigh all the options and decide." He gives me a searching look. "You do realize that as soon as I told them about the drive, they and the FBI could have just demanded it?"

"I knew that was a risk, of course." I drop my eyes to the floor and tap the bottle of wine against my leg. "Why do you think I came to you? I believed you wouldn't let that happen."

When I glance back up, his expression is more shuttered even than usual, but something flares in his eyes as they rake over my face, and I'm sure he's fighting the same attraction I've tried to ignore.

"You were right," he says, his voice soft, but with an edge. "I was prepared to do everything in my power to make sure you and your daughters got out of this as unscathed as possible."

Hot emotion gathers behind my eyes at his kindness, his care for the girls and me when my own husband hasn't shown even a measure of it. I clear my throat, testing the steadiness of my voice before speaking.

"I appreciate that, Judah."

"Luckily I didn't have to do much convincing. Delores insisted anyone who would tell her to her face that her pan sucked would not be in *cahoots*—her word. I've never used the word *cahoots* in my life—with her husband to steal millions of dollars."

"Seriously?" I gape at him, a wide smile breaking out on my face. "That's amazing. Delores in my corner. Who would've thought."

"That's what we get for sending you to fetch the..." Hendrix lets her words trail off and her gaze wander up and down and up again over Judah's tall, athletic build. "The wine. Well, hello. Who do we have here?"

"Oh." Yasmen is close on her heels. She pings a look from Judah to me a few times, interest sharpening in her eyes. "Sorry. We didn't know you were expecting company, Sol. I mean other than us."

She stretches out her hand. "I'm Yasmen. Nice to meet you."

"Judah Cross," he says, accepting her hand with a brusque shake.

"The accountant?" Hendrix demands, disbelief loud in her response. "My taxes would stay done if my CPA looked like you."

I'm mortified, but to my surprise, the straight line of Judah's full lips twitches.

"I'm not that kind of accountant," he answers teasingly. "But if I were, I'd take care of you."

"Oh, I just bet you would, honey." Hendrix steps closer and I stop her with the wine bottle shoved in her chest.

"Here you go, Hen," I say pointedly, nodding to the bottle and handing her the bowl of olives. "I think you were looking for this."

Humor and speculation light her eyes. "Come on, Yas. They obviously want to be alone."

She weighs the last word with suggestion, and I roll my eyes, silently begging her not to embarrass me any further. Blessedly, she and Yasmen return to the living room.

"Sorry about that," I apologize, sliding my hands into the back pockets of my jeans. "They're . . . well, they are—"

"Friends," he cuts in, his voice softening, his usually cool eyes warm. "I'm glad you have people who care about you the way they seem to. The FBI will unfreeze your assets, and CalPot won't go after your property when you turn over the drive, but you still have a long road ahead."

"Long road ahead, huh?" I spew a sour laugh. "The father of my children most likely going to prison. Me having to figure out how I'll support us. Divorce."

His gaze latches onto my face. "Divorce?"

"Did you think I'd stay with Edward after all he's done? I'm getting my divorce as soon as legally possible."

"I'm glad."

I can't force myself to look away, and I don't think he's even trying. There's a filament connecting us. It burns hot and bright and is impossible to ignore, but also impossible to pursue. We both know it.

"I better go," he says after a moment of charged silence. "I need to pick up Aaron and Adam from my ex's."

"Of course." I move with him toward the door.

"Could you bring the drive to the office tomorrow?" he asks from the front porch. "I knew you would want terms in writing. An agreement has been drawn up. You come in tomorrow and sign, then hand the drive over to us, and we'll share it with the FBI."

"And you'll have more than enough evidence to prosecute my husband." A brief prickle of guilt disrupts my relief. "He'll never forgive me."

"He should be the one begging for your forgiveness," he says, his words as harsh as the scowl on his face. "And he left you no choice."

"I agree, but it feels very cut-and-dried until you have to explain to your children that their father is in prison because of you."

"He's in prison because of himself. Not you. They'll understand."

"I think you're right for the most part," I say, "but one of my daughters, the middle one, is a real daddy's girl. Edward can do no wrong in her eyes."

Judah clasps my chin between gentle fingers, tipping my head back so I have to look at him. "Edward did a lot wrong, and once she sees that, it'll work out."

My breath hitches and my heart sprints at his touch, at the light caress on my cheek before he releases me. I resist the urge to put my hand there to relive that gentle touch.

"Are you always so sure?" I ask, half laughing, half really wanting to know. "I don't think I've ever met anyone so certain."

"There's one thing I'm not sure what to do about," he says, his gaze intense and unwavering on my face.

Somehow I know he means me. Or this thing that's been tugging me toward him since the second we met. And I'm not sure if there *is* anything to do about it. I need to focus on rebuilding a life for me and my girls from the ground up. I also need to rebuild *me*. A me who doesn't need a man, stands on her own, and gets what she needs to survive, even if she has to make it herself.

"I better go," he says again. "See you tomorrow."

"Tomorrow, yeah." I stand at the open door and watch him walk the driveway to his car, a black Audi Q8. Even after he pulls away, I can't seem to drag myself from this spot.

"Um, at what point were you planning to mention the accountant is bae?" Hendrix asks behind me.

I smile, close the door, and turn to face my friends.

"You mean Judah?" I ask innocently.

"*You mean Judah?*" Yasmen imitates my lighter voice. "That man smolders. He fine as hell."

"Do I need to remind you that you're a married woman, Yas?" I laugh.

"Definitely not." She smiles dreamily. "Josiah is it for me, but that doesn't mean I can't appreciate when a man like *that* enters the chat."

"And he was eating you up with his eyes," Hendrix says. "I never knew that was a real thing, but he needed a bib to look at you the way he did. Invisible drool everywhere."

"That makes no sense," I giggle. "I admit there's an attraction, but the last thing I need to be thinking about right now is a man."

"Since you don't want him," Hendrix says with a smirk, "tell him I like long walks on the beach and my safe word is *Popeyes*."

Who said I don't want him?

I shut that voice down because what kind of woman thinks about a man romantically in the middle of a DEFCON crisis? When she's still married to a lying, cheating scumbag of a criminal?

A woman who hasn't been touched with any real passion in months. Years? How long has it been since things felt right between Edward and me? Now I just want him out of my life, which leaves a void I probably shouldn't fill with another man right away. I have other things to focus on.

I let my gaze wander the high ceilings and hardwood floors of my foyer, of the house that is my little castle in the world. CalPot may not be taking it, but if I don't find a way to pay my mortgage, the bank will. Realistically, how long will my savings carry us? Maybe I should be frightened that for the first time everything will fall on me, but the prospect exhilarates me. My whole life is now DIY...or rather DIM. Do it *myself* because there's no one else who will.

"So, Hen," I say, linking one arm through Hendrix's elbow and the other through Yasmen's. "You said the seeds of an empire are right here in my house, right?"

"For damn sure." Hendrix squeezes my arm reassuringly.

I split a smile between my two best friends. "Then let's grow it."

PART II

"I am out with lanterns looking for myself."
        —Emily Dickinson, personal correspondence

CHAPTER THIRTEEN

SOLEDAD

Eight Months Later

I needed this." I release a pent-up breath and stretch out on the luxe white rug covering Hendrix's living room floor. "A night out of my house where no one is calling me Mom or asking me for anything."

"Honey, you just described my whole life." Hendrix chuckles. "Welcome to Chez Single Bitch and Glad About It."

When she passes me a drink, I prop myself up on my elbow to accept the glass with strawberries and lemons afloat in the slightly fizzy liquid. After one sip, I moan, bringing the glass back for another.

"Hen, this is incredible. What is it?"

"Strawberry-lemon prosecco sangria." She settles on the sleek white couch that dominates her living room. "One of my clients made these at her birthday party last week. Love them so much, had to share."

"Add this drink to the list of things I needed after the week I've had." I scoot over and rest my back against the couch beside her legs, placing my glass on the coaster on the glass coffee table.

"That's two of us." She sets her drink down, too, crossing her legs in the blush-pink silk loungewear I've seen on several celebrity favorite things lists.

"You look like an ad for luxury lifestyle," I tell her, resting my head on her knee.

"What can I say? I *am* the *rich Black girl* aesthetic." She pats her braids, which are pulled into a casually elegant topknot. "Now catch me up on this hellacious week you've had."

I let out a hollow laugh and reach for my drink again. "I'm too exhausted to even tell you how bad it is. You ever just get sick of hearing your own problems? Let's talk about something else, like dinner. You got eggs? I could make that frittata you like."

"Forget the frittata. I don't want to talk about something else. Tell me what's going on, Sol."

I lift my head and implore her with a look. "Can we skip it? It's the same shit you've been hearing the last nine months. I don't have enough money. I may have to pull the girls out of Harrington. All their friends and teachers they love are there, but if it comes to that, I will do it. I'm barely keeping a roof over our heads."

The same pathetic litany. I shove down the rising anxiety at the thought of the collectors calling, the teetering pile of bills stashed in my bedroom where the girls won't see it, and my half-empty closet, stocked only with the remnants of my wardrobe I haven't consigned yet. I'm on the verge of being house poor because I actually started selling furniture from spare bedrooms and other places I could find. One room is completely empty now. I go in there sometimes when I'm alone in the house, staring at the blank white walls as they close in on me.

"The savings running out fast, huh?" Hendrix asks.

"Yeah. CalPot unfroze our accounts, but that just gave me access to what was there. I had a nice little nest egg saved for emergencies, but nine months of emergencies? Not so much."

"You get any catering jobs this month?"

"I did, a couple here and there, and a bit of interior design work for some of the moms at Harrington. I had my first few sponsored ads on my socials, so thanks for the connection, by the way."

She inclines her head. "You know I'mma always look out for you, but it sounds like the expenses are outpacing the income."

"A little bit." I draw my knees up and wrap an arm around them. "I've gotten more orders for my pear preserves. Once Yas started selling them at Grits, a few other restaurants requested them. I got some personal orders too."

"That's great, Sol," Hendrix says, giving me a little fist bump.

"Yeah, and Yasmen says I could always come work at Grits. Right now, I'm at least making through my side hustles as much as I would at the restaurant, and this way allows me to make my own schedule so I can be there for the girls. It'll be fine."

I have no idea if it will or not, or what it will cost me to make things "fine." Whatever it is, I'll do it.

"The influencer thing will take off. You're starting to build an audience," Hendrix says. "You know I be checking your socials."

"It's been a slow start." I grimace. "But I did set up my storefront, so now when folks see things on my page and use my links to buy them, I get a cut."

"You just keep sharing good content with your *romanticizing your life, but still accessible* aesthetic."

"If by 'accessible' you mean broke." I choke out a laugh. "That's me. I try to stay consistent, posting my recipes and cleaning hacks and lifestyle stuff. I did a video earlier today making that vinaigrette you guys love so much."

"And you got a million things like that people will love and spread the word about. It's only a matter of time."

My phone buzzes on the floor by my feet, and I glance down at the now-familiar dreaded number, groaning. "Not today, Satan."

"Who is it?"

"My mortgage company." I decline the call and reach for my glass again. The glass is not deep enough to drown all my sorrows, but I'm gonna try. "The night shift."

"Past due?"

I shoot her a glance and take another sip, not wanting to answer. It's shitty being broke, but being broke with rich friends is a different level of embarrassment. I know Hendrix and Yasmen don't look down on me, and they know my full story, but it just gets awkward. I've found myself refusing to go out because they always want to cover my tab. A night in drinking or a meal at home I can swing. Anything else usually goes beyond my purse's reach fast these days.

"I believe things will pick up on the influencer end," she says. "I know you've gotten a few small-brand deals, and they were so pleased with the traction on the post. The cool thing these days is that you don't have to have a huge following to get results for a brand. I think they'll be back."

"I agree, and it's the kind of thing that feels most natural to me. Talking about my fave recipe or cleaning product or Dustbuster or whatever, but the bills keep piling up faster than the money comes in."

"Let me help."

My fingers tighten around the fragile stem of the glass. "Thanks, Hen, but you've done enough."

She and Yasmen have helped so much without me having to ask. Groceries from Yasmen have shown up at the house several times. Hendrix has been going around me to sneakily investigate how much Lottie's gym fees are and pay them. They're my best friends, and I know I have nothing to be ashamed of, but a helpless rage claws at my heart when I think about how desperate things are getting as the last of my savings dwindles. I can't just lean on my friends' generosity indefinitely. I won't. My eyes burn and I bite my lip to fight back a scream at the unfairness of the situation Edward has left us in.

"This drink is going right through me," I say, forcing a smile and standing. "Bathroom break."

I feel Hendrix's perceptive stare on my back all the way down the hall to her gorgeously appointed powder room. The soft lights rimming the mirror over her sink expose the defeat in my eyes, the bitter set of my lips. I brace my hands on the vanity and stare back at a stranger, a woman who looks lost and let down, my expression belying the high pony tied atop my head this morning in hopes it would make *me* feel bouncy.

I'm not bouncy.

I'm not buoyant.

I'm sinking.

I'm so fucking tired of holding back my tears for the girls, for my friends, for the moms at Harrington whose judgmental stares noted when I had to trade my new Rover for a secondhand Honda. I had to avert my eyes when I saw someone wearing my favorite off-the-shoulder cashmere sweater. There was the tiniest irregularity in the pattern, so I recognized it immediately. That was *my* irregularity. I paid four hundred dollars for it and accepted a fraction of its worth at the consignment shop so I could cover the gas bill.

Every month I ask myself how much longer I can hold on to our house. I could sell it and make things easier on myself, but I don't want easy. I want my *home*; I want the place in the world I carved out for my family. It holds all our memories, and I'm not ready to surrender it. On some level, I think I just can't take another loss. The marriage I thought was this family's anchor forever has dissolved, and even though I know Edward destroyed it, not me, the divorce still left me with an unreasonable sense of failure.

As I stare at that defeated stranger in the mirror, the weariness of just getting up every morning and keeping this ship afloat bends my will. My backbone feels like a Twizzler, and I can barely stand under the weight of impending doom.

As soon as I lower the wall holding them back, the tears fall, burning my cheeks and surprising a sob from me. I cup my mouth, afraid of what else will come out. A primal scream of frustration? A wail? I flush the toilet a few times to camouflage my sniffles and hiccups.

"Shit," I mutter, assessing my splotchy cheeks and red nose in the mirror. Like sharp-eyed Hendrix needs physical clues to my despair. Turning on the cold water, I splash my face and flush my eyes, trying to clear the telltale signs of breakdown. I probably reek of crisis, and Hendrix will start digging for answers right away.

If she does, what will I say? That I think I'm going to lose the house that means so much to me? The one I dedicated years to renovating and decorating and making a haven for my family? The one I thought I'd see my grandchildren running the halls of?

"It's just a roof and some walls," I remind myself. "You can find another roof and cheaper walls if it comes to that."

I stride back up the hall, smile pinned in place. "That drink hit the spot, but we need to eat. Want me to see what I can whip up? A frittata?"

"Or we could order. Give you the night off. You choose." Hendrix studies her phone. "Yas says she and Josiah are meeting with their adoption counselor tonight. They're still trying to decide if maybe fostering is a better option, I think."

"Okay. So it's just you and me, huh?" I sit beside her on the couch and reach for my phone, frowning at the email notification. Same old pattern. The collectors call and then send an email saying *We called and you still owe us money, bitch.* I hit the notification to clear it from my screen without reading too closely. The email opens up and I do a double take. It's a notification from my bank that I've received ten thousand dollars from…

"Hen," I whisper. "What did you do?"

"Same thing you'd do for me if I was about to lose my house and you had the money." She looks up from her phone, the regal lines of her face softening. "I spent that in bags and shoes last month, Sol. I'm doing really well. Ain't no way I'm standing by and watching you and your girls get put out when I could help."

"I—I can't accept this." I click my banking app, my mind spinning, hoping I can figure out how to reject a transfer. She snatches my phone and shoves it between the couch cushions.

"You gonna." She huffs a short laugh. "'Cause I ain't taking it back and you ain't sending it back. Girl, pay your mortgage and whatever else that can help with."

The tears I thought I'd gotten out of my system in secret make a public appearance, falling heedlessly. "You and Yasmen are the best friends I've ever had. We wouldn't have made it the last few months without you."

Hendrix circles an arm around my shoulders and tilts her head to press against mine. "We believe in you, Sol. If there's anybody on the face of this earth who can make something out of nothing, it's you. You just need a little time to make your something."

"Thank you." My voice breaks and I give up on that steel backbone, abandon that tough shell, and cry. Hendrix doesn't *shhh* me or spout platitudes. She lets my tears flow until there is nothing left.

"Love you, Hen," I say, linking our fingers on my knee.

"Love you too." She grins at me, the usual teasing glint restored to her eyes. "Now did you say frittata?"

An hour later, we're seated in her kitchen nook, enjoying the last crumbs of our meal, when my phone lights up with a text from Lupe.

"Let me see what this girl wants," I mumble into my sangria. "She and Inez better not be fighting. Can't leave them alone for one night."

Hendrix chuckles and licks her fork clean. "Thank her for lending you to me for dinner."

I smile and open the text message.

Lupe: Mom! Have you checked your last post? It's blowing up.

Me: Which one?

Lupe: The vinaigrette! Like...really blowing up.

"Lupe says my last post is doing well." I navigate over to my account, and a gasp escapes me. "Oh, my God."

"What is it?" Hendrix leans over to check my phone with me. "Does that say two million views?"

"Yeah." I laugh, covering my wide smile with my hand. "It does."

"Get it going." Hendrix nudges me, grinning and doing a shoulder bounce. "I told you it was only a matter of time."

CHAPTER FOURTEEN

JUDAH

Can we have pizza when we're done?" Adam asks.

I consider his request while we cross the parking lot to the Cut, the barbershop in Castleberry Hill where we've been going for years. A stack of paperwork I didn't get to this week in the office waits, so it has crept into my weekend. I'll have to get right on it as soon as we get home, but I think I can spare the time for pizza. After I drop them off at Tremaine's, it'll just be me, so I'll be able to focus.

"Sure," I tell him. "Guido's on the square sound good?"

He nods, but Aaron tugs my sleeve and starts scrolling on the communication device hanging around his neck. It's more portable than his old one, not much bigger than a phone. He pulls up a picture of Hops, his favorite game shop. There's a new special-edition Megaminx twelve-sided cube he's been asking for, and Hops usually carries all the toys and games he prefers, even the obscure ones I have trouble finding online. His teacher mentioned he got stuck a few times this week, perseverating and mentioning the cube repeatedly. It interfered with his work some, but she didn't have much trouble redirecting him.

"Hops is right across from Guido's," Adam implores on his brother's behalf. "One of the guys at school said they're the only ones who still have it in stock. It won't take long."

"It's not how close it is to the restaurant," I say dryly. "It's how hard it is to get him out of there once he's in, but okay. Twenty minutes at Hops. That's it."

I'll have to use the timer on my phone to help Aaron transition out of the store because that place is like heaven to him.

When we enter the Cut, Preach greets us with a smile over the head of the customer he's finishing.

"What's up?" he asks. "Man, thanks for being flexible with the time. Had a wedding party this morning, if you can believe. All the grooms-men wanted fresh fades."

"It's fine. The boys enjoyed sleeping in."

We've always been Preach's first customers on the Saturdays when we come because the later it gets, the more crowded and loud the shop becomes. Neither of my boys responds to all that stimulation well. They carry noise-canceling headphones in their backpacks in case it gets to be too much.

"Who's up first?" Preach asks, patting the barber chair.

Aaron takes one of the seats in the waiting area, puts his headphones on, and pulls out his cube.

"Guess that means you, Adam," Preach says, amused. He's used to my boys by now. When they were much younger, haircuts were hell. They were incredibly sensitive at their napes and around their ears. I could write a thesis specifically on haircut meltdowns. A mom men-tioned Preach to Tremaine in the waiting room of the boys' speech therapist. The rest is history. Preach is patient and not intimidated by the sensory issues that defeated so many barbers before him.

I check emails on my phone while Preach cuts the boys without incident. He's still cutting Aaron's hair when the bell dings above the door to herald a new customer.

"What's up, Si?" Preach shoots a wide grin at Josiah Wade. I don't know him well personally, but we've often been in the shop at the same time. Preach cuts his son, Kassim.

"Hey, Adam," Kassim says, and takes the seat beside Adam in the waiting area.

"Hey, Kassim," Adam replies.

I know Kassim attends Harrington, but he's younger than Adam, and I don't see him often. There aren't many Black boys at the exclusive private school, and though Adam has adjusted well so far and made new friends, I make a note to connect with more of the Black families there. Tremaine is much better at that kind of thing than I am. She's more plugged in at Harrington, maybe because she does that commute and I handle Aaron's, but I want to make the effort.

"'Sup." Josiah lifts his chin in my direction, and I return the greeting and the gesture. "Preach," he says, holding up a fistful of orange flyers, "you mind if I leave a few of these here in the shop?"

"Go for it." Preach glances up from the buzzing clippers. "What is it?"

"Soledad's doing this porch-drop thing," he replies.

"Oh, yeah." Preach grins. "I heard about that salad dressing of hers that went viral. Liz made it for dinner a few nights ago. It was good."

"Yeah." Josiah shrugs. "She's been getting lots of traction over the last couple weeks from it. Anyway, Yas asked me to leave a few here in the shop in case anybody wants one."

"What is it?" I ask, stepping over to the counter where he placed the flyers.

"Soledad Barnes." Josiah proffers a flyer. "She's doing this thing called Fall Focaccia. People order the focaccia in a basket she stuffs with some other fall shit, and she delivers it to their front porch when it's ready."

"Shit," Aaron repeats, not looking up from his device.

"Oh, sorry." Josiah sends me a chagrined grimace.

"It's fine," I reply, even though Aaron will probably randomly say "shit" forty times through the rest of the day and maybe half of next week. "Can I have one of these?"

"Sure." Josiah grins. "You like focaccia?"

"Love it." I've never had it and don't actually know what it is.

But I do like Soledad. Did Josiah's wife, Yasmen, say anything to him about the night I was at the house? Then again, what would she say? There wasn't much to tell, and I've kept my distance, knowing this has been a huge transition for Soledad and the girls. In the nine months since I've seen her, no one has captured my interest that way. I didn't want to be insensitive or raise any suspicions at CalPot after she turned over the thumb drive.

Edward is serving an eighteen-month sentence in Atlanta's low-security facility, just as he predicted. Only when he gets out, that huge nest egg won't be waiting for him.

But I've watched Soledad on social media enough to know she has been doing what she set out to do—standing on her own two feet and building a life she can be proud of. She's the kind of woman anyone would—

I haven't allowed myself to complete thoughts like that the last few months, but maybe now I can.

As Preach finishes the haircut, Aaron pulls out the device and displays Hops again. I'm surprised we made it through the haircut without hearing about it a hundred times.

"Cube," Aaron says, pointing to the picture of Hops.

"I know." I pull out the cash to pay Preach.

"Take care." Preach removes the cape from Aaron's shoulders and uses the neck duster to rid him of stray hairs. "Good job today, guys."

Preach high-fives Adam, but Aaron walks past the barber's suspended hand, grabs his backpack, and heads straight for the door.

"Guess that's my cue to roll out." I laugh, hand Preach the money, and dap him up. "We'll see you in two weeks."

Adam and Aaron stand by the door, both silent but brimming with impatience. Adam wants pizza, one of the few foods he'll actually eat, and Aaron can practically taste that new cube.

"Hops first," I tell them once we're in the truck, sensing that lunch at Guido's might go left real quick if we don't address the growing urgency of the cube situation.

As soon as we cross Hops's threshold, a large poster by the door proclaims they have the new special-edition Megaminx twelve-sided cube.

"It's here!" Adam turns to Aaron with a huge smile, like it's what he wants more than anything too.

"Thank God," I mutter, trailing Aaron, who's speed walking several steps ahead of us in his quest for the Holy Grail cube.

When I round the corner, I bite back a curse. The brightly colored Megaminx poster hangs over a bank of shelves.

All empty.

I should have called ahead. Ordered online. Waited. Anything but leave this to chance. I know better. I usually *plan* better. I can berate myself later. Right now...

"Cube." Disappointment flattens Aaron's voice. He stands in front of the empty shelves repeating "Cube" several times as if it's the password to reveal what he came for.

"Looks like they've sold out, Son." I keep my voice even and matter-of-fact. "Let's go check some other stores, or I can order it online."

"Cube," Aaron says, his voice pitching higher, eyes bouncing between me and the barren shelves.

"It's okay, Aaron," Adam soothes. "Let's eat pizza and then go look for it somewhere else."

"Cube."

The word fires from my son this time, loud enough to draw the attention of a few kids farther up the aisle. Aaron's fingers flex, curling and uncurling. Staccato breaths storm through his nostrils. He bounces on his toes a few times, gripping the device around his neck like it might anchor him to the calm slipping through his hands.

"Let's go." I reach for his arm, and he turns wide, distressed eyes to me.

"Cube!"

He slams his fist three times against his forehead and paces in a circle before the empty shelves, tension building and encircling the three of us in a tight, familiar ring. We've lived this before, done this so many times over the years, but it's been awhile. I had almost forgotten how this feels, but my body remembers. My pulse spikes and my stomach knots, and my heart thrashes in my chest and my teeth grit because I'm so helpless. I always try to catch these meltdowns before they escalate because once they start, you almost just have to ride it. And I don't want that for him. Years ago I cared what people around us thought. I'm not that guy who ever wants to draw attention to myself. Tremaine was always better at getting Adam to calm down. I always had Aaron, and I reach for the things that have helped in the past, praying they work.

"Son." I step in front of him as he paces, take his elbow gently. He tries to jerk away, his fist pulled up to hit himself again, but I don't let go. "It's okay. We'll find it somewhere else."

"Cuuuuuuuube!"

It's extended and explosive, the word strained to its limit and bouncing off the ceiling, ricocheting throughout the entire store. The hum of conversation around us dies. People stare. I ignore them, locking eyes with Aaron, rubbing his back. Sweat dots his forehead, and his chest rises with each ragged breath. He's taller, bigger now than when this happened last. When the boys were small, we could play it off as a toddler having a tantrum or just another kid in the store giving his parents a hard time. But he's fifteen now and stands only a few inches shorter than me, with tears in his eyes over this damn cube. I hear Adam sniffing behind us. He doesn't have meltdowns as frequently anymore, but he's so attuned to Aaron, like the thread of tension from his twin has wrapped around him too.

"Is there a problem?"

I spare a glance at the manager, who walks up the aisle, approaching a few measured steps at a time, cautiously, like we might strike at any moment.

"We're fine," I tell him.

"Cube! Cube! Cube!" Aaron yells, making a liar of me. We are not fine, and he doesn't care who watches or wonders if we are.

"You don't happen to have any more special-edition Megaminx in the back, do you?" I ask the manager.

"Sorry, no. We sold out fast, but a new shipment's expected Thursday." His gaze flicks past us to a mother and her son, who stand there half gaping, half trying not to stare. "Um, is there anything I can do to help?"

"No, I've got him." I look away from Aaron long enough to show the manager the calm in my own eyes, or at least I hope that's what I project. He doesn't leave but backs away a few steps, looking relieved he won't have to intervene.

Aaron is all that matters, and I annex the onlookers, the manager, even my own anxiety to the back of my consciousness until my sole focus is my son. Aaron's fear, his panic, his dismay swallow even my periphery, and there is only my boy and these few seconds where to him it feels like the end of the world.

In this moment he may even feel like a threat to the people around us—a nearly grown man angry and volatile. To me he is just *mine*, and more than anything, I want to make this better. All I have are these words, though, which sometimes prove useless, but I have to try.

"Calm down, bud." I press my forehead to his, clasp his nape. "Breathe with me, okay? Remember how to do that?"

He nods, tears streaking his smooth brown cheeks, his face caught between that of a child and that of a man. A muscle in his jaw bunches, and his eyes meet mine, flared with panic like this situation is a balloon he let the air out of and he's holding on for dear life even as it flails all over the room. Like even he couldn't have anticipated its frenzied trajectory and now he can't seem to release it from his grappling hands.

My eyes dart around the small store, searching for a quiet place where I can take him. I want to get him away from the discreetly— and not-so-discreetly—gaping shoppers and give him a private place to decompress, but I don't see a quick option for that strategy. I'm about to ask the manager when Adam steps beside Aaron and nudges his brother's clenched fist with a fidget toy. Slowly, finger by finger, Aaron's fist unfurls, accepting the six-pronged weighted rubber toy. Chest still heaving, eyes tightly closed, he presses the ball into his palm and weaves his fingers through the toy's arms. It disrupts his climbing agitation just enough for me to slip in with calming words.

"I got you," I tell him, pitching my voice to a timbre of acceptance and love that I hope breaks through whatever grips him. "I love you. I got you. You can do this, Aaron."

"Cube." It's a broken whisper with a softening edge, his anxiety melting slowly like ice cream left out in the sun. "Cube."

"I know. We'll get you one. I'll find it, but you gotta calm down, okay?"

The tension in his shoulders and arms under my hands leaks from his body in slow seconds. We managed to pull the stopper, and the anxiety and frantic indignation of the last few minutes drain away, leaving him shaking. Somehow smaller in his contrition.

"Sorry, sorry, sorry," he says, pressing his forehead harder into mine, holding my hand as if I'm the thing anchoring him to the ground as that balloon drifts away. "Sorry, sorry, sorry."

"You don't have to be sorry," I reassure him. "We all get anxious, right? It happens. We're okay now."

"You're okay," Adam parrots the words as if to reassure himself as much as his brother, wrapping his arms around us both. "You're okay, Aaron."

With both my boys trembling and tearful, we stand in front of the empty shelves, and I draw a deep sigh of relief.

"I got you," I tell them. Maybe to remind myself. "We're okay."

CHAPTER FIFTEEN

SOLEDAD

Whose brilliant idea was it to make a hundred focaccias?" I ask through bleary eyes. "Whoever it was, we should lock her up and never let her have any say in anything ever again."

"Pretty sure that was you, Mom," Lottie reminds me, not looking up from the basket she's stuffing. "But it's gonna make us a ton of cash, so a win is a win."

"You got a point, kid." I reach over and high-five her, and we share a quick grin.

I thought assuming complete responsibility for our household would create a lot of pressure, but it instead feels like a privilege. I always thought of myself as taking care of them, but all the shit that happened with Edward forced me to lean on my girls in new ways. From necessity, I had to ask and expect more from them because so much was being demanded of me. For our survival. They have become invested in the business in unexpected ways, especially since they made the connection between my success as a content creator and their way of life.

It's hard to keep my home separate from my work when my home *is* my work. The food I prepare for my family, the systems I use to clean my house, even my skin care products—all of it has become business. There's always a phone or camera and a light ring set up in my kitchen, in my garden, by the bathroom mirror. Lupe, Inez, and Lottie, as much as I initially resisted, have become a part of my "brand." My followers are so invested in our all-girl crew carving out a life for ourselves. I thought the girls would hate it, inviting people we don't know into our space the way we have, but the opposite has happened. They love it. I limit how much their faces are seen, but they're as much a part of this enterprise as I am. It's created an *us against the world* dynamic that has made us even closer.

I promised I wouldn't protect Edward from the consequences of his actions, not even with his daughters. I told the girls about the crimes he committed and the evidence I surrendered to the authorities. One, because it was the right thing to do. Two, because it was what I *had* to do if I wanted to save our house and provide for them. They understand that this house, the clothes they wear, the school Lottie and Inez attend—all of it could go away if I don't earn money to support us.

So when I thought of doing focaccia porch drops here in Skyland to make some extra money, they all agreed to help.

I inspect Lottie's work, making sure she's sealing the plastic on the basket tightly enough. "Keep up the good work in here. Lemme go check on your sisters."

My dining room has become an assembly line, the table littered with ribbons and tissue paper. Deja, Yasmen's daughter, is stuffing the baskets with packets of salted pumpkin seeds, hot chocolate, and marshmallows, which kind of garnish the basket. The main attraction is the focaccia. Lupe, wearing rubber gloves, has a stack of the loaves and is carefully wrapping each of them in wax paper.

I had no idea what I was getting myself into using this business to support us full-time. Lottie's gymnastics training is not cheap, and if I wanted her to continue, I needed extra income. I've done whatever keeps us living indoors with the lights on. The fall baskets seemed like a simple thing to do, but I didn't expect all the orders we received. Even limiting delivery to a ten-mile radius, I still had to bake more than a hundred. Fortunately, Grits, the restaurant Yasmen and her husband, Josiah, own, is closed on Mondays. We used their industrial ovens and made a huge baking party of it.

"Are mine ready to go?" Hendrix asks, slipping on a lightweight jacket.

"We got fifteen here," Lupe says. "They're all for the east side."

"Good." Hendrix grabs two by the handle and heads out of the dining room. "Let's get them loaded into the car, and I'll start the first round of deliveries."

"Hey, Hen," Yasmen yells from the kitchen. "I just texted you the east side addresses."

Hendrix pulls out her phone and nods. "Got 'em."

"I'm your sidekick, Aunt Hen," Lottie says, her face lit up as she scrambles to get her jacket.

"Grab some baskets, then, and let's roll," Hendrix replies. "But I warn you right now I'm in my nineties R & B era, so if you don't want to hear Brownstone, you better bring some headphones."

"We can totally do Brownstone," Lottie readily agrees, following Hendrix but turning around to whisper to me. "Who's Brownstone?"

I laugh, shaking my head. "Just grab the baskets and prepare to have your mind blown, little girl, by some real music."

"I'll help load into Aunt Hen's car," Lupe says. "I think we're just about done with the west and south side orders."

"That's me," Yasmen says, walking into the dining room. "Lupe, you coming?"

"And me!" Deja chimes in. "This is the most orders, so we figured we'd both go and can fan out faster in the neighborhoods to get it done."

"Sounds good." Yasmen grabs her jacket from the back of one of the dining room chairs. "Let's get it, girls."

"And we meet back here for my famous chili when we're done," I yell so everyone hears.

"Do you have to call everything you cook 'famous'?" Hendrix laughs.

"You're my 'manager.'" I tug on one of the goddess locs hanging down her back. "It's you who's trying to make all my food famous, though you won't take a commission from any of my brand deals yet."

"Oh, don't worry." Hendrix shoots a knowing look over her shoulder.

"When you get the big deal, it'll be time for me to take my share. Right now, I'm just investing in you."

"Well, I appreciate it."

"Just have a good red to go with that famous chili when I get back," she says. "That'll be thanks enough."

We take the next fifteen minutes to load up Hendrix's and Yasmen's cars with baskets, and they all leave to do their porch drops, while Inez finishes stuffing the last few baskets for my part of town, the north side.

When I come back into the house, everyone's gone, and it's just Inez and me. I told Yasmen and Hendrix I wanted to spend some time alone with Inez. Of my three daughters, she's had the hardest time adjusting to our new life, especially the fact that her father is in prison.

And that I helped put him away.

She hasn't been acting out, but she has been more distant. I think she's sorting through a lot of things she's not voicing. I want to be here whenever she's ready to open up, ask me questions, or even express her anger with me.

Yasmen and Josiah's family has experienced a lot of loss, and all of them have been in therapy at various stages. At her urging, we did family therapy to give the girls a chance to process an incredibly complex situation. I've been doing individual therapy too, and it's a lifesaver.

"Guess that leaves us." I wrap one last focaccia loaf and double-check the items that go in the basket. "You ready?"

"Yeah. How long do you think this'll take? There's a tournament tonight."

"Gaming?" I ask.

"Yeah. I mean since I don't get to play much during the week..."

She suspends the thought as an accusation because that's been a point of contention lately. I don't address it while we load the first round of baskets into the back of the Pilot and head inside for more. I touch her arm to halt her progress and get her to look at me.

"Hey, Nez. You know why I limit gaming during the week. It's too much of a distraction, and your grades suffer."

"Like gymnastics doesn't distract Lottie?" She lifts her brows and gives me a *so there* look.

"All right. I'll give you that." I head back into the dining room to get the next round of baskets, addressing her over my shoulder. "It definitely takes a lot of her time, but that's an extracurricular activity and a discipline. If she doesn't keep her grades up, she knows she loses it. Plus gymnastics could very well be Lottie's ticket to a college scholarship."

"Gaming requires discipline." Inez hefts two more baskets and walks out to the car. "I mean a different kind, but there's hand-eye coordination."

"Okay." I grab two more baskets and head to the garage. "That's a stretch."

"There are professional gamers making millions, Mom. Who needs college if that happens?"

I stop in the middle of the garage, my horror probably scrawled all over my face. "Did you say, 'Who needs college?'"

"I mean, you went to an Ivy League school, and a lot of good that did you. You got married, had kids, and stayed home. You could have skipped college with the same outcome. The major thing you accomplished at Cornell was meeting Dad."

I let those thinly veiled barbs sink into my flesh. How much of that insult is the insensitive oblivion that usually accompanies adolescence, and how much is her deliberately provoking and demeaning me? Motherhood truly is a thankless endeavor sometimes. We sacrifice everything for these *people* who never really understand what we've done for them.

"So my greatest accomplishment was marrying your father?" I ask, smoothing the irritation from my voice, unwilling to give her the satisfaction.

"I didn't mean it that way," she says half-heartedly.

"But you did, Inez." I slam the trunk and walk to the driver's side, angling a look at her. "We both know you did."

I climb in and start the car, waiting for her to take the passenger seat. After a few moments, she does and puts her earbuds in right away. I jerk the left one from her ear.

"No, ma'am." I toss it into her lap. "You just said something I believe was aimed to hurt me, to make me feel less. When have I ever said something that was designed to hurt you? Specifically to make you feel smaller?"

I pull out of the garage and let the silence stew, not offering relief but waiting for her to speak.

"Never," she finally says.

"Had to think about it? Had to review every conversation to look for a time when I deliberately hurt you with my words the way you just did me?"

"No, I...I'm sorry, Mom. I just...I didn't mean to hurt you."

"You did mean to hurt me, Inez. I just want to know why."

"I guess I lash out sometimes and I don't think before I say stuff." Eyes cast down to her lap, she fiddles with her seat belt. "I said I'm sorry."

"Do you want to talk to someone about it?" I spare a brief glance from the road to her profile and gentle my tone.

"You mean more therapy?" she scoffs, rolling her eyes. "No thanks."

"Those sessions were for us as a family, Nez, but if you need—"

"Mom, please." She grips her head in her hands and blows out a quick breath. "Can we just drop it?"

"Look, I know this hasn't been easy, and our whole lives have changed, but—"

"You act like he doesn't exist," she says abruptly.

I know exactly who she means, but I ask anyway. "Who?"

"See?" She tilts her head back into the headrest, eyes fixed up. "Dad. You act like he's just gone, instead of in prison."

"Inez, he is just gone for now. He has another year on his sentence."

"And when he gets out?" She twists in the passenger seat to watch my profile. "How's it gonna be then?"

"I don't know what you want me to say, Inez. He's your father, but he's not my husband. We're divorced. When he gets out, there will be space in your life for him if you want that. I won't keep you from him, but there is no place in my life for him. That's over."

"What if I want to see him before he gets out?"

My fingers tighten on the steering wheel. That's not something Edward has wanted. The one time he called the house after the sentencing, it was to lambast me for turning over evidence and to say he didn't want the girls seeing him in prison. He hasn't called, and they haven't asked for him. I knew at some point that would change.

"Let's talk about it later, Nez," I say softly.

She watches me for a long moment before facing forward and looking out the passenger window. The wall I've sensed her raising between us is only growing higher. The last nine months have been hell in so many ways, but what kept me going was knowing it was for my girls. Now I feel like I'm losing something precious with one of them.

"We, um, got our first stop coming up here on the right," Inez says after a few moments of tense silence.

"Okay." I glance over and force a smile to try to ease the tightness in the car. "One down. Twenty-five to go."

Fortunately, Yasmen did a great job plotting the stops, and they're mostly clustered together, a few on each block. Some houses are right across from each other or just along the block, so I take a few on one side of the street, and Inez takes the other.

"Last few," Inez says after about an hour and a half of deliveries across the north part of town that have taken us to the edge of Skyland's borders.

"You take these." I hand her the last two from the trunk. "I'll deliver mine and we'll be done."

We high-five, sharing an easy smile. After the initial tension, we found our footing, getting into the rhythm of making deliveries. Seeing people's pleasure at receiving the prettily ribboned baskets with the delicious-smelling baked bread improved our moods. After each drop, our grins stretched a little wider. We blasted some Lizzo, and it was about damn time before we knew it.

I walk up the steps of the last house, a four-sided white-brick traditional with navy-blue plantation shutters. Based on the look of it,
I'd estimate it was originally built in the 1920s, maybe '30s, with the
wraparound porch and arched dark wood front door. I ring the bell,
but after a few seconds no one answers. I ring the doorbell again, prepared to leave this one on the porch. I smile when the door swings
open but am disoriented to see Judah's son standing there.

"Aaron, oh, my gosh! Hi!"

"I'm Adam," he says, the look he gives me only vaguely curious.
"Aaron's my brother."

Twin brother, Judah said. From what I remember of Aaron, the boys
are startlingly similar. Same medium-brown skin and dark, slashing
brows. Judah's bone structure is sharper, but I suspect that as the boys
mature, they'll only become more like him.

"Oh, right. I met your brother last year at..." I bite my lip, not sure
what to say. "Well, at your father's job."

"You know my dad?" He tilts his head, skepticism in the question,
like there couldn't possibly be someone his father knows and he doesn't.

"Adam, who is it?"

That deep, rich-toned voice precedes him, but I only have a few seconds
to prepare before Judah appears at the door, a slight frown crinkling
the thick line of his brows.

"It's me." I half smile and wave awkwardly with the hand not holding the basket. "Special delivery."

"Oh, uh...hey." Judah reaches out to take the basket and stares
back at me. The porch is like quicksand beneath my feet, and it feels
like I'm sinking, losing myself in that steady, dark-eyed gaze that is at
once patient and probing. I'd forgotten the hot rush of sensation being
around Judah brings, but it crashes over me, scrambling my senses and
shortening my breath.

"Soledad."

My name is spoken, not by Judah, but by Aaron, who has come up
on the other side of his father.

"Aaron," I say, a genuine smile coming to my lips. "Hi!"

I'm surprised and delighted that he remembered my name. He doesn't say anything else but watches me with the same unwavering regard with which his father usually does.

"Guys, why don't you take this inside?" Judah suggests.

Adam walks into the house carrying the basket.

"Nice meeting you, Adam," I call after him, needing to leave the porch and get back to the car but finding it hard to move.

"Aaron," Judah says, his voice firm but gentle, "inside, please."

"Bye, Aaron." I wave, grinning even though he hasn't cracked a smile.

"Bye," Aaron answers, turning to walk inside, leaving Judah and me on the porch alone.

There has been no contact between us for the last nine months. After I signed the agreement and turned over the drive, CalPot left me alone. It had the information needed to recover most of its money and to prosecute Edward.

"It's good to see you." Judah shoves his hands into the pockets of his dark slacks.

"You too," I say.

"You look good."

His gaze wanders over me, leaving heat and chills in its wake. I shiver a little and wonder if I look as different to him as I feel on the inside. I'm still the same Soledad to the naked eye. He probably can't detect how changed I am from the desperate woman who stood in his office all those months ago taking a chance that he would help.

"So do you," I say after a few seconds. "Look good, I mean."

Understatement. He looks even better than the last time I saw him, and that's saying something. The top two buttons of his dress shirt are undone, and his sleeves are rolled above the elbows, exposing sinewy forearms and deep brown, taut skin. A man's forearms shouldn't have this effect on me. I glance down at my feet before he reads something I don't want him to see. With such a discerning stare, I wonder if he'd see how often I've thought of him. How I've touched myself sometimes at night, the memory of his voice and his gentle hand on my face enough to undo me with a few strokes of my fingers.

"I didn't expect it would be you." He shifts, pulling the door closed behind him and stepping a few inches closer to me on the porch.

"Um, what?" I frown, sure that I missed something vital when I lost myself in fantasy. "Expect...huh?"

"The basket. When I ordered it, I didn't expect you to personally deliver it."

"You knew I was making the basket?"

"Of course. That's why I ordered it." One side of his mouth skews into a wry grin. "I've actually never had focaccia, but I figured if you were making it, it would be good."

"So you ordered the basket to...like help me?"

"You don't need my help. You seem to be doing well enough on your own. Viral salad dressings and millions of followers."

"Just two million," I say with a smile. "Have you been stalking me, Mr. Cross?"

I allow my tone to tease, but when he looks up directly at me, catching my eyes and holding my stare, I'm mesmerized by the intent there.

"Is that bad?" he asks. "That I wanted to know how you were doing?"

My heart abandons any normal rhythm and just hammers, pounding beneath my ribs, where my breath is being held hostage.

"Bad?" I finally manage. "No. I...uh...we haven't talked, so I get it."

"I figured you wouldn't want contact with anyone from CalPot for a while. I didn't want to bother you, but I hoped you and your daughters were doing well."

"We have been." I run damp palms down my jeans. "It's been an adjustment, and there were times when I thought...well, that maybe we'd have to leave Skyland, but so far we're making it."

"I never got to personally thank you for the tip about Amber and Gerald," he says. "I missed them, but Edward rubbed me the wrong way the moment we met. I have an instinct about people."

"What was your instinct about me?" The words barged right out of my mouth without my permission, and I drop my gaze to the wide wooden planks of his porch. I didn't mean to say that. I shouldn't have said that. "What I mean is—"

"Oh, I liked you a lot right away," he answers, his voice dipping to a low rumble. "I still do."

I glance up sharply to meet the warmth of his stare. I lick my lips, push my hair away from my face, touch my throat. The restlessness of a schoolgirl, ill fitting on a woman my age...and yet I can't slow my heartbeat. I can't catch my breath with the scent of him—clean and distinct and masculine—overwhelming me. Those penetrating eyes resting on my face must see beneath the skin-deep disguise of my composure. Does he know how he affects me?

"You, um, were saying something about Amber and Gerald," I remind him, swatting at the butterflies fluttering in my belly. "I heard Gerald cut a deal."

"Yeah, he and Amber got off pretty light once they agreed to give up any info we were still missing."

The judge held Edward and Gerald primarily responsible for the scheme and deemed Amber's involvement only "limited," resulting in a much lighter sentence.

"In some ways," I say, hearing a touch of bitterness in my voice, "seems like my daughters and I got the shortest end of the stick."

His smile fades, and he reaches for my hand.

"I know you probably won't take me up on this, Soledad, but if you ever need anything, you can call me."

It would be so tempting to lean on him when times are hard because a man like him will always be harder. Judah would be a wall, a fortress. A shelter. He's the kind of man you can count on, but I'm done counting on men. He's the kind of man who, with just a touch of his hand on yours, sends you into fantasies. I carefully withdraw my hand and give him a smile.

"That's kind of you," I tell him. "But I think we've found our footing."

"I was thinking, now that things have settled down some, maybe we could grab coffee or—"

"Mom!"

Oh, shit.

Inez.

It's illogical and unfair, but Inez still places a lot of the blame on Judah Cross simply from Edward's consistent bad-mouthing of the man. She's never seen Judah and wouldn't make the connection, but I still turn immediately and dash down the steps before she comes closer. She's standing by the Pilot, staring up the street at Judah's house.

"I gotta go!" I yell, trotting down the porch steps. "Hope you enjoy the basket."

I hazard a quick glance over my shoulder for one last glimpse of the man I've thought about so many times since we first met. Even when it was wrong and impossible. Even when it was unwise. He looks from me to Inez waiting by the car, and I think he understands. He doesn't wave or say goodbye but simply nods, his mouth set in a firm line, and goes back inside.

CHAPTER SIXTEEN

∞

SOLEDAD

Okay," Hendrix says, laying her spoon beside her bowl on the dining room table. "You were right. Your chili should be famous."

"Told you." I shrug. "I add *sofrito* for a little sweetness and deeper flavor. Picadillo style."

"You have to show me how to make that," Yasmen says. "You know I've been stepping up my cooking game."

"I hadn't made it in a while, but I found my mother's *pilón* she used to mash the ingredients, and it prompted me to start."

"Well, it's delicious," Hendrix says. "Thanks again for dinner."

"It's the least I can do after all your help," I tell them. "Not just today with the deliveries, but the lead-up. I really started feeling like I had bitten off more than I could chew."

"Friends help friends chew." Yasmen smiles. "And I hope you've been considering that other thing I asked you to do."

"What'd you ask her to do?" Hendrix queries, picking her spoon back up to stir the last of her chili.

"You know I'm planning the Harvest Festival for the Skyland Association," Yasmen says. "Great way for local artisans to display their stuff and businesses to find new customers, et cetera, while the community gets to have a good time."

"Yas, you the planningest somebody I know." Hendrix chuckles.

"It's a gift." Yasmen fake-buffs her nails. "Well, I had the *brilliant* idea—"

"Jury's out on 'brilliant,' " I interject.

"The *brilliant* idea," Yasmen continues, "of setting up a pavilion called Sol's Farm-to-Table. People could experience one of her dinner parties, have her food, see how she creates the environment. We'd ask servers from Grits who aren't working that night if they want to help. Give them the chance to make some extra money. We wouldn't need many."

"I like it," Hendrix says, casting a questioning look across the table to me. "You don't want to?"

"I didn't say that," I reply. "I just don't know that people would be into it."

"They totally would," Yasmen says. "We need to strike while the iron is hot. You're TikTok famous."

"No, I'm not."

"Getting there," Hendrix says. "You have real momentum. In this age, a creator can go from obscurity to verified in no time. I think you should do it."

"It'll be extra work," I groan.

"It'll be money," Yasmen counters. "You know the Skyland Association got more money than we know what to do with half the time. They'd pay well."

Gymnastics, tuition, mortgage, car loan, college funds, utilities, HOA... to name a few things that require more money than I seem to ever have.

"Okay, I'll do it," I concede, and roll my eyes when they squeak in unison.

"I gotta give it to you, Sol," Hendrix says. "You *stay* hustling. These baskets today are just the latest example. Keep putting the work in, honey. It'll pay off. We're proud of you."

"You guys." I push out my bottom lip and fake-fan my eyes. "Don't make me emotional. I've already almost cried once today."

"Good cry?" Yasmen asks, pressing a spoon to her bottom lip.

I lean to the side and peer into the kitchen, making sure none of the kids are still in there eating. I'm pretty sure Lottie and Inez went upstairs.

"Lupe and Deja are gone. They went to see their friend Lindee," Yasmen says. "Her mom's cancer came back."

"Jesus." I close my eyes for a second. "You think you got it bad, and that gives you perspective fast. Do we know if anyone's organized a meal train for them?"

"I'm not sure," Yasmen says, a little dip between her brows. "We should."

"I'll check tomorrow and see what we can do." I pull out my phone and make a note to remind myself.

"So about this cry you had," Hendrix presses. "What was that all about?"

"I didn't cry," I correct. "Just almost. Inez was pressing my buttons. The usual teenage stuff. She hurt me, but it's not important. I'm good. The really disturbing part was that she told me she wants to see Edward."

"Oh, shit." Hendrix pours another glass of wine. "Why?"

"He *is* her father, Hen," Yasmen says. "Are you gonna take her, Sol?"

"At some point, if Edward will see her, yeah. Of course, but he doesn't want the girls coming there. I don't either, but I think she has a lot of questions that maybe only Edward can answer."

"Keeping her from doing it will only make her want it more," Yasmen points out.

"God, how y'all do it, I don't know." Hendrix shakes her head.

"Do what?" I ask.

"Be moms," Hendrix laughs. "That shit is not for me."

"You really don't want kids ever?" Yasmen asks.

"I would have kids, if my love language was drudgery," Hendrix drawls. "They be doing too little and needing too much. I got clients. I don't need kids too. Everyone's not made like that, and there's a lot of folks walking around here who should never have tried being parents. I'm not gonna be one of them."

"There are plenty of times I've asked myself if I was cut out for it," I laugh. "This afternoon, for example, the clash with Inez had me questioning. And then we had a close call with Judah Cross. If Inez knew it was him, it would only have made things worse."

As soon as I say his name, I fix my eyes on my bowl of chili, feeling the weight of both their stares.

"Don't even act like you can just leave it there," Hendrix says. "You invoked the name of that fine-ass accountant. Tell it."

I can't stop the smile from spilling onto my face. "He was my last delivery."

"Wait." Yasmen sits up straighter. "He bought a basket?"

"He did." I nod, biting my bottom lip. "He said he didn't expect me to deliver it personally. We were both kind of shocked. I haven't seen him since everything went down."

"Why was it a close call?" Yasmen asks with a small frown.

"Because Inez was headed back from her last delivery and saw me on Judah's porch with him. She blames him for Edward's situation, which is ridiculous, but Edward always talked so badly about Judah in front of the kids. He was the one who discovered the theft, but Edward did it."

"And you didn't want her to see you making heart eyes at him?" Hendrix teases.

"I was not making heart eyes," I say, feeling my cheeks heat.

"Was he still fine, though?" Hendrix asks.

"As hell," I reply without missing a beat. I bounce a glance between the two of them, and we all laugh on that invisible cue that comes with familiar friendship.

"I know he was." Hendrix *hmm hmm hmm*s. "How was seeing him again?"

"I don't know." I shrug. "Weird. Great. He helped me when he didn't have to."

I hesitate before confessing. "I met him at Edward's Christmas party last year before all this happened, and we kind of had a moment or something."

"Do tell," Yasmen leans forward and rests her elbows on the dining room table, chin in her hands. "You been holding out on us."

"Not holding out." I pull my hair over one shoulder and toy with the curls restlessly. "I was attracted to him. Like, really attracted to him, and I felt guilty because obviously I was a married woman."

"You ain't now," Hendrix says. "Was he feeling you too?"

"I . . . I think so." I close my eyes and draw a sharp breath. "It felt like it. Feels like it. Even today it was like if you lit a match in our general vicinity, we'd combust."

I lean in conspiratorially and lower my voice to a whisper. "And he asked if I'd have coffee with him."

"Coffee?" Yasmen clutches imaginary pearls. "Scandalous."

"It's not the coffee itself that's the problem." I split a look between them. "I'm not ready for anything with anyone right now, much less something as complicated as going out with the man who put my ex-husband in prison. It's too . . . messy, and I don't want messy."

"You could just fuck him," Hendrix says. "There's no law against that."

"Hen! She wouldn't do that." Yasmen slides a *You can tell me* look my way. "Would you?"

"Of course not." I gather my empty bowl and stand. "I'm really enjoying this time on my own, if I'm being honest. I spent my whole adult life with Edward. I poured a lot into him. It's time to pour into me."

"I like the sound of that," Hendrix says. "I'm sorry I suggested it. You know my horny ass denies myself *nothing* when it comes to sex."

"I'm horny too," I admit shamelessly. "But my vibrator won't break my heart and won't set unrealistic expectations for what I'm getting from a relationship. I've been talking with my therapist about self-partnering."

"Girl, I've been accidentally self-partnering for *years*." Hendrix grabs a slice of mango from the fruit tray I laid as dessert. "I haven't been in a relationship in a long time. Now, dick? That I would miss, but some dude all up on me and expecting me to put him first all the time? And getting my spare pillow hot and drooly? Oh, hell no."

"If there's ever a woman *not* in need of self-partnering," I joke, "it's you, Hen. All the stuff my therapist is talking through, it sounds like you've already learned."

"Well, she wasn't married to a con man," Yasmen asserts. "You were."

"I'm only now realizing how Edward subtly cut me down all the time to keep me feeling dependent on him for my worth. All these years I thought we were working together, but Edward thought I wasn't working at all. He viewed me as a dependent, not a partner, even though he couldn't have accomplished half of what he has without me."

"He's a narcissist," Hendrix says. "He needed to be the center of everything."

"If you need a season of being alone," Yasmen says, "take it."

"Maybe that fine-ass accountant will still be available when you're ready," Hendrix teases with an affectionate smile.

For a moment I consider confessing the clandestine touches beneath the sheets to my memories of Judah, but I decide against it. I don't want to muddy the waters any more than they already are. I said I'm happy being by myself for the first time, and I am. I need this. I just wish my body had gotten the memo because it lights up around Judah Cross.

I'm loading my bowl into the dishwasher when my cell rings in my back pocket.

"Hello," I answer, accepting Yasmen and Hendrix's bowls when they enter the kitchen.

"Mrs. Barnes?" A man's voice, brusque and businesslike, comes over the line.

I don't bother correcting that I've gone back to my maiden name, Charles. "Yes, this is she."

"I'm calling from Spiros to confirm your reservation for this Saturday night."

It's the reservation I made last year for our wedding anniversary.

"Oh, yes," I answer, forcing myself to focus. "The reservation. I actually..."

Actually what?

I've wanted to eat at Spiros for two years, but they've always been booked. Why should I pass up a chance to have a superb meal at a place I've wanted to try for years simply because I no longer have a man to take me?

"Mrs. Barnes?" he asks, a touch of impatience coloring his voice. "Do you still want the reservation?"

"It's actually Ms. Charles now." I swallow the last of my uncertainty and take the plunge by myself. "And yes. I still want it."

CHAPTER SEVENTEEN

JUDAH

I have to stop doing this. It's becoming...obsessive.

Before the thought has even fully formed, I'm picking up my phone and going to Soledad's profile. This is the shit high school boys do when they have a crush, not forty-one-year-old men with kids and responsibilities. Not directors working on a Saturday night who have presentations Monday. I have no excuse for being distracted. The boys are at Tremaine's for the weekend. I have the house to myself and an uninterrupted evening to catch up on some work.

And what am I doing?'

Lurking on Soledad's socials hoping for a glimpse of what she's doing right now.

"I know what she's *not* doing," I mutter, navigating to her profile. "Having coffee with you."

I blurted some half-formed invitation to grab coffee, and she literally ran screaming from my front porch. Her daughter was waiting by the car, so I know she had to go, but still...it was definitely not an *I'll think about it.* I was just so unprepared to see her at my house. I ordered the basket because I wanted...I don't know. To be connected to her? Involved somehow? I didn't analyze my motivation when I grabbed that flyer in the barbershop. I acted without thinking.

Also uncharacteristic.

Like it belongs to the teenage boy I'm apparently reverting to, my heart beats heavily when I see the notification that she's live right now.

She's tagged the post *Get Ready with Me*. I click on it and lean back in my chair to see what she's up to today.

"So," she says to the camera, pretty face clear and fresh looking. "Help me choose what to wear on my anniversary date."

What the hell?

Aren't they divorced? Is she visiting Edward in prison for their anniversary? Is it a conjugal visit? It can't be. Only five states still allow those, and Georgia isn't one of them. I know. I googled it when Edward was sentenced. Now if this were Mississippi...

"It would be none of your damn business." I return my attention to Soledad. She's seated in front of the mirror putting on makeup. Her hair, held back by a terry cloth band, streams in deep waves over the silk robe on her shoulders.

"This concealer, you guys." She displays the tube and uses the wand to apply some brownish-beige liquid under her eyes and over the tops of her cheeks. "Great dupe for NARS. I grabbed it at the drugstore for ten bucks."

She pauses to wink at the camera and whispers, "They'll never know."

She reaches for a brush and smooths foundation over her face. "Back to my anniversary date. There's a restaurant I've wanted to try for years, but it's always booked. So last year I made a reservation for my wedding anniversary."

Her half-made-up face clouds for the briefest moment before clearing.

"If you've been following me, you may know that my husband and I divorced this year. My first instinct when they called to confirm the reservation was to cancel, but I've been challenging myself to enjoy this journey of self-partnering."

She pauses to pop on lashes.

"Through therapy, I've come to realize I was married to a narcissist. How might one know if one is married to a narcissist?"

She gives a wide-eyed look and twists her lips.

"I'm glad you asked. Do they dismiss your feelings as 'crazy,' but others in your life don't agree? Do you often feel manipulated? Controlled?

Like you're losing your sense of self? Then you might be married to a narcissist."

She gives a quick shrug and goes on.

"Part of my recovery process is engaging in what's called self-partnering. I'm learning that to love and be loved is a perfectly healthy desire, unless we believe that relationship is somehow supposed to make us feel worthy or fulfilled. There's so much pressure not to be alone that sometimes it makes you feel like as a single person you don't have as much identity. It compels us to search for that person who will make us feel whole."

She lines her lips and looks right into the camera, her dark eyes sober and set.

"Well, I'm searching for myself. That's not to say I won't ever date again or have a relationship, but when I do, it will be in addition to the love I have for myself, not replacing it."

She stands and grabs two dresses on hangers from nearby hooks on the wall.

"I have a lot of love to give. I know I do because I've given it to everyone else in abundance my whole life. In this phase, I'm asking myself this question."

She tucks her chin into the collar of one of the dresses pressed to her chest and looks directly into the camera.

"What would happen if I turned all that love on myself? Not in a narcissistic way, but in terms of unconditional acceptance? Of truly attending to my hurts instead of expecting someone else to heal them?"

She holds up the two dresses again, one black and slinky and the other red and equally slinky. Both would look fantastic on her, but I want to see her in the black.

"So," she continues. "Instead of denying myself an experience I've wanted for a long time because there won't be anyone to meet me there, I'm meeting myself, which reminds me. I've been thinking of doing an online book club. Nothing too formal. Just me reading a book and anybody who wants to, reading with me. I want to read things that reinforce what I'm trying to accomplish. Let me know in the comments if that's something you might be interested in."

She grins and holds both dresses out.

"Which should I choose?" she asks. "Let me know in the comments, red or black."

"The black," I mutter, still mentally turning over everything she said. I never comment on her posts, of course, but I'm pulling for the black.

"Self-partnering, huh?"

No wonder she ran like I was some kind of threat. Maybe I am to what she's trying to accomplish right now. As much as I want to get to know Soledad Charles (yes, I know she reassumed her maiden name. I approve), right now it seems she's getting to know herself.

Who am I to stand in the way of that?

CHAPTER EIGHTEEN

SOLEDAD

R ight this way, ma'am," the host says, walking ahead of me as we cross Spiros's discreetly luxurious dining room.

"Thank you," I murmur, taking the seat he pulls out for me, because you don't just *say* things in a place like this. You have to *murmur* them.

"It's just you?" he asks with a quick frown. "The reservation was for two?"

"Oh, yes. Sorry. My husband is . . . well, not my husband anymore. It's just me."

He considers me with what looks like sympathy. "I'm sorry."

"Oh, believe me. I'm not."

"Good for you," he says, a grin cracking the careful veneer of professionalism. "I'll take this, then."

He clears the other place setting, removing the plate and silverware for my missing companion. There's a finality to it, him creating that empty space across the table from me. If he'd left it, those around us would assume I was waiting for someone, but that empty space is a declaration that no one is on the way. That could be the theme of my life this last year.

No one is on the way to rescue you. No one is on the way to save you and your girls. At the end of the day, it's up to you.

And so it is.

I catch the eye of a man dining with his wife, if the ring on his finger is any indication. He semi-leers at me when she isn't looking. Does he assume that since I'm alone I'm desperate? I've never felt less desperate in my life. I feel powerful, like I no longer need to squeeze myself into smaller spaces to clear room for others. Maybe I was afraid I wasn't big enough to occupy all this space alone.

Before the server comes and we start adding bottles and dishes, I want to capture a shot of the table with just me. I've become one of those people who take pictures of everything instead of just enjoying it, but documenting my life is work now. I'll grab a few shots here and there so I have content, but then I'm going to fully engage in this process tonight. Check my heart for any loneliness or regret, deal with it, and make room for contentment.

I snap a quick selfie of me and my one table setting and type out a caption.

Meeting myself! And I went with the red!

#SelfPartnering #MeetingMyself #Divorce

CHAPTER NINETEEN

JUDAH

I thought the idea of joint custody," I tell Tremaine while we buy tickets to the event she persuaded me to attend, "was that I have the boys during the week, and you take them on the weekends. Yet, here I am on a Saturday with my ex-wife, our kids, and her husband instead of catching up on my work. What's wrong with this picture?"

"Oh, stop complaining." Tremaine grins, looping her arm through Kent's. "Be glad someone cares enough to drag you out of that house instead of letting you brood all weekend with your spreadsheets."

"She's got a point," Kent says, giving me a wry look. "You do tend to brood."

"Dude, whose side are you on?" I grumble, shoving the ticket stub into the pocket of my jeans.

"You're not my wife." He shrugs. "Sorry."

An inch or so shorter than Tremaine, Kent is the perfect foil for her lean elegance. He's a tech guy and always looks slightly disheveled, like you caught him between software updates. The only time he appears truly tuned in is when he's seated in front of a machine. And when he's with her. Together, somehow her propulsive energy and his scattered wits seem to find rest.

I split my attention between our conversation and the boys, who are walking a few feet ahead. Too many people can overwhelm them, but so far so good. We used to stay home a lot, especially when the boys were younger and had more frequent meltdowns. Because Adam sometimes makes noises to self-soothe or when he's agitated, we've been kicked out of restaurants, churches, stores—you name it—for being "disruptive." Negotiating public spaces has gotten easier over the years.

And we just stopped giving a shit.

We have as much right to go out and explore the world with our family as anyone else. We'll be respectful, but we don't stand for people disrespecting our boys or making them feel that just because they may be different they are less or deserve less.

Maybe it's because I've been locked in my office all day, but the landscape seems almost Technicolor, with a sky so blue and bright I have to squint when I look up. This crowd is thick and the air is cool. Kids dart from booth to booth, squealing and laughing. The muscles of my shoulders, tensed while I hunched over my laptop for hours, slowly relax.

"Too bad you don't have a girl, Judah," Tremaine muses. "I could find you somebody. There's a nice woman at my firm who—"

"How many times do I have to tell you it's weird for my ex-wife to set me up on dates?"

"That is a little weird, honey," Kent agrees. "Besides, they have dating apps now. Remember? That's how we met."

"Can you imagine *him*," she says, nodding pointedly to me, "on Tinder? Oh, my God. I'd love to collect data on that social experiment."

"That won't be happening." I smother a laugh and shake my head. "It's bad enough you dragged me to this fall feast shit."

"Harvest Festival," she corrects.

"Whatever. It's bad enough you dragged me to this on my day off."

"Is it really a day off when all you do is work from home?" she asks.

"I'm behind and catching up." I survey the field of food tents, face-painting stations, trucks piled with hay, and a few pavilions. "I'm only staying twenty minutes, and that's for the boys."

Kent fit right in with our unit. Things are not always easy, but Kent knew what he was signing on for. Anyone who gets involved with Tremaine or me has to understand that ours is not the typical parenting journey. Aaron may always require intense support. He may live outside of our home someday, but it probably won't be entirely on his own. I'm very conscious of the fact that we may be fiscally responsible for him, not only until we die, but until he does. That sounds morbid, but when I work, when I save, when I invest, it has to last two lifetimes. Mine and his. He can still make progress, of course. Hell, he could become a world-renowned cuber and outearn all of us. Who knows? We hope for the best and prepare for...well, anything.

Adam's journey is different, but no less complex. He's academically gifted but still has a lot of sensory, behavioral, and socialization issues. Nothing we haven't learned to handle. I worry constantly about his seizures, though. He used to have fifty of them a day. Sometimes he would fall during one, bump his head, and end up in the emergency room.

Yeah, anyone who joins our crew needs to understand what they're signing on for, and Kent definitely did. I smile as he tries to convince the boys to go on a hayride. He's not having much success.

"If you go," Tremaine whispers to me, "you know they'll do it."

"You didn't say anything about riding a pickup truck through the woods."

"Woods? Judah, I see the parking lot of Walmart from here. They play tag football on this field. This is the closest Skyland can get to rustic, though, so throw yourself into it for the boys."

"Okay. I'll ride the hay thing, and then I have to get back to the house and finish these reports."

"I hope those reports keep you warm at night."

I don't answer because my nights recently have been filled with the memory of one woman whom I would deeply enjoy keeping warm. Soledad appearing on my front porch was torture and a blessing. I was thrilled to finally see her after so long, but I can't stop fantasizing about her. Even the word "fantasize" feels weird because I generally don't *have* fantasies, but the smell of her on my porch that day. I don't even know what scent she wears, but it haunts me, the way it's light and sweet and hangs in the air after she's gone.

Her hair was longer, swinging past her shoulders. From a distance, you assume it's just black, but what a privilege, being close enough to pick out the amber that streaks subtly through the dark strands.

And her mouth.

That damn mouth.

Her lips are the color of crushed plums, like the juice that oozes out. I know because I bought plums and squeezed one to see if it matched my memories of those pretty, pouty lips. It absolutely did, and the thought of Soledad's lips wrapped around my dick. I just want—

"Earth to Judah." Tremaine snaps her fingers in my face. "If you could stop dreaming of tax write-offs for a second, we could get you on this truck and back to your home office in no time."

I disguise my mortification with a droll look and a roll of my eyes before agreeing to the hayride.

As Tremaine predicted, the boys acquiesce as soon as they find out I'm willing. At first the three of us are stiff, which seems to be our default setting, but we loosen into laughter as the trip goes on. It's the crisp autumn air on our faces, the smell of fresh hay and trees all around, leaves spiced with the colors of saffron, turmeric, and sumac. Adam is smiling, and he may not be talking to the other kids on the ride, but he enjoys being with them. Aaron just watches and takes the occasional photo with his phone. With so much of his communication reliant on pictures, he's constantly adding to his encyclopedia of images.

By the time the ride ends and the truck returns to the small shed where we started, the boys are more eager to explore.

"Can we get our faces painted?" Adam asks.

"Sure," I agree. We head for the group of kids waiting their turn.

Maybe most fifteen-year-old boys aren't excited about getting their faces painted, but these guys have their own timetable. So many societal "norms"—like at what age you should stop playing with certain toys or indulging certain interests—are actually pretty arbitrary and don't make sense to a lot of autistic people. They don't make sense to *me*. Why should I hold my kids hostage to useless constructs that deny them things that make them happy? Aaron still carries a stuffed Cookie Monster in his backpack at all times. Adam has "Twinkle, Twinkle, Little Star" in his playlist for when he feels anxious. Small comforts in a world filled with sounds and sensations that, though completely harmless to most of us, sometimes feel hostile to them.

Sometimes feel hostile to *me*.

When I was growing up, tags in my shirts bothered me so badly, my mother cut them out of everything. To this day tags agitate me. If a shirt has a tag, I won't rest till it's gone. Should I have grown out of that? Like Adam and Aaron, I often find the world too loud, too bright, scents too strong. I don't judge where they find comfort or tools to help them navigate a life that feels like one of Aaron's cubes—pieces sliding and shifting until a picture forms that makes sense. I don't try to make them fit in with anyone else or compare them to their peers. I remember how that feels. Our family is on its own journey, and we'll take it at our own pace, one day at a time. It's how we've gotten this far.

Tremaine stops at one of the artisan tents.

"I wanna see if they have any beaded bracelets," she says.

I glance at my watch. I said twenty minutes, and I've given it an hour. I'm poised to extricate myself when a stack of floral bookmarks catches my eye. They're clear, with flowers pressed inside.

"Pretty, right?" the lady running the booth asks, walking over and picking one up. "Made these myself."

I reach for one and, before I can talk myself out of it, respond, "I'll take it."

Tremaine eyes me with surprise. "Need to mark your place in one of your accountant handbooks?"

"Something like that." I grin but don't look at her as I pay for the bookmark. "Speaking of which, I think I'm gonna take off. Get some work done."

"All right." Holding Kent's hand, she rises up on tiptoe to kiss my cheek. "Thanks for coming. I know you had other—"

"Farm to table!" A tall woman dressed in a discreetly expensive, deceptively casual dress brandishes flyers. "We have a few more spots for Soledad's Farm-to-Table Experience."

I stare at the woman, not just because she said Soledad's name, but because she looks vaguely familiar. She must feel the same because she narrows her eyes and tilts her head like she's trying to place me.

"You're the accountant," she finally says, a smile on her striking face. "I met you at Soledad's house. It's Judah, right?"

"Uh, yeah," I say, surprised she remembers. "Great memory."

"I'm her friend Hendrix."

"Nice seeing you again." I try not to sound too interested. "What's this for?"

"Soledad's dining experience." She waves the flyers. "Food she's prepared at a table she's set. Basically like attending one of Sol's dinner parties."

"Soledad with the vinaigrette?" Tremaine asks, her voice perking up. "Oh, I follow her. She's here?"

"Yeah." Hendrix smiles broadly. "She's prepared a meal completely sourced from local growers, butchers, and fishermen. We had a three o'clock and a six o'clock seating, but those are sold out. We had to add a nine o'clock to meet the demand."

"You said the three and six are sold out?" Kent asks. "That's too bad. I would have loved to go, but we'll be leaving soon."

"Yeah." Tremaine pushes her lips into a disappointed moue. "I need to get back home."

"Maybe next time," Hendrix says.

I must be eyeing those flyers like they're winning lotto tickets because Hendrix smirks knowingly and hands me one. "Just in case you change your mind."

"You're leaving, right?" Tremaine turns to me.

"Uh, yeah," I answer absently, my attention following Hendrix walking away. "I really need to go."

"Can we check out the pumpkin carving, Mom?" Adam asks.

He takes off as soon as she says yes, but circles back to grab Aaron's hand and drag him along. Aaron has his cube out, a sure indicator that he's losing interest in this event.

"We better go after them," Tremaine says. "See you tomorrow. I'll drop the boys off around six."

"Got it," I acknowledge. "Bye, Kent."

In moments, they're swallowed by the bustling crowd. Instead of heading for my car, I search the field for the pavilion with a sign that reads *Soledad's Farm-to-Table Experience*. It's only five o'clock. Hendrix said the six o'clock seating is sold out.

I could go home and work for a while... and then come back at nine.

CHAPTER TWENTY

SOLEDAD

Last dinner of the day," Yasmen says, setting a mason jar of flowers on one of the long tables lined up under the pavilion. "I always have great ideas, but even I didn't realize how successful this would be. We had to add another dinner, Sol."

"I know." I shake my head, still flabbergasted.

I take in all the details of the pavilion. The fairy lights strung overhead and candles glimmering on the tables make it feel warm and intimate. Rows of long wooden tables lined up and trimmed with wildflowers splash color in the dimness of evening. There's a poignancy the night lends the space that day didn't allow.

"This is the hottest date in Skyland tonight," Yasmen says.

"It's the hottest," Josiah says, grabbing her from behind, "because you're here."

"Oh, dropping lines, are we, Mr. Wade? You don't have to prove to me you still got game," Yasmen says, turning to loop her arms around his neck.

"I want to keep you interested, Mrs. Wade." His smile is loving, and his eyes never leave her face, as if they're alone.

"Hey, Sol," he says, turning his smile on me. "This is amazing."

"Thank you," I answer. "Didn't expect to see you away from Grits on a Saturday night."

"The manager's got it," he says. "Though it was definitely busy. The kitchen is slammed. I'm going back. I just had to see my girl."

"Oh, because it's been so long since we saw each other." Yasmen laughs. "A whole six hours."

"I missed you," he whispers, kissing her cheek.

She casts an unrepentant look my way. "Sorry, Sol. I promise you'll have my undivided attention as soon as I get rid of this guy."

My heart burns for a second with a desire to have that, but I shelve it. My desire for a meaningful, passionate connection with someone doesn't go away while I'm "dating myself." I'm working on me, so when I do find that person, I'm the most whole version of myself I can be. For now, the occasional twinge of longing is nothing compared to what I'm learning. Nothing compared to how I've been loving and knowing myself.

Josiah kisses Yasmen goodbye. They're a fairy tale. Divorced and remarried, they are couple goals for so many. There is no reunion with Edward in my future, but these two were meant to be.

Josiah heads back to the restaurant, and Yasmen and I handle the final details—checking tickets, place settings, food. Hendrix had an event for one of her clients downtown but gave us strict instructions to "fix her a plate." I'm making enough money today to cover my mortgage plus some this month. I'm so glad I agreed to do this, and even more glad that Yasmen thought of it.

"Reporting for duty," Inez says, playfully saluting, a few minutes before diners are scheduled to arrive.

"Did you squeeze in one more hayride?" I laugh, glancing up from the flowers I'm arranging on one of the long tables.

"Yes." She points to her brightly decorated cheek. "And face painting, but I'm all yours now. Remember I'm the daughter who showed up for you when it counted."

"I think I'll give Lottie a pass since she has a meet today. And Lupe has a debate team trip. I do appreciate you coming, though *maybe* the money I promised you'd earn should be factored in."

"I would have done it for free, Mom." She grins mischievously. "But I'm glad I don't have to."

"Just like at the other two dinners, you can hop in if you see the servers need help, but your main job is to capture footage so I can make content for the socials."

"I think that's a great idea, Sol," Yasmen calls from a few tables over, where she's folding napkins. "I could see folks asking you to throw their dinner parties after this."

I hadn't anticipated that as a by-product of this decision, but I guess that could happen if I offer it as a service. It's highly labor-intensive, so I'm not sure I would do much of it, but occasionally and for a steep price, I would consider it.

A few minutes later, the diners for our last meal start arriving and taking their seats at the long tables. The seating is not arranged for privacy, but for community and conversation. Folks are squeezed in, elbows and knees occasionally bumping. Candlelight illuminating not only the people they came with but also the ones they'll get to know. My hope is that my food will do what it's always done: lower people's guards, loosen their tongues, warm their hearts, and satisfy their hunger.

"Thank you so much for coming," I tell the packed pavilion once everyone is seated. "I'm so pleased to see you all. Before we get started, I want to let you know that a portion of your admission to this dinner tonight will go toward a GoFundMe for Cora Garland, a Skyland mom fighting cancer for the second time. We're all with her and want to help any way we can."

I point to a small wooden stand by the door. "There's more about her journey here in case you want to donate additionally and help her family offset medical costs."

I clap my hands together and spread a smile over the crowd. "Now for what you all came to do. Eat!"

I nod to the servers lining the walls, a signal for them to begin.

"We're bringing you water now, but I've pulled a few wines from which you can select. We have four courses, the first of which is my favorite salad topped with my"—I pause and air-quote with a smile—"viral vinaigrette."

Several folks whoop and applaud. This is what they came for.

"After the salad, we'll have a few shareables for each table," I say. "Fried truffle *burrata*, some stuffed portobello mushrooms, and a few other light items to prepare your palate. For the main course, we've got a grilled chop, a delicious grouper, and a superb risotto if you need a vegetarian option.

"For dessert," I say with a secretive smile, "I'm trying something here for the very first time. My peace cobbler, which has a made-from-scratch crust, locally grown peaches and blueberries. I also made it with homemade cake batter. You're my taste testers."

I'd anticipated this last dinner would be the least attended, but it's as packed as the other two. I'm pouring water for a few diners when Yasmen calls my name.

"Hey, Sol," she says, her eyes suspiciously bright. "Do we have room for one more?"

I almost drop the carafe of water I'm holding when I see Judah Cross standing beside her. I walk over to the pavilion entrance on unsteady legs. That's the effect this man has on me just by standing still and staring. He doesn't simply look at me. He takes inventory, slowly considering every detail from my head to my feet. The look is so discreetly hot and wanting, my toes curl in my shoes, like that look is a lick that runs the length of my body, stopping to sample secret places along the way. Am I making this up? Is it my imagination that each time we're together, it feels like he's hoarding every second, storing away images of me for later? Am I that conceited?

"Judah, hey." I tip my head back to smile up at him. "What a surprise."

"I was here earlier with my family," he says, looking away from me for a moment and then returning that penetrating gaze to my face, "and heard about this from your friend Hendrix. I didn't have any dinner plans, so thought this was better than DoorDash and fourth-quarter projections."

"Oh, good for Hen." Yasmen beams, flicking an avid glance between Judah and me like we're two gazelles on Animal Planet preparing to mate right before her eyes. "I need to go help."

"Help with what?" I ask, letting her know she ain't slick trying to leave us alone.

"Just help," she says, fluffing her curly Afro with one hand. "I'm helpful like that."

She walks away, leaving the two of us standing together, wrapped in warm light and the savory scents of dinner. My breath stutters at his nearness, at the smell of him, the look of him, so tall and broad and imposing. Yet safe. Really safe. And after all the shit Edward put me through, safe is the new sexy.

"I hope it's okay that I came?" he asks.

"Of course. It's open to the public, and you bought your ticket like everyone else. Glad you came."

"Good, because I'm starving."

We share a grin, and I set my nerves aside long enough to enjoy that he's *here*. That he came knowing I would be here too. That I get to see him again, even if it's surrounded by lots of people, with no privacy. That's probably the only way I *should* see this man.

I point him toward one of the few tables with a vacancy. "Let's get you fed."

For the next two hours, I do what I've done all day. Flit from table to table making sure everyone is enjoying the food, the wine, the company. I never linger too long with any particular group, but my attention is continually drawn to the quiet man eating his food, only occasionally acknowledging the diners around him. He's probably clueless that the brunette across the table has been making a play for him all night. The thirst on that lady is so real. I wonder if he'll take her up on what she's offering. My gut twists at the thought of those dark, steady eyes trained on another woman with that unwavering focus. I'm sure he dates. A man like him? Handsome, fit, successful, single. Kind and brilliant.

He dates, Sol. Of course he does.

Should he decide to date his eager dinner companion, that's none of my business.

My feet are killing me by the time dessert is done and guests start departing. I take up my spot by the door, thanking them for coming and giving everyone a sachet of potpourri I made as a parting gift.

"Wow. You make potpourri?" one diner asks.

"You can make it at home easy. Just slice up some apple, orange, add cloves, cinnamon, and vanilla. Bring it to a boil and let it simmer. Your house will smell divine."

"You really are the house lady," she laughs.

The moniker has started to stick, and I'm not sure how I feel about it.

"Have a good evening," I say, pressing the bag into her hands.

I try not to search for Judah in the thinning crowd. I've had sonar for that man all night, constantly aware of what he was doing, what he was eating, and how he seemed to be enjoying it. Did he realize the woman at his table wanted to box *him* up with her leftovers and take him home? My attention has been split between him and everyone else since he entered the pavilion, and now I can't find him.

The last of the guests leave, and I push down the rising disappointment that Judah left without saying goodbye.

"I'm gonna grab some photos of the empty pavilion still lit from outside," Inez tells me, her expression bright with exertion and excitement. She's been all over today, capturing shots and helping out.

"You've been amazing, Nez." I tug one of the long braids hanging over her shoulder. "Yasmen had to go pick up Lupe and Deja from their field trip. The bus just got there, but she left a crew to clean up, so we get to leave soon. How 'bout that?"

"Cool!" She takes off, phone and light in hand.

"Okay, that's it." I kick my foot behind me and grab the strap of my slingback, tugging it off and repeating with the other foot. I pad over to the wine station, grabbing an unopened bottle.

"You're coming home with me," I tell the merlot.

"Lucky bottle."

I swing around, and at the sight of Judah, my synapses start frying and my heartbeat starts tripping and something flutters in the belly region. I'm having an all-over startled reaction to this man.

"Oh!" I press the wine to my chest. "I thought you were gone."

"No, I just went to the car to get something."

"I thought maybe...well, that lady at your table seemed kind of... friendly. I thought you..." I stop, mortified that I let this private thought out and that he knows I was so aware of him all night. I can't lift my eyes from my bare toes against the dark parquet flooring we laid in the pavilion.

"I don't know her. I didn't come for her." One long finger lifts my chin, and the sincerity in his eyes reaches through my chest and squeezes my heart. "I came for you, Sol."

"Oh. Okay." It's all I can manage.

He pulls something from the pocket of his slacks and holds it out to me. It's an acrylic bookmark, clear with purple and white pressed flowers inside. "This is for you."

"Judah." I look up from the bookmark, so small and fragile in his wide palm, to his face. "It's beautiful."

"I saw you talking about starting a book club and thought..." A smile that mocks himself comes and goes, briefly softening the stern lines of his face. "It's kind of silly now that—"

"It's not. It's one of the sweetest things anyone's done for me in a long time."

His teeth flash, white and straight against the darkness of his skin. "One of the artisans had a lot of them at her tent, but I saw this one and I thought you might like it now that you're reading more."

"I want to read more. We haven't even chosen our first book yet." I bite into a smile and tease him through my lashes. "And have you been stalking my socials?"

"I can't seem to stop."

Our smiles fade together as his words drift down between us, soft and so revealing.

"And I keep asking myself: Why can't I stop watching this woman restock her refrigerator?" He shakes his head with a smile that's not quite comfortable. "Or wash her sheets? Or organize the cabinet under her sink?"

A laugh bolts out of me at the unexpected comment. "That's ASMR."

"What the hell is ASMR?"

"Autonomous sensory meridian response. It's like feeling soothed or stimulated even by certain sounds, background noise, whispering, pages being turned. All kinds of things, but it makes you feel good when you watch it."

"It's not that." He takes my hand and folds my fingers around the bookmark but doesn't let go. "It's you. I like watching you."

I'm trapped in this moment—the clean, intoxicating scent of him, the heat of his body this close, the intensity of his eyes caressing my face, my neck and shoulders bared by my dress—but instead of fighting my way out, I long to burrow in for a few stolen seconds.

"I saw your anniversary dinner," he says softly. "When you went to Spiros by yourself."

"You did?" I ask, barely breathing.

"I was rooting for the black dress," he says, his eyes never leaving my face. "But you looked so good in the red."

"Th-thank you. It turned out to be a great night."

"You have a way of doing that, taking shitty things and making them turn out great."

I don't know what to say. I blink at him, astounded by his unexpected sweetness. He's always so serious and brusque. That *I* bring this out of him is humbling.

"It sounds like you're on a self-partnering journey right now," he says. "No dating, right?"

"Right." I lick my lips and nod numbly. "None."

"I think that's great, especially so soon after your divorce." He squeezes my hand, which he's still holding. "And I don't want to distract from what you're learning about yourself."

It's what he should say. It's what I *want* him to say, what I need him to say, but Judah is something rare. I think we could be spectacular together. I'm not ready, though. It's like feeling him with just the tips of my fingers and not being sure I'll be able to hold on.

"I guess I wanted to let you know that when you *are* ready to spend time with someone else," he says, "I'd like to be someone."

"You are very much already someone, Judah," I whisper, and press the bookmark to my lips. "I'll keep that in mind."

"Hey, Mom." Inez pulls up short, stopping at the pavilion entrance, her sharp gaze traveling from me to Judah. "I'm, uh, finished."

"That's great, honey." I take a subtle step back, putting a bit more distance between Judah and me. I offer him a polite smile, hoping he takes the hint. "Thanks for coming tonight. Hope you enjoyed the meal."

I reach into the basket on the table holding the small bags of potpourri.

"Just a little something I made for all the guests," I tell him, keeping my tone neutral as I hand one to him.

"Thank you." He presses the bag to his nose for a deep inhalation. "Smells good."

"Take care." I don't know when I'll see him again, and I wish I could say more, but under Inez's watchful gaze, this will have to do.

"Night." He turns to the entrance, nods at Inez as he walks past, and disappears into the dark.

I sigh, reminding myself that I'm not dating anyway and can't do anything about the buzz beneath my skin every time this man comes around.

"You ready?" I ask Inez, slipping the bookmark into the pocket of my dress. "I'm exhausted."

"Who was that?" There's more than curiosity in her voice. There's suspicion. "Wasn't he one of the people we delivered baskets to last week?"

So she *had* been close enough to see him. I have to be honest with her. Hopefully she'll be reasonable.

I slip my shoes on but leave the back straps undone. "That's Judah Cross."

For a second she just stares at me, then she shakes her head. "You're being nice to the man who got Daddy arrested?"

"How many times do I have to tell you?" I struggle to keep the frustration out of my words. "Your father broke the law. It was Judah's job to tell their employer. That's all he was doing. His job."

"And was it his job to come here tonight? Daddy said Judah liked you. Do you like him too?"

"Your father was paranoid because he knew he'd done things that were wrong and he was afraid of being exposed. He pinned all that to Judah, when really he was to blame for everything that happened."

"But none of it would have been exposed had it not been for him." She tips her head toward the pavilion door Judah just passed through. "And, of course, all the information you turned over to them."

"What would you have had me do, Inez? Ignore what he did? Help him so I would get arrested too? Leave the three of you to end up God knows where with two parents in jail?"

"I *didn't* expect you to flirt with the man who sent Daddy to prison."

The words explode in my face like a grenade, but I don't flinch. I hold her accusing stare.

"There is nothing going on between Judah Cross and me," I reply, so glad I can say that with honesty. "He has been concerned about us, believe it or not. He never wanted us caught in the crosshairs of your father's lies. He helped us before and wanted to make sure we are okay."

After a final searching glance, she nods. "I just remember Daddy saying that guy was after him, and it was true. And saying he had a thing for you at the Christmas party."

"Your father was mistaken." I grab my bag and walk toward the exit. "Now can we drop this?"

I want to shift from this dangerous topic where I'm barely able to tell the truth. Something *is* going on with Judah and me, but it's subterranean. I'll keep it that way as long as possible.

"All right," she finally says.

"You did good today, kid," I say, linking my arm with hers and taking slow steps across the field of grass wet with evening dew.

"You did good too." She puts her head on my shoulder. "I'm sorry I came at you like that. I know nothing's going on with Judah Cross."

I smile and touch the smooth coolness of the bookmark in my pocket. Nope. Nothing at all.

CHAPTER TWENTY-ONE

∞

JUDAH

"They never learn," Perri tsks, setting a stack of reports on the edge of my desk. "Glad I don't have to eat it."

"What are you talking about?" I ask absently, glancing up to see if the reports are the ones I requested. I know I'm killing trees, but there's something about seeing the numbers in print. "Who never learns?"

"Them Callahans." My assistant takes the seat across from my desk—uninvited—and crosses her legs.

"Why don't you make yourself comfortable?" I lean back and hook an elbow on the back of my office chair.

"Oh, I am." Perri studies her white-tipped nails. "I heard they're using their cousin Eileen again to cater the executive Christmas party."

"It was pretty bland last year."

"Bland?" Perri sucks her teeth. "Everybody talks so bad about her food. They say she makes 'mediocre and cheese.'"

I have to laugh at that. "I don't remember macaroni and cheese at the party last year."

"No, she saves that for the company picnic." Perri shudders. "You know I already don't eat just anybody's food. Everybody don't keep a clean house. You know what I mean?"

"You sound like my mama." I chuckle. "She never ate at the office potlucks."

"Smart woman. Seems like the Callahans would want to pull out all the stops for their executives, but no."

"The sweet taste of nepotism," I say, recalling Soledad's assessment of the food at last year's party. Was it only a year ago? I knew I didn't imagine the pull between us as soon as we met, but I also knew she would never do anything about it. She's not that kind of woman.

Hell, I'm not that kind of man, but when I'm around her, the lines blur and I forget the boundaries that have always been a hallmark of my life.

After I left the pavilion Saturday night, I couldn't focus on my reports. I couldn't sleep. That damn scent she wore had somehow made its way onto my clothes. Just a hint of it, but it stole my focus and made me hard. A late-night run through the neighborhood didn't help. A cold shower didn't help. Watching videos she'd posted on her socials made it worse. I know she's self-partnering, not dating. I wasn't lying when I told her I don't want to disrupt the process she needs to go through.

I just like being around her. She makes me feel lighter. After all the anxiety and responsibility I've lived with for so long, "lighter" is an addictive feeling. I don't have to date her to get to know her, to be around her. I'm disgusted by the compulsive way I replay in my head our interactions at dinner on Saturday, though. The way I turn over every word, looking for hidden meaning.

Maybe Cousin Eileen's mediocre and cheese presents another opportunity.

"I had a great meal this weekend," I offer, studying the report on the iPad in front of me.

"Oh, yeah?" Perri asks.

"It was the best meal I've had in a long time, actually." I pick up a sheaf of papers from the stack she laid on my desk, considering it instead of meeting Perri's eyes. "It was at an event. I wonder if they'd be available to cater the executive Christmas party?"

"Hey, it's worth a shot." Her smile is sly and delighted. "But you'd have to convince Delores."

Which is how I find myself stopping Delores on her way out of our directors' meeting that afternoon.

"Hey, Delores. Can I ask you something about the executive Christmas party?"

She studies me with one lifted brow. "What about it?"

"Hiring your cousin every year kind of smacks of nepotism."

"Why do you care?" She starts down the hall and I match her steps. "Nothing matters to you except the bottom line."

"It's the principle of it," I lie. "And have you eaten the food?"

"Oh, I have." She grimaces. "It's bad."

"Well, why keep subjecting your highest-ranking employees to the worst food?"

Delores's thick brows bend into a frown. "Why do I get the sense that you have something in mind for the Christmas party?"

"I mean," I say with a casual shrug, "I did have a great meal at the Harvest Festival this weekend, and thought if we ever want to serve food that's actually edible at the holiday party..."

"Who is it?" she glances at me, her eyes narrowing, assessing.

"Soledad."

"You mean the wife of the man who stole over six million dollars from the company?"

"I mean the *ex-wife* who gave us the means to recover said six million dollars, yes."

"Oh, my God." She stops in the middle of the hall, catching my arm to stop me too. "You like her." Her eyes are wide and shining with some mischievous mixture of shock and delight.

"So do you," I say, casting a self-conscious glance toward the break room with the door open and employees heating up their lunches inside. "And would you keep your voice down?"

I start walking down the hall again, not waiting for or *wanting* Delores to join me, but she does, matching her pace to mine.

"You were the one going to bat for her when all that shit went down," I remind her.

"I distinctly remember *you* always up at bat for her, and me cheering from the sidelines."

"Look, she has to support her daughters alone. Edward left their lives in shambles, and she's catering, decorating, and doing whatever she can to make money."

"I know." She sighs. "It's crossed my mind more than once that she got hurt the most in that situation."

"Exactly," I say, pouncing on her compassion. "And considering how much she helped us, it's kind of the least we can do."

Delores examines me with X-ray vision, and I'm sure she sees through every excuse and half-truth I used in hopes of seeing Soledad again. "I'll see what I can do."

"That's great." I turn on my heel and start walking toward the elevator before I reveal something embarrassing.

"Oh, and Judah," Delores calls from behind me.

I turn to face her, brows lifted and waiting. "Yeah?"

"It's kind of cute."

"What?" I ask cautiously.

"The crush you have on Soledad."

I expel a harsh breath, roll my eyes, and stalk into the elevator as soon as it opens, but her guffaw chases me.

So much for not embarrassing myself.

CHAPTER TWENTY-TWO

SOLEDAD

Y ou guys ready?"
     I look over at Lupe in the passenger seat and glance to the back, where Deja sits.

"I guess so." Lupe pushes a chunk of fiery red hair behind her ear, eyes cast down to her lap.

"Lindee says Mrs. Garland has been really sick," Deja offers from the back seat, her voice hushed. "Like from the chemo or whatever."

"I remember that from when my mother had cancer," I tell them. "It's the worst. Exhausting. You don't feel like doing anything." I smile at them both. "That's where we come in."

I get out of the Pilot and go to the trunk, which is loaded with my favorite cleaning supplies and several large reusable bags of storage containers for food.

"A clean house makes most things a little better," I tell them. "Or at least it makes me feel a little better most of the time."

"Should I grab footage for CleanTok?" Lupe asks. "That last post of your cleaning hacks got like three million views."

"Nah. This is just for us." I glance up at the two-story redbrick house, which seems a little desolate and bleak. "And for them."

The porch could use some brightening. A quick Target run may be in order. One of the Harrington moms *did* give me a gift card for organizing her pantry. I was saving it for a rainy day, but Cora's gloomy porch seems an even better reason to use it.

"Put your masks on, girls. Cora's immune system is probably some-what compromised." I pull out a mop and my favorite vacuum. "Now let's get to it. The sooner we start, the sooner we can wrap up and you can get on with your weekend."

Lupe grabs two bags and strides toward the house. "Lindee's been bummed big-time. I can't imagine how she feels."

I can. Terrified. Irrationally angry because *Why my mom?* Sad most of the time and guilty when she's *not* sad. I ran the gamut of emotions when Mami was diagnosed. I had so much hope, though. I had never seen anything beat my mother. Cancer wouldn't be the first.

It was the first. And the last.

When Lindee opens the door, her face brightens immediately.

"Hi!" She gawks at all the stuff crowding their front porch. "Oh, my gosh. What *is* all this?"

"Did you not tell her we were coming to clean, Lupe?" I turn con-cerned eyes to my daughter. I don't usually like people coming to my house unannounced. I certainly wouldn't want to spring this on Cora.

"She did. I just didn't expect..." Lindee waves her hand at the bags of food and mounds of cleaning supplies. "All this."

"My mom is a general. Cleaning is war," Lupe says. "And we're her soldiers."

"Not exactly how I would put it, but close enough." I smile at Lindee. "Could we come in and get started?"

She steps back, waving us into the foyer. "Of course."

A boy, maybe a few years younger than Lupe, comes down the stairs. He, like Lindee, has golden-brown skin and dark, curly hair. His is cropped close.

"What's going on?" he asks, eyeing my cleaning supplies and the items still on the porch.

"They're here to clean, George," Lindee offers cheerfully.

"Does Mom know?" He frowns and glances up the stairs. "She's resting."

"We'll be quiet." I turn to Lindee. "Or if you want us to come back another time—"

"No." She shoots her brother a pointed look. "Mom does know and was happy. She's fine and will appreciate the help."

"Well, if that's the case," I say, looking questioningly at the scowling boy. "Maybe you could help us load some of this stuff into the house?"

With dragging steps, George goes out onto the porch and grabs a few bags of food. It's obvious the house has been neglected. The kids have probably tried to help, but what I've seen so far is in need of a deep clean.

I peer into the fridge. My fingers itch to scrub this thing from top to bottom.

"Okay." I turn to the four young people watching me. "Everybody ready for their assignments?"

The girls nod, eager to get started, while the semisulky boy stands off to the side.

"What about you?" I ask him. "You wanna help? You don't have to if you—"

"I'll help." He shuffles his feet and surveys the kitchen. "Tell me what to do."

Over the next two hours, we work together to get the house sparkling and smelling fresh. I usually like to clean alone, but I sense that George might need to talk. He resists my first tentative attempts to draw him out, but after a few minutes starts sharing a little at a time. He's a good kid, but confused and scared. I remember feeling that way, and I was an adult when my mother was diagnosed. I can only imagine how unmoored he feels by the threat of losing his mom this young.

"We've cleaned every room but Mom's," Lindee says, parking a bucket of supplies by the fridge and blowing her bangs from her eyes.

"We can do that another day," I say. "I don't want to wake her up."

"I'm up."

Cora Garland stands at the kitchen doorway, and if I weren't in her house, I would never have placed her. She looks so different from how I remember, from the glowing woman with the lustrous hair in the photos gracing the mantel and walls. Her skin is dark brown and ashen. Her hair—gone. She's not wearing a wig or a turban or a cap. She is bold bald, with no lashes or eyebrows. Her body, once round and pleasingly thick in all the *sistah girl* places, is reduced to a bony frame drowning in a sweatshirt that reads *F*ck Cancer*.

"Got it the first time I beat this bitch," she says, touching the letters across her chest. "Still holds true."

"I have several of those," I admit.

"You a survivor?" Surprise lights her expression.

"No, my mother had cancer."

"Did she make it?"

I wish I hadn't mentioned it. I hate to tell her my mother is gone. That Mami won so many battles, but the one Cora herself is fighting right now, she ultimately lost.

"No. She passed away." I grab one of the glass storage containers from the counter. "I was just putting these in the fridge. Pasta salad. There's some salmon. I left that uncooked but marinated. Lindee, maybe you can just pop it in the oven for a bit. Or even the air fryer. I've left instructions for everything."

When I stop talking and look back to Cora, her mouth has relaxed into a loose smile.

"Why don't you come on up to the bedroom," she says, turning her back to leave the kitchen. "If you can get it looking like the rest of the house, I'm not gonna turn it down."

I grab my bucket of cleaning supplies and follow her out into the living room and up the stairs, which seem tough for her to negotiate. Some of her spunk in the kitchen was probably for her kids' sake. I know that feeling, and the relief of letting it go as soon as you're alone.

"Maybe you could sit there," I say, nodding to an armchair in the corner, "while I get the bed together."

"Sounds good to me." She falls into the seat and closes her eyes immediately. "Clean sheets in the linen closet."

"I hope I didn't forget the..." I dig through my supplies until I find what I need. "Aha! Got it!"

"What is that?" Cora asks, one eye open and on the small white item in my hand.

"Denture tablet." I grin and strip the sheets with quick efficiency. "I toss one in with my whites to brighten."

A slow smile works its way onto her chapped lips. "Oh, that's right. You're the house lady. You got all those tips and recipes and hacks and shit on Instagram and TikTok or whatever. And you made that salad dressing."

"I guess that's me," I reply ruefully. "The house lady." I hold up the tablet. "Let me get this into the washing machine and then get some sheets on here for ya."

"There's a really faded set that you can almost see through," she calls after me. "I want those."

When I reenter the bedroom, she has drifted off again. I make the bed quickly but don't wake her to get in right away. I go, instead, through to the en suite bathroom and clean the counters and the sinks, then scrub the toilet and the shower. For good measure, I toss a eucalyptus tablet down the drain, releasing the sharp, minty scent into the room. Once the mirrors have been cleaned with my special lemon-and-vinegar mix, I inspect the bathroom with satisfaction.

When I tiptoe back into the bedroom, Cora still sleeps. I start clearing off her bedside table to dust. Reading glasses, old Kleenex, cough drops, water bottle. And then my hands pause over a book.

All About Love by bell hooks.

To find the book from Mami's chest here on Cora's bedside table coils a knot of pain under my ribs for a second, and I can't breathe. It's an old pain and yet timeless because I know I will miss my mother this way until the day I die—with the sharp cut of sudden memory, realizing anew that she is gone and I can never have her again. Seeing this book with Cora, who is fighting the same fight, is almost too much. The melancholy I've been fighting off all day crashes over me. I sniff and swipe at the tears streaking my cheeks.

"What's wrong?" Cora rasps from her armchair in the corner.

Startled, I look up to meet her steady regard and set the book down. "Nothing. I just...My mother left me this book. Or rather I took it from some of her things when she passed away."

"Is it any good?"

"I haven't read it." I laugh. "I was gonna ask you the same thing."

"Deidre, who owns that bookstore—"

"Stacks?"

"Yup. She brings me books." Cora rolls her eyes but manages a smile. "Like every week. She was bringing me romance novels, but I told her I like nonfiction better. So Deidre brought me some, and that one interested me."

"I may start this one to launch my book club. We'll have an online discussion, but...you wouldn't want to buddy-read, would you?"

"Like we have to read together?" Cora asks, skepticism spanning her narrow features.

"Not in the same room or at the same time, but like we both read on our own," I tell her, warming to the idea. "And then we come together to talk about it."

Her smile falls away. "Not sure how I'll feel about going out for a book club. Lately I haven't much felt like leaving this house."

I sit on the edge of the bed and hold the red book, flipping through its pages. "I could come to you."

Her eyes widen beneath her naked eyelids. "You'd do that?"

"Of course. Sounds like fun."

"I don't trust 'fun' from someone who enjoys cleaning as much as you do." She laughs. "But we can give it a try."

"Good." I stand, put the book back on the nightstand, and pull the covers back. "Come on. Your bed awaits."

It's late afternoon by the time we're done cleaning. Cora went back to sleep and didn't surface again. We got all the food put away and left instructions for storage, freezing, and prep. In the end, I couldn't resist a Target run for the front porch. I grabbed a new welcome mat on sale, a few cheap pots, and several pumpkins from the produce section.

"Wow," Lindee says. "You decorated our porch."

"You think your mom will mind?" I ask, biting my thumbnail. "It's fall, and I wanted to give it a little pop. Make it kind of festive and cheerful?"

"She loves stuff like this," George volunteers. "She usually does it every year. It'll make her happy to see it. Thank you."

"It's nothing." I loop my elbows through Lupe's and Deja's. "Come on, girls. Let's load up and move out."

"Bye, Mrs. Barnes," Lindee calls from the porch.

"It's Charles now," Lupe corrects. "That's her maiden name."

I stare at my daughter because, if I'm not mistaken, there's a touch of pride in her voice.

We leave Cora's house and drive back through Skyland. In the last nine months, I've come close to losing our house and being forced from this place more than once. It makes me appreciate the charming square where the gurgling fountain holds court. The restaurants with tables set out on cobblestone sidewalks. The verdant lawn of Sky Park and the ornate gate that guards it. This is our home, and I allow myself a moment of gladness that I keep fighting to stay here.

"Am I dropping you off at home, Deja?" I ask.

"Yes, ma'am." She grins at me through the rearview mirror.

"Can I hang out at Deja's for a little while?" Lupe asks.

"Sure." I smile at them both. "You guys were amazing today. Thank you for giving up your Saturday."

"You're pretty amazing, Mom," Lupe says softly from the passenger seat.

Surprised, I glance over to her, and when I meet her eyes, there's a serious expression on her face.

"People don't do that," she continues. "What you did for Mrs. Garland, most people don't do. Most people aren't you."

I jerk my eyes back ahead, as much to compose myself as to keep the car on the road. Emotion heats my throat, and my eyes burn.

"Yeah, Ms. Charles," Deja adds. "My mom says she wishes you were the president."

My shoulders shake with a laugh. "America would be clean, if nothing else."

"Deja and I were thinking." Lupe glances to her best friend in the back seat and then to me. "What if we donate our hair for cancer patients who need wigs?"

For a moment I can't even speak, I'm so moved by these young girls' generosity, their compassion. As a mom, you often wonder if you're getting it "right." Moments like these make you feel that all the shit you go through from the time they come out of you squawking might actually be worth it.

"I think that's such a good idea," I reply, reaching over to squeeze Lupe's hand. "How about if I do it with you guys?"

"Oh, my God. Ms. Charles!" Deja squeaks. "That's so cool!"

"I'll check to see what we need to do," Lupe says, a bright smile on her face. "Like how long it needs to be and where to send it."

"Sounds good." I hand my phone to Lupe, hoping to shift the tone so I don't cry and can keep it together. "Now find us something to listen to in there. I've got it all. Doja Cat, Megan Thee Stallion, Bad Bunny."

"Oh, my God." Lupe rolls her eyes, but grins. "It's giving very much *I'm the cool mom* energy right now."

"But I *am* the cool mom," I tease.

"If you have to say it," Deja giggles from the back, "we know you're not."

We get through a few songs before I pull into Deja's driveway.

"Tell your mom I'll talk to her later," I call as Deja and Lupe climb out. "Call me when you're ready, Lu. I'll come get you if Yas can't bring you home."

"It's just a few blocks," Lupe protests, her hand on the door. "I can walk."

"Not at night. Nope. Either they bring you home or I do, but you are not walking."

"Whatever." After a beat, she leans over and kisses my cheek. "Love you, Ms. Charles."

I grin like I just won the lottery. My daughter is proud of me. "Love you too, baby."

I'm still grinning when I pull into my driveway and my cell rings. It's an unknown number, and I would usually let it go to voice mail, but at the last PTA meeting, a few Harrington moms mentioned calling about some spaces they needed redecorated.

"I'm gonna regret this," I mutter before accepting the call. "Hello."

"Soledad, hi. This is Delores Callahan."

I almost drive through the garage door without lifting it, I'm so taken off guard.

"Oh. Delores." I put the car in park so I can focus. "Hey. How are you?"

"I'm fine, but let's skip the pleasantries."

Right. Because who wants to be pleasant when you can be... Delores?

"Of course," I say. "Was there something you needed?"

"Yes, we're looking for someone to cook for the Christmas party at the house."

"I cater some small dinner parties, but I'm not—"

"I would consider our executive Christmas dinner a small party. Smaller than three parties in one day at the Harvest Festival."

I wouldn't think Delores would have heard or *cared about* the Harvest Festival.

"You could prepare the food on-site if that's easier," she continues as if I weren't in the process of turning her down. "A small city could fit in Pop's kitchen. He has like three ovens. And you wouldn't have to worry about cleanup. The same company that cleans the offices comes to clean up at the house after the party."

"Look, Delores, don't you think it would be kind of awkward for me to handle the food considering my ex-husband stole a lot of money from your company?"

"We bear you and your girls no ill will," Delores says, her usually gruff voice smoothed with something close to kindness. "And we probably wouldn't have gotten most of that money back without your help."

"If I do this," I say, "and that's still a big if, I would prepare the menu we agree on and I'll make sure everything's set up, but I don't want to attend the party. I don't want to see everyone."

"Pop's assistant, Willa, usually handles a lot of details and hosting. You could hand most of the on-site stuff off to her."

"I'm not sure," I hedge.

"We pay generously."

Now that gives me pause. Christmas *is* coming. I'd like to be able to get the girls a few things they really want, but even more, I'd like to not work much at all once they're on holiday break. I could do a few easy sponsored posts, but otherwise, I want to get some quality time with my family.

"Can I think about it?" I ask, rubbing my tired eyes.

"Yes, but don't take too long. Typically we'd have this settled already."

"Typically your cousin Eileen does the party, and we know how vile her food is."

Delores makes a strangled sound between a chuckle and a harrumph.

Shit. When will I learn to govern my mouth? Delores seems to bring out the sassy in me.

"True. Her food is inedible," Delores agrees with no apparent animosity. "It's been pointed out to me that using her every year could smack of nepotism."

I stall, hearing the echo of a past conversation in which I told Judah the exact same thing. "Hey, Delores, what prompted you to approach me?"

"Didn't you have a salad dressing go viral or something? A lot of people in the office were talking about that. We want that too."

"So I had a vinaigrette go viral," I say, allowing a sliver of my disbelief to creep in. "And now you want me to cater your holiday party?"

"So you'll do it?"

"Send me the details and we'll see."

"Check your text messages."

I pull the phone away and check my messages. The amount she's proposing is as much as I made in the last three weeks combined. How can I not?

I pull the phone back to my ear.

"I guess we have a deal."

CHAPTER TWENTY-THREE

JUDAH

I'm tempted to ignore the phone when it rings. For once I'm not working on a Saturday night. I was excited to give my career the attention I hadn't been able to early on and am grateful for the opportunity at CalPot, but being a director at one of the largest companies in the state is incredibly demanding. The boys need so much during the week that I often bring lots of work home on the weekends.

But even I have to watch when Georgia plays Florida *at* Georgia. I'm kicking myself now for turning down the season tickets we get through the office, even though I, like the boys, sometimes get overwhelmed in crowds that huge. I haven't gone to as many games the last few years as I would have liked.

But I do watch.

I ordered wings. I have cold beer. I'm set for a kid-less, workless night. But my phone ringing on the weekend is usually the boys or my job. I can't ignore either.

When I dash from the living room to the kitchen to catch the call, I'm not expecting to see Soledad's name on-screen. Definitely worth missing kickoff.

"Soledad, hey."

"Oh, I wasn't sure you saved my contact from when we texted before."

"I did, and apparently you saved mine," I reply, leaning back against the center island.

A breath of a laugh drifts across the line, and I smile because that's as close as I ever come to flirting, and I think I did okay.

"Yeah, well, Delores called me."

"Huh. Okay."

"She asked me to cater the Christmas party."

"Which Christmas party?"

"Really, Judah?"

"What?" A low laugh slips out, and I cross one arm over my chest. "You think I had something to do with that?"

"I do, and..." She draws a quick breath. "Is it okay if I come in for a bit to talk?"

I straighten up. "Come in where?"

"In your house. I'm parked outside. I remembered you saying your ex usually has the boys on the weekend. I just want to talk for a few minutes."

If this woman comes into my house, I may not let her leave. Is that kidnapping? Abduction? I'd have the best intentions. I almost tell her it's a bad idea. What if I kiss her? I don't know how much longer I can be around her believing she's attracted to me, too, and not kiss her. How ironic. I haven't been interested in anyone since my divorce, and the first woman I'm interested in is initially unavailable because she's married and now single and unavailable because she's dating herself.

"Uh...Judah?" she asks, her voice turning tentative. "If you're busy or—"

"No, come on in."

I take a quick swig of beer and go to open the door. She's standing on my porch, her hair in one long braid, silky curls fighting their way loose from the confinement. Her nose is pink from the cold and her lightly floral scent reaches me before she even crosses the threshold.

"Can I come in?" she asks, looking over her shoulder like someone might report her to the neighborhood watch.

"Sure." I step back and gesture her inside with my bottle. "Be my guest."

She walks in and grimaces. "Sorry. I'm a mess. Been cleaning all day."

"You clean houses too?"

"What?" Understanding dawns on her face, and she shakes her head. "No. I have before. Believe me, and was glad to have the work, but no. One of Lupe's classmates, her mother has cancer, so we've all been chipping in. Meals and helping out. If I smell like lemon and vinegar, you'll know why."

"You smell like you always do to me," I tell her. "What's that scent you wear?"

"Oh." She smiles. "Jasmine oil. It's my favorite."

Her Cornell T-shirt peeks out from beneath a half-zipped pink puffy vest, and gray sweatpants hug the curves of her hips and ass. Even dressed down and with a small streak of dirt on her cheek, Soledad is a feast. I'm always starved around this woman. Always want to consume her through every sense. It's disconcerting because I've never felt this way. Even early on, my relationship with Tremaine was never like this. She often jokes we were better friends than lovers. When I see her with Kent, I know what she means.

I loved Tremaine the way I knew how, and I absolutely believe we were supposed to be together for that time of our lives. That marriage gave us our boys. We navigated them through some of the toughest years of their lives. Of ours. We needed less from each other, and wanted everything for them. But at a point, Tremaine started wanting something for herself that I wasn't the one to give.

I think it was this.

This yearning. This burning hunger. This all-consuming feeling that you could eat every bit of someone and never be satisfied. That you would lick their crumbs. That's how I feel around Soledad, and it is out of control. I hate being out of control, but I keep finding ways to be around her so I can *feel* this way.

She takes in the foyer with its original hardwoods and the thickness of the crown molding. We renovated this place but kept all the things we loved about the period when the house was born.

"Oh, this is gorgeous." She turns in a circle, staring up at the design etched into the ceiling. "I love all the things you've preserved."

"Would you like a tour? I'm not a decorator like you by any means, but Tremaine did a pretty good job before she moved out."

"Tremaine? Your ex-wife?"

"Yeah, the boys are with her."

"And you do what when they're gone and you're not working?" She peers into the living room at the huge plasma mounted over the fireplace. "Watch football?"

"If Georgia's playing Florida, yeah." I gesture to the living room. "You wanna sit? I have wings, beer."

"No, I'm going home. I'll make dinner."

"I'm sure something fancier than beer and wings. What's on the menu tonight?"

"All veggies." She smiles and toys with the end of the braid over her shoulder. "Black-eyed peas, creamed corn, and stewed tomatoes."

"Not exactly a Puerto Rican classic."

"My mother was Puerto Rican *and* African American, so I grew up with the best of both kitchens, so to speak."

"Where'd you learn to cook all the fancy things?"

"I went to Cornell's School of Hotel Administration and ended up working in a really nice hotel all through college."

"Wow. Impressed."

"Whatever, MIT."

"How'd you know I went to MIT?"

"Edward always said, 'Just because that asshole went to MIT, he thinks he knows everything.'"

"Ahhh." I slide my hands in my pockets and lean against the wall, smiling a little arctically at the mention of her repulsive ex. "You two met there? At Cornell?"

"Yeah. I had a scholarship to cover tuition, but everything else was on me. With two parents who were librarians, we weren't exactly balling." She shrugs. "When I graduated, I had trouble finding a job right away, so I stayed on working at the hotel. Learned a lot about hospitality, ambience, food, service."

"So that's how you got so good at what you do?"

"I always say I have a bachelor's in hotel admin and a master's in Pinterest."

I smile at that and proffer the bottle in my hand. "You sure you don't want a beer? Wine? Water?"

Her easy humor melts away, and she shakes her head, sobering. "Did you ask Delores to offer me the Christmas party?"

I could lie, but what would be the use? "Yes."

"Why?" Her pretty, lush mouth thins into a flat line. "And don't bullshit me, Judah. Tell me the real reason."

"I wanted to see you again. Do I seem like the kind of man who would leave something I wanted to chance?"

"I can't say. I don't know you that well."

"We could fix that. Besides, I figured you could use the money."

"You're right. I can. Well, thank you for—"

"But mostly I just wanted to see you again."

She frowns at me like I'm a riddle she's not sure how to begin solving.

"You said no bullshit." I don't look away from her and will her not to look away from me. "Both those things are true."

"I can't..." She licks her lips and lets out a long sigh. "You know I'm not dating."

"I don't plan to ask you out."

"Then what...I don't understand your endgame here."

"It's not an endgame." I push away from the wall and step close, carefully lift the curls around her hairline away from her face. "It's a begin game."

I pull away almost before I get to feel the soft fineness of her hair, but she goes still, like she's glued to the spot.

"What does that mean? 'Begin game'?"

"It's a long game. I don't want to interfere with all you're doing, how you're working on yourself. I think it's awesome, but if I can find a way to see you, I will."

Her fine brows pinch, and she fiddles with the zipper on her vest. "And if I don't want to see you?"

My heart pauses in its beating, the thought of her not wanting to see me apparently causing cardiac distress. I cup her chin, and it feels completely natural for my thumb to brush the fullness of her lower lip. To trace the deep, wide bow of her mouth. Her breath fans across my palm and my fingers literally tingle.

"Then tell me to stop."

This woman is an electric storm, but I have no caution and don't want shelter. Her lashes fall to cover the heat in her eyes, but I *feel* it between us. It takes all my willpower not to haul her close. Not to kiss and claim her. Just when I think I'll have to do it because the desire is so overwhelming, she steps back. Her breasts rise and fall with stilted breaths, and she takes the few swift strides from the center of the foyer to the door.

She jerks the door open and doesn't look back, but says, "Don't stop."

And walks out the door without another word. She races down the steps to her SUV, hops in, and drives away.

"Oh, don't worry, Sol." I take another swig of my beer, barely registering that in the next room, the Bulldogs just scored. "I won't."

CHAPTER TWENTY-FOUR

SOLEDAD

Hang out with me for a spell while I work on my she shed."

I smile into the camera and into my phone. I'm live on one platform, but I'm also recording myself now to edit later for YouTube. A year ago, I didn't know how any of this could actually equal a paycheck. Now I understand sponsored ads and brand deals and all the things that seemed like another world not long ago. It *was* another world, one where Edward paid our bills and I didn't have to think about any of that.

I like this world a lot better.

"If you're new to me," I say, leaning against my worktable, "I'm renovating the storage shed in my backyard. It was my ex-husband's man cave." I roll my eyes and angle an exasperated look to the camera that every woman who has ever had a trifling man will understand. "Long story, but I'm taking it over and reclaiming it. He had all his Boston Celtics stuff here."

I gesture behind me to the space missing chunks of plaster and drywall.

"As you can see, I got an early start on the demolition. I'm gonna do a little work for my accent wall. Maybe paint it like a seafoam green. Any thoughts for color?"

I point down.

"Leave them in the comments." I glance up at the ceiling. "I know I'm putting in a skylight. I want it brighter in here."

I stomp the floor a few times with one sneaker. "Definitely taking up this nasty dookie-colored carpet. Maybe some engineered hardwood. I could make this my office. I think I might get a desk in here."

I walk over to a corner occupied by a leather recliner.

"I could make this my reading corner." I squee and wiggle my fingers. "Almost forgot. We have our first book club pick. It's *All About Love* by bell hooks. I'll be meeting in person with a few friends to discuss, but I'll come on here to do a live discussion with you guys who read along too."

I walk over to my phone so I can read the comments in real time, a smile blooming on my face.

"I feel you, 492GirlGetAGrip. I haven't read as much lately as I've wanted to either, so this is a perfect opportunity for us both."

I squint at the comments, making sure I'm reading the next one right.

"ComeHithah2004 says, 'we love a reading-ass bitch.' Girl, you always crack me up." I grin and shake my head, moving on to the next comment. "ViralVixin says, 'I went to dinner by myself this week and had a great time.'"

I lift my arms like it's a touchdown. "That's incredible! Love that for you!"

Four more commenters say they went on solo dates this week.

"This is great. After my solo anniversary date, I decided I'll take myself out once a week. You wanna join me?"

So many comment "Yes" and "For sure" and "I'm in" that I lose count. Someone comments "#datingmyselfchallenge."

"Oh, I love that!" I say. "Hashtag datingmyselfchallenge. Let's do it. And *All About Love* is the perfect book for us to start. It's about loving yourself and healing yourself. At least that's what I think it's about. I'm gonna read some tonight. We'll find out together, huh?"

I grab my safety goggles and turn up the music on my pill, the wireless speaker blasting Backstreet Boys' "I Want It That Way."

"Any BSB Army out there?" I ask, chuckling as I check my table saw.

"I'mma ride this playlist till I'm done in here. I want to get some of this finished before I have to start dinner. It's Taco Tuesday. The link to a supersimple recipe that my girls love is in my bio. I substitute meatless beef for the vegetarian in my bunch. I swear you won't be able to tell the difference."

I pull my goggles down.

"This she shed is on my Me List," I tell them, "which is a list of things I'm doing solely for my enjoyment. Not about my job or my kids or my friends or my family. Just for me."

I glance at the phone to check the comments again.

"ComeHithah2004, did you say, 'add a pole'?" I laugh. "Like for pole dancing?"

I glance over to the space where Edward's pool table sat before I butchered it with my machete.

"Pole dancing, huh? Now there's a thought." I turn to the camera and give them a little half-hearted, full-assed twerk. "I'll think about it."

Later that night, once the girls and I have eaten our tacos, finished homework, cleaned the kitchen, prepped lunches, and made sure uniforms are pressed and ready for tomorrow, I finally get to settle down in bed with my book in a moment of pure silence.

Until my phone dings with a text.

"I meant to mute you," I mutter, but can't resist checking to see who it is. I'm halfway to convincing myself I don't want it to be Judah. My lady parts and heart parts can calm down. They don't get a vote in the Judah situation. This is a dictatorship.

It's not Judah.

Yasmen: Hey! Have you guys gotten to chapter four?

Hendrix: I haven't even started. You know I'm out here in LA working. I thought you weren't gonna pressure us???? What happened to reading at your own pace?

Yasmen: LOL! Girl, ain't nobody pressuring you. There's just something cool in that chapter and I wondered if you'd read it yet.

Me: Literally in bed now starting that chapter! Will I know it when I see it???

Yasmen: Oh, yeah. You will for sure, Sol.

Hendrix: I'll start on the flight home. Love you, bitches.

Yasmen: Travel safe. Love.

Me: Love

I prop the book on my knees, which are pulled up under my cloud-esque duvet. It's such a great chapter on self-love and fragile self-esteem and breaking from old patterns. My hands can't keep up with my heart while I try to highlight all the truths dotted throughout these pages. It's like a treasure map I've found at exactly the right time. bell hooks is reaching through the years to tell me I should take responsibility in all areas of my life, to believe I have the capacity to reinvent my life and shape the future around my well-being. There's even a whole section on satisfied homemakers and the joy of self-determination and being your own boss. Each word is like a punch to the chest and a pat on the back. I'm encouraged and provoked at every turn. So much of it connects to my own life deeply that I consider stopping for the night to fully process all I've read.

"I'm still not sure what Yasmen thought was so special for me," I tell my empty bedroom.

I decide to read a little more to finish the chapter. I'm nodding when she discusses creating domestic bliss, a household where love can flourish.

"Spot on," I say, reaching for a handful of the roasted almonds I keep by my bed for the night growls. My hand stills midreach when I read the next line. hooks calls her house in the country a sanctuary and refers to it as "*soledad hermosa.*"

The brakes in my head screech, bringing me to a complete stop.

My name. Right here in the book that is slowly but surely restitching the fabric of who I am.

Soledad hermosa. *Beautiful solitude.*

Tears prick my eyes, spill over my lashes. It feels like a sign that I'm headed in the right direction, like a letter hooks sent encouraging me that I *can* be alone and not lonely. That this journey I'm on solo right now can be beautiful. I can be content. That my very name reflects this pursuit I'm on of renewal, understanding who I've been and who I'm becoming. Seeing my name in ink on paper in this context sprinkles goose bumps along my arms.

I close the book and, instead of returning it to my nightstand, lay it on the pillow where Edward used to sleep. My dreams aren't haunted by the past or all the cruel things *he* did to me. I dream about a bright future of my own making.

CHAPTER TWENTY-FIVE

JUDAH

MawMaw."

Aaron's voice gives me pause during dinner as I'm making sure none of my foods touch. I detest close food proximity.

"What about her?" I ask, giving him my full attention.

He lifts the communication device hanging around his neck and scrolls for a few seconds before finding what he's looking for. When he turns it toward me, he displays a photo of my mother.

"Yeah!" Adam says from his side of the table. "Let's FaceTime MawMaw!"

"Maybe after dinner." I scoop string beans onto their plates.

"Or we could eat while we FaceTime," Adam wheedles, rocking on the yoga ball he brings to the dinner table sometimes. He has one at school too, for his desks there. When he's forced to balance on the ball, it gives his extra energy somewhere to go, engages his core, and helps him focus.

Aaron again turns around the device showing my mother's face, his insistent bid to eat and talk. He prefers FaceTime. Sometimes when he's talking to someone on the phone, he just walks away. Something about the phone up against his ear starts to bother him. That's how I feel half the time when I'm on the phone too. Like just dropping it as soon as I'm bored and walking away without even saying goodbye. The world would be a simpler, albeit ruder, place if we all lacked the ability to dissemble that way.

"She may not even be available," I warn them.

But she is, so we find ourselves all sitting on one side of the kitchen table with my phone propped up so we can chat with MawMaw.

"What is that you're eating?" she asks, narrowing her eyes from the screen. "Chicken?"

"Yeah," I confirm, taking a bite. "Ms. Coleman made chicken, brown rice, and string beans. The boys have mac and cheese, but will eat some string beans."

I aim my fork at the untouched green beans on their plates.

"Thank God for that woman helping around the house," Mama says. "And cooking, but I want to make you some of my stew. I could ship it."

"Ship it?" I pause and send a skeptical look to the screen. "How about you ship yourself on a flight? Maryland isn't that far from Atlanta."

"If Maryland isn't that far from Atlanta," Mama says, "and flights go both ways, ship *yourself*. Why haven't you brought my grandsons to see me?"

"Lots going on. We'll see you for Christmas."

"What's Tremaine doing for the holidays?"

"The boys will spend Christmas Eve with her, and then she and Kent are going to his parents' for Christmas Day."

"How her folks doing?" Mama asks, the tiniest bit of reserve entering her voice.

"They're good. The boys will see them maybe on winter break."

Tremaine's parents weren't as understanding as mine about autism. They kept thinking we could just discipline the boys out of meltdowns. That the boys weren't sleeping because kids don't like to sleep and if we imposed restrictions, they would "cave" and sleep more at night. When we were trying elimination diets to identify any allergies the boys might have, they would ignore our instructions and feed Aaron and Adam whatever was in the house. It was always *something* with them, and I refused to subject my boys to their ignorance and stubborn insistence that they knew best when they didn't know jack shit about what we were dealing with. They've gotten better, but I'm still wary about leaving the boys alone with them for long.

"Goodbye," Aaron says, standing. He takes his dish to the sink, rinses it off, and loads it into the dishwasher.

Mama doesn't miss a beat but just waves. "Bye, baby. You be a good boy for your daddy."

Aaron doesn't respond but climbs the stairs.

"Bye, MawMaw." Adam stands and clears his plate, too, loading it into the dishwasher and following Aaron.

"I really know how to clear a room, huh?" Mama laughs.

"They love you, but the pull of their video games got to be too strong," I joke, scraping the last of my rice and green beans up, grinning while I chew. "Where's Dad?"

"On my nerves. Ever since that man retired, he's been like a caged animal, prowling around here all the time looking for stuff to fix or hang or trim. It's downright unsettling."

At seventy, my father is nearly ten years older than my mother. She was twenty and he was twenty-nine when they had me. She'll retire soon from her job as a nurse, but for now she's still going strong at the hospital.

"Hey, at least you come home to a clean house and a home-cooked meal every night now that Dad's home, right?" I deadpan, knowing damn well he's asking her what's for dinner as soon as she walks through the door.

"Boy, you know your daddy better than that." She rolls her eyes and laughs. "But I will say he found all these easy Crock-Pot recipes online. He even made one last week. It was pretty good. I was shocked."

"My father, Belmont Cross, cooked a meal?"

"He's on the internet all the time now. Mostly Facebook, and he found this lady who has a recipe and a life hack for everything. She's in Atlanta, I think."

It could be anyone. Atlanta's a huge city, and the internet makes the possibilities infinite, but something makes me ask, "What's her name?"

"That Puerto Rican lady, Soledad something," Mama mutters, brow furrowing, possibly with the effort to recall more. "Pretty. Smart. Your dad loves to watch her."

"Must run in the family," I mumble.

"All I know is I came home and one of her recipes was in that Crock-Pot and he wasn't asking *me* for nothing. I approve. She's great."

"She is. I, um, know her. I mean, like in real life."

"How so?" Curiosity spikes in Mama's eyes.

"Remember that huge embezzlement case I worked on at CalPot?"

"Yeah."

"Her husband was the thief."

"You sent her husband to jail?" Mama whistles. "Bet she can't stand the sight of you."

"Actually"—I suppress a grin—"I think she likes me a lot. Almost as much as I like her."

It's so quiet, the hum of the refrigerator is the only sound for a few seconds.

"Do you mean *like?*" Mama's eyes saucer. "You *like* her? She *likes* you?"

My almost-grin drops into a scowl. "You don't have to sound so shocked that she would like me. Wow."

"You've been divorced almost four years, Judah, and, as far as I know, have never shown much interest in anyone besides your boys and your laptop, so forgive me if I wasn't expecting that."

"Not like we're in a relationship or anything," I admit . . . reluctantly.

"Well, no, because your daddy told me she's not dating. Got that whole hashtag datemyself thing going on."

"You know about that?"

"Is she dating you?" Mama frowns. "Now that just don't seem right to have all these girls running around here dating themselves when she dating you."

"We're not dating."

"But I thought you said you *liked* her *liked* her."

"I do."

"And she likes you?"

Don't stop.

Soledad's parting words have haunted me ever since she spoke them, had me tossing in my sleep, playing on repeat in my head. I've taken those two words as something to hold on to until I can hold on to her.

"Yeah, I think she likes me, but she's self-partnering."

"Lord, if these girls don't be making stuff up."

"It's not made up, Ma. Her divorce wasn't that long ago. She wants to heal and make sure she's ready for..."

Me.

Not me, but a relationship.

It's more accurate to say she wants to make sure she's ready for *her*, to be exactly herself when she is ready to be with someone again, but I hope she'll be ready for me too.

"Ready for what?" Mama presses.

"She was a stay-at-home mom most of their marriage, and loved it," I answer indirectly. "Now her ex is in prison, and she's providing for herself and her girls. Standing on her own. Has her independence. She wants to enjoy that and make sure she's healthy."

"I admire that," Mama says. "What does Tremaine think?"

"I haven't talked to her about it."

"You want *me* not to talk to her about it?"

Divorce didn't change anything between Mama and my ex-wife, who bonded like mother and daughter almost from the beginning. They talk all the time, not having missed a beat when things changed between Tremaine and me.

"I'd prefer to bring it up with her myself, yeah," I tell her. "And there's not really much to say at this point. We're not dating or anything."

"Oh, I hear some *anything* in your voice, and that's saying something."

"I like her a lot," I reply quietly, not embarrassed by my feelings for Soledad, but also not wanting to pull them out for someone else to poke at and examine. "And I hope when she's ready, we can see where that could go. For now, we're just friends."

"'Just friends,' huh?" Mama teases, but she shrugs. "Okay. I'll let it be until further notice. Does she know about the boys?"

"You mean that my situation is complicated by two amazing boys who need a lot of support? She does. Her situation is involved too. She has three daughters who are adjusting to everything being different, especially their father being incarcerated."

"Do they know you were the one who discovered what he was up to?"

"Yeah, they know. I can't imagine I'm their favorite person."

"They don't know about...whatever is *not* going on between you and their mother?"

"Correct."

"Whoo-wee, you getting messy down there in Atlanta, but what's supposed to be, will be."

"Yeah, how's Dad?" I ask, wanting to talk about anything other than my would-be love life. "Taking his meds? Sticking to his diet?"

"I watch him like a hawk, but he cheats from time to time. His numbers look good, though. Cholesterol down. Blood pressure down. What about the boys? Any changes to their meds? You look at that study I sent on coadministering clobazam with CBD? May help reduce seizures."

The nurse has entered the building. From the beginning Mama has been involved with the boys' treatments and medications, even several states away.

"I saw it. Tremaine and I heard about it too. We're talking to some parents who tried it about the efficacy, side effects, et cetera...Adam's in a pretty good place right now. Not nearly as many seizures as before."

"I just don't want my baby to end up in the emergency room again." Mama draws and expels a deep breath. "I'll be down there so fast."

"I know, Mama," I tell her, letting her love and concern for the boys touch me by extension.

"I better go," she says. "Your daddy will be back from Home Depot soon. Got it in his head to plant a garden. May be something your girlfriend put in his head."

"She's not..." I shake my head and give up because this woman has been pushing my buttons since before I had buttons. "Bye, Mama."

"Bye, Judah." She smirks, but the look in her eyes tells me she likes the idea of me finding someone, even if that someone isn't ready to be with me...yet. "I love you."

"Love you too, Ma."

CHAPTER TWENTY-SIX

SOLEDAD

"The Boricua High Council is now in session," Lola says, banging her imaginary gavel to start our FaceTime call.

"Can it not be in session more than ten minutes?" Nayeli asks, carrying my nephew Luca on one hip and brushing cereal from my niece Ana's hair. "Some of us have six kids and are running on green juice and adrenaline."

"Did Luca's fever break?" I ask, glancing from the screen of my iPad and back to the ingredients I'm sorting on the counter.

"His fever didn't break, but I have. These kids have shattered all sense of time and space."

I herd a group of green peppers into a row. "Did you try the bone broth I told you about, Nay? And the elderberry? That might help with the fever."

"Yeah." Nayeli frowns and kisses Luca's hair. "I'm going to do a bath. I'll take him to the doctor if it doesn't break soon. So again, can we hurry this along, *mija*?"

"I won't hold you up," Lola says. "You're not the only ones with pressing things to do. I'm watching season two of *Fleabag*."

I point to her and grin. "Told you it's the best. It's a crisis of faith and a sexual awakening."

"I couldn't go to confession for a month." Nayeli crosses herself. "God forgive."

"Okay." I take a stool at the counter. "I really do need to start this 'Cook with Me Live' in a few minutes, so what's this about, Lola?"

"I'm moving to Austin." Lola *eeeeks* and covers her face.

"As in Texas?" I ask, willing all my frown muscles not to flex.

"Yes, Texas," Lola says.

"And you're endangering your reproductive rights for what?" I ask.

"Books," Lola says simply. "I'm opening a bookstore with Olive."

"Olive, your best friend," Nayeli clarifies, "who you recently realized you're in love with? You're following her to Texas?"

"I'm not 'following her,'" Lola protests. "We're doing this together."

"And if you just happen to slip and fall between her legs"—I shrug—"oh well."

"That is only a possible enjoyable by-product, not my primary motivation." Lola's expression loses all levity. "I'm done teaching. I need to do something different. You know I love books the way Mami did. This is what I want to do. I'm even gonna have Cat's Corner."

Catelaya.

"It'll be a section for Mami's favorite books," Lola says, her eyes bright with unshed tears and enthusiasm. "And we'll have a banned books library. If a kid's school doesn't carry those books, they can come to us and check them out. Can't you see it? This will be amazing."

"I see it," I say softly. "If this is what you want, I support it."

"I guess I do too," Nayeli says grudgingly. "Just make sure you're chasing dreams, not a piece of ass."

"That's a really crude thing to say." Lola beams. "Proud of you, Sis."

I roll my eyes but can't suppress a grin. "So when will this move happen?"

"I'll finish this school year," Lola says. "But come summer, we're packing it in and relocating. Olive may go ahead of me and move in the next few months."

"You have money saved up?" I ask. "Like for the transition?"

"I do," Lola says. "But I thought a cushion might be good too."

"Cushion?" Nayeli walks through her house, holding the phone to stay on FaceTime. "Sorry. I need to check upstairs. It's too quiet, and I should make sure no one has done a sibling bodily harm."

"We have to think about what we'll do with the house when I move," Lola says.

I freeze, shocked that wasn't the first thing I thought about. I love that house. We all do.

"Do we want to sell it?" Lola asks.

"No!" Nayeli and I say in adamant unison.

"Don't get your panties twisted." Lola laughs. "I figured as much, but we can't just have it here empty and collecting cobwebs. I wondered about using it as an Airbnb. It would generate some income, which I need during this transition. And I know you could use the money, too, Sol."

"Always," I agree. "Though things have been good lately. I'm getting the hang of this influencer thing."

"You have videos go viral like every other week," Nayeli says. "I'd say you are."

"That doesn't always translate into cash," I tell her. "Matter of fact, most of the time it doesn't. But the more visibility, the better chance I have at getting brand deals, ads, et cetera... Anyway, the moral of the story is that I always need more cash."

Which reminds me I should finalize the menu for the CalPot Christmas party. I've been trying *not* to think about it because there's a chance I'll see Judah there. Bad enough I think about him all the time. Dream about him. Fantasize about all the things he could do to me. The things I could do to him. How good we might be together.

"Did you hear me, Sol?" Lola frowns at me on-screen.

"Huh?" I mutter, sitting up straight. "What was that?"

"We asked if you want to give it a shot," Nayeli replies.

"Um... sorry. Give what a shot exactly?" I ask.

"Updating the house before we start using it for Airbnb," Lola says.

"Yeah, that could be cool." I force myself to tune back in.

"Okay. I just wanted to run all that by you," Lola says. "We can talk more details later. In the meantime, Christmas is coming. What we doing?"

"I'm sorry," Nayeli says, her tired eyes flicking from me to Lola. "Six kids traveling cross-country is hard at any time, but the holidays, and they've all been so sick? I think it's best if we stay here in Cali this year."

"Ain't no thang, Nay," Lola reassures her. "We get it. Olive and I are going to Austin after Christmas to look at spaces and get the lay of the land, but I was thinking of visiting you guys the week before, Sol."

I wish I could reach through the screen and squeeze her. I've been blessed to have Yasmen and Hendrix here with me through all the shit Edward left me to deal with, but the ache of missing my sisters is tangible and deep.

"Oh, Lola, please come." The prospect of a week with my big sister lifts my heart. "The girls would love to see you. So would I."

"Consider it done," Lola says, her smile gentle and understanding. "Anything for you, *mija*."

"Love you guys." Nayeli shoots us a harried glance. "But I gotta go. I knew those heathens were too quiet. Now I have to cut gum out of this child's hair."

We chuckle and disconnect. And not a moment too soon. I need to set up for the "Cook with Me Live" broadcast.

"Dammit," I say. "Already late."

I get my phone set up and start the session.

"I know I'm late." I shake my head and chuckle. "It's been a day, but come cook with me. If you're following along, get your ground beef going. I have two pans here. One for my carnivores and one for my vegetarian. If you were wondering what's for dinner..."

I look into the camera and wink, already feeling like I'm among friends as I see the comments flooding my feed.

"Don't worry. Sol's got ya."

CHAPTER TWENTY-SEVEN

SOLEDAD

"Knowing how to be solitary is central to the art of loving. When we can be alone, we can be with others without using them as a means of escape."
—bell hooks, *All About Love: New Visions*

A day in the life of an influencer dating herself.

That could work as a title for my next post. My followers like seeing the times I carve out to be alone each week. I'm still blown away by how many of them have started their own "dating myself" journeys. I hope these times alone provide them with the same comfort and contemplation they afford me.

Walking through Skyland is a different experience on a Sunday morning at seven than at any other time. Shop windows are shuttered, *CLOSED* signs turned to the street, café tables stowed inside. The only signs of life are in nature, like a choir of birds waking up to sing their Sunday-morning hymns.

It's nearly two miles from my house to Skyland Square, and I relish every step through the deserted cobbled streets. I pull in a bracing breath, let the cold air go to my head, and clear my jumbled thoughts. I like coming to Sky Park before the hard-core alfresco yoga girlies venture out. There's a Sunday-morning class that meets here till Christmas, weather permitting. Bundled up and ready to pose and flex, they arrive around nine.

I'll be long gone by then.

I walk through the high arched gate of Sky Park and find the limestone bench I've come to think of as mine. It's planted in the shadow of a dogwood tree that flowers white for a few glorious weeks in spring and richly green in summer. A layer of autumn's purple and red leaves blanket the ground, shed from the spindly branches stretching to the sky, naked and shivering in the early-morning chill.

I set my bag on the ground at my feet, sit on the bench, and close my eyes. The first few times I came here, it was hard to silence the voices in my head. The questions I don't want to consider bombard me as soon as I'm not driving Lottie to gymnastics or taking the girls to school or cooking dinner or volunteering at Harrington. Or...and the list of things I'd rather think about than my mistakes goes on and on.

When conversing with the heart, expect it to talk back, to revisit the pains and disappointments that left the deepest dents and scratches.

Infidelity from a man you thought you knew will have you rethinking everything. Replaying each argument and reliving all the moments you saw one way but that surely had to be another. The voices in your head tell you it was because you took too long losing the weight after that last kid, or maybe it was him being in the delivery room. Some men never see their wives the same after that. You should have given him more blow jobs. Cooked better, cleaned better, anticipated his needs.

He wanted someone more ambitious.

No, more docile.

No, more outspoken.

Because he obviously wanted someone who wasn't you.

It's in these quiet moments, in these conversations with my heart, that I realize I can never take responsibility for someone else's bad character. Edward made a vow and broke it, underestimated forever. He is the past. At this point the only questions I'm interested in are the ones about myself. Shouldn't I have known? The fundamental question becomes not *Can I trust another man again?*, but *Can I trust myself?*

He was a bad man, yes, but was I a bad judge of character? And would I be again? What will I accept in my next relationship? Will there *be* another? What are my boundaries? My desires? My limits?

The answers surface in my heart, often surprising and sometimes frightening. Once I jot my thoughts down in my Sunday-morning journal, I rise, glancing at my watch to make sure I won't be late for my reservation at Sunny Side. Yasmen, Hendrix, and I love this place, but I've started hitting it solo on my way home after the park. It opens at eight, and the first ten customers get the half-price early bird special. Best believe I'm always first in line. I requested a gift card to this place in exchange for meal prep for a busy neighbor. A week of meals in exchange for a Sunny Side gift card. If she'd given me cash, I would have found something for the family to spend it on. This time alone is a discipline I invest in, so each Sunday I use her gift card with its dwindling balance to meet myself here.

As soon as I'm seated at my small table by the window, overlooking the street, the server takes away the other place setting. It's become my thing to grab a quick shot for the socials of me and my table for one, so I do that and then order my usual stack of buckwheat pancakes, turkey bacon, and two egg whites. There's something bold about eating alone, enjoying your own company and not waiting for *nobody*.

I don't linger today but pay for my cheap meal, gather my bag, and strike out for the short walk home. What a difference an hour makes. By nine, Skyland is buzzing with activity. The mimosa crowd is out and about. Pups walk their owners to the dog park. Strollers line the sidewalks as busy families venture out for a slice of leisure before the week revs up on Monday.

I take it all in, feeling rather zen by the time I reach my house.

"Forgot to check the mail," I mutter, opening the box and pulling out a few letters. One name above a Boston address stops me in my tracks.

Oneida Barnes.

Dear God, what does my ex-mother-in-law want?

Keeping quiet because the girls sleep in hard on Sundays, I let myself in through the front door and make my way to the kitchen. I set my bag and the other correspondence on the counter. I take a stool and pick up the letter with a sigh. Edward's mother and I have had very little contact since I "betrayed" him, as she likes to call it, by sharing information with the Feds.

"Maybe she's finally breaking her silence through snail mail," I say, sliding a nail under the envelope flap, "to let me know what a deceiving, backstabbing bitch I . . ."

A check flutters from the envelope and onto the counter.

"Five thousand dollars!" I stare at the check like it fell from space, and it may as well have, considering how little contact I've had with Edward's mother. The memo line on this extraterrestrial check reads *Tuition for the girls*.

There's no note. The check is simply wrapped in her monogrammed stationery.

Relief and reluctance wrestle in the pit of my stomach. Relief because keeping this house and keeping two girls at Harrington are the banes of my existence. I've been tempted to send them to public school. That is not off the table. Lupe loves going to an Atlanta city school, but if I can keep Lottie and Inez where they have friends, love their teachers, and are thriving, I will for as long as I can. This money is right on time, but I hate that it comes from Oneida. I can't help but wonder what she wants in return.

"Guess I should call to thank her," I grouse to my empty kitchen, half hoping the cabinets will open and say, *That won't be necessary.*

I pull up the contact I haven't used in nearly a year and dial.

"Soledad," she answers without preamble, her voice cool and liquid. "I wondered if you would call."

"Oneida, hi." I clear my throat before going on. "I hope you're doing well."

"As well as a mother can be when her wrongly accused son rots in prison for crimes he didn't commit."

"Um...you do realize Edward pled guilty when it became apparent the evidence was overwhelming?"

" 'Evidence' "—she says the word as if it's a tenet of a conspiracy theory—"that you magically produced to save yourself and your house and your car and all your designer dresses. And then to abandon him in his hour of need."

Anger bubbles in my blood, and there's so much steam building inside, my head might whistle if I don't let some of it out.

"First of all," I say, my jaw clenched hard enough to hurt, "I don't have the fancy car your son insisted on buying anymore. I sold it for something more affordable. Other people walk around in my clothes now because I consigned most of them. And I bust my ass to keep this house because it's my daughters' home, and it will have to be pried from my cold, dead fingers."

"Well, it's about time you downsized anyway."

"On that we can agree. I had so many things in my life that really weren't necessary, including a lying cheat of a man. Consigned him too. To a federal prison."

"And here I was thinking you called to thank me for the tuition payments I sent," Oneida says, huffing her outrage on the other end of the line.

"And here *I* was thinking you wanted to help your granddaughters since your son stole six million dollars and left me to provide for them all by myself. Guess we were both wrong."

"Well, a thank-you would be nice," Oneida says. "And to see my granddaughters every once in a while. Even if it's only Lupe."

I tighten my hand on my cell.

"She's at an age now," Oneida continues, "where she'd perform so well in pageants. She's such a beautiful girl."

"They're all beautiful," I interject stiffly. "Lupe hates pageants. And just because one looks like your side of the family and the other two look like mine doesn't make one better than the others."

"Of course it doesn't," Oneida gasps. "I resent what you're implying."

"And I resent you thinking you can control me or my girls through your money."

"That is not at all what I'm doing," Oneida returns hotly. "What Edward ever saw in you I don't know."

"I believe it was my ass and the fact that I basically put him through grad school. He knew my ambition was to raise a family and build a wonderful life for them and decided he should be the primary beneficiary of all this talent."

"Look, do you want the money or not?" she snaps, her tone as frigid as a Boston winter.

"Not if it comes with strings. You don't get to tell me how to raise my daughters or run my household or anything. By necessity we've built a life for ourselves that doesn't include Edward, and by choice I want to keep it that way. If you want any role in my daughters' lives, you need to figure out what's important. Defending your lying-ass criminal son and constantly demeaning me or finding some way to be in your grandchildren's lives that aligns with our values. You don't get both."

The silence on the other end elongates, stretchy and sticky.

"Keep the money," she finally mutters. "They're my son's daughters. *They* deserve the best."

The obvious implication that I do not rolls right off my back. There was a time when my pride wouldn't have let me keep this money, would have had me tossing it in her face—a grand gesture I can no longer afford. I'm depositing this check as soon as I hang up.

"You're right, Oneida," I simply reply. "They do."

And with that we disconnect.

CHAPTER TWENTY-EIGHT

SOLEDAD

"You've checked everything like four times," Rhea says, spooning fondant potatoes onto gold-rimmed plates. "I think we're good to go."

"We wouldn't be without your help." I start one more circuit around the Callahans' huge kitchen, inspecting the plates we've loaded up so far. "Thank you for everything."

"Hey, thank *you*. I love cooking at Grits, but anytime I can make some extra cash, I'm down." She smiles. "Besides, I'm low-key clout chasing. When I post that I did an event with you, I'm bound to get new followers and lots of engagement."

I shoot her a disbelieving look. "Whatever. Just make sure to keep the shots generic. I don't want the Callahans thinking we put their business in the streets."

"Will do, Boss."

CalPot booked ten servers for the fifty people attending the party. These are skilled workers who do events all the time and could handle this with one hand tied behind their backs, but I still review the plan for the evening with them carefully, leaving time for questions or suggestions about more efficient ways to manage the dinner.

"I think we're about ready," I tell them, walking down the line to high-five them. "Let's do it."

"Perfect timing," Delores says from the kitchen entrance. "I was just coming to say we're ready when you are."

"Great. Then they'll get the food out."

"Not so fast." Delores raises a staying hand. "I'd like for you to open by providing an overview of the menu."

"Me?" I press a hand to my chest. Preparing the food and making sure it's plated beautifully is one thing. Walking out there and facing a room full of Edward's former coworkers is another. "But doesn't your mother usually give opening remarks before dinner? I wouldn't want to step on her toes."

"She's the one who requested it, actually." Delores tips her grin to one side. "She heard you're like an internet sensation."

"But I'm not." I shake my head vigorously. "It's just a lot of views on a pretty ordinary salad dressing."

"Ma wears the pants here at home." Delores shrugs. "What Ma wants, Ma gets."

"But we agreed that—"

"I know. I know." Delores waves a dismissive hand. "You didn't want to see anybody, but you're just telling us about the menu and then you can skedaddle."

Hmmm. I got her skedaddle right here.

This is not what I signed up for. It was only a year ago I was on the other side of that door as a guest, complaining about the food. Tonight, I'm serving it. I'm the help, aren't I? My name is mud here.

Correction.

Edward's name is mud. I did nothing wrong. As a matter of fact, I did something *right*. I turned over evidence I found and helped this family, this company, recover millions of dollars. And instead of losing our home, we are still in it.

I did that.

I glance down at my clothes. I'm not bummy, but I'm not dressed for a dinner party. The black vegan leather dress buttons up the center and clings to all my curves but is easy to move in. And though I wore my low-heeled boots mostly for comfort, they aren't shabby. I guess I'll do, but the plan was to help set up, give direction, and leave it in Rhea's more-than-capable hands. It wasn't to see these people Edward cheated and stole from. It certainly wasn't to see Judah, but I'm avoiding him for a very different reason. I've been dating myself, reading about loving myself, and enjoying the community of women who have joined me on this journey. I don't want this persistent attraction to Judah distracting me from what I'm learning and who I am becoming.

Still... I can't get that man out of my mind. I know he's out there. As long as I'm not alone with him, I should be okay. Open dinner and jet. I can do this.

"Gimme a sec," I say, grabbing my Hermès knockoff from where I stashed it in the butler's pantry. All my real bags have long been sold online or consigned.

I don't have my good makeup, but I have some lipstick and powder I always carry, which I apply quickly. I unknot my hair and shake it out, letting it fall over my shoulders and nearly to my elbows. Lupe, Deja, and I have stuck to our pledge over the last month not to cut our hair, so it's a little unruly. It is healthy, though, and longer than it's been since high school.

Delores runs her glance up and down me, shaking her head at my minitransformation. "It's like magic."

"Magic, huh?" I scoff. "Wish I could make myself disappear. Let's get this over with."

The huge dining room is packed, and I immediately note many familiar faces. I lift my chin a notch, refusing to be cowed by any judgment or speculation. In a quick scan of the round tables, I don't see Judah. I'm not sure if I'm relieved or disappointed, but I need to power through this and go home.

"Good evening, everyone," I say, giving the room a slow sweep with a relaxed smile. "I'm Soledad Charles."

I pause to let that sink in. I may have been on Edward's arm the last time they saw me, but I've shaken that man off, and even his name is no longer attached.

"It's been my great honor to prepare the food for this evening."

To my utter surprise, many applaud. Some whoop. I'm not sure if it's a ringing endorsement of my rumored competence in the kitchen or an indictment of Eileen's past cuisine. Probably the latter.

"Thank you," I acknowledge. "We have four courses tonight. The first course..."

Movement at the door distracts me. I falter when my eyes lock with Judah's. He stops at the threshold, making no move to find his seat but simply staring back at me. My heart stammers and my pulse leaps. Dragging my gaze away, I refocus on the roomful of waiting guests.

"Where was I?" I ask, clearing my throat. "Oh, yes. The first course is a simple salad of spinach, feta, olives, and tomatoes. What makes this special is the vinaigrette. Some of you may have heard it called my 'viral vinaigrette.'"

I smile when several people whistle and tap their plates lightly with the silverware.

I zip through the other three courses and the wine selections and end with the dessert.

"A variety of desserts are courtesy of Skyland Bakery," I conclude, "located in Skyland Square. I hope you'll love what you taste tonight and try them again later."

Now that I've gotten through what I need to say to people I hoped never to see again, I allow myself to really look. I don't find any judgment or dislike. Only curiosity and, if I'm not mistaken, goodwill.

"It was great seeing so many of you again," I say. "I wish you all the best and a happy holiday."

I nod to Rhea, who stands at the entrance with her small contingency of servers behind her. On my cue she and the others come in, carrying plates of delicious-smelling food. I start toward the door, carefully avoiding the side of the room where I saw Judah settle. I'd hoped to get out fast, but people keep stopping me. They tell me it's good to see me, that they've been watching my posts. One young VP even tugs me to the side and whispers that she's started dating herself once a week.

"That's amazing." I squeeze her hand and share a smile with her.

"My last partner cheated on me," she goes on. "At first I felt like I lost the love of my life, but taking this time for myself, now I realize without honesty and respect, that wasn't actually love."

The word "cheated" tears through me like a Band-Aid being ripped off. Does she know Edward cheated? Surely they all do. The affair with Amber was an integral part of cracking the case. Everyone knows how he betrayed me, and suddenly I just want to get out of here. Not to be the object of anyone's scrutiny. Or worse, their pity.

"I'm so glad you're enjoying this process," I tell her with all sincerity. "It's been transformational for me too. You'll have to excuse me now, though, because I need to get home to my girls. Have a good one."

Lupe is old enough for them to stay alone, which they do all the time, but I need to get out of here before I turn maudlin, down a few bottles of wine, and end up drunk, dancing on a table and sobbing through all four courses.

"You got this?" I ask Rhea once I reach the kitchen and find her directing the servers rushing to get the plates out.

"Got it." She sends me a harried glance. "Glad Ms. Callahan asked you to do that, not me."

"It wasn't part of the bargain. I want to get out of here before she finds something else I didn't agree to do. Have a great night. Their crew will handle breakdown and cleanup."

"Thanks for the opportunity," she says, giving me a small salute.

I grab my purse from the pantry and head for the back porch since all the servers parked on the rear lawn. A gentle grip on my elbow stops me before I get out of the kitchen. I look up over my shoulder to meet Judah's eyes.

"Leaving without saying goodbye?" The sculpted curve of his mouth settles into a disapproving line. "Or even hello, for that matter."

"Uh . . ." I slide a look to Rhea, who seems to be very purposely *not* watching us right now. "No."

"So you were just carrying your purse and headed to your car, but not leaving?"

"Judah." I cast a self-conscious glance around at the kitchen and the servers rushing in and out. "Can we not do this here, now?"

Without replying, he takes my hand and leads me through the bustle of the kitchen and out into the hall. We keep going past the dining room, where guests have started eating and drinking. Laughter and the muted tinkle of glasses follow us down the quiet passageway. I love how his fingers curl around my hand. The contrast between strength and gentleness in the span of his palm. I relish it as a small thing I don't have in this period of my life. With unhurried steps, he takes me to a room down the hall. When the door closes behind us, I look around, a small smile forcing its way through my wariness. It's the same room where I found Aaron at this party last year. Same book-lined shelves and well-used armchairs. Even the faint smell of cigars still hangs in the air like a ghost.

Judah turns to face me, sliding his hands into the pockets of dark slacks. With his lean, athletic build, broad shoulders, and narrow waist, clothes love him, draping and clinging in all the right places. He slowly takes in the details of my face, my hair, my clothes. An inventory that ends when he meets my eyes.

"You look good," he says. "You always do."

"Thanks." I clasp my hands behind me, gripping my purse to keep from reaching for him again. That simple mingling of our fingers was better than a kiss in some ways, and I want to hold on to it. "I assume you didn't bring me back here to compliment my outfit."

"No, I brought you back here because you weren't even going to speak to me." One side of his mouth quirks up. "It defeats the purpose of me arranging ways to see you if I don't actually get to see you."

"I told you I'm grateful for this gig."

"You don't owe me anything, but I thought we were friends."

"Is this what friends do?" My laugh comes out like forced air, rough and short. "Want each other?"

In two strides he's much closer, towering over me, pouring a devouring look down the length of my body. He leans into me until our noses brush and our parted lips nearly touch.

"You want me, Sol?" he asks, his breath fanning my lips.

"Yes," I pant.

He grips my hip with one hand, pulling me flush against him so I feel how I've affected him, how hard he is for me. He lowers his head, and I know that if I don't speak now, our first kiss will consume all thought.

"But I want myself more than I want to fuck you."

My words hang between our lips, which are only separated by a paltry centimeter. His thick lashes flick up and his eyes meet mine. "Elaborate."

"I want what I'm learning about myself, what I'm fixing about myself, how I'm standing on my own," I say in a rush. "I want that more than anything. Even you."

I reach up to touch the hard, high slant of his cheekbone.

"And I do want you so much," I confess, letting my thumb drop to caress the full, soft anomaly of his lips in the rugged beauty of his face. "But this is something I have to do on my own. If I don't do it now, I'll repeat my mistakes, Judah. And I can't go through it again, what I went through with Edward."

"I'm not Edward."

"But I *am* Soledad. I'm that girl who chose comfort over truth. Did I ignore what was wrong in my marriage, with my husband, because I wasn't sure there was anything else for me? Did I not want to disrupt life for my girls? Or was it that I didn't want to disrupt life for myself? Those are questions that demand answers."

I don't look away even when shame curdles in my belly at how weak that could make me appear to a man who's so incredibly self-assured and strong.

"Maybe I didn't see how I could do better on my own." I lift my chin, even though it brings my mouth dangerously close to his. "But I'm learning what I'm capable of without a man. Just me."

"And you want to be alone?"

"I want to know that if I am alone, it doesn't mean I have to be lonely. That I can be content. I'm taking time to know and understand myself better. To converse with my heart. To listen to it."

"I get that. I respect it." He glances up, searching my eyes. "Is this forever? Are you saying that I can't ever have something with you?"

A muscle twitches in his jaw while he waits, and I clearly see so much hangs on this question.

"No, I'm not saying that."

He presses closer, laying his nose against my neck and breathing me in.

"Then I'll wait." His lips brush the soft skin of my throat, and I stifle a moan and pull back enough to find his eyes.

"I'm not asking you to, Judah. That's not fair."

His hand at my hip coasts up my back, sliding between my shoulder blades to caress my nape beneath the heavy fall of hair. "And what do you think I would be doing if I wasn't waiting for you?"

I shrug, as if I don't know, but I do know. I do know the risk of refusing to be with a man like Judah—eligible, successful, handsome, kind, generous, an amazing father. The risk is losing him before I ever get to have him.

"I guess you could find someone else and—"

"I've been divorced almost four years," he says, lifting my chin and capturing my gaze. "Haven't been in a relationship. Haven't even been on a date. Haven't been tempted to."

I must do a bad job of hiding my shock because he chuckles and says, "I see that surprises you."

"Well, yeah."

"Why?"

"Have you seen yourself?" I laugh up at him. "I bet every single woman you meet and a few married ones are after you."

"Can't say I've noticed."

"Liar."

"Nope." He shakes his head. "I'm cursed or blessed, depends on how you look at it, with this hyperfocus. I latch onto something—a goal, something I want—and it's the only thing I see. The only thing I pay attention to. My boys have it. Sometimes for Aaron it's an action figure or a particular cube or...whatever. It consumes him. I didn't understand it when he was younger, but it seems some people on the spectrum fixate. Adam does, too, but not to the same extent as Aaron."

"Are you autistic?" It's not the first time I've wondered, but it's the first time I've asked. I hope he doesn't mind.

"I might be. When I was growing up, no one was paying attention to that kind of thing or naming it like we do now. I was the nerd. The odd one. The quiet one. The loner. I adjusted. It's harder for Aaron and Adam, but I see myself in them and I see them in me, yeah."

He shrugs.

"Anyway, our divorce was amicable, but it was a huge transition for my boys. They have been my main focus for a very long time, but after the divorce, I became kind of obsessed with making sure they would always be okay. And as they get older, I find myself focusing a lot on earning and saving for their futures even after I'm gone. There was little else that interested me."

His smile dies and his expression sobers.

"Until you." He pulls a long coil of my hair away from my shoulder, then frees it to spring back into place. "I can't stop thinking about you."

Perversely, even knowing I'm not going to start a relationship with him right now, it's exactly what I want to hear. His admission blows off dusty places in my heart. After so long with Edward, who, near the end, didn't seem to give me a second thought, it feels good to have a man like Judah unable to get me out of his mind.

"Well, since I'm not available," I force myself to say, "maybe you should find someone else. I'm sure you have needs."

I know I do.

I don't voice it, but my needs where Judah Cross are concerned torture me. They keep me up at night. They would run my vibrator into the ground if left unchecked.

"Sol, when I say I haven't had a date or an attachment since my divorce," he says, "I mean I've been celibate."

My jaw drops and I can't even play it off.

"Are you serious?" I gasp.

"I've never been into casual sex." He quirks a dark brow. "You find that unusual?"

"Well, most guys from puberty till the grave are all about pussy. So...yeah. A little."

"Don't get me wrong. I love sex, and I'm not saying I only ever had it with Tremaine, but I *was* married to her for over a decade. Before that, it was usually in a committed relationship. It's...well, I guess it's a trust thing. Is there anything more intimate? And I don't trust easily."

"And you're saying you trust me?"

"I'm saying," he replies, dragging his thumb over my ear, down the curve of my jaw, over my lips, "that when I fuck you, it will mean something to me."

His words are as raw as the need in his voice. The rough edge of it mirrors mine like a shard of glass, slicing through inhibitions and reservations. Through my resolve. It's been so long since a man looked at me the way Judah does, with blazing interest. With such steady, heated intent. But his touch? It has been centuries since I was *touched* this way. With tenderness. With barely checked desire. The longer we stand together like this, the harder he becomes. His arousal insists where our bodies touch.

I can't give him everything, can't *have* everything, but maybe tonight I can give him one thing. I can have one thing.

"Kiss me."

The words bolt from my mouth before I have time to stop or rethink them. He doesn't hesitate, dragging kisses over my jaw, under my chin, along the curve of my neck. It's torture the way he explores me with soft presses and tender licks, like he's sampling me before he takes his first bite. Open-mouthed, he sucks at the tendon running along my throat, and a current runs to my core. The purse drops from my nerveless fingers as his touch cracks me open and strokes the center of my body, lighting me up until I'm like a wax candle burning down to the wick. He's everywhere but where I need him. I want to taste him too. I fist his shirt and yank him forward until our lips meet. He smiles into the contact.

"Had to make sure you really want it," he says.

"I do." I cup his face, bracketing the high cheekbones between trembling hands. "Just one kiss."

"Then I better make it count." His hand travels up the center of my body, up my torso between my breasts to grip my jaw. "Open your mouth."

As soon as I do, he dives in. The seeking, searching kiss goes fathoms deep, and all rational thought flees my mind. Judah is so controlled, so meticulous in all he does, I expected his kiss to be like that. It is instead a force unleashed on me. Wild and sure and ferocious in its hunger, like he's been starving it in a cage and now... the feast. He presses my lips against my teeth and presses my body into the door. I widen my mouth for the deep stroke of his tongue as he tastes me, takes me. His other hand grips my hip and he pulls me impossibly closer until the fabric, the millimeter separating us, the reasons I shouldn't do this— they all dissolve and it's just naked desire writhing into naked desire. It takes flight and catches fire. I know I need to smother this flame, but can't bring myself to do it.

He dips his head, breaths ragged at my neck. "I don't want to stop, Sol, but you said one kiss. I don't want to take advantage of you."

I bury my head against his shoulder, face on fire, lungs burning with labored breaths. I'm not sure I would have stopped if he hadn't. I think I would have screwed him against this door, fully clothed, panties pushed aside, legs wrapped around him like ivy. Screaming his name while they ate their fondant potatoes up the hall. My knees wobble and my heart slams against my ribs in a frantic fuck-me rhythm. I force myself to pull away, out of his arms. With the cool air of our separation comes a rush of reality. So much for my resolve to not get involved any deeper with this man.

"Thank you," I tell him, running a hand over my unruly hair. "I probably look a mess."

He smiles faintly. "You have lipstick everywhere."

"Shit." I wipe my mouth with the back of my hand.

"Let me."

He pushes aside my hand and with gentle fingers wipes around my mouth, his eyes fixed on my lips. Brushing the tousled hair away from my face, he lowers his forehead to mine. Every touch with him feels as intimate as a kiss. Even something as simple as this is charged with potent possibility. This nameless thing I feel when he is near, it lurches in my belly. It brushes across my heart and heats between my legs and rips through my good judgment. With no more than a glance, he can enflame my senses. It frightens me how little command I have of myself when he's this close. He draws me in, and if I'm not careful, he'll draw me away from the work I know still needs to be done in *my* life before I tangle it with someone else's.

"I'm...I'm still not dating, Judah." I force myself to pull back far enough to look at him directly. "I shouldn't have...I don't mean to string you along."

"You're not." He cups my chin, lifting it, his long fingers splayed over my throat. "It was a kiss. I won't pretend I don't want you, and I hope you won't pretend what just happened didn't just happen, but I respect your decision."

"That kiss was—"

"I don't regret it." He bends down to kiss my hair, brushes it behind my ear and over my shoulder. "But I get it and I'll wait."

"Thank you," I whisper.

"That doesn't mean we can't see each other at all," he continues. "We did say we're friends, right?"

"Friends. Yeah," I agree cautiously. "I bet I look like I've been dragged through a bush, so I'm gonna try to sneak past the dining room and out to my car."

"I'll walk you out."

"No, you don't have to." I bend to grab my purse, long forgotten, from the floor. "I'll be fine on my own."

He gifts me with one of his rare wide smiles. "Of that I have no doubt."

CHAPTER TWENTY-NINE

SOLEDAD

"Ho! Ho! Ho! Merry Christmas!" Hendrix says, loaded with shopping bags, when she enters the kitchen. "Bringing tidings of joy and rich-auntie energy."

"Gifts!" Lottie claps. She knows Hendrix is heavy on the "rich" when it comes to presents. "Thank you, Aunt Hen!"

A glance into the bag confirms that Hendrix really outdid herself spoiling the girls this year.

"Now you showing out," I tell her, shaking my head and smiling down into the bag.

"Just acting my wage," she laughs. "What else am I gonna spend my money on?"

Lottie takes the bulging bag from Hendrix, visions of sugarplums and gift cards no doubt dancing in her head.

"We're not opening gifts until midnight, Lottie," I remind her.

"Awww, Mom." She half-heartedly stomps one slippered foot.

"You girls are the ones who said you wanted a traditional Nochebuena." I glance up from the fresh pan of *pasteles*. "Gifts at midnight. How you coming over there, Inez?"

"I'm making the achiote oil," she says, pouring the red annatto seeds into a pot to warm.

"Good." I nod to Lupe and her cutting board filled with vegetables. "When you're done, help your sister with the yautia and malanga for the masa."

"This batch is ready to go," Lola says, entering from the butler's pantry carrying a crate of brightly colored gift boxes and carafes of coquito.

"Oh, thank you," I say, turning to Hendrix. "I told Cora I would swing by to drop off a batch of *pasteles* and some coquito. When I was over there for book club, she said she wanted to try them. I won't be gone long, Lola."

"Lola?" Hendrix looks from my sister to me. "Finally we meet!"

"Hendrix!" Lola sets the small crate on the counter and waves her arms, stutter-stepping toward one of my friends she's heard so much about. "I feel like I already know you."

Seeing my sister and one of my best friends hug like they've known each other forever when it's their first time meeting makes me pause and smile. I've been going all day, trying to give the girls a true Nochebuena experience, but also pulling some last-minute gifts together to deliver to friends. Seeing people I love happy together makes all the rushing around worth it.

"Let me take your coat," Lola says.

"Oh, I can't stay." Hendrix pulls the faux fur lapels of her coat up around her face. "Just left a mixer downtown for work. Now I gotta catch my flight to Charlotte. Spending Christmas with my mama, but I needed to swing through and get the *pasteles* Sol promised me."

"I got you." I reach into the crate of gift boxes and hand one to Hendrix. "As promised. You just missed Yasmen and Deja. They swung through to get theirs 'bout an hour ago."

"We're on the second batch." Inez grins, now standing at the chopping block with Lupe, cutting up malanga.

"Y'all running a little *pasteles* factory up in here." Hendrix eyes the banana leaves lined up, the *pasteles* machine, and the ingredients in various stages of preparation.

"It feels like the holidays when we were growing up," Lola says wistfully. "Only we had Mami, all us girls, and a houseful of friends. We played dominoes all night. Our house was rocking for Nochebuena. Mami'd be blasting El Gran Combo's *En Navidad*."

"Our *abuela*'s favorite group," I tell the girls, who appear to be riveted by this glimpse into the childhood Lola, Nayeli, and I cherish.

"'They coulda been your *abuelo*,'" Lola says, imitating our grandmother's heavily accented English. "'All of 'em.'"

"Remember that time Abuela *and* Grammy came for Christmas?" I ask Lola, catching her eyes to resurrect a memory only we can truly appreciate.

"*Ay, Dios mío*," Lola cackles. "We had *pasteles* cooking over here, oxtails and collard greens over there. Salsa blasting in the front room and Nat King Cole singing 'The Christmas Song' in the back."

"It was one of the best Christmases of my life." I swallow the hot lump filling my throat. "That was the last time we saw Abuela before she passed away."

The laughter slowly fades from Lola's face. She nods. "And Grammy wasn't far behind."

You feel the loss of those you loved most acutely at the times when they made you feel so alive. At some point every year, I relive that Christmas when my whole family came together and celebrated the season and life and each other. I hear the echo of their laughter and feel the warmth of their hugs as if their arms surround me again during the holidays. Which reminds me of one very important delivery I need to make.

"Let me get this over to Cora's," I say, grabbing a few of the red-and-green boxes of *pasteles*. "I wanted to check on her before it gets too late."

"Who's Cora?" Lola asks, walking over to lift the lid of the picnic pork cooking for our second batch.

"My friend Lindee's mom," Lupe says, some of the joy in her face dimming too. "She has cancer."

"Oh." Lola watches me, concern creeping into her eyes. She knows how hard Mami's death was on me. "How's she doing?"

"Hard to say." I walk toward the mudroom and grab my coat. "This is her second time fighting cancer. It's more aggressive, and the chemo is wearing her out."

"Mom's organized a meal train," Lupe says. "And cleaned their house a few times and does a book club with her."

"Not much of a book club." I shrug. "Just me, Cora—"

"And me and Yas," Hendrix cuts in. "We just started *All About Love* by bell hooks."

"A classic." Lola presses her hands over her heart. "Mami loved that one."

"I'm reading Mami's original copy," I tell her. "It has her annotations and notes in the margins. It's fantastic."

"I want to see that," Lola replies. "There's probably a lot of her stuff still up in the attic. We'll find it when we clean the house out for the Airbnb."

"Lola's moving to open a bookstore in Austin," I tell Hendrix. "She and her best friend."

"Oh, I've heard about this best friend." Hendrix wags her eyebrows.

Lola flashes a look at the girls managing their cooking assignments and grabs my and Hendrix's elbows, dragging us out of the kitchen and into the living room. Hendrix and I sit on the sectional, and Lola plops onto the tufted ottoman in front of us.

"What has my little sister told you?" Lola asks, eyes narrowed, but a smile playing on her lips.

"Only that you've fallen in love with your best friend." Hendrix grins. "I hope that was okay."

"It's fine. I could use some advice, actually. We kissed." Lola bites her fist, wide eyes pinging between Hendrix and me.

"Oh, my God, " I say. "Isn't Olive straight, far as we've ever known?"

"She did experiment in college," Lola corrects. "Unfortunately never with me, but yeah. She's only ever been in relationships with guys. We were packing up some boxes at her house for the move and it just happened."

"How was it?" Hendrix asks.

Lola sighs dreamily, leaning back on the heels of her palms. "It was like...coming home. I know I can be dramatic sometimes..."

"Sometimes?" I lovingly scoff.

"But," Lola says pointedly, "when we kissed, it felt like this was what every other kiss in my life wished it could have been. It was natural, but otherwordly. I can't describe it."

"You just did. Very well," Hendrix says. "And now I want a kiss like that. I met a couple of guys at this mixer tonight who could get it if they play their cards right. May have to put some girls on the roster too."

"As a happy hybrid"—Lola grins salaciously—"I ten-out-of-ten recommend expansion-league dating. I've tried 'em both, and can say with all confidence, pussy is superior."

The three of us laugh. Hendrix and Lola have a lot in common, not the least of which is their outrageous sense of humor.

"What about that guy you met on Tinder?" I ask Hendrix. "He was cute."

"He pronounced the 'l' in salmon." Hendrix sucks her teeth and shakes her head, disgust evident. "I said check please immediately. You mispronouncing fish. How can I trust you?"

"What about that guy you met at the Black Entrepreneurs Summit?" I ask.

"His rich ass," Hendrix says, "flying private and driving a Lambo, had the gall, the Black-ass-ity, to say we should split the check. Making all that money? If you ain't splitting the check with them light-skinned chicks, them white girls, them skinny li'l hos you Instagrammed on the yacht in Saint Bart's, don't try to dutch nothing with me." She gestures to her ripe figure. "Getting more fabulous for your money and gon' be cheap? Not over here."

"I know that's right." Lola high-fives Hendrix and cackles. "Know your worth, *dulzura*."

"Um, and the guy your cousin introduced you to from church?" I suppress a grin, already anticipating an excuse for why this one *also* failed to meet Hendrix's exacting standards.

"*I* had bigger dick energy than that man, which means we were basically unequally yoked. *How* can I be my ancestors' wildest dreams settling for some mid dick? I can't let them down like that."

"It's the dickmatization of it all," Lola laughingly agrees. "If I want it like that and there's no man around worth my time, I can always grab a strap-on."

"Please keep your voices down," I hiss, throwing a cautious look back toward the kitchen. "I don't want to spend Christmas morning explaining strap-ons to my eleven-year-old."

"I'm just saying," Hendrix whisper-laughs. "I told Santa all I want for Christmas is an orgasm that rolls my eyes back past my lace front. Something I need three to five business days to recover from."

"Oh, my God," Lola gasps. "I see why Sol loves you so much."

I shake my head at them both and try one more time. "What about that manager you met on set with your housewives, Hen? He seemed to have some potential."

"My first foray into the palm-colored of the male species." Hendrix crosses her long legs. "He was attractive, but he said 'malarkey' and 'rigamarole' *unironically*. My Blackness won't let me, at least not with him. If I'm dating a white dude, he better be invited to the cookout. A man with that Christopher Jamal Evans energy."

"While we're on the subject of white men we never shoulda let in our drawers," Lola says caustically, "how's Edward doing in that low-security resort of a prison?"

That sucks all the fun out of the conversation for me.

"I have no idea, and that suits me just fine," I reply, not even trying to strip the bitterness from my voice. "He's pissed at me, of course, and has only talked to the girls a few times. He doesn't want them to visit him in prison, which...good call."

I flop back against the cushions, fixing my stare on the coffered ceiling.

"I talk it through with my therapist, and the girls have talked with a family counselor about it. Overall, they've adjusted remarkably well, maybe because Edward was around so much less the last couple years."

"You still think Inez seems to be taking it the hardest?" Hendrix asks, brows pinched.

I sigh and squeeze the bridge of my nose. "Edward could never do any wrong in her eyes, and even with all the undeniable evidence that he did indeed do wrong, she's still on his side."

"I know this is a lot to navigate," Lola says, "but I'm glad it all came out. Glad you got rid of him and have taken your power back."

"Not only was Edward *not* invited to the cookout," Hendrix interjects, "he was the raisins in the potato salad. Like, who let *you* in? Good riddance and good for nothing."

"I never liked him." Lola offers her best big-sister sneer. "Uppity. And that mama of his, never trusted her."

"We agree on that point," I say dryly. "Can you believe he thought I would pack up the girls and move to Boston to live with my mother-in-law who doesn't even like me?"

"I'm still not over that Boston Celtics jersey he loved so much being his downfall." Lola chef-kisses.

"No, his downfall," Hendrix says, "besides your fearless sister, was that fine-ass accountant Judah Cross."

A Whitney Houston sweat breaks out across my top lip as soon as Judah's name enters the conversation.

"The accountant who busted Edward is fine?" Lola glances at me accusatorially. "Why is this the first I'm hearing of it?"

"Because it's irrelevant." I ball my hands into fists on my lap.

"Girl, the way he looks at your sister is not irrelevant." Hendrix casts me a knowing sideways glance.

"How does he look at her?" The expression on Lola's face can only be described as rapt.

"Like a dog with a juicy bone," Hendrix whispers.

"I should get these *pasteles* over to Cora," I say, standing.

"Or a juicy ass." Hendrix slaps my butt and tugs my waistband, forcing me back to the couch. "Sit down."

"You've barely seen us together," I tell Hendrix. "You don't know what you're talking about."

"I saw him here at the house," Hendrix counters. "And even then he looked like he wanted to fix all the shit Edward had caused and then take you to the nearest bed for some nerdy back cracking."

"Once. You saw us together once," I concede. "And he did not look at me like—"

"And chile, you shoulda seen his face at the Harvest Festival where Soledad was cooking," Hendrix barrels on.

"That Soledad experience thing?" Lola asks. "What happened?"

"When I was calling her name selling tickets," Hendrix says, "you woulda thought I used a dog whistle the way that man's head whipped around. Nearly detached his retina."

"These canine analogies really are unfortunate," I mumble.

"He was with his family," Hendrix continues as if I hadn't spoken. "His ex-wife, her husband, and Judah's twin sons. All Black, blended, and healthy. It was a beautiful sight to behold, honestly. They wanted to go to Sol's pavilion, but the only tickets left were for the last seating of the night, and they had to leave. But guess what?"

"What?" Lola asks, elbows propped on her knees.

"Judah left with his family." Hendrix allows a dramatic pause. Of course she does. "And came back, honey. Came back to see our girl, and I wasn't there, but Yasmen said that man was following Soledad all night with his eyes."

"That is so dramatic," I say.

Hendrix points one almond-shaped nail at me. "But accurate!"

"You weren't even there," I tell her with an exasperated laugh.

"Did Yas lie?" Hendrix challenges. "Be honest, and remember I haven't even told Lola yet how he ordered your focaccia basket so he could see you when you delivered it."

"He didn't even know I would be the one who brought it," I say lamely. "He just wanted...he wanted to support me."

"Awwwww." Lola presses one hand over her heart. "Sol, why haven't you told me and Nay about this man?"

"There's nothing to tell," I lie, picking up a decorative pillow to give my hands something to do. "He's a great guy. I admit there's an attraction." I close my eyes and lick my lips, memory tasting the scorching heat of Judah's kiss at the Christmas party. "But I'm dating myself right now," I remind them... and myself.

"You can't fuck yourself," Hendrix blurts.

"Well, technically...," Lola ventures with a wicked note in her voice.

"If you mention that strap-on again," I hiss, "and Lottie walks in here, your ass is mine."

Hendrix and I fall back into the cushions laughing, and Lola bends over, shoulders shaking with her own mirth. And I needed this. Talking with them feels like a gasket has been twisted loose so all the emotions and doubts I've bottled up can finally fly free.

"I really like him," I whisper in the after-quiet of our bawdy laughter, swiping my hands over my face. "I mean... like *really* like him."

I look up to find both women watching me with a mix of curiosity and surprise.

"We kissed," I confess.

"Bitch, when?" Hendrix demands, sitting up straight and poking my shoulder.

"Owwww." I massage the sore spot. "Hen, I hate it when you do that. What the hell?"

"No, you what the hell," Hendrix fires back. "How you not gon' tell me and Yas you kissed the accountant?"

"Or your sisters." Lola reaches toward me.

"If you pinch me," I warn her, "I swear I'll put you in a headlock."

Lola slowly withdraws her hand. "She's small, but wriggly. I never won a wrestling match on our living room floor with this one."

"When did you kiss the accountant?" Hendrix asks.

"Shhh." I crane my neck to peer down the hall. "I don't want the girls to hear. We've gone through too much over the last year. Too much transition and all the confusion with Edward for me to even think about dating this soon. Not to mention Inez still blames Judah for Edward being in prison."

"Okay," Hendrix says, her voice lowered. "But when did it happen?"
Single-minded heifer.

"At the CalPot Christmas party last week," I admit.

"How was it?" Lola whispers.

"It was...good." I understate, unwilling to go much further for fear of revealing how many times I've replayed that kiss. "Really good."

"He knows you're on the self-partnering tip right now?" Lola asks.

"Yeah. He said he'll wait for me." I hazard a look from one to the other, finding the swoon response I knew would be there. "That's good, right?"

"Well, yeah." Hendrix shrugs. "But only if you're into patient, kind men who look like Idris and could save you thousands on your taxes."

"I can't believe you didn't tell me this was going on," Lola says.

"It's not going on exactly." I twist my fingers in my lap. "It's not something that can happen, at least not right now, for several reasons, so I don't talk about it much because it might make me want it to happen even more and *now*."

"If it's like that"—Lola grabs my hand and squeezes—"maybe it wouldn't be so bad to explore a little of what it could be."

"Edward took so much from me." I release a hollow laugh. "Not to mention all that I surrendered because I thought we were in this together when he was in it for himself. I just need some space of my own. I don't trust myself right now, much less trust another man. I'm building a new foundation for me and my girls, and I won't compromise that for the first man who shows interest in me."

"Just don't think that self-partnering has to be cold turkey," Hendrix says. "I know you are learning a lot about yourself right now, but you deserve some pleasure, Sol. Being powerful means you can set your own boundaries. Make your own rules. If you want to kiss a guy but not be in a relationship, kiss a guy and don't feel guilty about it."

"You've been through so much, Sis," Lola seconds. "And you're always sacrificing for other people. Don't be afraid to get a little something for yourself unapologetically."

"I'll keep that in mind," I say, standing abruptly because I'm tired of being the focus of the conversation. "Okay. I need to take these *pasteles* to Cora's so I can get back and spend the rest of Christmas Eve with the girls."

"And I cannot miss this flight. Just think about what we said." Hendrix stands and grabs her purse. She smiles at Lola. "It was so good to finally meet you. I hope you come back real soon. You're much more fun than your sister."

"The story of my life." I roll my eyes but watch fondly as the two of them hug their farewells. "Travel safe and kiss your mama for me."

"Will do." Hendrix smiles, though without her characteristic easy humor and warmth. Her mother's dealing with some form of dementia, and it continues to worsen. It weighs heavily on Hendrix, and she visits her in Charlotte as often as she can.

"The two of you doing anything special over the holidays?" I ask, reaching to squeeze her hand.

"I do have tickets to a Broadway show. Mama loves them, and we used to..." Hendrix's smile is a little reminiscent, a touch sad. She sighs and squeezes my hand back. "We'll see how she's feeling."

"Merry Christmas, Hen." I kiss her cheek. "Love you."

"Merry Christmas," she says, finding her usual bright smile. "Love you too, Sol."

Once Hendrix leaves, I load the small crate of *pasteles* and coquito into the Pilot.

"I'll be back soon," I tell the girls, who are still busy working on the next batch.

"Can we play Uno when you get back, Mom?" Lottie pleads.

"We're playing dominoes," Lupe says. "All Nochebuena traditions, remember?"

"I think one game of Uno won't hurt." I give my youngest a wink and head toward the garage. "Be back."

My heart constricts in my chest when I pull up to Cora's house. The last time we came over for book club, Yasmen, Hendrix, and I helped Cora's kids put up Christmas decorations. I know there is a cloud of uncertainty and fear hanging over Cora's house as they enter this next phase of battling the illness, but the warm glow of lights adorning the porch and twinkling from the tree in the front window adds at least some exterior cheer.

I shift the two boxes cradled to my chest and ring the doorbell with the hand holding the carafe of coquito between my fingers. The door opens and a man I haven't met, but have seen in photos on the wall, stands at the threshold.

"Hi," I say, smiling tentatively. "I'm Soledad."

"Oh, I know who you are," he answers. "I travel a lot, so I've been away the times you've come, but Cora and the kids told me all about you." A half smile settles on his mouth between the lines of fatigue marking his face. "They even showed me some of your videos."

"Oh." I manage a laugh. "Those. Yeah, well. It's nice to finally meet you. Robert, right?"

"Right." He gestures inside to the small foyer. "Cora's asleep, and the kids went to a movie. Figured they deserved a little escape, but you're welcome to come inside."

"Oh, no." I proffer the two boxes along with the carafe. "My girls and I made *pasteles*, and I promised Cora I would bring her some."

"What're *pasteles*?"

"They're kinda like tamales. In Puerto Rico, we make them to celebrate Nochebuena...uh, like Christmas Eve. Anyway, we've been making them all day, and I wanted to bring some over. You can try them whenever. Freeze them. Up to you."

"And this?" he asks, tipping the carafe.

"It's coquito. Kinda like eggnog. Rum and coconut. I think you'll like it."

"I'll have this tonight," he says. "And thank you."

"Oh, it was nothing. I had told Cora I would bring it by, so—"

"I mean for everything," he interrupts softly. "For the meal train, cleaning the house, coming to see her. Being a friend. It means a lot to her and the kids. To all of us."

I blink back tears because the things I've done seem so inconsequential in the face of what Cora and her family are experiencing. I know firsthand how terrifying this fight is. I know how it feels to lose it, to do everything everyone told us, and it just wasn't enough. The helpless rage of losing Mami too soon swells in my chest, vises my heart. I hate that my new friend has to battle the same foe.

"Merry Christmas," I say after a few moments. "Tell Cora I'll check on her soon."

"Merry Christmas," he replies, his solemn eyes dropping to the boxes of *pasteles* in his hands.

I turn and take the porch steps quickly. Even with my back to him, I'm afraid he'll sense my tears somehow. Stumbling through the slightly neglected yard, I force my feet to keep moving until I reach the Pilot. I climb in and glance back to the house. I can see Robert through the screen door, holding the two festive boxes and the coquito. He hasn't moved from the spot, but just stands there looking a little lost, like he's not sure what's next.

And I know that feeling too.

I start my car, but don't drive off immediately. Instead, I glance over at the passenger seat, where one last box of *pasteles* and a bottle of coquito rest. I can lie to myself, but when I packed the extra box, I knew who it was for.

I drive almost on autopilot for the few miles it takes to reach my destination. I pull out my phone to send a text.

Me: Hey! What are you up to?

Judah: Nothing much. The boys are spending Christmas Eve with Tremaine. We fly out tomorrow to see my parents.

Me: So you're home?

A string of dots hovers, and my heart seems to be suspended too. Waiting to beat.

Judah: I'm home, yeah. Why?

Me: I'm outside.

Judah: Then come in.

CHAPTER THIRTY

JUDAH

It's like I "talked her up," as my mother used to say. I've been thinking about Soledad a lot since the kiss at the party. I'm usually focused on whatever is right in front of me, and my attention rarely wavers. But since she came into my life—since the first night I met her—she has intruded on my thoughts and broken my focus more than anyone or anything ever has. I don't want to crowd her, so I haven't called. I'm resigned to this friends-at-a-distance arrangement, even though I've wanted to touch her every day.

Guess not reaching out paid off, because she came to me.

I leave my suitcase open on the bed, already filled with neatly folded clothes for tomorrow's flight to see my parents. I force myself to take the steps slowly, like an adult man who helps manage a multibillion-dollar budget for one of the state's largest corporations instead of a horny, nervous teenager anticipating his date to the prom.

Not that I had any interest in going to the prom. I wasn't so much a late bloomer as a disinterested gardener for a long time.

The doorbell rings as I reach the foyer, and I refrain from yanking the door open. How is it possible to miss someone you've barely gotten to spend any real time with? But I've watched Soledad's platform grow, her confidence soar over the last year. I, like so many of her followers, feel like she's a friend. Someone I can trust and am rooting for. She's an influencer. She influences *me*, and she probably has no idea.

"Hi." She stands on my front porch, bathed in the glow of Christmas lights and early-evening moonbeams.

"Hi." I step back. "Come in."

She glances over her shoulder and bites her bottom lip, the battle clear on her face.

"Did I imagine a text message where we said you'd come inside?" I ask, her obvious reluctance drawing a smile to my lips.

"No." She clutches a gold box and a glass bottle of milky-looking liquid to her chest. "You're right. I just..."

She's obviously conflicted about coming inside. Maybe even about coming here at all. I hope that means she has to fight the desire to seek me out the way I fight every day to stay away from her. A noble impulse urges me to take the box and the bottle and send her back to her Honda... for her own good. It's been a week since I saw her. Since I tasted her sweetness for the first time. Felt the effect of our kiss on her, how her heartbeat answered mine, knocking between our chests. Even if I can't have another kiss, I could have that. The closeness and the hunger, even if I must deny it. The possibility of even a few minutes with her crushes my noble urge.

"Five minutes," I negotiate, stepping back to clear her path into the foyer. "And then you can leave."

She still hesitates, looking down at the box and the bottle and drawing a deep breath.

"What could happen in five minutes?" I ask, even though myriad things I could do to her in five minutes that would satisfy us both filter through my thoughts.

She gives me a *Really?* look but finally relinquishes half a smile and steps inside, holding out the box and the bottle.

Accepting both items, I frown. "I didn't get you anything. I didn't think—"

"It's nothing. Believe me. *Pasteles* and coquito. I'm giving them as gifts to friends this year."

I lift the box to my nose and inhale. "This smells fantastic. You made it?"

"Well, the girls and I made them. And my sister who's in town. Making *pasteles* is always a family affair."

"I can't wait to taste." I nod in the direction of the kitchen. "Have one with me?"

She clutches the strap on her bag and gives a tight smile. "Seems like that might take more than five minutes?"

I turn down the corners of my mouth. "Ten tops."

She rolls her eyes but nods and follows me into the kitchen.

I set the box on the counter and pull back the lid. An unfamiliar but enticing scent wafts up from the leaf-wrapped treats nestled together on wax paper. They are bundles of two *pasteles* each tied together with string. Soledad pulls a pair out and unties them, then unfolds the paper. She opens the green leaves to reveal what resembles a tamale.

"Wow. Thank you. These look delicious." I glance up. "You still down to taste?"

"One." She holds up her index finger. "And then I need to get back to the girls."

"And your sister, you said?" I walk over to the cabinet and pull out two plates. "Which sister?"

She tilts her head, a querying brow lifting. "How do you know I have more than one?"

"I've heard you talk about them online." I snag two forks from the drawer. "Lola or Nayeli?"

"You are such a stalker," she laughs, shaking her head.

I grin, unabashed about how much I've studied her the last few months. "I think we've established this."

"It's Lola. Nayeli stayed home. She has six kids and they've been sick."

"I'm glad you'll have some family with you this Christmas."

Her smile fades, and she reaches into the box to lift one of the *pasteles* out and onto one plate, then does the same with the other. "Me too. It's our first Christmas with Edward in prison."

"I hadn't actually considered that, but yeah. I try to think about Edward as little as possible."

"That makes two of us." The sour twist looks incongruous on her sweet lips. "You mentioned that you and the boys fly out to see your parents tomorrow. Where do they live?"

"Silver Spring, Maryland." I slice my fork into the *pastel* and lift it, holding it poised at my mouth. "I've been working so much, it's been too long since we visited."

I grunt at my first bite, then let out an extended groan on the second.

"Damn, this is good, Sol. The boys may not get any."

"There's like ten of them in there," she laughs, but she looks pleased. "Save some for them. Don't be greedy."

"I am greedy." I run a slow glance up the length of her, from her boots hooked over the barstool rung along the lean legs and the full curve of her hips and the subtle swell of her breasts beneath her sweater until I reach her pretty face. Pink sifts into her cheeks, turning them rose gold. "You're blushing."

"Because you're trying to make me blush." She bites into her grin and then into her *pastel*. "Are you close to your parents?"

"Yeah, very. They've been amazing with the boys, even though they don't live that close."

"Who are you most like?" She props her elbows on the counter and leans forward.

"Mostly my dad. My mom is..." I give a vague wave of my hand in her direction. "Like you. One of those glittery people who enjoy being around others all the time. *Life of the party* kind of person."

"You mean an extrovert? That *is* different from you, then."

I chuff a laugh. "Thanks a lot."

"You said it first. It's not bad, just different." She glances up through a veil of long dark lashes. "I like it. I like you."

Those words dangle between us from a tantalizing thread, shimmering with the possibility of pleasure we tasted together only a week ago. A pulse of *again* and *more* and *now* clamors through my body, but I subdue it and wait for her to move because *she* has to control this.

She clears her throat. "Um...sorry. You were saying."

"Just that I'm a lot more like my father."

"What do they do? For a living, I mean? Or are they retired?"

"My mom is still going strong as a nurse, but she'll probably retire in the next couple of years, if only to be at home with my dad. Though right now he's driving her out of her mind. He's bored."

"What did he do?"

"He *was* an FBI agent."

Her eyes go wide and round. "Are you kidding me?"

"No. Hundred percent. He'd come home talking about his cases, at least as much as he was at liberty to. The embezzlement stuff always fascinated me the most. Or anything where someone stole something and tried to get away with it."

"I'm envisioning ten-year-old Judah walking around with a calculator, solving fifth-grade crimes."

I chuckle and shake my head. "Not quite. I did love numbers. Like they came so easy to me, which actually I think I get from my mother. She's great at math. And I loved puzzles. Solving things."

"Like Aaron."

I glance up from my plate, where only a little of the *pastel* remains. "Yeah. I guess like Aaron. I got a full ride to MIT and wasn't sure what I wanted to do at first."

"It's hard for me to imagine you not being sure what to do. You always seem to know."

A self-deprecating smile tips one side of my mouth. "You should have seen me when we got the boys' diagnoses. I didn't know what any of it meant. I was kind of a wreck for years, but didn't realize it until Tremaine insisted I start therapy. Thank God for her."

"When were they diagnosed?"

"Around two years old, and around the same time. For a while they presented very similarly. As they got older, Adam started making gains that Aaron wasn't. Well, I don't know if it's actually quite that simple."

"What do you mean?"

"Adam made the gains people pay the most attention to. Like he started talking again. He's very academically gifted, so teachers were dazzled by his intelligence. They just weren't always sure what to do with a ten-year-old who could do high school–level math but wasn't potty-trained and couldn't tie his shoes. He wears Crocs or slip-on sneakers to this day because he still can't. Aaron has incredible bodily kinesthetic intelligence but can never learn to ride a bike. There are these...gaps sometimes. Development is not a straight line, and it misses some stops altogether."

"Sounds challenging," Soledad says.

"At various points, yeah. Tremaine and I took turns staying home or working from home. There was a time when both of us working outside the house was impossible, but there were things we wanted to do for the boys that weren't covered by insurance. So we needed money. We got calls from school constantly because of Adam's seizures or Aaron's meltdowns or any number of things. Not to mention driving back and forth to after-school therapies."

"So you stayed home?"

"We both did." I shrug. "I would take on freelance stuff so I could work from home. It slowed my climb up the ol' corporate ladder. Tremaine's too. She should have made partner years ago."

"We do what we have to for our kids, huh?" Soledad pierces her *pastel* with a fork and slides part into her mouth.

"Almost forgot the *coquito.*" I walk over to the cabinet and grab two stout glasses.

"Only a sip for me. I'm driving, and the rum is actually pretty strong in this batch. Courtesy of Lola's heavy hand."

"Tell me about your sisters." I pour a small amount of coquito for her and a little more into my glass.

"We've always been close. Lola has a different father from Nay and me, but we always joke half sister, whole heart."

"Nice. I know Nay is married. What about Lola?"

"So your cyberstalking didn't reveal everything about my siblings?" she teases.

"I didn't want to be nosy."

"Ha!" She sips her coquito and looks back to me. "Yeah, Nay is married. Lola is single, but in love."

"Really? A relationship?"

"Not yet. It's her best friend, actually. They're moving to Austin to open a bookstore."

"Unrequited love?" I ask with a small smile.

"Maybe not as unrequited as she assumed. They kissed." She scoops a swath of dark hair over her shoulder. "I'm so loose-lipped tonight. Not sure why I told you that."

"Maybe subconsciously you wanted to talk about *our* kiss," I venture, only half teasing. "Have you thought about our kiss last week?"

My tone is even, light, as if the words don't matter, when they really fucking do. I don't want her to move faster than she needs to, but for some reason I need to know it's not easy for her when it's so difficult for me.

"I've thought about it a lot." She sets her glass down carefully and looks up to meet my gaze. "You know I have."

"I hoped you had, but I wasn't sure. I like knowing I'm not the only one having to exercise an inordinate amount of discipline to not act on what I feel."

"You are definitely not alone in that," she says, picking up her glass for another sip.

"Good to know." I decide to shift the subject to something that won't have me kissing her again. "How's your Me List coming?"

"Oh, wow." She eyes me speculatively. "You saw that?"

"I didn't just see it," I tell her. "I made a list of my own."

"You have a Me List, Judah?"

"Recently made one, yeah." I run a hand over the back of my neck. "My ex-wife, Tremaine—you'll love her, by the way—she gets on me all the time about making my whole life about our sons and my job."

"You said she's remarried?"

"Yeah. By the end we were glorified roommates. Great friends, but it was not a passionate marriage. The boys were everything to us both, and we knew the easiest way to take care of them was together."

"And then she wanted more?"

"Then she wanted more, yes. And it wasn't with me."

"I've come to realize that a woman who wants more and realizes she deserves it is a dangerous thing."

I know what she just said is really empowering, but it's also so damn hot. Hearing her roll *"pasteles"* off her tongue got me hard. That statement is even more arousing because I wonder if I could be part of the *more* Soledad deserves. A man who would cherish where Edward disrespected. Who would protect when he left her vulnerable. Who would stay for all the treasures that piece of shit abandoned.

"So Tremaine got more," Soledad says, bringing me back to our conversation. "And now she wants you to have more too."

"She does. As parents—I guess it's true for most parents, but I've definitely noticed in parents of disabled people—sometimes we fall into the trap of thinking sacrificing everything is the greatest measure of our love. We devote everything to our kids who need more than most. That has consumed me for years. I thought that kind of singular focus expressed the highest form of love for my boys. Your journey, your list, has shown me how much I'd neglected anything just for me. Maybe there's value to them seeing their father happy."

"I believe so, or at least I've started to understand the value of that over the last year," she says. "Will you tell me what's on your list?"

I stand and step between her knees, absorbing her scent and her heat, losing myself for a few seconds in the dark infinity of her eyes.

"I'll do even better." I take her hand and pull her to her feet. "I'll show you."

CHAPTER THIRTY-ONE

SOLEDAD

Never has a man so affected me by simply holding my hand, but every time Judah takes my fingers in his, it's like the sun trapped between our palms. And that point of contact is both searing and a comfort. He leads me out back, behind the house to a small shed.

"If you tell me you have a she shed too," I tease, "I'm getting a restraining order."

"Somehow," he says, catching my eyes with his over the muscled contour of his shoulder, "I don't think you will."

I release his hand and playfully slap his arm. "Cocky?"

"Hopeful," he corrects, opening the door to the shed and pressing a hand to the small of my back to guide me inside. "Watch your step. I left in a hurry last night and may not have put everything away."

He flicks the wall light on, and I'm completely unprepared for what's in his shed.

"A truck?" I gasp. "You're fixing a truck?"

It's an older model, but that's as far as my limited knowledge extends. It appears that either there wasn't much to repair or he's advanced in the process. The wheels are on. The parts seem shiny and relatively new.

"Not just any truck," he says. "A classic, a 1964 Chevy C10."

"You've done this before?"

"My dad and I used to restore classic cars and motorcycles, so yeah." He walks around to the front, lightly tapping the hood. "He's got a

1981 Honda CM400 waiting for me in his garage right now that we plan to work on over Christmas."

"I don't know much about motorcycles, but that sounds really cool."

"It is, and you probably know this bike. It's the one Prince rode in *Purple Rain*."

"Shut up! How'd you get that? It's not part of his estate?"

"Not *the* bike, Sol." His shoulders shake with a deep laugh. "Sorry. I should have been clearer. *A* 1981 Honda CM400. Not *the* one, and it's not purple. I don't think I could pull that off."

"Well now I feel silly." I cross my eyes, drawing a low chuckle from him, which makes looking a little silly worthwhile. "My sisters and I watched that movie a hundred times. Shame yours isn't purple. That's my favorite color, you know."

"I'll see what I can do," he laughs.

"Whatever. Tell me about this truck."

"Ramjet 350 engine," he says.

"And, of course, I know exactly what that means. Go on."

He grins, pounding the roof lightly with his fist. "Custom interior, automatic transmission with overdrive, Positraction rear end with 3.73 gears, coil-over front suspension with rack-and-pinion steering. And for your ultimate posterior comfort, Tahoe leather bucket seats."

"You know all of that sounds like gibberish to me, right?"

"But are you impressed?"

"Oh, very." I widen my eyes. "Tell me more."

"If you mean that literally, and I can't imagine that you don't," he says, smoothing a palm over the hood, "anodized aluminum grille. I already repainted it. It was this gross green color, but I blocked and sanded it and painted it black."

"Looks like you're almost done." I walk slowly around the truck, pausing at the back and peering into the truck bed. There's a blanket and two pillows laid out.

"Is this a setup, Mr. Cross?" I ask with mock sternness. "Thought you might get some action?"

"No, I swear it's not. Aaron and Adam come out here sometimes and hang out in the truck bed while I work on something under the hood."

He grabs me by the waist and lifts me to sit on the lowered lip of the truck bed, making me laugh and squeal.

"But you can sit here for a minute and trust that I won't take advantage of you."

I smile up at him and pat the space beside me. "And I promise not to take advantage of you."

"Oh, please do." He chuckles and hops up beside me. "I'd like that a lot, actually."

"I just bet you would." I pull my knees under me and lean back on my palms, trying to regulate suddenly shallow breathing. He's big and handsome and warm, and his clean, masculine scent encircles me. His stare stalks me, and every cell of my body is screaming, *Catch meeeeeee.*

I clear my throat and ask, "So restoring this truck is on your Me List?"

"Yeah. I haven't done this since summer of sophomore year when I was home from college." He shrugs. "I forgot how much it calms my mind. Sometimes I spend all day trying to figure something out at the office. An hour out here after dinner and the solution just clicks into place. There's a correlation for me between working with my hands and with my mind. Sitting at a desk all the time, that's easy to forget."

"Anything else on your list?"

His grin builds slowly, and then he dips his head a little closer like he's sharing a secret. "Running the New York City Marathon."

"For real?" I twist to face him, see him better. "You're a runner?"

"The boys and I run most mornings. It helps them self-regulate better throughout the day."

"You're a fantastic father."

"Is it sexy?" he deadpans.

I know he's joking, but I can't find the light rejoinder because it is one of the sexiest things about this man, and that is saying something because even his Adam's apple turns me on. I lower my glance to my lap, tamping down the desire to straddle him.

"Should I tell you what I think is sexy about you?" he asks, his voice almost imperceptibly hoarser. I'm afraid to look up, to look at him, in case the same desire raging inside me is reflected on his face.

"You don't have to—"

"Your resilience. The way you make me laugh when you don't mean to be funny. How smart you are."

Sometimes I forget I graduated with a higher GPA than Edward did. Forget the times he used my notes because they were so much better than his, and that he wouldn't have gotten his MBA if I hadn't drilled him, hadn't pushed him to be better. How he would come home talking about a difficult account because he knew I would see something he had missed. I forgot so many things I was capable of because he wanted me to believe I relied on him, when actually he relied on me much more.

"I love the way you care about people," Judah continues. "Like your friend Cora."

I do look up then, touched that he remembered her name. The harsh overhead light in the shed hones the angle of his cheekbones, exposes the full, firm lines of his mouth. Burnishes his skin a deeper brown.

"Your ass," he says softly, completely seriously.

Laughter erupts from me, and I flop back on the comforter, squinting up at the overly bright light. "My ass is my most noble quality."

"Pretty close," he says, leaning over, smiling down at me.

I can't seem to find the will to resist reaching up, tracing the curve of his bottom lip. The shallow cleft in his chin. He stills, eyes locked with mine so intensely, I almost forget we're in a shed in the back of an old truck. We could be in an orchard, on the side of a mountain, in a vineyard. I'd be anywhere with him right now, and the way he devours me with one hot look, it feels like he'd choose to be anywhere with me. And yet the restraint is evident in the fists clenched at his sides, in the muscle flexing in the taut line of his jaw. If I kiss him now, I won't have anyone to blame but myself because I know I can trust him not to cross the invisible line I've drawn between us. Lola and Hendrix's words echo back to me from just an hour ago.

You deserve some pleasure.

Make your own rules.

Get a little something for yourself.

Judah Cross is something for myself, and I want him now. It's Christmas, and I want to feel like a gift, like someone to cherish. He makes me feel that way now with just a look. Imagine what a kiss would do.

I reach up, slowly in case he doesn't want to do this, and cup his neck, drawing him down to me. His brief moment of hesitation leaves a tiny breath between our lips.

"Are you sure?" he rasps.

"A kiss, okay?" I whisper. "We can do just a kiss, right?"

He nods, sliding his fingers into the hair at my nape and pulling me close, so close our lips brush, pull away, brush again. A dance of *should we, will we,* and *God, yes, let's,* ending with his mouth sealed over mine in a kiss that once it begins, does not hesitate. He dives in, and the desperate force of it matches my own. He said earlier that he was greedy, and the kiss reflects a deep, banked hunger that mirrors mine. Like the desire that has driven me more than once to touch myself under cold sheets and think of him has burned through him too. The kisses he trails down my throat torch my control, and my hands glide over the hard muscles of his back beneath his sweater.

He groans into our kiss. "Touch me, Sol."

I want to so badly, and my wandering hands aren't shy, gripping his shoulders and caressing the lean muscles at his waist. Learning his body with the tips of my fingers, I kiss the column of his throat. His grip at my waist tightens, and the tether on his self-control seems strained. He breathes heavily into the curve of my neck. His erection presses into my hip, and I know that if we don't stop now, it will go beyond a kiss.

I want it to.

I find one of his hands and guide it to my breast. My nipple buds into his palm, a flower turning to the warmth of the sun. Watching me closely, he squeezes in rhythm with my ragged breaths. I hold my bottom lip hostage between my teeth to keep from screaming. It has been so long since I was in the palm of a man's hand like this—with a laser desire that takes my every response as a cue to how to pleasure me next.

"Can I see?" he asks, his hand poised at the hem of my sweater.

Inside this cocoon we've woven from ardor and desperation, I can't deny him anything. I nod, closing my eyes when he peels the sweater up and unlatches the front closure of my bra. Cool air christens my nipples, drawing them into hard, tight points.

"Jesus," he breathes, his breath fanning warmly over the curve of my breast. "You're so fucking perfect."

"I'm not." I force a laugh out, ready to detail all my flaws and sags after breastfeeding three babies. "My—"

I choke on my words when his mouth closes over the tip of one breast.

The soft pressure of his mouth sucking gently on me is torture. I squeeze my thighs together, seeking some relief from the throbbing there. From the heat building in my core and spreading across every centimeter of skin and nerves. He increases the pressure, alternating bites, nibbles, sucks, licks with his mouth, while his hand rubs my other nipple, tugs and pinches and flicks. It's an unrushed seduction, so persistent and patient and precise that the pleasure steadily climbs up my body. My back arches and my legs fall open and my head tips, mouth widening on a silent scream.

"I'm gonna come," I gasp, incredulous because I never have from just this. It's been a long time since a man's touch coaxed this response from me, but I recognize the tension crawling up my legs and wrapping around my spine.

"Good," he breathes, not relenting.

I whimper and moan and pant while he keeps at it, confining his focus to my breasts. My hips twist and I writhe, but he doesn't let me get away. Finally I can't take it anymore and I explode in a clap of thunder. With a crash of lightning behind my eyes, I unravel like a loose thread that he keeps tugging and tugging until it dangles. *I* dangle over an open canyon, waiting to be dropped, but he never does. He holds me through the trembling shock of a pleasure so intense it feels like a discovery. I hide my face in the warm skin of his throat, my sweater accordioned between us, bra open, breasts bare and heaving into his chest.

"I've never..." I draw in a ragged breath, helplessly trying to calm my racing heart.

"Never what?" He strokes my hair away from my face and dusts soft kisses across my hot cheeks.

"Never come from just that," I confess in a mortified rush.

"Really?" His eyes are riveted on my face. "Can I...never mind."

He moves to sit up, but I grab his arm to keep him close.

"What is it?" I whisper. "What do you want?"

He hesitates for a moment before meeting my eyes directly. "Can I feel?"

"Feel?" My mind is scrambled, an orgasm omelet, with all my thoughts whisked and tossed. "Oh, you mean *feel*."

He offers a terse nod, lips and jaw tight, but he doesn't withdraw his request. In answer, not breaking our stare, I unzip my jeans, wriggling to loosen them around my hips. I take his hand and guide it into my panties. Both of us are breathing harshly by the time his warm, blunt fingertips reach me, explore the wetness flooding my underwear. I clench my eyes shut. He said he just wanted to feel, but I drop my legs open in case he wants more because I do.

Unhesitating, he grazes my clit with his thumb and I arch, staring up at the light on the ceiling as if that one point of brightness anchors me to the world, to my body.

"Sol," he breathes, lowering his head to my neck and kissing the dips and hollows of my collarbones. "You're so wet."

"I know," I pant, involuntarily rolling my hips into his touch, into the probe of his fingers parting me. "Please do it."

"Do what, sweetheart?" he asks, his fingers going still, poised at the entrance to my body. "What do you want?"

"You know, Judah." A sob catches in my throat. "You know what I want."

He brushes my clit again, sending a jolt through my legs and curling my toes in my boots.

"You know I want you inside," I choke out.

Two big fingers plunge into me, and we gasp together when he breaches that most intimate place for the first time. He begins slow and steady, then becomes urgent and ruthless. He wrenches a second orgasm from me, this one accompanied by a scream that flees my body and climbs the walls of the shed. I almost clench my legs together to keep him when he withdraws from me. I search for the embarrassment, for the shame of coming all over his hand. Of screaming his name in the back of his 1964 vintage pickup truck. Of taking pleasure in the sweet, soft, rough, right places I find it.

But there's no shame. No embarrassment when he looks at me and smiles, eyes searching my face.

"That was..." I sigh and rest my hand on his chest. "If I smoked, I'd have a cigarette."

His rich, throaty laughter coaxes a chuckle from me too.

"You didn't..." I falter, my amusement withering when I notice his erection. "We can—"

"Not necessary," he assures me, his deep voice rumbling under my palm. "I'll be fine."

"But you—"

"We said ten minutes and it's been thirty." He drops a kiss to my forehead. "You need to get back to your girls and your sister."

"Shit." I cannon up and scramble off the truck bed. "How could I forget..."

His usual impassive expression doesn't hide the smug satisfaction lurking beneath the strong planes of his face.

"Oh, God." I laugh and point at him. "You're so happy you made me forget."

"Not happy, no." He takes my hand and kisses the back of it. "But I don't regret that. I don't want you to feel guilty being here with me too long on Christmas Eve with your family waiting for you."

"Thank you." I step close, tip up on my toes, and kiss his cheek. At the last minute he turns to capture my lips with his, groaning when our tongues tangle. His hands slide down my back to cup my ass, lifting me closer. When I'm drowning in sensation and oblivious to time, rolling my hips into his hardness, he's the one to pull away.

"You should go," he says, strain laced in the words and on his face.

His hand rests possessively at my hip, and he slaps my ass lightly. It seems like such an un-Judah thing to do, it makes me laugh. It's a happy, unfettered sound that floats around us in the cool night air. He takes my hand and walks me into the kitchen to grab my purse and then on to my car.

Has it only been a year that I've known him? It feels like our times together have been concentrated—so much has been poured into every interaction. We've learned and revealed so many things about each other. He's a friend who, as much as I resist it, becomes more every day.

"Fly safe," I tell him when we reach my car.

"Enjoy your sister," he says, opening the door for me. "Thank you for the *pasteles*."

"Make sure the boys get some."

"They only eat about four things," he laughs. "But I'll try."

Once I climb in, he presses one arm against the car over his head and leans in until our mouths align. He takes a slow, thorough kiss, and I give him everything he wants.

"Can I call you?" he asks.

It's an innocent question, but it holds significance. We're not meeting "by coincidence." We're not running into one another. Even if I wanted to reduce what happened tonight to merely a physical connection, there is an honesty in the way we touch each other, look at each other, that would call me a liar if I tried to pretend this was casual.

"You can call, yeah." I brush my knuckles over his cheek, and my heart turns so tender it hurts. "Merry Christmas, Judah."

He kisses my forehead and cups the back of my head gently. "Merry Christmas, sweetheart."

CHAPTER THIRTY-TWO

SOLEDAD

We want to see Dad."

My hands freeze over the cake I made for tonight's dessert, fingers tightening around the piping bag of strawberry icing.

"What?" I ask numbly, knowing damn well what but still unprepared for this inevitable moment.

"We want to see Dad," Inez repeats, standing in the kitchen's arched entryway, her small hands twisting nervously.

"Oh." I set the piping bag on the counter and wipe my hands on a tea towel. "Um...I'll have to check the schedule to see when visiting hours—"

"There's visiting hours on New Year's Day," Lottie says from a few steps back.

My youngest averts her eyes to the floor, not quite meeting my gaze.

"He may not..." I stop myself, refusing to tell my girls their father does not want to see them. Or at least doesn't want them to see him in prison. "I need to check with him to coordinate, if you're sure you want this."

"We want it," Lupe says. "We know he broke the law, and we know he hurt you, Mom. I'm so mad at him for all of that, but he's our dad. It's the holidays. We want to see him."

"Is that okay?" Lottie asks, her voice wobbling and crystalline tears trembling on her bottom lashes. "We love you. I promise. We just—"

"Love him too," I finish for her. "Of course you do. That's natural, baby."

Yet it feels like the most unnatural thing in the world to arrange for my daughters to visit the man who upended their lives, who betrayed me and left us to fend for ourselves. Left *me* to fend for myself. If I never saw Edward again, I would die happy, but it's not just about me. It is, as it always is, about my girls.

I'm reminding myself that this is for them when we pull up to the prison parking lot on New Year's Day. Last year at this time, I was blissfully ignorant of the avalanche poised to dump all over my life. I had my suspicions, sure, and my concerns about the state of our marriage, but nothing was certain. And there were days I could even pretend everything was fine. I'll never take solace in a fake fine again.

"Ready?" I ask, turning to study Lupe in the passenger seat beside me and Lottie and Inez in the back.

"Yeah, but..." Lupe bites her lip, toys with the ends of the long red braid flung over one shoulder. "Do you have to come inside?"

I frown, tossing the keys in my purse before meeting the concern in Lupe's eyes. "You're minors. I have to accompany you, and there's no way I'd let you go into a federal prison without me. You know this. Why don't you want me to come?"

"He cheated on you," Inez says, surprising me since I know how hard it has been seeing her father's feet of clay. Her soft response barely cloaks the disbelief and dismay of a little girl who thought the sun rose and set on her father. When I glance back, her eyes hold an incongruity of emotions I wish she didn't have to sort through yet.

Fury. Disappointment. Longing.

She loves an undeserving man. It's a sorrow most women experience at some point in their lives, whether it's a father who neglects or a son who forgets or a husband who betrays. These men let us down and we pull ourselves back up, hopefully with the help of other women who love us in ways that heal. Lola and Nayeli held a Boricua High Council FaceTime this morning over breakfast. Nayeli prayed that I would have peace that surpasses understanding, the kind that rises when your heart would drag you to fall. Yasmen came to the house this morning carrying a bouquet of yellow roses from Stems, my favorite florist in Skyland.

"For friendship," she whispered into my hair. But I knew she really meant *for courage*. She hugged me tight, squeezing, not letting go until a few tears trickled over my cheeks because she knew I needed to cry *just* a little.

My friends, my sisters, my daughters. My great loves.

I look at each of my daughters with deliberate care, wanting them to see strength and resolve. I love that I've raised girls who think about me, who care about me as a human, not just their mother who exists to serve their every need. There's an honesty in that. I think I saw it in my mother because I knew she stayed with my father, loved him in her own way, while the deepest parts of her heart belonged to another. I saw her not just as Mami, but as a woman in all her full, flawed dimensions. I want my girls to have that too.

"Your father broke my heart," I tell them, "and he broke the law. He is not, in my estimation, a good man. I wish I could have protected you from the truth, but that was impossible. So you understand why I had to divorce him."

"I would have been mad if you hadn't," Lupe says, traces of bitterness in her words. "He doesn't deserve you, Mom."

"No, he doesn't, and he doesn't deserve you either, yet here we are." I gesture toward the imposing white building of the prison. "He's all the things we said, but he's also the man who taught you to ride a bike, Lupe."

She drops her eyes to her lap.

"And always played video games with you, Inez," I say, glancing back to meet my daughter's eyes. "And did handstands with you in the backyard, Lottie."

"He wasn't very good at them." She snorts, but a small smile cracks the corner of her mouth.

"My point is that it's complicated," I say. "He's not all bad and he's not all good, and he's still your father. Finding out he's not perfect doesn't erase all your love for him."

"You're sure you're okay with us seeing him?" Lottie whispers.

"I've told you from the beginning and I mean it now. I don't want to keep you and your father apart. He will never—hear me when I say this—*never* have custody of you. No judge would award him that, and I would move heaven and earth to stop that from happening. You can love him, but I will never trust him with my heart again. The three of you are the most precious things in the world, and I will not trust him with you."

I let the words land in the quiet interior of the car before going on.

"And seeing him today may bring up some really big feelings. I'm not leaving you to process that on your own. So yeah, if you want to see your father before he gets out, I will be with you." I grab my purse and open the car door. "Ready?"

Am *I* ready?

As we check in, go through the metal detectors, get our hands black-light stamped, my stomach roils. My last visit with him traumatized me in ways I have only revisited in the safety of a therapy session. Edward did not see me as an equal. He did not appreciate the years of labor and counseling and love that I gave freely to our relationship, to this life I was stupid enough to think we were building together. I was merely unpaid labor to him, and he treated me like shitty tissue paper. Flushed me for someone he hadn't gotten to use yet.

"It's a lot of people," Lottie whispers, reaching for my hand.

"Yeah, we don't get, like...a private place to talk?" Inez asks, glancing around the visiting room, where several other prisoners are receiving their families.

"I told you it would be a communal visiting room," I remind them. "Your father only gets a private room with the lawyer."

"Dad!" Lupe gasps, her eyes going wide.

Edward stands at the door with a group of inmates, all similarly garbed in khaki pants and button-up shirts to match. He swings his head around when Lupe calls him. His face lights up at the sight of the girls. Even though he didn't want his daughters to come here, he looks happy to see them, immediately stretching his arms out for a hug. Inez and Lottie run to him, flinging themselves into his arms. I hate this bastard, but seeing his brows knit with emotion, the flush crawling over his cheeks, and the dampness on his lashes elicits a tiny twitch of pity.

Lupe hangs back, still standing with me, but staring intently at her sisters and her father.

"What's wrong?" I ask, brushing a hand over her head.

She looks at me, and even though she has Edward's eyes, I see myself in her. I see the deep concern she has for me warring with the love she still holds for her father, despite what he's done.

"You sure you're okay, Mom?" Tears fray the ends of her words, and she blinks with wet lashes.

"I'm fine," I reply, keeping my voice level despite the emotion her concern causes to well up inside me. "Baby, go see your dad."

My permission seems to uncork the last of her reservations, and in a few steps she adds herself to the group hug still going on with her sisters and my ex. Edward glances up from the cluster of black and red heads to catch my eye.

"Thank you," he mouths.

I don't respond, only give him back a hard stare to let him know I'm not playing with his trifling ass. Me he can no longer hurt. These girls...he's already damaged them in ways I may not even know yet, in ways the family therapist may have missed. I'll never forgive him for what he's put them through.

"Let's sit down," he says, pointing to a small cluster of chairs in the corner of the room. There are only three seats available. He takes one and pulls Lottie onto his knee while Lupe and Inez take the other two.

"We can share, Mom," Inez offers, scooting her slim frame over to make room for me.

"I'm fine here," I tell her, softening the stiffness of my tone with a smile and leaning against the wall.

For the next twenty minutes, Lottie regales Edward with stories of her meets and medals. Inez talks nonstop about *Animal Crossing* and school, and after a few watchful moments, Lupe starts opening up and talks about her grades, the debate team, and finally Lindee and Cora.

"Mom and I are growing our hair out to donate," she tells him, flags of pink in her cheeks. "Isn't that cool?"

"That's amazing, honey," Edward says, glancing at her braided hair. "How long is it now?"

With a huge smile and deft fingers she unravels her braid, freeing the thick, bright strands around her shoulders and down her back. She gets that red hair from my father, and when I see it, I thank the recessive gene that defied all odds to gift this tiny piece of my dad to me through her.

Edward eyes the spill of hair down to her waist, and something shifts in his expression. A sadness I don't understand at first.

"You've grown up so much, baby girl," he tells Lupe, then glances to Inez and Lottie. "You all have. It's only been a year, but I already feel like I've missed a lot."

"When are you coming home?" Inez asks, then shoots a repentant look at me. "I mean getting out. When do you get out?"

"It'll be over before you know it," he replies. "And I can get back to my life. Back to you."

"Why did you do it?" Inez asks, her tone injured.

In the difficult silence following Inez's question, Edward seeks me out where I stand apart. And I realize that, like so many times in the past, he's waiting for me to speak. For me to fix. For me to clean up a mess he's made.

The hell I will.

I cross my arms over my chest and leave my mouth shut, zipped into a stubborn line while I wait with his daughters to hear how he'll explain his deception.

"I wanted more for our family," he finally says. "I made mistakes I'm not proud of. I shouldn't have stolen from CalPot." His eyes harden to flint. "Especially with that Judah Cross on my tail."

"We saw him," Inez offers. "At Mom's event."

All eyes snap to me, and my spine stiffens, but I don't move.

"What event?" Edward demands. "Why was he there?"

No one else speaks, of course, so I draw an irritated breath and muster a response. "I was cooking for the Harvest Festival. Judah and his family were there, and he came to eat."

I don't owe Edward an explanation, and he knows it, but his lips tighten and his jaw is a line of granite. "That guy's got some nerve."

"Let's not talk about nerve, huh?" I say. "Your audacity far out-reaches anything he's done."

"What's he 'done,' Sol?" Edward's words come out like knives drawn, suspicion in the look he runs up and then down my body, like he's checking for Judah's fingerprints.

Oh, I'd just love to tell you where Judah's fingers have been.

The stare I level back at him warns him to back down. He has no moral high ground, and if he presses me, I'll remind him of that in front of his daughters and anyone around who'll bother to listen. He finally shifts that censorious gaze from me to the clock on the wall behind us, his eyes widening.

"Look, girls," he says, kissing Lottie's head and reaching across for Lupe's and Inez's hands. "I have to get back. It's time to go."

"But...we...," Inez sputters. "We just got here."

"It's been thirty minutes," I say, but I frown at Edward's sudden urgency for us to leave. "Your father's right. Time to go."

"Can we come back soon, Dad?" Lottie asks, her skinny fingers gripping the sleeve of his prison-issue shirt.

"Baby," Edward says, standing hurriedly, "I've missed you so much, but I don't want you seeing me here. And I don't want you visiting prisons. This isn't the place for my princesses."

He draws them into his arms, the three of them huddled around him in a chorus of sniffles. My heart bends, not for him but for the girls, who know what he's done—know what this situation is and that it is completely of his doing—but still love and miss this scoundrel.

"I'll be out soon," he says, kissing the top of each head. "But we can talk more on the phone. How about that?"

Inez nods, wiping at the tears on her cheeks. Lottie leaves his arms and rushes over to me, burying her little face against my chest, wetting my dress immediately with a flood of sorrow. I blink at the hot tears rising with the evidence of my daughter's pain. Rage and helplessness careen through me, and I glare at Edward over her head.

You did this!

The furious scream is trapped in my throat, clawing to break through the cage of my teeth. I'm so angry that Edward demolished life as our daughters knew it, shattered their illusions and introduced struggle into their lives that I had to rescue them from. But I wouldn't trade the truth for the ease of the life we had, not when it came with the paranoia his sneaky behavior caused or the insecurities he planted trying to manipulate me into being the wife he wanted. It's shitty that our girls had to find out what a termite their father was, but I'll guide them through recovery and healing, and they'll come out stronger, their eyes wide open about how people will exploit your weaknesses if you let them.

And it's petty, maybe immature, but I can't leave without leveling at least one punch.

As we're going, I turn to Edward, reaching to yank him into a tight hug. Surprise stiffens him against me, and I pull his head down as if whispering a secret.

"Just thought you should know," I hiss into his ear. "Found out the problem wasn't that my pussy was loose. I just needed a bigger dick."

I jerk back and glance down between us, then up to meet his angry glare. "So we have that in common."

I don't know yet if Judah's dick is bigger than Edward's, but let this bastard stew on the idea of me getting mine while he's locked behind bars. I don't give him time to respond but grab Lottie's and Inez's hands and move swiftly toward the door. "Come on, girls. Time to go."

"Thanks for bringing us, Mom," Inez says when we reach the car.

"Yeah." Lupe opens the passenger door and looks at me over the roof of the Pilot. "I think I needed to see that he was okay."

"We'll get to talk to him on the phone, right?" Lottie asks. "He said we could sometimes."

"Of course, honey." Noting their long faces, I force a smile. "Hey, what do you say we do a vision board party tonight? That'll be fun, right? Set some goals and dream about what you want for the New Year?"

"That *could* be fun," Lupe says, her lips twitching.

"And we could have a dance party." I do my best running man right in the middle of the parking lot. They act mortified but crack up like I knew they would.

"No Backstreet Boys," Inez grumbles, her lips fighting a grin.

"You're killing me, Smalls." I shake my head in mock injury.

"Smalls?" Inez frowns. "Huh? Whadda ya mean *smalls*?"

"It's from her generation," Lupe explains sagely.

"Can we make a s'mores charcuterie?" Lottie asks, her face brightening.

"Yeah." I nod and stretch my smile a little broader. "Now you're talking. And we can order something good for dinner."

I open the driver's-side door but am distracted by a flash of blond across the parking lot. It takes a few seconds for my brain to catch up to what I'm seeing. It's like some freakish déjà vu. The last time I visited Edward, I spotted Amber leaving, and now as I'm going she arrives.

"Um, girls," I say, not taking my eyes off the door Amber just walked through. "Go ahead and get in the car. I think I left something."

"Left what?" Lupe asks with a frown.

"I'll be right back," I say. "Get in the car, please."

I speed walk to catch up to the woman's confident strides before she gets any farther.

"Amber!" I call, not pausing to see if she'll answer. I know it's her.

She pauses but doesn't turn around. I walk ahead to step in front of her, blocking her path. The words I've been holding for months die and my mouth falls open when I see what she's holding.

Or *whom* she's holding.

It's a baby boy, bundled in a white blanket. Golden-blond hair peekaboos from beneath the green wool hat on his little head. The shade perfectly matches his eyes, a unique leaf green. I gasp, recoiling from the evidence, the confession of those eyes. Eyes I've seen nearly every day for half my life.

They're Lupe's eyes.

They're Edward's eyes.

"Jesus." I stumble back a step. "What the..."

"Soledad," Amber says, shifting the baby's weight against her chest. "I didn't...I thought you'd be—"

"Gone? No wonder Edward was rushing us out. He didn't want us to run into family number two."

"I know this is a lot." Amber dares to meet my stare head-on for a second before looking away quickly. "We never meant to hurt you."

"Liar," I rasp, poison dripping from the word. "Bitch. Home-wrecker."

Her eyes snap to mine, and her pale throat bobs with a deep gulp. Her arms tighten protectively around the baby.

"I did not wreck your home," she answers. "*My* life is wrecked. I'm on probation. I have a record. I lost my career. I'm barely making ends meet."

I take in her professional blowout, the perfectly manicured nails patting the baby's back, the laminated brows, the dress and shoes and bag my expert eye clocks at more than two thousand. I think of the Porsche she was driving when I last saw her. Barely making ends meet, my ass.

"So how'd this work?" I gesture to the baby. "This threesome, you and Edward and Gerald? How do you even know whose baby this is?"

The green eyes have already told me the truth, but I'm curious how she'll respond.

"The thing with Gerald..." Amber's gaze shifts away and she licks her lips nervously. "It shouldn't have happened, mixing business with pleasure."

"Um, isn't that exactly what you did with Edward?" I choke out a laugh and nod to the corridor leading deeper into the prison. "That turned out great for everyone."

"That was different. We're different, Edward and me. Gerald knows it's over between us." She kisses the baby's cheek and meets my eyes defiantly. "Edward will finish his time, and we'll be a family."

"Great way to start a family, with cheating and lying and scheming. I wouldn't put it past the three of you to have a little nest egg the FBI never found."

It's a shot in the dark, but as soon as the words leave my mouth, I know it's true. Her panicked gaze flies to me and her red-glossed lips O with shock. She clamps her mouth closed and smooths her face into a neutral mask. Too late. I peeped her, but I find I have no desire to use this information against her, against them. Edward can do whatever the hell he wants as long as he leaves my girls and me out of it. He has no power over me anymore. And for this woman? I have only pity. Yes, I'm shaken by this new development, but she won't know it. I won't show it.

"Good luck, Amber," I say, forestalling any more of her lies and taking one last look at the little boy with Edward's eyes. "You'll need it."

CHAPTER THIRTY-THREE

JUDAH

You sure you're okay with the boys staying over?" I ask Tremaine, the phone pressed between my ear and shoulder as I walk a sandwich and a beer from the kitchen to my office.

"Of course," she says. "We missed them while you were in Maryland. Kent mentioned a New Year's Day hike up Stone Mountain."

"They'll love that," I reply, not sure they actually will but already turning my mind to the pile of work I've neglected over the holiday break.

"They can stay with us a few more days if you want them to," she says. "Since they don't have to go back to school yet."

I pause at the double doors leading into my office, plate and frosted glass still in hand. "Do *you* want them to? They can anytime. I don't have to tell you that."

"Of course. It's not like I don't see them every day. I sometimes miss having them in the house during the week, though. Having them just on the weekends and holidays…"

"It's not set like that." I frown. "You know you can have them whenever you want."

"Yeah, but I hate disrupting their routine. Besides," she says softly, "they prefer being with you."

"That's not true, or at least it's not that simple." I walk into the office and set the sandwich and drink down, then perch on the edge of my desk. "Aaron prefers being *here* and got really attached to me when he was having a hard time sleeping. And Adam doesn't want to be anywhere Aaron is not. It's a miracle we got him to attend Harrington on his own."

"I know it's not personal, but at first it kind of felt that way. Kids always choose their moms, right?" Self-mocking laughter threads her words, though the tiniest fiber of hurt ribbons through them.

"I'm sorry." I blow out an extended breath. "We don't have the typical setup, and our life looks different from most. We made the best choices we could for each other and for them."

"I don't want you to feel bad, Judah. Do you know how many women in my parent support groups wish they had a partner as involved as you've been? Or even around? So many of them just leave and send money, if that."

Her deep inhalation reaches across the line.

"You did not only what was best for them," she continues, her voice softening, "you did what was good for me. So many moms lose their careers until their kids are almost grown. You didn't let that happen to me."

"How would that have been fair?" I ask. "We both had goals, careers. Why would I let that happen to you?"

"You're so used to being this way, you don't even realize how extraordinary it is, but I do."

It's silent for a few moments because I don't always know how to respond in conversations like this. It feels so self-evident. We were partners. We were a team. We still are.

"Anyway," I say, shifting the conversation to more comfortable ground. "Thanks again for taking them tonight, and they can stay until it's time for school on Monday if you want."

"We both know Aaron will want his bed before then," she laughs. "But tonight for sure. Let's see how long he lasts."

"Sounds good. Mama told me to tell you not to be a stranger."

"She called me this morning. She was cooking black-eyed peas, collards, and cornbread when we talked. Inspired me to make my New Year's meal too. We'll see if the boys eat it."

"Don't set yourself up for disappointment," I chuckle. "You better have a box of macaroni and cheese on standby because you already know that's what they'll want."

"I gotta try." She laughs. "Hold on. Okay. Kent says it's time for the hike. We'll chat later."

After we hang up, I sink gratefully into the chair behind my desk, slip on my reading glasses, and open the laptop for the first time in days. There's a comfort in the familiar cells of the spreadsheet. I get stressed about my money, always making sure there will be enough of it to take care of the boys when I'm gone, but other people's money is like a playground, especially when there's as much of it to manage as CalPot offers. And as stressful as my job should be, it never really is. My work has been an outlet, something to relieve whatever challenges I have at home. Something I'm good at and always get right. In parenthood, especially with our circumstances, I've often felt like I was failing. Not for want of trying, but just not having all the answers or ways to make things better.

But things *are* better.

My sons are in a good place, generally, besides the usual speed bumps. Tremaine is happy, which is really important to me.

But what about *me*?

I hadn't thought much about being happy for years. It felt like a luxury, something I'd never get for myself. I've been thinking about it lately, though. Possibilities have flooded my mind since the last time I saw Soledad—what-ifs I never entertained teasing the back of my consciousness.

What could we be together?

Happy? Deliriously content?

I take a few bites of the sandwich and a sip of the beer, work for a few minutes on the spreadsheet, but finally push away from the desk, unable to focus.

I want to see her.

She said I could call, but I haven't. Her sister was visiting. She was spending time with her girls. I was with my boys and my parents. I reach for my phone, staring at the dark screen for a few seconds before tossing it onto the desk. Leaning back in my chair, I crack the door open for the memory of that night in the shed. How she felt in my arms, how she smelled, the sounds she made, the way she screamed my name the second time she came.

"Shit." I run an agitated hand over the back of my neck and just barely stop myself from taking my dick out right here in the office. "I should go for a run."

I've stood and headed off to change into running clothes when the buzz of my phone from the office catches me at the bottom of the stairs.

I head back to the office and flip the phone over, almost dropping it when Soledad's name flashes on-screen.

"Sol," I say, forcing myself to sound normal. "Hey, happy New Year."

"Hey," she replies. "Yeah, happy New Year."

I frown, hearing the catch in her voice. "You okay?"

"Um, not really." She laughs, but it's high and false. "Could I... Are the boys there?"

"No, they're with Tremaine for the next couple of days. We just got back this morning, and they basically went straight to her place. She missed them."

"Oh, so are you... Could I come over?"

"Sure." I pause for a breath in case that came out too eager. "Yeah. I'm here."

"Do you mind if I pull into your garage? I don't want rumors or gossip... The girls—"

"No problem. Let me know when you're outside and I'll open it."

She chuckles. "I'm outside."

As soon as she enters my kitchen from the garage, I know something's off. Her eyes are like bruises against the honey gold of her face. Her hair is always wavy, but it riots in tousled tangles like she's been shoving her fingers through it. I take her coat, and when she hands it to me, I'm momentarily distracted by the black dress hugging the cursive shape of her petite form. It's a modest dress that covers her with its high neck and the long sleeves that gather at her wrists, but Soledad doesn't have a modest body. It's bold in the flare of her hips and the tight swell of her thighs, juxtaposed against the exaggerated jut of her ass. When I'm able to tear my eyes away from her figure to meet her gaze, she's watching me watching her.

"Uh, sorry." I turn to hang her coat in the mudroom. "So what's up?"

"I probably shouldn't have come." She walks over to the counter and takes one of the high stools, covering her eyes with shaking hands and pushing the hair out of her face. "But Hendrix is still in Charlotte. Yas and Josiah took a trip to the mountains."

"You don't have to explain why I was your last resort," I say with wry amusement. "It's fine."

"You were actually the first person I thought of," she says, narrowing her eyes on my face. "You wear glasses?"

"Oh." I take them off and rub my eyes, setting them on the counter. "Just for work. Reading."

"I like them."

I slip a finger under her chin, turning her face up to me. I've been good, but good is gone when she looks at me with the same desire I've tried to ignore since the last time she was here. I lower my head for a kiss. It doesn't occur to me to ease in or start slow. I tug her jaw open and dive in, licking inside and tasting the raw reply of her hunger. She grips my shoulders, tugging me to step into the V of her thighs. I shove the dress up so I can get closer, baring the firm lengths of her legs and stepping between. She strains up, stretching to wrap her arms around my neck. I break contact with her mouth to dust kisses along her hairline and across her cheeks, but pause when my lips encounter wetness.

I pull back, peering down at her face. "Sol, are you crying?"

She clenches her eyes shut and shakes her head, tears slipping from beneath her long lashes. "No."

"Hey." I gently scrub my thumbs under her eyes, swiping at the tears. "Tell me what's up."

"Way to shatter the mood, Sol," she says, rolling her eyes and dropping her arms from around my neck. "I'm sorry. I thought I could... forget for a while, but it's not working."

"Forget what?"

"Edward."

His name drops into the conversation like an icicle. I step back and shove my hands into my pockets, leaning against the counter and fixing my gaze on the hardwood floor of my kitchen. When she's in my arms, in my house, with me, for her to be crying over that piece of shit? It lights a new fire in me, one I'm not sure I've experienced before. There is a bright blue flame at its center, and I think this must be what jealousy feels like.

"That came out wrong," Soledad says when I don't respond but stand stiff and taut. "I wasn't thinking of him when we... I mean, I was, but not—"

"If you could just say what you mean because this is making me... I don't like feeling this way, Sol."

"What way?"

"Like punching a hole through a wall because you're kissing me and thinking about him," I admit through gritted teeth.

She gets off the stool and walks over to stand in front of me, linking her fingers with mine.

"We went to see Edward in prison today," she says, her voice subdued but her eyes connecting with mine, hiding nothing. "The girls asked if they could."

"Shit. I'm sorry." I rest my palm flat against the base of her spine and draw her closer, surrendering to her heat and the enticing scent of jasmine.

"The visit itself was fine, I guess." She shrugs, bites her lip, and tucks a wavy lock of hair behind her ear.

"What happened?"

"When we were leaving..." She closes her eyes and releases a stilted breath. "I saw Amber."

"She was visiting Edward too?" I ask, my brows going sky high at this plot-thickening detail.

"She had a baby, Judah." She blinks wet lashes up at me. "Edward's baby."

"The fuck?" I mutter, completely nonplussed. "Are you sure?"

"I confronted her about it, and she admitted it, so yeah. I'm sure." She drops her head to my chest, muffling her next words with my shirt. "But I would've known. The baby has Lupe's eyes. Edward's eyes."

My muscles tense with rage on her behalf. "I'm sorry. Did your daughters see?"

"No. I'll have to tell them eventually, of course, but I spotted her in the parking lot when we were getting in the car. A secret baby with his secretary? What a fucking cliché."

"If he hadn't gotten caught, there's no telling how long he would have maintained the lie."

"Oh, I think at least part of it would have collapsed." She laughs humorlessly, her gaze trained on her ankle boots. "He would have eventually left me."

"Why would you think that? Because of Amber?" I shake my head. "He had to recognize what he had in you, Sol. He was a fool, but he was always bragging about his beautiful wife and how she was such an asset. Threw the best parties, hosted clients better than anyone. He wasn't trading that for a side piece."

"But he had a shinier, newer model." She bites her lip. "Eventually he would have left. I'm just glad I saw him for what he was."

"So what did she say when you confronted her?"

"She just insisted she wasn't a home-wrecker, which is true. Our home was already wrecked. I just didn't want to face it because that would have capsized my entire existence." Soledad looks up at me and offers a one-sided grin. "I was so afraid of losing a life that wasn't serving me well just because I wasn't sure what else there was. I should thank Amber, if I'm being honest."

"For real?"

"For real, because now she has to put up with him for at least another eighteen years. Besides whatever limited contact he has with the girls," she says, her shrug philosophical, "I'll be free of him."

"You seem to be coming to terms with this."

"I think I'm still processing. I'm shocked and angry, but it also gave me perspective. I didn't escape a bad marriage and an awful husband just to go through life half-living. I want more than what I have now. In a few months, Edward will walk out of prison a free man. He finally got his boy. He'll have everything he wanted, and I have taken so little for myself."

I stiffen. "Is that why you came here today? To take something for yourself?"

"What would you think if I said yes?"

Though everything in me screams that I should take her upstairs before she changes her mind, I pause and consider. I've wanted Soledad for a long time. I've invested in getting to know her, in understanding what motivates her, and this isn't like her. I won't toss all of that away for a quick fuck, though my persistent erection thinks that's exactly what we should do.

"I'm not sure how I feel about being your revenge sex, Sol," I tell her.

"You're not. This was spurred by the realization that Edward gets what he wants, and I don't, but reducing my story to revenge makes it about *him*. His betrayal was a catalyst, yeah. It was a spark that set fire to an unsatisfying existence. I had silenced the woman screaming inside of me so much, I didn't even realize just how unsatisfied she was. *I* was. This life, this adventure I'm on—I'm orchestrating. Edward is a footnote written in afterthought ink."

"What about self-partnering and dating yourself?"

"I'm still on a solo journey," she says, her eyes meeting mine frankly. "That doesn't mean I can't have something that is strictly for my pleasure. For our pleasure, if you'll accept my conditions."

"Which are?"

"This is a one-time offer. If I want to do it again, I'll ask you again."

"And what if I want to do it again? Are you the only one who gets what they want out of this?"

"I thought you wanted me."

"You know I do."

"Then what's the problem?"

What if I want more?

I don't say it, but I know by the veil she pulls over her expression that my thought reverberates in the room all around us. It's not what she wants tonight—to discuss the deeper waters we may wade into if we take this step. She's fooling herself if she thinks anything we do together will stay shallow. She's clinging to an illusion of control, and I think that's what she needs to do after what Edward has put her through. It's just an illusion, though. I know what control feels like. I've pursued it, insisted on it whenever I could. This is its opposite. This is free fall. It's careening into a glorious unknown. It's running full speed ahead into a burning promise.

It's a risk, and not even a calculated one because how do I know Soledad will ever be ready for the kind of relationship I want with her? How long could I do this? Want her as a partner while she only wants to partner herself?

But she does want to fuck you.

It's a dangerous whisper, one I try to ignore, but it scratches my ears and whirs inside my mind. Our fingers are still linked, and her head is bent. There's tension to the slight curve of her shoulders, as if she's braced for something.

Rejection?

After the day she's had, that's the last thing she needs from me. And maybe this is serendipitous. Before she arrived, wasn't I thinking about how I've put everyone's happiness ahead of my own? And I don't resent that, but I've decided I want some happiness for myself.

And she may still be figuring out exactly what she wants, but I'm absolutely sure. I want a future with her. It would be complicated. I have a complex situation with my boys and an unconventional setup with my ex. Soledad has...all that shit Edward has done. Her daughters probably hate me and think I put their father in prison. There are obstacles, but with Soledad standing so close, warm and soft and willing and wanting me, none of them feels more important than this moment.

I capture her stare, searching for uncertainty or reluctance and finding none.

"You're sure about this, Sol?" I ask because I have to be certain.

"I know what I want," she says, the delicate line of her jaw tense and tight.

I take both her hands in mine and drop a kiss at her temple.

"Then let's go upstairs."

CHAPTER THIRTY-FOUR

∞

SOLEDAD

Sometimes when I'm nervous, I say weird things.

"I reviewed a dupe for that comforter last week."

Judah stands beside his bed with its slate-gray duvet and tilts his head to consider me. "What exactly is a dupe?"

"Oh, um...a duplicate. Like a cheaper version of the real thing." A breathy laugh slips out. "It wasn't as good as this one. You made the right choice."

A smile cracks Judah's serious expression, and he slides his hands into the pockets of his dark jeans. He's wearing an MIT sweatshirt.

"MIT," I prattle on. "Very prestigious."

"So is Cornell."

"True." Excitement and nerves have apparently atrophied my brain. I gulp and lick dry lips.

Dry lips?

Oh, my God.

Where is my lip balm? I'm having sex with someone who is not Edward for the first time in nearly twenty years, and I have chapped lips.

"I think I left my purse downstairs," I say, my voice emerging high and strained. "I need my lip balm...um...my purse. I'll be right back."

He grabs my hand before I reach the door and turns me to face him. He frames my face with big, gentle hands and dips to my height, holding my eyes with his. "We don't have to do this."

"What?" I cover his hands with mine, blinking at stupid tears. "But I want to."

He breathes out a shallow laugh. "Are you sure? Because I haven't done this in a long time, but I don't remember conversations about comforters and lip balm as foreplay."

"Then I guess you weren't doing it right." I smile into the warmth of his palm. "I'm sorry. I'm nervous. I haven't been with anyone except Edward since college, and for the last two years our sex life was almost nonexistent."

"You know I haven't been with anyone other than Tremaine since college, and we've been divorced almost four years."

He towers over me, strong and virile, and my curiosity overtakes my nervousness. "How did you do it? Abstain for four years?"

"I told you I'm not into casual sex. I know that's unusual, but—"

"Do you masturbate a lot?" The words shoot out of my mouth like bullets from a misfiring rifle. "Oh. I'm sorry. I didn't mean..."

I close my eyes, mortified, but let out a sigh of relief when I see him grinning.

"Well, do you?" I ask again, grinning back.

"When I need to. I run more, though lately..." He gives me an assessing look and then a *what the hell* shrug of his wide shoulders. "Since I met you, I would say the rate has probably tripled."

"You mean running?" I tease.

One of his hands slides from my cheek to splay across my throat and tip my chin back until I meet the molten want in his otherwise inscrutable expression. "No, the other one."

"I think about you when I touch myself," I confess.

He goes impossibly still, like a statue burning from the ground up with all the heat gathering in his eyes.

"How long have you been doing that?" he asks, and the studied evenness of his tone is as telling as if he had roared the words.

I drop my head, and his fingers spear into the hair at my nape. "The first time was a few days after we met, after the Christmas party." I bite my lip, blowing out a sharp exhalation. "I felt so guilty. I didn't mean to. I had never thought of another man that way."

"Tell me." He leaves one hand at my throat and slides the other to my back, a caress in long strokes that burn through the material of my dress.

A harsh laugh grates my throat, and I swallow the hurt that's not quite healed. "The night you and I met, Edward and I argued before coming to the party because we hadn't had sex in two months. He knew how much I . . ."

I falter, unsure how this man, so disciplined and controlled, will respond to the truth about me.

"He knew how much you . . . what?" Judah asks, pushing the hair away from my throat and rolling his thumb over the sensitive skin there.

"He knows I have a high sex drive," I say in a rush, not meeting his eyes.

His thumb at my throat pauses for a second but then resumes the caress that is sending sparks over my collarbones and across my chest. I watch as my nipples peak and pebble beneath the thin wool of my dress.

"Take off your clothes."

His words, hard and flat, yet with a sudden urgency bubbling beneath them, stall me.

"What?" I blink up at him.

"Whatever this thing is you were telling me, this Edward thing, I don't give a fuck." He runs his hands over my stomach and over my hips, my ass. "Do you want me to do it? How do I get this off of you?"

"Um, there's a zipper at the—"

Shock strangles the words as he turns me around abruptly and tugs the zipper at the top of my neck, dragging it down with swift decisiveness to the base of my spine. He peels the sleeves down over my shoulders until the bodice pools around my waist.

He shoves the dainty straps of my bra away with his lips. "God, your skin, Sol."

He rakes my hair aside and blesses the back of my neck with

open-mouthed kisses, hot and worshipful. He sucks the curve of my shoulder, unhooks the bra at my back. The lacy cups slump forward, falling to the floor and leaving my breasts bare in the cool air. They're not uncovered for long because he reaches around, cupping them in his hands, rubbing and tugging the nipples with firm, sure fingers.

"Oh." I go limp against him, the sensitive skin of my naked back prickling against the softness of his sweatshirt. "I had no idea how sensitive my breasts were until—"

"You said you'd never come from just that," he whispers into the curve of my neck, never letting up on the peaks in his palms hardening, begging for his attention. For more. "Let's find all the other ways we can make you come."

His hands leave my breasts and I almost weep at the loss, but he *doesn't* leave me. He pushes the dress over my hips, over my ass, and down my thighs.

"Soledad," he rasps behind me. "If I had known you were wearing this thong, we'd already be fucking on my kitchen table. There's no way I could have waited."

I'd forgotten. The dress fits so closely, and I hadn't wanted panty lines. I'm forming the words to explain, but I yelp at the wet heat of his mouth on the curve of my ass.

"Judah!"

I twist my head to peer at him over my shoulder, and my knees go completely weak. He's kneeling, eyes squeezed shut, mouth open on one generous globe of my butt. He rains kisses over it, licks the curve, coaxes the strip of silk down until it slides around my ankles, joining the dress and bra in a silky heap at my feet.

"Fuck, fuck, fuck," he mumbles, squeezing my butt, sucking it, licking it. "This ass."

His hand disappears between my legs.

"Ahhh!" I gasp when two big fingers slip over my clit, rubbing me and exploring my pussy freely. I can't even be embarrassed at the sounds in the quiet room, the sounds of my sloppy wet pussy as he strokes me. His fingers leave me for a moment, and when I peer at him over my shoulder again, both fingers are in his mouth.

"You taste..." He stands, coming around to face me, bending to put his shoulder at my waist and lifting. I'm in the air before I even know what's happening, dangling over his back.

"Judah!" I half laugh, half protest. "Put me down."

He drops me onto the bed, and I bounce a little, which makes me giggle. I sound like a giddy virgin. I feel like one, instead of the forty-year-old mother of three who has done this half my life.

"You, Soledad Charles," he says, standing between my knees at the foot of the bed, famished eyes roving over my naked body, "are fantastic."

I let my eyes run down the length of my body, and I can't help but notice the imperfections. All the ways I'm *not* fantastic. The stretch marks from three kids. A bit of a mommy pouch that no amount of ab work will make go away. The skin around my belly button, a little looser than the rest, that only a scalpel would dispatch.

None of it seems to matter to Judah, who kneels at the foot of the bed to unzip one sharp-toed ankle boot and then the other. He kisses the arch of my foot, licks up my calf, sucks the inner skin of my thigh until he reaches the core of me.

"I've waited for this." His voice goes even deeper and rougher than usual. I meet his lust-drugged eyes over the tiny tuft of hair—

HAIR!

Dear God, no.

"Um, Judah." I squeeze my knees together. "I haven't done this in a long time, ya know?"

"I know." He nudges my knees an inch apart. "And it's been a lot longer for me."

"Uh-huh." I snap my knees back together. "I just...but I...the thing is I didn't know this was happening."

He coaxes my knees apart, hope in the eyes that meet mine again. "But now it is, right?"

"Yes, but I didn't...I haven't waxed." I slide my eyes away from him, flick them up to the tray ceiling.

"I want you however you come."

My eyes zip back to his. My breath hitches, and a hot lump swells in my throat. I try to swallow but can't, and a little whimper escapes my lips.

"Spread your legs for me, sweetheart," he says, running a palm up and down my calf. "I would hack through a forest to get to this pussy, and I've waited long enough."

As soon as I open, he drags me to the edge of the bed, until my ass is almost hanging off, and takes my legs over his shoulders. His fingers peel me back and then his mouth is on me. He groans, grunts, slurps. He bites, sucks, invades. It is thorough, like Judah is in all things. There is not an inch of me left dry when he's done. I'm dripping, screaming, straining to get away because it feels unbearably good, but he holds me in place and eats me out until I come so hard the blood pounds in my ears and my clit throbs. This orgasm hits my system hard, and I'm so drunk on it, I'm barely lucid. He licks at the slickness between my legs, his hunger building again as he bends my knees up so my heels hang at the edge of the bed. I'm delirious, so limp and half out of my mind, I barely think about how exposed I am. The cool air on the hot, wet strip of flesh revives me long enough to see him, rubbing the insides of my thighs and dipping his head to start all over.

"I can't, Judah," I moan. "Not again."

And yet I grip his head with both hands, pull him to the center of my body, begging for his lips, his teeth, his lust. There is a bottomless well of need inside me, and he keeps pouring and pouring until miraculously I start feeling full.

When I come again, he stands beside the bed and strips his clothes off with quick efficiency. I crack my eyes open to watch him and lift up on one elbow.

"You're the fantastic one," I say, my voice cracked and hoarse from screaming his name, alternately begging for mercy and for more.

He is long, sinewy lines and ripples of well-conditioned muscles. He has a runner's body, but bulkier at the biceps and thighs than I would expect. His shoulders and back are a landscape of sculpted male beauty.

And his dick.

It juts proudly erect from a stack of ridged abs. I swallow, not nervous because I've had three kids. I know I can take him, but it's been so long since anyone was up in there. So long since I had the intimacy of a naked man staring at me the way Judah stares at me now. I would love to gape at him for a few minutes.

He has other ideas.

He reaches into the nightstand and pulls out a condom, making quick work of opening it and sheathing himself.

"For someone who hasn't done this in four years," I say, grinning up at him, "you sure are prepared. Exactly how old are those condoms?"

"When was the Harvest Festival?" He climbs onto the bed wearing nothing but a condom and a smile. "I bought them that night on the way home."

"Cocky," I say, reaching to wrap my hand around his dick.

"Hopeful," he chokes out, the smile dropping from his face. "You do know it's been four years. You do much of that, and this won't last long."

I open my legs and nudge his hip, inviting him to come to me.

"Four years, huh?" I wrap my legs around him, hooking my ankles at the base of his spine. "I hope it's worth the wait."

I push up at the same moment he thrusts down, and we both go completely still. The first thing I note is how incredibly right it feels, like someone molded me to his proportions. Then I notice that inside this deep pleasure, there is the slightest bit of discomfort.

"Sorry," he mutters into my neck. "It's tight."

I freeze. Edward's taunting words walk the corridors of my mind, blow through the chambers of my heart.

Things get loose down there.

"What did you say?" I ask, breathing through the discomfort and the shock of pleasure that is not only physical but the bliss of healing.

"It's just a little tight." He raises his head to look at me, concern in his eyes. "You okay? Do we need to—"

"Don't stop." I explore his back with wandering hands, roam down to the firm curve of his ass, and press him deeper into me. "It feels good."

He drops his head again, burying it in the curve of my neck, dipping and taking a nipple into the seeking heat of his mouth. "I don't want to hurt you, but I want to fuck you hard, Sol."

An electric shock zips up my spine, and I tighten my legs around him.

"As hard as you want," I whisper into his ear, wrapping my arms around his shoulders to brace myself. "I can take it."

Bold words because this man tests me, hooking an elbow under my knee and sliding in by slow inches, blunt, hard, heavy. The impact whooshes air from my lungs. He doesn't pause but finds a spot I didn't know existed and strokes it over and over and over. He never breaks pace, never loses momentum, never lets up.

"This pussy is so good, Sol," he groans, flipping me over to my hands and knees, knocking my legs apart. He wraps the length of my hair around one hand and grips my hip with the other, anchoring me in place before he drives back in. "You okay?"

Okay?

Is that weak word supposed to describe how it feels to receive the unrelenting, pounding worship of a man twice my size, but who makes me feel absolutely in charge one second and then completely subbed, bottomed out the next? He puts me how he wants me, turning me onto my side, lifting my leg and taking me with my knee resting on his.

I have no idea how long it goes, but I know I've never been fucked like this. We are soaked with each other's sweat, and my legs are shaking by the time he flips me to my back again, pulls my legs flat against his chest, ankles on his shoulders, and pushes into me.

"I want to see your face," he says, a gentle hand coaxing my damp hair back. He reaches between us and strokes me, slowly at first, then quickening the pace as my expression crumples with new pleasure. In this position, the penetration is so deep, I come with a crash, screaming so loud I feel the veins straining in my neck.

"Sol!" My name is torn from him, and he stills, trembling over me, his eyes clenched shut, his powerful body taut and somehow vulnerable even in its strength.

I know we've both been married before. This wasn't the first time for either of us, but something broke through inside me, and I think in him too. The clues are in the kisses he drops into my hair. The soft words of praise he leaves along my collarbone, the undersides of my breasts, my rib cage, like even though we are done, he can't stop loving on me. He looks into my eyes and I can't help but think he feels it too. It's a shoot bursting through fallow ground, and as I fall asleep in the cradle of his strong arms, I recognize that it may have just begun to grow, and it may still be tender, but it's already fierce.

CHAPTER THIRTY-FIVE

JUDAH

I know I have to let her go, but dammit, how?

Not just let Soledad leave my house. Of course she has to return to her girls. Aaron will probably only last another night at Tremaine's before he packs his bag and stands at the door. He's been known to sit in the back seat of the car, waiting for them to bring him home. So I have to get back to my life, to my responsibilities, to my boys too. I don't mean how will I let her leave tonight, but what will I do if this is it? She said one night.

The hell.

One night? With her? Impossible. But I don't know how to ask for more without derailing what she's trying to do for herself now. I don't want her self-partnering anymore. *I* want to be her partner. I want to be the one she leans on and for her to be whom I lean on in return. I want us to sort the tangled fibers of our lives, to knock down the barriers to being together. I want her to be whole.

I just want to be whole with her.

How do you fix something that doesn't feel broken? Because her in my bed, naked, with her hair flowing all over my pillow, feels right. And however I can have this, I will. I already know I'll take this however I can get it. However she will give it.

It's getting late, and a sense of unease starts to creep in. I should wake her. Her kids are fine at home by themselves. She said they stay home alone often, but still. It's been a rough day for them. Seeing their dad in prison has to have been hard. I glance at my watch on the nightstand. This woman tipped my whole world on its axis, and she has been here less than two hours.

"Maybe she can stay a little longer," I mumble, sliding back under the covers and reaching for her. She's petite... but the ass, the hips, the legs—perfectly thick. The sheet falls away, and I caress the velvety mole in the center of her spine, like a drop of midnight on a gold shore of smooth back and shoulders.

"Damn," I groan into her neck, unable to resist rolling her over, kissing down between her breasts and taking one berry-colored tip into my mouth. "Shit."

"You're a very profane lover," Soledad grumbles, gripping both sides of my head and running her hand over my face. "But I like it."

"You do?" I release her breast with a pop, grinning up at her. "So you'll keep me?"

The laughter slowly fades, and she runs her thumb across my brows, down my jaw, and over my lips. "We'll see. That was a test drive."

"Then let's take another ride." I rise up on my knees and grab her by the thighs, crawling between her legs, only to start tickling her ribs.

"Judah!" she gasps, rolling away from my fingers. "Stop! I can't take it."

"I see that."

I laugh, sitting with my back against the headboard and pulling her up to straddle me and then closer for a kiss. The kiss starts playful but heats and boils over until she's rolling her hips over my hardening erection. We're lost in each other again, but some distant sound breaks the flow of the kiss.

"Oh, shoot!" Soledad rolls away, leaving my arms and bed empty. She grabs my sweatshirt, scrambling to push her arms and head through it. "That's my phone. We're supposed to be doing a vision board party tonight."

She rushes out, and her footsteps thud down the stairs. I pull on my jeans, not bothering with a shirt, and follow.

"Yeah, honey. I know," Soledad says, the phone at her ear, her hip propped against the kitchen counter. "But could you just calm down? Tell Inez I said to give your sweater back. I'll work on the stain when I get home, and you should be fine for pictures this week."

She shoots me an exasperated look and rolls her eyes, one bare foot crossed over the other.

"Lupe, if I got blood out of our white sofa, ice cream on your sweater is child's play."

I come to stand beside her at the counter, taking her free hand and twining our fingers. I turn her hand over, frowning at an angry scar streaking across her palm like a bolt of lightning.

"You want Indian?" she asks. "Call it in to Saffron's. Yeah, the one on the square. Order me butter chicken. I'll pick it up on my way in. Gimme...I don't know. Thirty minutes? Okay. No more fighting. I'll be home soon. Yes, vision board party is still happening, but tell Inez Backstreet Boys is back on the table after this foolishness. Love you too."

She disconnects and glances at our entwined fingers, a tentative smile on her bare lips. The lipstick is long gone. Her hair is in complete disarray. She's outwardly discomposed, and that's how I feel—like a storm blew through and disheveled my mind, my will, my emotions. Sex with this woman overturned my soul, spilling all the contents, and she stands here calmly talking about ice cream stains and takeout.

"I have to go." She carefully extricates her fingers from mine. I recapture her hand and turn the palm over.

"What happened here?" I ask, tracing the long scar.

Her face clouds. She pulls her hand away and runs it through the hair curling around her shoulders. "Long story."

"And you only have thirty minutes." I walk over to the refrigerator to grab a beer.

"You know I have to get home to my girls." She frowns and heads for the stairs. "You understand, right?"

I take a deep breath and a gulp of my beer before following her upstairs. By the time I reach the bedroom, she's already wearing her underwear and bra and is on her knees looking under my bed.

"The other boot's behind you," I say, my arms folded over my chest, the neck of the beer bottle trapped between two fingers.

"What?" She looks over her shoulder, ass in the air, reminiscent of one of several positions I had her in.

I had *her*? This woman had *me*. Owned me between her legs. She must know that.

"If you're looking for the other shoe, it's behind you," I reply, clenching my teeth tighter with every piece of clothing she puts on, with every minute that goes by, taking her closer to walking out of here like this was some kind of one-night stand—like I'm her fuck buddy, not the man who has been falling in love with her incrementally since the moment we met.

And now I'm too far gone. The intimacy we shared pushed me over the edge into something I've never felt before. I knew what this was, though. Soledad told me it was one night. She told me she needs to be alone right now. She didn't lead me on, but frustration seethes under my skin as I watch her struggle with the zipper of her dress.

"Here, let me." I step behind her to drag the zipper up the last few inches. Her hair falls in thick waves to the middle of her back, and I bury my face in the fragrant cloud of it, breathing in the scent of jasmine oil and the traces of us that still cling to her skin.

"I gotta go." She turns to face me. "You know how it is."

"Yeah, I know how it is." Even I hear the tension in my words, but I keep my gaze on the floor when I feel her eyes on me.

"Are you mad at me?" she asks, her brows bunched into a frown. "I would stay if I could."

"Is that true?" I meet her gaze before it skitters away again. "Because it feels like even if they weren't fighting, even if there wasn't a stain or pictures, or takeout, you would find some reason to run from this."

"No." She bends to retrieve her other boot, sits on the side of my bed, and slips it onto her bare foot, but leaves it unzipped at the ankle. "I'm not running. I'm just sticking to what we said. One time and..."

She stops, scooting on the bed closer to the nightstand and opening the drawer wider. There's a really big box of condoms in there. I don't want her to think I planned some kind of orgy.

"This was the only box they had," I explain, closing the drawer quickly. "I wasn't—"

"You're reading *All About Love*?" she asks, her voice soft, her eyes trained on the drawer I slammed shut.

"Um...yeah."

"So am I."

"Right." I tilt my head, frowning at her. "Why do you think I'm reading it?"

I could tell her I've come to understand showing interest is part of how *she* shows love, and that I wondered if that's how she receives it. I could tell her everything that interests her interests me because it's a clue to how I can reach her, how I can love her the way she deserves, but she already seems a little freaked out by the book, so I hold that back.

She releases a shaky breath, burying her face in her hands and propping her elbows on her knees.

"Shit, shit, shit," she chants, the words muffled against her palms.

I sit beside her and pry her hands away. "Sweetheart, what's wrong?"

"This is not how it's supposed to be," she says, her voice wobbling. "I'm supposed to be able to fuck and go. I'm on a solo journey. It's just the first sex since my divorce. It's not supposed to feel like..."

She bites her lip, cutting herself off.

"Not supposed to feel like what?" I ask, holding my breath, silently urging her to articulate what sang between us like a tuning fork when I was inside her.

"Like I went to outer space." She closes her eyes, biting into the quiver of her bottom lip. "Like I discovered a new planet. Like I walked on air."

All the tension I've held in my muscles since I realized she was going to leave without acknowledging just how epic the lovemaking was drains from me, and my shoulders slump. I take her chin between my fingers and turn her head so we're looking at each other, our faces only inches apart.

"Does it make it better to know it was the same for me?" I ask.

"Not really, no. I'm... I'm scared, Judah. I can't do this again yet. I'm not ready. I shouldn't have—"

"I won't rush you." I brush my thumb over her cheekbone. "But I told you sex isn't casual to me, so when it felt like this was something you could brush off—"

"It's not." She takes my hand and kisses my knuckle. "It's definitely not, but that doesn't mean I'm ready for a relationship. This can be special and also something I'm not ready to take any further."

"I respect that. Does that mean we won't do it again?"

I went four years without sex, but I didn't know about *her*. Now I do, and I'm not sure I can go four *days* without this.

"I don't know." She swipes both hands over her face. "Can we take it one day at a time?"

"Yes, of course." I kiss her forehead and bend to zip her other boot. "Now you better go get dinner from Saffron's."

"You're right." She stands and hesitates at the table by my bed, then opens it, staring down at the gigantic box of condoms and the shiny red copy of *All About Love*. "Did you finish the book?"

I nod, taking it out and handing it to her. Little Post-its feather as she flips the pages and pauses to read things I scribbled in the margins. Remembering some of the notes I made, I want to grab it back, but I restrain myself and let her look. She pauses in chapter four where her name appears, the tip of her finger caressing the line where I highlighted and circled *soledad hermosa*. She pulls out a pink slip of paper I was using as a bookmark. Shit. It's that damn grocery list of hers from months ago that I found in my wallet and couldn't make myself throw away. If she thought I was a stalker before...

She doesn't comment but rubs the pink slip of paper between her fingers before slipping it back into the pages and placing the book into the open drawer.

"Am I allowed to ask when we'll see each other again?" I smooth all expression from my face, not wanting to project anything that will make her feel guilty or obligated, but I do want to know.

"Call me." She folds my sweatshirt neatly and places it on the bench at the foot of the bed.

"Sounds good." I follow her out of the room and down the stairs. When she enters the garage and opens her car door, she whirls back to me and grins, unruly waves fanning out around her.

"You really thought you were gonna make up for lost time with that huge box of Costco condoms, huh?"

I laugh and flash her a middle finger. "Get out of my house and don't come back."

"You don't mean that." She pokes out her tongue, climbs in, starts the car. She drives down my driveway, and a hollowness settles in my chest as soon as she's out of sight.

"No," I tell the empty garage. "I don't mean that at all."

CHAPTER THIRTY-SIX

∞

SOLEDAD

I have a bruised poontang thanks to you."

I snort laughing at Hendrix's outrageous—and incidentally accurate—statement.

"They're called pole kisses," I say, grinning at her and Yasmen over my menu. "We'll all have them in unusual places tomorrow, but they say it's hardest the first time."

I lay my menu down and smile at Cassie, Grits's head chef, as she approaches our table.

"Have you ladies decided what you're having?" Cassie asks, setting down a basket that is half corn muffins and half biscuits.

"To what do we owe this honor?" Hendrix smiles up at her. "Not every day the chef herself comes to take our order."

"Heard the boss was out here with her girls." Cassie nods to Yasmen, her face smooth and unlined beneath the pristine white scarf covering her honey-blond locs. "Wanted to take care of you ladies personally. Any questions about the menu?"

"Yeah, why does everything look so good?" I scan all the high-fat, hearty-helpings items. "I just worked out, but that loaded mac 'n' cheese...hmmm. At least those ribs aren't on the menu anymore to tempt me."

"You can still get 'em at the Grits in Charlotte," Hendrix says, sliding Yasmen a sly look. "I swung by there when I went to see Mama last month. Vashti's recipe is still bringing folks in by droves."

Yasmen offers a wry look at Hendrix's subtle dig about their attractive employee who transferred from Atlanta to their North Carolina location.

"It's not the ribs I'm glad are gone." Yasmen smirks. "It's the woman who makes them. Let the good people of Charlotte enjoy them ribs. We good over here."

And that's all we'll say about that.

"I'll have the turkey wings." Hendrix closes her menu with a decisive snap. "Fried green tomatoes and corn off the cob."

"The usual shrimp and grits for me," Yasmen says, handing her menu to Cassie. "If it ain't broke."

"Let's go with the catfish." I give a quick glance at the sides. "Rice and gravy, green beans."

"Sounds good," Cassie says, giving me a wink. "And I'll bring some of Soledad's pear preserves out for your biscuits."

I grin at her comment, sharing a smile with Yasmen over that small, but consistent, contribution to my monthly income. A few Atlanta-area restaurants carry Sol's Secret Preserves now. It's still in relatively small batches, but every little bit helps.

"I just wanted to give pole a try." I pick up where we left off. "A few tries, actually, before I commit to installing one in my she shed. So thank you for indulging me and venturing out."

"I don't think it's for me," Hendrix says. "If I'm hanging upside down, some man better have me in his red room."

"I'm not sure I'm down either, Sol," Yasmen agrees. "You might be on your own for this one."

"That's fine," I say. "I may not even end up installing the pole, but it does seem like a fun way to stay in shape, and I've been pushing myself to try new things."

"How's the she shed coming?" Hendrix asks.

"Have you not been watching my live updates?" I feign affront. "And you're supposed to be my manager."

"Oh, I am your manager, little girl." Hendrix gives me a secretive look. "I got some things up my sleeve for you."

"What things?" Yasmen asks, munching on a muffin.

"In due time," Hendrix replies cryptically. "It's in the oven. I'm not pulling out till it's done."

"There's some sophomoric humor to be had in that statement," I laugh. "But I'm taking the higher, more mature road."

"Speaking of the high road," Yasmen says, sobering, "which you definitely took by not punching Amber in the face, have you thought any more about when you'll tell the girls they have a little brother?"

I crumble a biscuit onto my plate. "I'm just gonna hold for now. Why should I have to tell them all the hard shit?"

"That's right," Hendrix says. "Let Edward deal with it when he gets out. You just keep working that pole."

I laugh, raising my water for a toast. "Here's to working the pole like rent is due, even though I'm making no money from my efforts."

They take me up on my toast, but Hendrix grimaces. "If my pussy hurts, I want at least three orgasms to show for it."

I choke a little, sputtering at the mention of multiple orgasms, but compose my features. I told Hendrix and Yasmen about the trip to the prison and about Amber's little bundle of joy, but didn't mention the world-rocking sex I had with Judah. They do usually offer great advice, and after the way I ran from Judah's house like I was being chased, maybe I could use it.

"So, I may have…Ahem," I say, pulling the silverware from its napkin blanket. "I may have had a little sex with Judah."

My announcement is met with two sets of shocked eyes and dropped jaws.

"You sneaky heifer," Hendrix laughs, giving me a congratulatory fist pound. "When?"

"New Year's Day," I confess.

"And you're just now telling us?" Yasmen asks.

"That was only like three days ago," I remind her.

"You gotta tell us this stuff immediately," Hendrix says. "We're in a drought and celebrate any rain in the forecast. At least one of us is getting some."

"Um, excuse me." Yasmen raises her hand. "To quote *Brown Sugar*, I get it on the regular and the shit is the bomb."

"Yeah, but you're married." Hendrix waves a dismissive hand. "To one guy. Twice. Booooooring."

We all laugh at her joke, but when the humor fades, Yasmen narrows her eyes knowingly on my face.

"So tell us what happened between *Oh, my gosh, my inmate husband has a secret baby* and *I smashed the man who put him in prison*," Yasmen says, resting her chin on her folded hands. "This is some *Days of Our Lives* shit."

"Now that's a show I miss," Hendrix says. "My grandmother used to watch her stories every day when we stayed with her over the summer."

"Same!" I say. "*General Hospital* with Grammy and all my *abuela's* telenovelas."

"Focus." Yasmen claps thrice and bends a semistern look on Hendrix and me. "Now, one of our own got her back broke by a handsome accountant, and I want all the details before mommy curfew kicks in and I have to leave to check homework and make lunches for tomorrow."

"Right." Hendrix sips her water. "Priorities. Spill, Sol."

"Well, I was distraught after seeing Amber," I tell them.

"And you said, *I know what'll make me feel better*," Hendrix says, imitating my higher-pitched voice. "*Judah's dick.*"

"Hen!" Yasmen's lips twitch. "Let her tell it."

I don't want to laugh, but they make it so hard—and everything so much better—a chuckle does spill out before I resume my tale of tail.

"Well it was actually your fault, Hen," I admonish. "You and Lola were the ones who told me that self-partnering didn't mean I couldn't take something for myself once in a while."

"I will gladly take the credit." Hendrix pats herself on the back. "If anyone deserves some pleasure, after what you've gone through this last year, it's you."

"I'm happy if you're happy, Sol," Yasmen says. "But why do I get the feeling it's more complicated than a hit it and quit it?"

"He likes me," I admit.

"We knew that since he came to the house looking at you like you were rolled in sprinkles," Hendrix says. "You like him too. We know all of this. What we don't know is how was the sex?"

I cover my face. "I'm in trouble."

Yasmen pries my fingers away one by one, catching and holding my eyes. "It was that good?"

I lower both hands and sigh.

"I think in the back of my mind, as soon as he said his boys weren't home, I knew it would happen." I pause to give my next statement the gravity it deserves. "He was wearing glasses when I got there."

They both gasp because we all know I have a spectacles kink.

"And you immediately wondered," Hendrix intones without a trace of humor, "*How does one best sit on a man's face when he's wearing glasses?*"

"I did wonder that and not for the first time, yes." I shrug helplessly. "They were black rimmed. I'm not made of stone."

"Girl, no one could blame you under those circumstances." Hendrix sips her tea. "Of course you went to him with legs wide open."

"You're two consenting adults," Yasmen says. "You're both single. You both knew what you were getting into, right?"

"Yeah, I told him that it was one time, and he understood. He asked if it was revenge because of what I'd just found out about Edward and Amber."

"And?" Hendrix lifts dark, querying brows. "Was this some *get your lick back* sex?"

"No, it really wasn't. I just wanted something for me. I wanted *him* for me, and I knew Judah wanted me. It felt good to be wanted like that. With him, it was the most beautiful..." I swallow a hitching breath. "It was so perfect. All I kept thinking was, *I'm forty years old. How did I not know it could be like this? How did I settle for less than this for so long? And would I have kept settling if Edward hadn't showed his whole ass? What if I had gone my entire life without this?"*

It's quiet at the table as my rhetorical questions hang in the air.

"He hasn't been with anyone since his divorce nearly four years ago," I go on, my voice weighted with the significance of that knowledge. "Like no dates. Nothing. He's been celibate and doesn't really do casual sex."

"And you believed him when he said it would be a one-time thing?" Hendrix lightly coats her words with exasperation. "That man's in love with you, Sol."

"No." I shake my head. "He can't be." I bite my thumbnail and give them a pleading look. "Can he?"

"How do you feel?" Yasmen asks. "Be honest with us. Be honest with yourself."

I gulp back the excuses and wave away the smoke screen responses to give them the unfiltered truth. "I'm scared. What if the feelings I have aren't just liking him, but not liking being alone? Not wanting to rely on myself because relying on a man was a habit?"

"You're not asking him to pay your mortgage," Hendrix says dryly.

"There are other ways to rely on someone, Hen," I say. "This chapter is supposed to be about contentment—about discerning the difference between being alone and being lonely."

"You had Edward, but weren't you lonely in your marriage?" Yasmen asks.

I was. They both know. Answering would be redundant, so I don't bother replying.

"Maybe the key is finding contentment wherever you are, whoever you're with," Yasmen goes on. "Knowing you always have you. Do you have to deny yourself happiness with someone else in order to be happy with yourself?"

"That's the problem." I look down at my hands in my lap. "I'm not sure anymore. Of all the things Edward took from me, the trust I had in myself seems to be the hardest to recover."

Servers bring food out before I get to say more, but as soon as we have our plates and are eating, my friends return to the subject, of course.

"I saw the way he watched you at the Harvest Festival," Yasmen says, a spoonful of shrimp and grits poised at her mouth. "That man been gone for you."

"He *has* been planning this for some time, apparently," I laugh around a mouthful of green beans. "You should have seen what he had in his nightstand."

"Condoms?" Hendrix asks, cracking a smile.

"Yes! So many condoms." I press a napkin to my lips to keep from spewing food on a laugh. "He was like uber-prepared, which is so Judah. I'm surprised he didn't have lube."

"Girl's gotta carry her own," Hendrix tsks. "I always have emergency lube."

"We know." Yasmen drizzles sarcasm over the words. "You gave it to us as stocking stuffers last Christmas."

"And you're welcome," Hendrix cackles.

"So how are you feeling about it all?" Yasmen asks, taking us back to the things I've been trying not to face.

"I don't know." I shrug miserably. "All I *do* know is that he's amazing. I'm not sure I *want* to go back to how things were before that night, but maybe I *should* go back so I don't start feeling too much or become too dependent."

"Don't overthink it," Hendrix says, the sobriety in her tone all the more marked because she's usually the one who keeps us laughing. "You like Judah. Judah likes you. Don't let Edward ruin your good thing."

"This isn't about Edward," I say. "It's about me. About being able to stand on my own and trust myself."

"You *were* standing on your own," Yasmen interjects. "Edward wasn't around at the end. He wasn't present. He wasn't loving. You were raising those girls, managing that house, building your investment portfolio. The only way that man could build real wealth was to steal it. He tried to tear you down. He needed more from you than you ever needed from him. It's his bad luck you finally figured that out."

"And as soon as he was out of the picture," Hendrix says, "you showed everyone, including yourself, exactly what you're made of."

"It was never you that couldn't be trusted, Sol," Yasmen adds, squeezing my hand. "It was always him you couldn't trust. You are the most capable, trustworthy person I know."

"And what about me?" Hendrix asks, allowing a little levity.

"Yeah, you too, whatever." Yasmen rolls her eyes and shoots Hendrix an affectionate smile. "My point is everyone knows how amazing you are, Sol. Edward's the one person who didn't want you to believe it. There's nothing he would like more than for you to waste another twenty years 'recovering' from him."

"I just didn't think I'd find something, *someone* who felt like *this* so soon after the divorce," I admit. "It's kind of terrifying."

"You know what Aunt Byrd used to say?" Yasmen asks, a brief shadow clouding her expression at the mention of Josiah's aunt who passed away, the woman who was like a second mother to her.

"What?" I ask, holding my breath.

"*As fast as God gives,*" Yasmen says, "*as fast as you get.* One thing you shouldn't second-guess is a blessing."

"And you think Judah's a blessing?" I ask.

Hendrix shifts a bite of fried green tomatoes to give me a half grin. "Don't you?"

CHAPTER THIRTY-SEVEN

SOLEDAD

"Anybody up?"

I aim the question at my camera from the chaise longue I picked up at an antique shop. Though I still have some DIY work to do on my she shed, I think I can make it fit in here once I ditch the Pepto-pink upholstery.

"In case you're wondering," I continue, "it's well after midnight where I am, and I'm still awake. I know. You probably saw my post earlier this week about making sure to get eight hours of sleep. I did try. I just keep waking up."

Comments jackhammer at the bottom of my screen as followers weigh in.

" 'Chamomile tea.' " I read one. "Great suggestion, MarilynMonMo. Let's see what else. DTF2000 says, 'Getting laid always knocks me right out. Some people still f*ck even when they're self-partnering. Go for it. #datingmyselfchallenge.' "

I clear my throat and hope the warmth in my cheeks doesn't actually show. "Duly noted. Thank you for that sage advice, DTF2000. And with that, I think I will log off and give it one more try. Night, my loves. Sleep tight."

I log off and kill the light on the ring stand but leave my phone in the holder.

"Getting laid, huh?" I mutter, flopping back down onto the chaise longue. "Not likely. Not tonight."

Judah and I have talked or texted most days since…the sex, but we haven't seen each other at all. We've both been busy. During the week, his sons are home, and their care takes a lot of time. I understand that. Between chauffeuring Inez and Lottie back and forth to Harrington, getting up early for gymnastics, staying late for clubs, and volunteering on parent committees, not to mention all the brand work I've taken on lately to make sure the ends keep meeting, when would we have had time to re-create the coital magic, so to speak?

And am I even down for that happening again?

My body screams *Yeeeeeessss, bitch. You definitely are.*

Making love with Judah uncorked something in me. I was horny before, sure, but this is different. I know exactly how Judah feels inside me. How he sounds when he comes. How ferocious and selfless and patient he is as a lover. My body wants that again and again and again and as many times as I can have it.

My mind is not as sure. My heart wants to be left out of it—let my body and mind fight it out because as soon as my heart takes a side…

I pick up a wallpaper book to flip through a few selections marked as possible for the back wall.

"This won't put me to sleep," I mumble, caressing a floral sample. "Swatches excite me too much."

A text notification chirps, loud and unexpected. I drop the wallpaper book and cross the room. Grabbing the phone from the ring light, I flip it over to read the incoming text.

Judah: Heard you can't sleep.

I bite into an irrepressible grin and sit on the arm of the chaise longue, almost dropping the phone, my fingers are so eager to respond.

Me: Stalker, but yes. I'm up.

Judah: You still in your she shed?

My heart performs a somersault in my chest, but I take a deep breath and type.

Me: Yeah. I'm still in here.

Judah: Are you alone?

Me: Lottie and Inez are asleep. Lupe's staying over at Deja's tonight. So…yeah. Out here all by myself. What about your boys?

Judah: It's the weekend. They're with Tremaine.

Me: What are you doing up?

Judah: Working on a presentation for Monday and just happened to catch you live.

Me: Just happened to, huh? LOL.

Judah: I have a few things that might help you sleep. Do you want them or not, smart-ass?

Me: I would appreciate these things of which you speak very much.

Judah: Good. Can I swing through?

Getting laid always knocks me right out.
Shut it, DTF2000.

Me: Sure. I'll unlatch the gate.

Judah: Gimme five minutes.

Me: That fast? That soon?

Judah: I was already on my way ☺

Of course you were.
"Five minutes?" I shriek with sudden realization. I run to unlatch the gate, then dash back to the tiny powder room at the back corner of the shed. Really no more than a toilet and a small sink with a mirror hanging above it. My hair is everywhere. I'm wearing a cropped T-shirt that says *JUST FOLD IT IN* and a pair of Lupe's jogging pants with *PINK* printed across the butt. They're too long, so I have them rolled up to the knees. And we crown this ensemble with a pair of white faux-mink slippers from a sponsored ad I did a few weeks ago. I'm a motley mess, but there's no time to fix any of it. I'm at least trying to finger-comb my hair when there's a *tap tap tap*.

"Crap," I whisper, but I cross the short distance from the powder room to the door.

Judah's outside on the postage-stamp cement stoop carrying a Harrington tote and wearing a black hoodie with gray sweatpants. The way those sweatpants hang on his lean hips and hug his ass—the night is not playing fair.

"I almost forgot Adam attends Harrington," I say, stepping back so he can come in. "I'm surprised I never see you there."

"He's older than your girls, so he's on north campus. Plus it's closer to Tremaine's office, so she usually takes Adam. Aaron's school is closer to mine, so I take him."

"Great system," I say, needing something to distract me from how good he looks. He has a fresh haircut, the edge precise and neat, but there's the slightest hint of daylong stubble hugging the carved line of his jaw, and it is sending me. If he were wearing his glasses, I'd be sitting on his face by now.

"When the boys can't sleep, especially Aaron," he says, reaching into the tote, "this helps."

He hands me a gray blanket. I accept it, surprised by how heavy it is. "Did they knit this with cement?" I joke. "It must weigh fifty pounds."

"Fifteen, actually. It's a weighted blanket. He has like five of them. Between the blanket, melatonin, and the tea I brought, you'll be knocked out before you count your first sheep."

"I hope you're right."

"I'm usually right." He eyes the letters emblazoned across my chest. "I like your shirt."

It's only then I realize I'm not wearing a bra and my nipples are happy to see him.

"Oh, God." I cup my breasts as if to shield them.

His sudden laughter startles me—not just the sound of it, which is rich and resonant, but the effect it has on his handsome face. How it cracks the austere lines and warms the usually serious dark eyes. It softens the stern set of his mouth. It opens him up and invites me in.

"Come here." He drops the tote, sits on the chaise longue, and pulls me onto his lap. "I missed you."

He says it so freely, and it's hard to believe I ever thought this man was reserved, cold. He's generous with his words, with his affection—at least to me. I drape one wrist at the back of his neck and press my hand to his chest, over his heart.

"I missed you back," I whisper, taking his bottom lip between mine. He eases me down onto the chair beneath him and cups my cheek, tugging my mouth open, and spoils me with caramelized kisses—sweet heat and sensuality melted, poured over us. I'm drowning in it. He doesn't let up, and I lose breath, coming up for air to pant at his throat. His hand explores beneath the hem of my cropped T-shirt, squeezing one bare breast and then the other.

"When you were doing your nightly cyberstalking," I gasp between kisses, slipping my hand into his jogging pants, "did you see what DTF2000 suggested I should do to put me to sleep?"

He groans when my hand moves up and down over him. He presses his forehead to mine, a long breath wrenched from him. "I did see her suggestion."

He pulls back to peer into my face, searching for the answer to a question he hasn't voiced yet, but it's clear in his eyes.

"Are you sure?" he asks.

Am I?

"I'm sure that I want you." I sit up and pull the T-shirt over my head, distracting him with my breasts as I knew I would.

He grabs his sweatshirt at the neck and pulls it over his head, exposing a T-shirt beneath that molds itself to the muscles of his shoulders, back, and chest. He tugs that over his head, too, and I trace the sculpted topography beneath with eager hands. He slips his jogging pants and briefs off while I shimmy out of Lupe's bottoms. Forgot I wasn't wearing panties underneath.

Ooops.

One thing I did take care of since I last saw him was tending the bush. Even though he didn't seem to mind a little bit o' hair down there when he ate me out *twice*, I still waxed her up real nice for such an occasion as this.

"Does it sound goofy to say I've been dreaming about this?" he asks, studying my naked body like I'm a buffet and he's been fasting.

"Not at all," I tell him, rushing to lock the shed door. "The girls are asleep, but just in case."

I cross back over to the chaise longue more slowly, stopping to stand between his knees. "Did you happen to bring a condom?"

"I did," he replies, pulling one from his pocket. "Just in case."

"Let me guess." I straddle him, setting one knee and then the other on either side of his powerful thighs. "You've got a jumbo box of condoms in that tote bag."

"Only need one," he says, his voice smoky and rough.

"Don't underestimate yourself."

He grips my ass, lifting me slightly above him to take one breast and then the other into his mouth. I drop my head back, my hair rushing down my spine in a river of cool waves. My hips start a rolling motion, readying for the rhythm that, even after only once, my body remembers. The wrapper crinkles as he unwraps the condom, and I glance down.

"Let me." I take it from him and clutch it in one hand for safekeeping. I scoot back but, instead of putting it on him right away, slide to the floor between his splayed knees and grip him in my hand. Holding his eyes, not breaking our stare, I bend my head and take him in my mouth.

"Sol," he moans, slumping back, the dark brown of his skin gleaming against the garish pink brocade.

I'd forgotten how good I am at this. How much I enjoy it. I roll him in my hand, work the length of him, suck and lick until his hand fists my hair and he forces my head down to take more. I gag a little but breathe through it, wanting him to have this, but he reaches under my arms after a few minutes, dragging me up to his lap. He grabs the condom, wraps up, and touches between my legs.

"I want to make sure you're ready," he says, his breaths ragged. "You're soaked."

"What can I say?" I shrug and rise, poised to take him in. "Making you feel good does that to me."

When he slides inside me, it's different from the last time. We stare into each other's eyes as I rise and fall over him. It's like our bodies bookmarked this spot so we could take up exactly where we left off on New Year's Day, dragging us deeper into a vortex of passion. And each touch, each stroke, each kiss is quantum, propelling us forward fast, far into a moment that exists nowhere but here. A place in time we claim as ours alone, insulated from the world beyond these walls. Sealed between our hips and bellies. Something made from our molecules meshing, cells colliding into a new *us* where we are inseparable and all things are possible. A miracle of intimacy. A faith grounded in the rhythm of our bodies and the gasps of our souls.

He tangles his hand in the length of my hair, dragging me forward and ravaging my mouth, plundering until I offer up all my secrets—until my lips tell him everything he wants to know without yielding one word.

"I want this all the time, Sol," he says, trailing kisses down my chin, my throat, over my shoulders. "Should I pretend I don't?"

I don't have words to answer him because this melding of our flesh and souls and spirits strips me of thought, blurs my reason and my reasons. Blocks my doubts and hesitations. When we're joined like this, I would give him anything, and that may be the most dangerous truth of it all.

When we've plastered the walls with our muffled cries, I lie against his chest and listen to his heartbeat. It races and then evens out, until it is once again steady as a metronome.

"I didn't mean to put pressure on you," he says after a few minutes of quiet, his fingers playing over the damp, naked skin of my back. "While we were...I shouldn't have said that."

I turn my head, twisting up to look into his face. "I'm still working through some stuff, but I don't want to hold you back, Judah."

"That's my line." He huffs out a humorless breath. "There are things you need to discover by yourself, about yourself, that I don't want to interfere with, but I'm finding it really hard to stay away."

Stay away? Go? Live without this? A tremor runs through me at the thought of losing that moment we made. Of never being able to find it again.

"Don't stay away." I trace the bow and line and curve of his mouth. "I'm learning to trust myself again."

"And me?" he asks, nipping the tip of my finger with his teeth. "Are you learning to trust me?"

I don't answer but lay my head back down on his chest, snuggling closer under the weighted blanket. "Maybe I'm learning to trust us both."

CHAPTER THIRTY-EIGHT

SOLEDAD

"Y̲ou cheated," Judah accuses me, sitting at the card table in my she shed wearing only briefs and one sock.

"How do you cheat at Uno?" I try to keep a straight face but can't hold back my laugh.

"You devised this game," he says.

"Uno is a real game. I've been playing it since I was like six years old. I play it with my girls all the time. I did not devise it."

"Right, but I've never heard of strip Uno."

"They play it this way in France." I grin at him over the one card left in my hand. "And how would I cheat?"

"When you persuaded me to call in sick to work," he says. "Which I've never done, by the way."

We've both done things that are out of character over the last two weeks. Playing hooky. Calling in sick. Sneaking around to see each other. It's been glorious.

"Oh, so now I've also corrupted you," I laugh. "Go on."

"You knew you wanted to play this perverted version of the game."

"Perverted?" I press my hand to my chest. "I didn't think you were so easily offended. I would never have guessed by the way you bent me over that table and had your way with me fully clothed as soon as you arrived."

His lips twitch. "That's neither here nor there."

"Actually it was here *and* there because you did it twice."

His eyes smolder and he goes on. "Like I said, you planned this, so you knew to wear all of that." He waves a hand to my winter coat, scarf, hat, and gloves over jeans, a T-shirt, two pairs of socks, and my faux-mink slippers. "And I came unprepared and am almost naked after an hour."

"Not naked enough for what I have in mind," I laugh, stretching my leg under the table to run my foot up his calf.

"Stop that." He aims a stern look at me. "I'm accusing you of something very serious."

"Wanting to see you naked?" I frown and tilt my head. "Or wanting to see you lose?"

"Both." He glares at the one card left in my hand. "And I bet that's a Wild card. That's the other way you've cheated. I can't figure out how, but you've had Wild cards every hand."

"What can I say? That card is drawn to me. I always get it at least once every time. I used to love it growing up because you could change the color to whatever you wanted."

"Well I have four cards," he says. "And you only have that one left, so we both know you're about to win. Just play it."

Instead of throwing down my final card, I stand and walk over to his side of the table. I toss one leg over his and straddle him in the chair, running the edge of my card down his chest and abs. His muscles flex beneath the card's trajectory. I turn it over and slap it against his naked chest. He glances down and roars a disbelieving laugh.

"You have to be cheating!" He takes the Wild card and tosses it across the room.

"Sore loser. Now let's see. You have a sock and this underwear. Which do I want to claim?"

"I don't like this game anymore," he says, tugging my hat off and tossing it to the floor.

My hair tumbles down and around my shoulders. "Now *that's* cheating. You can't just start taking my clothes off. You haven't won one hand."

"I can," he says, tugging at my scarf and throwing it over his shoulder. "And I will."

"Cheat!" I try half-heartedly to get off his lap, but he holds me in place, plucking at the buttons of my winter coat. "This has to go."

"This is a miscarriage of justice," I tell him, giggling and squirming as he takes the opportunity to tickle my ribs beneath the coat.

He grabs my hand and rips off one glove. The laughter dies from his eyes as he studies my palm, bringing it to his lips and leaving a kiss across the scar marring it. "You never told me what happened here."

"Did I not?" I breathe out the last of my amusement and stand, walking across the room to grab the Wild card and bring it back to the table.

"No, but I remember you had it bandaged the day you came to my office with the drive."

It's been so long since we discussed that day. It feels like another life, one where he was still an enigma, not the man whose body I know almost as well as my own now. A life where the only outlet I found for my rage was within the walls of this room. That was another woman, and I don't much want to revisit her.

"I cut myself," I finally say, taking off the winter coat and hanging it on the hook by the door.

"How?" he asks, leaning back in his chair, as confident in briefs and one sock as most men would be in an Armani suit.

"I found out some news about Edward that made me lose my mind a little," I say, forcing a laugh. "I took my machete to his clothes, his shoes."

My eyes stray to the holes and dents still in one wall.

"His man cave." I shrug. "I knew the Bird jersey was his most prized possession, so I shattered the glass, which is, of course, how I found the drive."

"And how you cut your hand?"

"Right."

"What did you find out about Edward?" he asks.

I settle on the chaise longue and pull my knees to my chest, shame seeping in, cold and familiar. "My doctor called and told me I had chlamydia."

"Sol, shit." He stands and crosses the small room to sit beside me on the chaise longue. "That motherfucker."

"It's curable...I mean, I'm fine now, but that was how I knew for sure Edward was cheating on me." I turn my palm over in my lap. "You know what I realized, though?"

"What?" he asks, tracing the ugly scar.

"It bisects my lifeline." I smile down at the lightning bolt of raised flesh across my palm. "And that's how I think of it. That day, that realization split my life into two parts, from blind trust to eyes wide open. I wouldn't trade the knowledge of who Edward really is for anything."

"I still can't imagine how you felt hearing that." He brushes my hair back with one hand.

"Hey, some good came of it." I smile up at him. "If I hadn't temporarily lost control, I would never have found the drive, and he might not be in prison."

"And we might not be here now." He links our fingers and sets our joined hands on his knee.

The idea that Judah would be out there in the world with someone else, or just not with me, and that I'd still be trapped in that plastic bubble Edward tried to maintain, makes me shudder. Terrifies me. I snuggle into Judah and reach up to cup his face, touching my mouth to his. It's as much an entreaty as it is a kiss—a soft pleading passed between our lips, an invitation to stay while I figure my shit out because I don't want to imagine him out of my life. I don't know exactly what this is we're doing, or what I'm ready to call it, but I want it. I want him, even if a part of me asks if I'm sure I'm ready.

I think he pretends not to see the tears at the corners of my eyes. It's a kindness because he likely assumes I'm at a breaking point. He would be wrong. I'm not crying because I might break. I'm crying because I'm healing, and I'm just so damn grateful for the journey I've chosen. I need to see it through, but will I lose Judah while finding myself?

He squeezes my shoulder and runs a finger down the bridge of my nose, which I'm sure is red by now.

"Also, should I be concerned at how casually you said 'my machete'?" he asks, the question lifting the somber tone of the conversation.

"No need to worry." I slant him a teasing look. "I don't think I'll ever need to use my machete because of your bad behavior."

He captures my chin between his fingers, holds my eyes, the humor fading into sincerity. "I promise you won't."

It's a pledge that lands like a balm on my injured memories, and I know I can trust him. I can't even bend my mind to imagine Judah doing the things Edward did, treating me the way Edward did.

"I know," I tell him, covering his hand where it rests on my face.

"Good," he says, grabbing my Wild card. "So what do you think? One last hand?"

I find a chuckle hiding somewhere and roll a look down his barely clothed body.

"You know you'll lose and end up completely naked, right?"

Bending his head, he kisses the curve of my neck and takes my earlobe between his teeth, whispering, "I thought that was the point."

CHAPTER THIRTY-NINE

JUDAH

"Tell me again how I ended up being the parent explaining what I do to Adam's class?" I ask Tremaine.

She laughs, writing her name on the guest badge at Harrington's front desk. "They already had three lawyers come this week. Nobody had an accountant, so short straw goes to you, buddy."

"And they'll be so excited to hear about me crunching numbers all day," I tell her dryly, affixing the guest badge to my sweater. "What made you want to come too?"

Her smile dwindles, and a frown takes its place. "I wanna see this new teacher of Adam's in action. There's some aspects of his IEP I want to make sure are being executed. This feels like a good excuse."

"There won't be any instruction happening," I remind her. "Just me talking about how titillating a career in accounting can be. So how will that give you a sense of what's going on?"

"I'll *know*, Judah." Tremaine watches me from under sleek, dark brows. "Do you doubt my detection abilities?"

Once Tremaine, based on gut alone, withdrew the boys from a school for autistic kids that later landed on the news for neglect and borderline abuse. My specialty is research and data, gathering all the facts, but I'll defer to that famous gut instinct of hers every time when it comes to Aaron and Adam.

"Do you know where you're going?" asks the woman at the front desk, studying us over the thin wire rims of her glasses.

I'm a lot less familiar with this campus than Tremaine, so I trust her when she reassures the receptionist we'll be fine.

"Shit!"

The soft-voiced curse from behind us prompts Tremaine and me to turn and look at the office entrance. Soledad stands at the door, dwarfed by a covered rolling cart. She looks up, horror stamped on her flushed face.

"Sorry, Diane!" She addresses the apology to the woman at the front desk. "For the cussing, I mean. This wobbly wheel is giving me the business, and I . . ."

Soledad's words die when her eyes meet mine. "Judah. Oh, hi. I didn't know you were . . . Hi."

"Hi." I feel the laser beams of Tremaine's eyes burning a curious hole in the side of my face. "You need some help?"

"No, I'm less of a mess than I seem to be," she laughs. "Promise."

She isn't a mess at all. Today her hair is tamed into a single braid, but those defiant curls sprout at her hairline. Her black denim jumpsuit nips in at the bust, revealing her exaggerated curves from the waist down. In the fashionable jumpsuit and New Balance sneakers with green and black accents she's pretty and pulled together, the classic suburban housewife. I can't shake the image, though, of all that hair unbound, pushed over one shoulder so I could kiss her neck while she rode me reverse cowgirl in her she shed on my lunch break a few days ago. Finding time to see each other has been hard, and we haven't been together nearly enough over the three weeks since I delivered that weighted blanket, signaling a new phase of whatever this is we're doing.

"Ahem." Tremaine clears her throat pointedly, bouncing a glance between Soledad and me. "Want to introduce us, Judah?"

"Oh, sure." I try to keep my face neutral, but I want to grin like a kid introducing one of the important women in my life to another important woman in my life. "Tremaine, this is Soledad. Soledad, Tremaine."

"Nice to finally meet you," Soledad says, offering a tentative smile to my ex.

"'Finally'?" Tremaine pounces on the slip. "You two know each other that well, huh?"

"Um...not really." Soledad shifts her attention back to Diane. "I'm here for the *bring your parent to school* thing."

"Oh, we know. The kids are excited." Diane walks swiftly from behind the desk and crosses over to Soledad and her wobbly cart. "They're already in the auditorium."

"Auditorium?" Tremaine asks.

"There was so much interest in what Soledad does," Diane preens, "she's doing a special presentation for her daughter Inez's entire grade."

"It's not a big deal," Soledad demurs. "I think they just want to eat."

Diane laughs and opens the door so Soledad can maneuver the cart back out into the hall.

"I didn't get to fill out my guest badge," Soledad says from just beyond the door.

"It's fine," Diane practically purrs. "We all know you here, Ms. Charles."

There's some clanking as Diane helps Soledad adjust a few things on her cart out in the hall.

"Wanna tell me about Ms. Charles?" Tremaine asks with low-voiced curiosity.

"Not particularly, no," I say, looking straight ahead and not meeting the rabid questions I know are in those eyes.

"Well, you will," she says. "As soon as we're done."

We're not "done" for another hour because Adam's class has a lot more questions about my job than I anticipated. I let it slip that I've worked with the FBI on several cases, and all of a sudden, I was fascinating. It's worth the hour or two away from the office to see Adam beaming and laughing with his classmates, relishing the new respect in their eyes when they hear I've helped put criminals behind bars. Socialization is still really challenging for him, but he tries hard. Social stories and groups have helped him a lot, but he'd still prefer home with Aaron and me over any social setting outside our home. But hell, so would I.

"Thank you so much for doing this, Mr. Cross," Adam's teacher Ms. Bettes says when we're done. "I didn't know how fascinating accounting could be."

Her light touch on my sweater sleeve draws Tremaine's eyes and lifted brows. Is this teacher... flirting with me? Couldn't be, but I'm usually oblivious to stuff like that. Tremaine jokes that she had to knock me over the head with a statistics textbook to get my attention.

"Ms. Bettes," Tremaine says, "while we're here, I just wanted to remind you that we're trying a new seizure medication for Adam. We're being really vigilant watching for any adverse reactions. Please let us know if you spot unusual behaviors or responses."

"Will do." Ms. Bettes slowly withdraws her hand from my sweater. "Thanks again for coming, Mr. Cross."

As soon as we've told Adam goodbye and are in the hall, I ask Tremaine, "So was it my imagination, or was she—"

"Pushing up on you?" Tremaine chuckles, looping an infinity scarf around her neck as we head back to the front desk to check out. "Yeah. Definitely, but apparently she's wasting her time since you're head over heels for Soledad."

"You're imagining things," I lie. I don't even know why I lie, except I'm not sure we're ready to share what's going on with the world. I know *she's* not. If her daughters found out, it might make things complicated. Even more complicated.

"You're a bad liar," Tremaine reminds me. "And the way you were salivating over that woman was frankly hard to watch. I was kinda cringing on your behalf."

"I was not salivating." I frown, wondering if I'm that obvious. "Was I?"

Tremaine stops in the hall to face me, setting her hands on her slim hips. She's lean and almost as tall as I am. When she wears heels, we're practically eye to eye.

"Should I be insulted that she's my opposite in every way?" Tremaine asks. Despite the amused glint in her eye, I rush to disagree.

"What? No," I say. "She's actually a lot like you."

"Light-skinned, hair all down her back, and not big as a minute?" Tremaine asks, but her eyes tell me she's teasing. "Seems pretty much opposite to me."

"You're both fantastic mothers. You're both smarter than me in the ways that actually count. She's diligent and innovative and resilient and determined and compassionate." I touch her shoulder, looking into her eyes to show my sincerity. "You're both such good people."

"I'm happy for you. Honestly, Kent and I had almost given up hope that you'd find anyone."

"Thanks," I say dryly.

"So how long has this been going on? Since all that shit went down with her husband?"

"Ex-husband, and no. We only recently started…"

I don't know what to say. There's no way I'm discussing sex with Tremaine. She'll make fun of me for years to come if she finds out about the industrial-sized box of condoms in my nightstand.

"We only recently started seeing each other," I settle on. "And it's not public. Her girls don't know. It's awkward."

"Because of the whole *You put our dad in prison* thing?"

"Yeah, a little. Well, for one of them in particular. The middle daughter has been having a harder time than the other two seem to be." I glance at my watch, grateful for an excuse to end this conversation. "Don't you have a deposition?"

"Yeah." She slants a knowing look at me. "Don't think we're done. I want to know everything."

"Well, you won't."

We turn in our guest badges to a woman Tremaine recognizes as the librarian and head back out. A burst of laughter from the auditorium up the hall grabs my attention as we're about to exit the building.

"You go on ahead," I tell Tremaine distractedly. "I'm gonna use the bathroom before I leave."

"The bathroom, huh?" Tremaine buttons up her coat and starts toward the door. "Tell your girlfriend I can't wait to have her over for dinner. She can make that viral salad dressing for us."

I don't dignify that with a response. Keeping an eye out for Diane in case she drags me back to the front desk for a guest badge, I stealthily make my way toward the auditorium. I poke my head in just enough to see but not be seen. Soledad stands onstage behind a table, stirring something in a bowl and wearing an apron over her jumpsuit that says *I'M THE COOL MOM.*

"This dish is one of my girls' favorites," she tells the assembled sixth graders. "It bakes all in one pan. This one's vegetarian because Inez's sister doesn't eat meat. Promise you won't miss it. I brought some samples for everyone. How's that sound?"

The crowd cheers when students from the class walk the aisles carrying trays with little cups of the food and tiny plastic tasting spoons.

"Pass me that salt, Nez," Soledad says to the young girl standing beside her. I've seen photos of the girls on Soledad's social media, and I knew her oldest, Lupe, strongly resembles Edward but has red hair instead of his blond. Seeing them side by side, I notice for the first time the strong resemblance between Soledad and her middle daughter. Inez beams, pride in every line as she assists her mother.

"I know I'm here cooking." Soledad pauses to address the crowd, stepping out from behind the table. "But I'm not just a cook. I'm an influencer. A content creator. That wasn't even really a thing when I was growing up, but now it is."

She clasps her hands in front of her, smiling out over the crowd of students.

"You guys are the generation pioneering all this stuff," she says. "I'm playing catch-up. I've always wanted my girls to go to college."

She turns a playfully narrow-eyed glare on Inez. "I still do. Don't get any ideas, young lady."

Everyone laughs, and she turns that brilliant smile back on the assembly.

"But it's amazing what you can do in the time we live now, the career you can have with your phone, a ring light, a few good ideas, and consistency. This is the perfect career for me because it allows me to do what I love most." She pauses to shrug. "Make the best home possible for my girls and me. I share the meals I prepare, the ways I keep our house clean, the ways I manage our schedule and our budget with the world now. It's my niche, and it's changed my life. It's given me a lot more than just a way to make a living. It's given me new confidence and helped me value making a home as vocationally valid in a way that culture hadn't reinforced before."

She grins, watching the students chew on the samples. "Any questions?"

Hands fly up all over the room, and I hover in the hall for another fifteen minutes listening to her field questions and entertain her daughter's classmates. Finally they break and head back into their classrooms. I hang out around the corner, waiting for the crowd to clear. Eventually Soledad and Diane appear in the hall, wobbly cart in tow.

"I need to go relieve the librarian," Diane says. "She's sitting in for me at the front desk. I can find someone to help you get this stuff to your car."

I step out from behind the wall as if I were just casually coming from around the corner.

"Ms. Charles," I say. I know I'm bad at this stuff by the amused look Soledad shoots me. "Still here? How'd it go?"

"Great, I think." She turns to Diane. "Don't worry about finding someone to help me. I'll be fine on my own."

Diane shakes her head. "Oh, but—"

"I'm on my way out," I say, stepping in to steer the cart out of Soledad's hands. "I can help."

"If you're sure?" Diane asks, flicking a glance from me to the cart.

"I'm sure," Soledad and I say in unison.

"Okay." Diane looks over her shoulder toward the front desk. "I better get back, then. Thank you both for doing this."

She walks off, and Soledad and I watch each other for a few silent seconds.

"How serendipitous that you happened to still be around to help," she says, starting the walk to the car.

I push the cart and keep pace with her, following Harrington's camellia-lined brick path toward the parking lot.

"You may not believe this," I say. "But I kind of arranged to be around when you finished so I could see you."

"No!" Soledad turns mock-shocked eyes on me, pressing one hand to her chest. "Mr. Cross. If I didn't know any better, I'd think you're stalking me."

"Seems the only way I'll get to see you."

She sobers, an apology etched on her expression. "I know it's not ideal. I'm sorry. I—"

"You don't owe me anything," I say, parking the cart beside her Pilot. "It's not like we're in a real relationship, right?"

I regret the words as soon as they leave my mouth. She's turned away from me, loading dishes into the trunk, and the slim line of her shoulders tenses. She pauses, dropping her arms and her head. The side-opening trunk door shields us from the school's view, so I take a chance, gripping her arms gently from behind and bending to whisper in her ear.

"I'm sorry." I pull her softness into my chest and fold my hands over her waist, leaning down to the curve of her neck. "I don't mean to pressure you. You're doing what feels best for you right now. I respect that. I just..."

Want you.

I don't say it aloud, but the way her hands close over mine in front of her, the way she leans back into me, letting her head fall against my chest, tell me she knows. Tell me she feels it too. In her own time, she'll know how we should move forward. I can be patient and give her that space.

The sound of quick breaths and running feet approaching makes us spring apart, but when Inez rounds the car, there is still suspicion in her eyes as she looks between her mother and me.

"Inez," Soledad says, slamming the trunk door. "Hey. What are you doing out of class?"

Her daughter scowls, glaring at the two of us before tossing the apron to Soledad and turning on her heel.

"You forgot that!" she yells over her shoulder, taking off to run back to the school.

Soledad looks at the fabric clutched to her chest, then pulls it away and stares down at the vibrantly stitched message.

I'M THE COOL MOM.

CHAPTER FORTY

SOLEDAD

"So how was school?" I ask, my tone bright and false-sounding even to my ears.

"Great." Lupe serves herself some of the grilled chopped vegetable salad from the center of the table. "I got an A on that history test."

"That's amazing, honey." I smile with genuine pleasure. "Studying really paid off, huh?"

"Yeah." She nods. "Don't forget I need to pay for that SAT prep class."

"Right." I start adding and subtracting figures in my head to make sure I'll be able to handle even one extra expense. "We'll take care of it."

"I can get a job, Mom," Lupe says, ladling some of the tomato bisque into her empty bowl. "I can help."

"No." I release a sigh and shake my head. "What I mean is not yet. I want you focused on school right now and all the extracurricular stuff colleges will be looking for."

"What about this summer?" she ventures. "Deja and I thought about maybe working at Grits as hostesses."

"I wanna be a hostess!" Lottie says, a lettuce leaf hanging from her mouth.

"Be eleven, Lottie. I'll let you know when it's time to be something else." I turn my attention back to Lupe and spoon up soup from my bowl. "That might be a good idea, Lupe. We can talk about it later."

Inez, who has not said a word to me since "catching" Judah at the car, stirs her soup, her eyes fixed on the swirling liquid. We weren't doing anything, but my daughter isn't stupid. She has eyes and no doubt picked up on the connection between me and the man she holds responsible for her father's incarceration.

"What about you, Lottie?" I sip my water and smile when my youngest's face lights up.

"This morning," Lottie says, "Coach said my bar routine is one of the best he's seen in a long time."

"That's so great." I reach across and tug one of the braids on her shoulder. "Proud of you."

"He says he emailed you three camps for the summer. I need to make sure I get into one if I wanna keep up," she continues, piercing a few strips of grilled chicken on the platter and transferring them to the salad on her plate. "He asked if you got that email?"

"I did." I blow out a breath. "The camps are really expensive, honey. We'll have to see, okay?"

The light dimming in her eyes makes my heart clench. It kills me not to be able to give them things they want or need, but there is only so much I can do. I'm making steady money now, but it's not always predictable. I try to keep a good bit in savings as a cushion in case I have a really dry month or two. My parents didn't live in a house like this in a neighborhood like Skyland. It was public school from K to twelve for us. No exclusive private school like Harrington, but our basic needs were met, and we were loved. We all knew that, and that is the greatest gift I can give my girls, even if sometimes it feels to them like they need more.

"But Daddy will be out by then, right?" Lottie asks, her voice uncertain. "And we'll have a lot of money again?"

I grit my teeth. It's galling that after all this time working my ass off, figuring out a whole new career and path for myself to keep a roof over our heads and food on our table, my daughter still thinks it's her father who will swoop in and save the day. He's the one who ruined everything. *I* saved us.

"Your father won't be able to go back to his job," I settle on saying, stabbing the salad with my fork. "You know that. He may not be able to help out much financially when he first gets out."

"I'm sure your rich boyfriend will help us, Mom," Inez says, her first words to me all night.

Everything and everyone go completely still, like someone poured a bucket of ice water over the table and we're all frozen in place. Lupe's spoon dangles above her bowl. Lottie looks like a little guppy, her mouth stretched open in shock.

"You have a boyfriend, Mom?" Lottie asks.

"What's she talking about?" Lupe lets her spoon drop and clatter in the bowl.

"It's exactly like Dad said," Inez rushes on, her eyes narrowed on me accusingly.

"What do you mean?" Lupe frowns, looking between her sister and me. "You don't know what you're talking—"

"Judah Cross," Inez cuts in, giving up all pretense of eating and shoving her untouched food away. "I caught her with him in the parking lot today."

"Inez, you didn't 'catch' me doing anything." I clench my fingers tightly around my spoon like it's a lifeline.

"Mom, just tell us," Lupe says, a frown crinkling her brows.

"Girls, I don't... We aren't..." I go silent because it feels like a lie to say there is *nothing* going on, but I'm not telling my daughters, *We're just fucking*. And even thinking that feels wrong—cheapens what's happening between Judah and me. "It's not like that."

"But it's like something?" Lupe persists. "With Judah Cross?"

"Yeah," Inez says, hurt and anger bucking in her voice. "She's dating the man who put Dad in prison."

"I'm not dating anyone but myself. You know that. After all your father put me through, put us all through, I'm not sure I'm ready to jump back into a committed relationship yet, but I do like Judah Cross, yes." I'm not sure those were the right words to say and want to take the admission back immediately, but it's done, and maybe it's for the best. "And for the last time, Inez, Judah did not put him in prison. Your dad did that to himself."

"But he was telling the truth when he said Judah Cross had a thing for you," Inez fires back.

"Your father is the last person you should be thinking knows anything about the truth right now," I say, brittle derision all up and through my statement.

"You said yourself that he's not perfect," Inez says, "but he's still our dad."

"That does not make him a good man," I say, trying to keep my own anger tamped down. "Or someone you can trust."

Inez stands and turns, then takes a few stomping steps away from the dining room table.

"Where are you going?" I demand.

"To my room," she tosses over her shoulder.

"Sit. Down," I say, the two words like shots fired across the dining room. She doesn't stop and almost reaches the stairs.

"Inez Ana Maria, I said sit down. Now."

She stops in her tracks but doesn't turn around. Does not sense how close I am to snatching her up and sitting her narrow butt down myself.

"I don't care what you see your friends at Harrington doing," I say, my voice snapping like a belt, "or how they treat their mothers, but you do not storm off in my house. *¿Lo entiendes?*"

Silence.

"I'm waiting for your answer, Inez. Do you understand?"

"Yes, ma'am." She turns to face me, her mouth set, but doesn't move to take her seat.

"Then sit down." I nod to her place at the table. "And finish your dinner."

It's quiet and tense for the rest of the meal, with only the sounds of silverware scraping plates and the occasional slurp of soup breaking the silence.

"Put the food away and wash the dishes, girls," I tell them. "I'm going out to the shed to paint some before bed."

"You want any help?" Lottie asks, flicking a glance between Inez and me. My girls are extremely close, and I hate that two of them feel like they have to take a side in this.

"I only want you to do your kitchen chores," I say, cupping her head and kissing her cheek. "Make sure that kitchen floor is clean enough to eat off, okay? Do your homework and then go to bed."

"Okay." She grabs my hand when I turn to leave. "I love you, Mommy."

Her words are tender, like her mother needs to be handled with care. We so rarely get that with our kids. It doesn't always occur to them that *we* need care too. I know the fighting, the tension, the divorce, Edward's incarceration—it's all been a lot on them, maybe more than they've been able to articulate or realize. There's only so much of their innocence I can preserve.

I glance into the kitchen, where Inez and Lupe are having an intense conversation at the sink. Lupe thrusts her finger into Inez's face, a scowl snapping her brows together. Inez leans up into her sister's space, not backing down as they hiss at each other. I'm not even going to intervene. Enough for tonight. I slip out the back door and pad across the yard, wet grass cold on my heels in the faux-mink slippers I can't seem to stop wearing.

"Well, I know what my sisters are getting for Christmas," I mumble, letting myself into the she shed. Usually walking in here gives me a sense of pride, the progress I'm making serving to encourage me. Tonight, though, all I see is the shambles Edward left behind. The hole where his Celtics jersey used to hang. Wallpaper plastered to half the back wall, the dull paint Edward wanted still covering the other half. Everything appears undone, half-done, far from finished. And that's how I feel tonight. Like a messy room still marked by Edward's mistakes mingling with my own.

I half-heartedly pick up the roll of wallpaper, determined to make something in this room better before I go to sleep. My phone buzzes in my back pocket, and when I pull it out, seeing a text from Judah makes me drop the wallpaper.

Judah: Is it okay to call?

I don't reply but dial him, my heart hammering. Nervousness, excitement, dread—all the emotions buzz in an anxious hive under my rib cage.

"Hey," he says, answering before the first ring finishes. "How are you?"

"Fine. I guess. Inez tried to call me out at dinner." I laugh humorlessly and flop onto the chaise. "That probably didn't go the way she thought it would."

"What happened?"

"She said maybe my rich boyfriend can take care of us since her father won't be able to go back to his old job once he gets out of prison. The prison that you put him in, obviously and by the way."

"Ouch."

"My sentiments exactly. I think Lupe is reading her for filth as we speak, though, so I take small comfort in that."

"What did you tell them?"

"That we're not dating, but that I do like you and..." I trail off because it all sounds so inadequate. "It's complicated."

"I see," he says.

"Everything's mixed up. I want to do what's best for them, but I also want what's best for us. I want to be fair to you. I want to make sure I'm ready for whatever this is we're starting."

The air feels weighty with the words he hasn't voiced yet. "And I don't want to make things any harder for you, Sol. Maybe we should just not do this right now. It's causing complications for you at home with your daughters. It's making you feel conflicted. And for what? Just sex?"

"It's not, Judah." I pull my knees up and rest my forehead against them, closing my eyes at the hurt hiding beneath the cool tone he usually uses with the rest of the world, but not with me. "It's not just sex and you know it."

"You're not ready for more. It's the wrong time for your daughters with the Edward thing so fresh. It's the wrong time for you because you're not ready for a relationship. I don't want to take away from it, but I—"

"Are you breaking up with me?" I lift my head, pain gathering behind my breastbone so acute I press my hand there to relieve it.

"How could I be when we're not together?"

"We have something, though."

"You think I don't know that?" The words blaze through the cool wall he erected between us. "You are doing what you have to do, Sol. I've told you I understand. Do that. Handle that."

He draws in a harsh breath.

"You're very much occupied with cleaning up the past and getting things right for your new reality, as you should be, but the whole time you're trying to fix what was, all I can think about is what we could be. I want my boys to know you. I want you to meet Tremaine. Really meet her and her husband, Kent. I want you to meet my parents. Did you know my father is making your Crock-Pot recipes?"

"Your dad is wh—"

"Well, he is, and he'd be thrilled to learn that my girlfriend is that pretty woman from the Facebook because he's old and Facebook's about as much as he wants to manage these days."

"Judah—"

"Only you're not my girlfriend. You're this amazing woman I sneak around and sleep with on the weekends, on lunch breaks. Who I see more online than I do in real life. And I thought I could do this in-between, limbo thing where I get to share your bed, but nothing else."

"That's not true," I tell him, tasting salty tears in the corners of my mouth. "It's more than that."

"I don't want you to settle for anything less than what you want your life to look like right now, but I'm not willing to settle either."

"I don't know if I'll ever want to be married again," I blurt out because my heart won't let me hide that from myself or from him any longer. "I may never want that, Judah."

"Who the fuck cares?" He's louder than I've ever heard him. Harsher than he's ever spoken to me. "I'm not asking you to marry me. I'm asking you to *be* with me. I don't care if your friends get married twice, divorce, and marry again. I don't care how shitty your marriage to Edward was. I'm not looking at the forty-five years my parents have been married or the partnership I had with Tremaine. I want a life with *you* that *we* make, and who cares what the hell anyone else does or calls it or expects? This could be our Wild card, Sol. We can make it whatever we want it to be."

I sniffle, all the words I would say locked in my throat with no way out. That thing that withered and died inside me when Edward betrayed our vows, abandoned our family, reneged on promises—it could breathe again with a man like this. With Judah, my trust is regenerating, but I'm not sure if it will ever take the shape of marriage again. Even with him. It took me long enough to truly actualize into the woman I am becoming and am right now. I love Soledad *Charles*. I don't want anyone else's name. And even though Judah *says* he doesn't care...

"I love you, Sol."

"Judah, I—"

"No, don't. Because it doesn't matter what you feel if you're not ready for me."

"I don't want to lose you," I tell him, tears and snot and sadness streaking my face. "But I can't be ready before I *am* ready."

"I'm not going anywhere, and I don't want anyone else. I just think this thing we're doing now is confusing everyone, including us."

I want to tell him he's wrong and we can keep doing what we're doing, having just the little that we have, but I'm afraid he's right. That taking what we can instead of what we both deserve is a disservice to what we can be when the time is right.

"We're not breaking up?" I curl into a ball on the chaise and swipe at my wet cheeks.

"I think we have to date before we can *stop* dating," he says. "Focus on your girls. Focus on yourself, but when you *do* think about this relationship, don't compare it to anything else, to any*one* else. Draw a picture in your mind of what a future could look like and really believe this could be us. And whenever you're ready, I'm right here."

CHAPTER FORTY-ONE

SOLEDAD

Boricua High Council rides again!" Lola sings, and she rifles through a box of albums in the garage of the house where we grew up.

"God help us." Nayeli rolls her eyes, but a grin splits her face. "First time I've been in South Carolina in years."

"Nay, I'm not sure if you're so happy because you get to see us," I tell her, squatting to transfer clothes from a box to a bag for charity, "or if you're just giddy to be up from under all them kids of yours."

"Both!" She executes a body roll, tongue out. "Ayyyyeeee."

"You're not calling every ten minutes to check on them?" I ask.

"No, they are with their daddy." She does praise hands. "He can handle his own kids by himself for a few days. I do it all the time."

"Mine are probably having a party as we speak." I stand and rest my hands on my hips. "A weekend with Auntie Hen is like a dream. They'll eat out every night, probably go shopping for new shoes and video games, and be spoiled by the time I get home."

"It's good you have friends who can step in that way," Nayeli says. "It's a blessing."

"I need less talk," Lola calls out. "Get your asses to work so we can finish. The cleaning crew comes tomorrow and we need to have all this stuff cleared out."

"This idea of yours," Nayeli says, dragging a box from a corner in the garage. "Moving in with Olive early and starting the Airbnb now wouldn't have anything to do with that kiss before Christmas, would it?"

Lola pauses, turning to assess us over one shoulder, her hair braided and tucked beneath a bright red headscarf. "Absolutely not. She and I agreed that it would be smart to go ahead and start collecting money from this place as we prepare for the move to Austin this summer. So why not move in with her in the meantime?"

"And it hasn't occurred to you that it'll be just the two of you in that li'l ol' apartment?" I ask. "Just two horny besties?"

"She's not horny," Lola protests.

"Notice you didn't even try to front like you aren't," I laugh.

"Of course I'm horny." Lola rolls her eyes. "Don't be ridiculous."

"And you, Sol?" Nayeli asks. "How's your love life?"

"Nonexistent." I force a laugh, sorting a box of dusty books into keep and donate piles.

"What about that guy Hendrix mentioned at Christmas?" Lola asks. "Anything develop with him?"

Nayeli straightens from the stack of old vinyl records she's sorting. "Is this the one who prosecuted Edward?"

"He didn't prosecute Edward," I correct. "He was the accountant who uncovered the embezzlement. We, um…we're figuring it out."

"You're dating and you didn't tell us?" Nayeli asks, her voice tinged with hurt.

"We're not dating. We're…" I shrug, tired of hiding and trying to explain things to make anyone, including myself, more comfortable with it. "We started sleeping together, but—"

"Hold up!" Lola walks over and drags an empty crate to sit on beside me. "You can't just plow right past that. This is the first man you've been with besides your trifling-ass husband in almost twenty years."

"How was it?" Nayeli whispers, like our parents might hear in the next room.

"Was it good?" Lola asks.

"Best I ever had." I split an impish look between them. "Oh, my God. How did I not know it could be like that?"

"For real?" Nayeli's voice holds wonder and curiosity. "Like what?"

I turn to her, meeting her eyes squarely. "Like multiple orgasms, like eating me out for*ever* and making me come with just his—"

"Damn!" Lola laughs. "I rarely even do dick anymore and you make me want one of *dem*."

We fall into a laughing heap, and it feels like high school again, the three of us sharing secrets, sharing ourselves, unburdening. It's one thing to connect over FaceTime, but being together in this house again, surrounded by the memories that made us—it's priceless.

"So if you got it like that," Lola says after more squeals and revelations, "why did you call your love life nonexistent?"

My laugher dries up as the complexity of our situation hits me again. "The girls, especially Inez, are still adjusting to the idea of the man who put their father in prison dating their mother. And I'm not ready for a relationship, but he's in love with me and would prefer to wait until I'm ready to be with him fully. So technically we aren't together, no."

I don't look up, even when I feel their stares, but flip through a tattered copy of *Waiting to Exhale*.

"Forget the girls for a minute," Nayeli says. "Let's say they come to terms with you dating Judah. How do you feel about *him*?"

I'm not prepared for that question. Not talking with Judah or seeing him the last two weeks has been hell. Things seem to be leveling out with my daughters. Lupe gave Inez a good talking-to, apparently. Inez apologized and we hugged it out, but we haven't discussed Judah again. Yasmen and Hendrix continue to ground me and make me feel supported and loved. I have a thriving online community. A whole army of women who are dating themselves and figuring out a lot about what they will and won't accept in the process. It's amazing.

And yet...there is this ache, not a hole. It's not that part of *me* is missing. I feel whole on my own. Not an ache inside, but an ache *by my side*. That's where the hole is.

"I care about him," I finally reply. "I miss him so much it hurts, but, you guys, what if I make the same mistakes I made before? It hasn't been that long since my divorce. Don't I need more time?"

"You've taken time," Lola says. "And you've done a lot of work on yourself. When are we ever done working on ourselves? I believe wholeness is not a destination, but a lifetime process. Something that instead of waiting for, you could be living for."

"Hey." Nayeli touches my shoulder, prompting me to look at her. "If he makes you happy, be happy now. You deserve it."

I cover her hand and smile up at her. "Appreciate that, Sis."

"Okay. Back to work. If we gonna sit around chatting all day, we'll never get this done," Lola says. She stands and walks over to her phone, which is resting on one of the sealed boxes. "Music makes everything go faster."

Cherrelle and Alexander O'Neal's "Saturday Love" blasts from Lola's phone, ushering in memories of Saturday mornings cleaning this house under Mami's watchful eye. She loved this song, and I can't help but laugh remembering her dancing around the kitchen while dinner was cooking. We've reached the Sade stage of the playlist, with "Smooth Operator" crooning over us, when I find one of Mami's leather-bound journals with her initials engraved on the front. There's nothing more than loosely tied string protecting its secrets from prying eyes. I glance up, checking to see what my sisters are doing. Lola walks a box out to my Pilot, which is parked in the driveway.

"Quick potty break," Nayeli says, rising and rushing back into the house, leaving me alone with Mami's leather-bound memories.

I glance around the empty garage as if someone might catch me pulling the curtain back on my mother's inner thoughts from years ago.

"Fuck it," I mumble, and crack open the journal.

For the most part, it's mundane stuff, literally a record of life events. She wrote about things we achieved, like Lola getting on the honor roll and Nayeli winning first-chair flute. Me making cheer captain. She wrote about petty office politics at the library where she and my father had met and both worked—a stream of consciousness veering from the lofty to the base and banal, encompassing her everyday and her daydreams. On the rare page, she wrote about *him*, Lola's father, who was a mystery in shadows most of my life. But more than anything, she wrote about herself, revealing things that I'm not sure I ever knew.

My heart is not split in two. My heart is whole. When I'm with Jason, he has all of it. When I'm with Bray, he accepts nothing less than everything, so as much as I want him, our time has passed. He cannot come around anymore because his eyes betray him, and he is the kind of man who makes you burn your life to the ground. I won't do that to Jason, and I won't do that to my daughters and I won't do that to myself. Not even for him, the one who tutored my soul in passion.

I never thought I would forgive Bray for cheating on me, and there is a part of me that maybe never will. We were too young for all that emotion. It was like wrapping yourself around dynamite, reckless and exhilarating. We exploded, hurting everyone in our blast zone.

Lola is so much like him. Her heart is big and her spirit is free. Maybe that's why we clash. It crushed me to see her leave, but she is with Mami. It is best for now.

There are so many ways to break a woman's heart. Her children. Her lover. Her body when it betrays her. Life is clever that way, devising plans for our demise from the moment we're born. Death by a million heartbreaks, a thousand regrets, a hundred goodbyes.

When I dropped Lola off on the island, Mami asked who my one true love was. I knew what she meant. Was it Jason or was it Bray? I told her I am the love of my life. I have learned to love myself without judgment or condition. It's the only way I have enough love for everyone who needs it—to love myself. No one can love me like I do. No one knows me like I know myself.

I read that Richard Bach book everyone at the library was raving about. He said what the caterpillar calls the end of the world, the master calls a butterfly. I know what he meant. When we have hard times, huge changes that seem to be the end of the world as we know it, it's actually an incubator for metamorphosis. For a new beginning.

To me he misses the point, as men so often do. When you hurt the way we women sometimes have to, when you lose so much, when the world ends over and over and over again, we are no longer butterflies. Those wings are much too fragile to carry us on and through.

I'm a hornet. I can love. And I can sting.

I close the journal, retying the string that guarded Mami's inner life. I will show Lola and Nay. They need to know these facets of Mami revealed in crinkled pages and fading ink. Our mother, the librarian who preferred books over parties and game shows over just about everything else, saw herself as a hornet. Loved herself fiercely enough that if no one else ever saw her, ever loved her fully, she would love herself enough to have some left over for everyone else.

And it seems bold. That feels brave. A woman who knew and loved herself well enough to rely on no one, choosing to risk her heart with more than one. Choosing to make room for love in all its varied forms. In a way, I think she was talking about contentment, and it gets to the core of what I've been wrestling with.

Alone or lonely? Single or in a relationship? Can I love myself unconditionally? Accept myself, creating a foundation, a model, for how I want to love everyone else? Maybe it's not *Am I ready for love again?* but *Am I ready to love myself that fiercely no matter what?* It brings me back to the question I keep circling in my head.

Can I be the love of my own life?

CHAPTER FORTY-TWO

JUDAH

H ave you heard the news?"

I glance up from last quarter's financial report and suppress my annoyance. Why is Delores Callahan darkening my door on a Friday afternoon? I need to leave in a few minutes to pick up Aaron from school.

"What news?" I ask, keeping my voice disinterested, even though she walks farther into my office and takes a seat.

I give her my full attention, sharpening my gaze on her face. Something's changed about her, but I can't quite put my finger on it.

"What's different?" I finally ask.

"It's the eyebrows," she says, obviously pleased to have stumped me. "They really make a difference. I got them waxed. Soledad's got a place she recommended."

At the mention of Soledad's name, my teeth clench. As much as I've tried to convince myself that I just miss fucking her, I know it isn't true. I miss everything about her. The scent of jasmine oil. Seeing her small shoes kicked off in her she shed and watching her walk around barefoot. Her laugh. The feel of her under me, on my lap, in my arms. I haven't even allowed myself to watch her on social media. I think I'm going through withdrawal.

"You asked if I'd heard the news," I remind Delores without acknowledging her comment about Soledad. "What is it?"

"That hotshot lawyer of Edward's has managed to get him out earlier than expected."

"What the hell?" I take off my glasses and toss them onto the desk. "How is that possible?"

"He's a first-offender white male who committed a white-collar crime and cooperated with authorities," Delores says wryly. "Do the math."

"When did you hear this?"

"Pop told me a few minutes ago. The FBI wanted to make sure he knew."

"Is your father pissed? Does he think we should push for him to stay longer?"

My wheels start turning on ways I might be able to keep him in prison. Additional evidence that may have been overlooked. I feel myself tensing for battle, searching for what to do so that miserable motherfucker doesn't make life harder for Soledad.

"I don't think Pop much cares anymore." Delores shrugs. "Edward did his time, or at least most of it. He gave the money back and won't ever work in a corporate setting because this will follow him all of his days."

"When's he getting out?" I ask, glancing at the calendar on the edge of my desk.

"Next month. I figured you would want to know, considering… well, considering."

"Considering what?" I ask cautiously, frowning at her across my desk.

"That you like his wife."

"They aren't married anymore," I grit out.

"See?" Delores grins and crosses her ankles, leaning back and getting comfortable. "Like I said. You like her."

My ringtone cuts in, and Tremaine's contact photo pops up on-screen.

"I need to take this," I tell her, giving a pointed look toward my office door. "If you could close that behind you?"

She rolls her eyes but stands to leave.

"And Delores," I call, waiting for her to turn. "Thanks for the heads-up."

She smiles and waggles newly waxed brows on her way out.

"Tremaine," I answer the phone. "What's up?"

"Judah, he's...they've...He's at the hospital. Oh, God, if he—"

"Hey, slow down," I urge, even as I grab my jacket and walk out of the office as swiftly as I can. "Tell me what's going on. What's happened?"

"It's Adam," she chokes out. "He had a seizure, a bad one, and he hit his head. Just...Judah, just come."

CHAPTER FORTY-THREE

SOLEDAD

N ow, before I tell you what I've been working on," Hendrix says, leaning her elbows on my kitchen counter, "remind me who's the best manager in the whole wide world?"

"You are." I glance at my phone, noting a missed call from Brunson. I haven't heard much from the lawyer since Edward went in. I'll call him back later. I plate a slice of iced cinnamon loaf and slide it across the counter to Hendrix. "Now, what have you been working on?"

She takes a bite of the loaf and groans, dragging the whole pan to her. "This is all mine."

I drag it back, laughing. "No, it's not. I promised Yasmen I'd save her some. She's doing me a huge favor picking up Lottie and Inez. I had the live broadcast with that reality-chef person today."

"Ahh. Well, Yasmen's lucky she's doing us a favor, or no cinnamon loaf for her." Hendrix takes another bite, aiming her fork at me. "Have you heard of Haven?"

"Of course. The lifestyle brand by Sofie Baston Bishop. Really high end, right? Fashion, home, wellness." I serve up a small slice of cinnamon loaf for myself. "I used to love her stuff when I could afford it."

"What if her stuff"—Hendrix pauses to give me a huge smile— "becomes your stuff?"

"What do you mean?"

"She's looking for a partner for the budget-friendly tier of her brand, and she's seen you online. Been tracking you and is very impressed."

"What?" I'm left speechless for a few seconds, processing that someone as powerful and influential as Sofie Baston Bishop, a former top model known as the Goddess, wants to partner with me.

"She knows all the shit that went down with Edward," Hendrix continues. "Because of course she'd thoroughly vet anyone she's considering working with."

"And?" I ask, crumbling a corner of cinnamon loaf between my fingers. "Is she hesitant about working with a felon's ex-wife?"

"No hesitation at all. In fact, the way you've pulled yourself up and rallied to support your family makes the prospect of working with you even more appealing. Plus she really wants her brand to be inclusive."

"Ugh. Is it gonna be weird performative shit? Like *I'm white, but look how progressive I am working with fill-in-the-blank BIPOC?*"

"Not performative, but she does want to give back, and she would like her brand to be proactively inclusive. Her father-in-law is Indigenous. Sofie has already partnered with a few Indigenous creators on some projects. She'd love to work with you too."

"That's pretty incredible."

"It absolutely could be. She was thinking Haven x Sol, but is open to suggestions. It might be a precursor to your own lifestyle brand."

"This is big, Hen." I meet the excitement on her face with a smile of my own. "I couldn't be happier."

Hendrix chews thoughtfully, her eyes not leaving my face. "I'm 'bout to make you the mogul mama. Seems like you *could* be a little happier, actually. I expected through the roof. You're not quite at the rafters. You okay?"

"Yeah. No. I mean, I'm really happy about this. And I'm okay. Just turning a lot of stuff over in my head." I trace the pewter swirls in the marble counter. "Mostly what I'm gonna do about Judah."

"The drama with Inez?"

"Well, yes, that, but he kind of suggested we back off until I'm ready for an actual relationship."

"Were the two of you not *in* an actual relationship? Wasn't he hitting it every chance he got?"

I try to shame her with a chastising look, but this is Hendrix, and shame is not an emotion with which she's intimate.

"I'm just saying it's semantics." Hendrix shrugs. "You've come a long way since Edward left you high and dry. You needed that time right after to stand on your own two feet. You did that."

Watch me.

That was my response when Edward predicted I wouldn't survive without him. Subconsciously, his scorn was just as much a driving force as anything I'd needed to prove to myself.

"But—and correct me if I'm wrong—" Hendrix continues, "there were other things you needed too. I know you want to be whole, but I think being whole means acknowledging all your parts. And there are parts of you that want to be held, want to be needed and loved. That is just as emotionally valid as the parts of you that crave independence."

"Maybe I was so worried about making sure I'm independent," I admit, "that I didn't feel I could acknowledge those parts of me that long to share my life with someone."

"You know now that you *can* do it on your own," Hendrix says softly. "But you also know that when the right person comes along, you don't *have* to—at least not to prove something. Don't we spend enough of our lives proving shit to people?"

"He said he wants to build a life with me," I tell her, swallowing the emotion welling in my throat as I recall the rawness of his words that night. "On our terms, no one else's. I told him I'm not sure I ever want to remarry."

"And what'd he think about that?" Hendrix asks with lifted brows.

"I think his exact words were 'Who the fuck cares?'" I say, laughing a little, even while I swipe at the wetness under my eyes.

"Let's think about this, Sol." Hendrix starts counting on her fingers. "One, he stalks you online because he wants to know and understand you."

"'Stalk' is a strong word."

She bends a knowing look on me, twisting her lips.

"Okay, essentially stalking, yes." I giggle. "But in the best way."

"Two," she says, raising another finger, "Edward prioritized his goals over yours and didn't see you staying home as valuable."

"Right," I sigh, surprised to only feel a twinge of irritation at the memory, not the hurt it used to engender.

"And this man, Judah, actually stayed home with his boys, taking time from work so his ex-wife wouldn't get too far behind in her career."

"He's a saint among men, isn't he?"

"Three"—another finger—"you said he sees you reading *All About Love* and starts reading it, too, to interrogate his male privilege."

"When I asked, 'Are you reading *All About Love*?' he said, 'Aren't you?'"

"Girl, I know because he put your sperm donor in prison, it could feel like Judah is the last man you should be with," Hendrix says, putting down all three fingers to reach across the counter and squeeze my hand. "But it sounds to me like the universe delivered *exactly* the right one—someone who has seen the whole of your journey, watched you grow, understands your fears, your reservations, your boundaries, and accepts them all."

"You're so right, and it's like every time I raise the bar for what I should expect from a partner, Judah clears it. Easily. I've learned that revealing yourself to your partner should bring healing, not harm. That a true intimate relationship is a safe place with no facades. A space where you can be wholly yourself. I have that with Judah."

"Then don't throw it away. Give it a chance. Give *yourself* a chance."

The foyer door opens, interrupting us. Hendrix and I share a glance that promises to finish this conversation later.

"Hey, Mom!" Lottie bounces into the kitchen, her long hair braided into straight backs inspired by Lola's hairstyle during the holidays. "Hey, Aunt Hen."

"Hey, honey." I kiss her cheek. "How was school?"

"Great!" Her whole face lights up. "Coach said I—"

"*School.*" I wave a warning finger, but smile. "Not practice. Grades start falling and gymnastics goes away."

"That won't happen," she hastens to assure me. "I'm going to do my homework right now."

"You want a snack first?" I slide the cinnamon loaf across the counter in her direction.

"Homework!" She trots out of the kitchen. "I'll eat later."

Entering, Inez almost collides with her as Lottie leaves at a clip, following much more slowly from the front door.

"Hey, Nez," I greet her. "Yasmen with you?"

"No, she said to tell you she had to get to Grits," Inez says, "but to save her some cinnamon loaf."

I give Hendrix an *I told you so* look before returning my attention to Inez. "Good day at school?"

She hesitates, fiddles with the beads on her backpack strap. "It was... okay. Something happened. I didn't see it, but I heard about it."

"Really?" I stand and collect Hendrix's and my plates, walking them over to the dishwasher. "What happened?"

"The ambulance came," she says, her voice and eyes lowered.

"Oh no." I turn to face her. "I hope everything's okay?"

Harrington takes no chances and will call an ambulance for a hangnail, so it doesn't seem too unusual. If anything, a few parents have complained about having to foot the bill when "an emergency" could have been handled by the school nurse.

"Was it a student?" I press, trying to see the expression on Inez's lowered face. "A teacher?"

"It was Adam," she says, her eyes finally lifting to meet mine. "The ambulance came for Adam, Mom."

My heart stops—stills—sprints, and I grip the edge of the sink. "Do you mean... Judah's Adam? Adam Cross?"

Inez nods, her eyes clinging to mine. "Yeah. It was... I didn't see, but I heard he had a seizure and hit his head."

"Oh, God." My hand flies to cover my mouth and I try to catch my breath. "But he... he was okay? Was he conscious by the time the—"

"No." She shakes her head miserably. "They said he wasn't."

I don't wait for more information.

"I'll be back." I grab my purse from the mudroom. "Hen, Lupe should be home in like ten minutes. Would you—"

"Go!" she urges, concern drawing her brows together. "I got 'em."

I kick off my slippers and shove my feet into the sneakers by the door. Harrington always uses the hospital closest to the school for emergencies. I'll start there. I can't worry about Inez's speculations or if she thinks I shouldn't be with Judah, or if this will stoke her anger with me. I can't even care whether Judah would welcome having me there or not. In my mind's eye, I see my wrinkled pink slip of a grocery list tucked in the pages of Judah's copy of *All About Love*. I see bags and bags of groceries on my front porch when we had no food. I see the focaccia basket he ordered thinking I would never even know he'd done it to support me.

A collage of care, a dozen ways he has demonstrated his feelings for me. I know how fiercely he loves those boys. I'm sure his ex-wife will be there, and probably her husband too, but something screams in my head that *I* should be there. The hole that has been aching beside me since our last conversation—I can't let him feel that way now. This is what you do to support and be there for the ones you love.

Love?

I stumble, my shoe getting caught on the kitchen rug, or maybe it's my mind stumbling on this new realization.

Love?

"I'm sorry, Mom," Inez says, her words hitting my back as I race to the garage door.

I stop and turn, taking a second to study her. "Why, honey? It's not your fault. I just need to know Adam's... that Judah..."

Worry crowds my throat and lodges a knot under my ribs.

"I mean I'm sorry for..." Inez licks her lips, eyes cast down. "For before."

I walk over to her, bracketing her face between my palms and looking into her eyes. "We're good, honey. I love you."

"I love you too." She leans into my shoulder and mumbles into my shirt. "I hope he's okay."

"He will be."

I give her a quick kiss, rush out to the garage, and pray the whole way to the hospital that my words are true.

CHAPTER FORTY-FOUR

JUDAH

He's gonna be fine."

At the doctor's proclamation, I breathe for what feels like the first time in a year. The relief is dizzying, and I slump against the wall of the hospital room, swiping a shaking hand over my face.

"Jesus." Tremaine sinks to the chair beside Adam's bed and drops her face into her hands. "Thank you."

"I told you I'm fine," Adam says, though he looks worse for wear with the white bandage eclipsing part of his forehead.

"They probably just wanted a second opinion," the attending physician, Dr. Carolton, says with a kind smile. "I'm sorry your neurologist is on vacation, but I can assure you the CAT scan shows typical seizure activity for Adam's condition. We feel confident the complication came from the blow to his head when he fell."

"He's never been out like that," I say. "Even if he hit his head before, we were always able to wake him up."

"I wasn't on the scene, of course," Dr. Carolton says. "But the EMT indicated Adam gained consciousness very soon after they attended to him."

"Yeah." Adam nods. "My head hurt, but it was kinda fun riding in the ambulance."

Tremaine gives him an incredulous, chastising look. "Boy, if you don't—"

"Maybe we can talk later about how much 'fun' it was, Son," I say. "I don't think your mom's ready for that yet."

"He's on new medication." Tremaine shakes her head. "I knew we needed to monitor him more carefully."

"Hey." I touch her shoulder and wait for her to look at me. "The new meds have reduced seizures by seventy percent. They're working, but he probably won't ever be one hundred percent seizure-free. We know this. We're getting good results and doing the best we can do."

"Your husband's right," Dr. Carolton comments. "The complication came from the head injury, not the seizure itself."

"Oh, we're not married," Tremaine says. "Not anymore."

"You didn't have to say it like that," I half joke, glad after the last few harrowing hours to find some levity. "Damn, Maine."

She cracks a smile, the first since we arrived in a panic here at the hospital, and shakes her head, rolling her eyes. "You know what I mean. That reminds me, I need to call Kent. He was trying to get a flight out of Chicago when he heard what happened. I may just tell him to come home tomorrow like originally planned if we're out of the woods?"

She directs the last of the question to Dr. Carolton.

"Oh, yes." Dr. Carolton hangs Adam's medical chart on the foot of his bed. "In cases like these, we like to take precaution and observe overnight in case of concussion, but from what we're seeing, he should be fine."

"Can I stay with him?" Tremaine's voice breaks with relief, belying her placid demeanor.

"I think we can arrange that." Dr. Carolton offers an understanding smile.

"Cool," Adam says casually, but I'm sure he's thrilled he doesn't have to stay in the hospital alone.

"We'll get a cot in here," Dr. Carolton says before leaving with promises that a nurse will come through soon.

"Where's Aaron?" Adam asks.

"Ms. Coleman picked him up from school." Tremaine turns to me. "But with you *and* Adam not at the house by now, he might start to get anxious soon, Judah."

I walk over to the hospital bed. "I'm gonna go home to check on your brother, okay?" I lean down to kiss Adam's cheek.

"Okay." Adam raises anxious eyes. "Make sure he knows I'll be back tomorrow and that I'm okay."

"I will." I look to Tremaine. "Walk me out?"

She nods and turns to Adam, squeezing his shoulder. "I'll be right back."

As soon as we reach the hall and the door closes behind us, I stretch my arms out and Tremaine steps into them. "You okay?"

She allows herself to sag against me for a second, and I know that despite her apparent composure, she's shaken. Hell, I'm shaken. It's been a long time since we were in a hospital with Adam, and it never gets less terrifying.

"I'm fine." I can almost see her mentally pulling the pieces of her composure back into place. "You're the best dad. You know that?"

"Only if you admit you're the best mom." I pull away and give her hand a squeeze. "Tell Kent hello for me when you talk to him."

"Will do, and don't think you've gotten out of spilling all the tea about Ms. Charles," she says, the first sign of teasing since all of this went down today. "You've been dodging my questions for weeks."

I stiffen and force the sudden tension from my shoulders. "I've been busy is what I've been."

"Well, now that the crisis is averted, you'll have to tell me everything."

I twist my lips into a rueful curve. "Oh, there's not much to tell."

"It didn't work out?" Tremaine frowns, placing her hand on my arm to stop me from leaving.

I can't bring myself to admit that. I'm not sure it *won't* work out. I know Soledad cares about me, and I know she wants something with me, but I'm not sure it's the same thing I need from her. Until we're on the same page, what do we have?

"Let's just say it's still being *worked* out," I settle on. "When there's something to spill, you'll be the first to know."

"She seems amazing. Don't screw it up."

"Yeah, I'll try my best. I'll call from the house so you can see Aaron before he goes to bed."

"Thank you."

I turn my phone back on as soon as I walk down the hall. I called Ms. Coleman to ask her to stay with Aaron at the house, then turned the phone off because I was getting so many calls from the office. As soon as it's back on, sure enough, missed calls and text messages from CalPot flood my phone.

"They can wait till tomorrow," I mutter, looking up to orient myself and find the elevators. When I round the corner, I come to a complete stop, jarred by the sight of the woman alone in the waiting room.

"Sol?"

She's curled up in one of the pleather sofas, but she stands immediately and walks over to me, concern etched all over her face.

"Hey. Sorry to ambush you this way, but I heard about Adam and wanted to make sure he was okay. That you're okay."

"He's fine now."

"Oh, thank God." Her shoulders slump, and she closes her eyes, breathing out her relief.

Uncertainty pins my arms to my sides. I've missed her so much, and holding her, being held by her is exactly what I want after a day like this one, but I'm not sure where we stand after our last conversation.

"How'd you know?" I ask.

"Inez told me when she came home from school. She was worried about Adam. I guess a lot of students were after the ambulance came. She figured I would want to know."

"Oh, wow." I clear my throat and slide the phone back into my pocket. "Thanks for coming. For checking on us."

"Of course." She looks up and toward the bank of elevators. "Were you on your way out or..."

"Yeah. I need to get home to Aaron. Tremaine's staying here with Adam tonight."

Her face falls, her expression shuttering. "Oh. I don't want to hold you up. I know you—"

"I could walk you to your car?"

From habit, my hand strays to the small of her back, and her muscles tense. It's been two weeks, and this lightest touch feels incendiary, flaring heat from one tiny point of contact. The silence tightens around us, broken by the faint ping of the elevator as it descends.

"It's only one floor," she says, eyes lifted and fixed on the elevator's lit numbers. "I think I'll take the stairs. Get my steps in."

"Good idea." I turn to scan the smooth lines of her profile. "Let's take the stairs."

She turns to look at me, and the air between us is scorched with desire and longing and desperation. We walk swiftly to the stairs. As soon as the door closes and we're alone in the stairwell, we reach for each other. She presses me to the wall, which should feel comical since she's half my size but is such a turn-on because her hunger claws its way to the surface, calling mine out to wrestle with hers. Our teeth knock and our lips bump and our hands scramble to find purchase on any parts of each other's body we can. She clasps my neck, grips my ass, cups my face—all while straining up on her tiptoes to take the kiss deeper. It's a honeycomb kiss with sweetness hidden in crevices, tucked under her tongue and in the sweet lining of her mouth. I squeeze her butt and lift, grunting when she wraps her legs around my waist.

"I've missed you," she whispers between our lips, raining kisses over my neck and jaw.

"So much." I bury my face in the curve of her throat, inhaling the scent of jasmine. "God, Sol. Don't..."

Don't what?

Don't make me wait any longer?

Don't do this to us?

I swallow my words, the ones that would push her to move before she's ready. That would implore her to choose us. To choose the life we could have together *now*. I don't want to manipulate her, pressure her.

All the reasons that separated us the last two weeks rear in my mind, interrupting these heated seconds. I lift my head, drop my hands from her butt, and let her slide down the length of my body.

Nothing's changed. She still needs to figure out what she wants. I still want... *everything.* Not marriage or for her to sacrifice her needs, but I want a life with her on our terms with nothing held back. Until we can have that, sex is just a temporary fix. A very good one, but pale compared to what we could be.

"I better go." It takes all my willpower to set her away from me, and the few inches between us immediately pulse with need. I drag my gaze up her body with slow deliberation, committing every detail to memory. Compact and curvy, wavy hair spilling down her arms, kiss-swollen lips the color of plums.

"Judah."

Her voice, soft, urgent, prompts me to look into her eyes, something I didn't want to do for fear I might not be able to turn away. I might get lost there and forget half measures aren't enough and do whatever it takes to get me back in her bed, back in her arms, back in her life.

"Yeah?" I ask, but I take a step toward the stairwell door, backing away from the precipitous edge. From a long fall.

"Once Adam's feeling better," she says, digging her hands into her pockets and staring down at her sneakers. "I thought maybe you could come over for dinner. You and the boys."

I stop, staring at her lips even though they're no longer moving, wondering if I heard her right.

"I know they don't eat many things," she continues, eyes still lowered. "But you mentioned they love your mom's mac and cheese. Maybe I could talk to her and she could walk me through the recipe. I'm good at following recipes. I wanna at least try to—"

"You want to talk to my mother?" I demand, clarifying. "And you want us to come to dinner? At your house?"

She nods haltingly.

"Will your daughters be there?"

At that she glances up, her slight smile wry. "They do live at the house, so yeah. They'll be there for dinner."

"Soledad, what are you saying?"

"I'm saying I want what you want." Her brows knit over the earnestness in her eyes. "A life together on our terms."

For a second I don't even know how to answer, can't find words to ask about exactly what I want being dropped into my lap. It's disorienting.

"I . . . we . . . what's changed?" I ask.

She draws a deep breath and clasps her hands tightly in front of her.

"I just got back from South Carolina. My sisters and I had to clear out the house where we grew up, and I found some of the journals and diaries my mother kept."

She shakes her head, her expression self-deprecating. "I know. I probably shouldn't have read them, but I miss her so much, and there's a lot I never understood about her as a woman. Not my mom or my dad's wife, but as her own person. She shared that in her journal, and I needed to see it."

"That makes sense," I say. "Go on."

"She was in love with two men in her life." Soledad leans against the stairwell wall. "Lola's father and mine. Lola's dad was that passion that burns so hot it consumes you. Her love for my father was . . . softer, warm, not hot, but it was that enduring kind of fire that just keeps burning and lets you glow."

She bites her lip as if uncertain how to go on, but I let her figure it out in the silence, afraid anything I might say would ruin it.

"I used to think of that great passion as a vine that wraps around your soul, makes you feel wild and abandoned and almost out of control. And I thought of what she had with Dad as a seed that grows slowly within. Something you nurture over time that makes you feel safe and secure."

She looks up at me, resolve and wonder in her expression. "I was never sure I had either with Edward, but with you I've found both. You make me forget the world when you kiss me, and it's reckless and out of control, and yet there is no safer place. No one I trust more. You're a harbor, not just for me, but for your boys, for your ex, for anyone you love and who needs you. You are the seed and you are the vine, and I love you, Judah."

I let her words wash over me, soothing the uncertainty of the last two weeks, unsure of how to respond. I gather her close again, unable to stay away with what I've seen in her eyes, felt in her arms, finally spoken.

"I love you too, Sol. There's nothing I want more than a life with you."

The light in her eyes dims a fraction, and she bites her lip, squeezes her eyes shut as if afraid to see my face when she utters her next words.

"Judah, I love you, but I meant what I said. I don't know if I want marriage ever again. I do know I want *you*. Is that enough?"

I grasp her chin and wait for her to look at me, wanting to dash the uncertainty in her eyes.

"I don't care about that. By the end of my marriage, Tremaine and I were basically roommates and co-caregivers. It wasn't about passion or connection or love or any of the things that make a marriage real. I want *those* things. It doesn't matter to me if it's wrapped in a marriage license or secured by a set of rings that tell people we belong together. We know, and that may look different now than it will when our kids are gone. In my case, my kids may never be gone. I have no idea."

"And the way you're committed to them for life," she says, "is one of the things I love most about you. I'm not going anywhere either."

I can't help but think of the first time I saw her, of how Aaron reached out to her, connected with her, which is rare for him. People often underestimate him because he doesn't speak, but I think that even when he doesn't make eye contact, he's still watching. Even when he doesn't seem to be paying attention, he hears. He listens. I wonder if he saw Soledad that first night even in a way I didn't at the time—if he recognized her as someone special.

Stay.

He said it to me at one of the most crucial points in our life, and it reverberates through every cell of my body as Soledad snuggles close for one last hug.

Stay.

I haven't had much to smile about lately. Today has been hell, and the question of our future had me dragging around like I lost my best friend the last two weeks. Because in some ways I had. I've known Soledad a little over a year, but in that time, I've felt seen by her as I never have by anyone else in my life. And the possibility of having the camaraderie, the communion, the passion Tremaine said she and I both deserved—having that with the woman I've been drawn to since the moment we met? It paints a goofy grin on my face. I know it does. I can feel how ridiculously happy it makes me appear, but I can't hold it back.

"I've never seen you look like this," Soledad laughs, setting her palms on either side of my face and tipping up to kiss my nose, my cheeks, my lips.

"You've made me happy," I tell her, curling my arms around her waist and pulling her into me. "You *make* me happy."

It's true. Happiness for myself was at the top of my Me List, and I wasn't sure if I'd ever truly have it. Maybe that was the wrong thing to say since I know she's spent so much time over the last year ensuring she could be happy on her own, could be content alone, but doubt doesn't flicker through her eyes. Just a deep emotion that reflects the feeling banging against the door of my heart.

She smiles into our kiss.

"And I love being happy with you."

CHAPTER FORTY-FIVE

SOLEDAD

"That looks delicious, Soledad."

I absorb Margaret Cross's praise and study the macaroni and cheese fresh out of the oven.

"You think so?" I ask, doubt apparent in my voice as steam rises from the pan. "I hope they'll like it."

"Now listen," Margaret says from the iPad screen propped against my kitchen backsplash. "Those boys are as picky as can be. They still throw out some of Tremaine's food sometimes."

"I have actually experienced that for myself. We did three test runs. I made it and took it over to the house. The last time, Adam ate some. Aaron, however, promptly walked his over to the trash and dumped it."

We both laugh, and it eases some of my anxiety, not just about Judah's boys eating my mac and cheese but about our two families getting together for the first time.

"You nervous?" Judah's mother asks, a small smile playing on her lips.

"That obvious, huh?" I run damp palms down the front of my apron. "Very."

"There's nothing to be nervous about. You've met Tremaine. She's just glad Judah finally found someone. Kent likes whoever Tremaine likes. The boys already know you, and you have the boxed mac and cheese on standby, right?"

"Yeah." I chuckle. "I know I could just make the boxed stuff for them and save myself a lot of hard work and heartache, but I had to try."

"Then it must be *your* family you're nervous about," she says, her expression understanding.

I glance around, making sure my girls are all upstairs. "Yeah. A little. I assume you know about my ex and Judah and—"

"Yes, I'm aware. Life is always gonna be complicated, but the good stuff is worth fighting for. I know Judah thinks you're one of the best things that's ever happened to him."

Warmth blooms from my heart up to my cheeks. "I feel the same way about him."

"Then do what you gotta do to make this work. I have a feeling it won't be as hard as you think."

"I hope you're right."

A set of footsteps pounding down the stairs cuts me off.

"I should go. Thanks again for all your help with the recipe, Mrs. Cross."

"Now I done told you to call me Margaret," she chuckles. "I hope you can manage it by the time my son brings you to meet us."

"I'll try my best. Is your husband still making those Crock-Pot recipes?" I grin into the camera.

"Yes. That last one with the ground beef was the best so far."

"Awesome. Tell him I said hi. We'll talk later. Gotta go."

We sign off just as Lupe comes in.

"Need any help?" she asks, glancing around the kitchen.

"You can take these dishes into the dining room," I tell her, untying my apron.

"Okay." She grabs a serving dish of cabbage and peruses me critically. "You look nice, Mom."

I paired dark, wide-legged denim slacks with a simple white shirt embroidered with tiny orange and pink flowers. I got a blowout, and my hair hangs straight almost to my elbows.

"Thank you." I check to make sure my gold hoops are still there and didn't fall out while I was finishing the meal. "Guess it'll be time to cut our hair soon and donate, huh?"

A dark cloud passes over her face and my heart sinks. The news for Cora hasn't been good lately. She's in the hospital with an infection.

"Me and Deja are taking Lindee to the mall tomorrow to get her mind off everything," Lupe says, her voice subdued.

"You're a good friend, Lu."

"Learned from the best," she says, smiling and carrying the dish to the dining room.

"Can I help too?" Lottie bounces into the kitchen still wearing her practice leotard from gymnastics.

"You could change your clothes," I say, pulling the oven-fried chicken out and setting it on the stove. "You smell like floor exercise."

She sniffs under her arm. "Are you sure it's—"

"Yes, baby. It's you. Please take the fastest shower of your life. They'll be here soon."

She turns to leave but pauses at the door. "So Judah Cross is your boyfriend, right? That's what we're saying."

I pause, turn to face her, and prop my bottom against the kitchen counter. "Um, well, yeah. We're...we're dating."

I don't ask her if that's okay or if she has a problem with it. I love my girls, and they have been the center of my life since the day they were born, but they also deserve a happy mother. I'm happy with myself, yes, but I'm also happy with Judah. They'll leave one day, sooner than I want, and I'm not deferring my best life for anyone anymore.

A slow smile builds on her face. "That's cool, Mom."

Even with the resolve that I'll be happy with or without her approval, having it makes me feel so pleased. I step forward to whack her bottom with a dish towel. She squeals, covering her butt with both hands and rushing toward the stairs.

"Get your little musty self up to that shower." I wrinkle my nose, laughing.

I set the chicken on the dining room table and tell Lupe to go upstairs and change since she's wearing booty shorts and some tiny top that should have been retired or passed on to a younger sibling years ago. I take the next twenty minutes making sure the table is ready.

"Everything looks good," Inez says from the arched entrance to the dining room.

I turn to consider her, schooling my face into a neutral expression. Lupe and Lottie have taken the situation with Judah in stride, but Inez and I have, seemingly by silent mutual agreement, not discussed it much at all.

"Thanks." I set rolls on the table and cover them with a tea towel. "I made your fave fried chicken."

"The one you cook in the oven?" she asks, taking a tentative step into the room.

"Yup." I walk back into the kitchen and grab the mac and cheese. "This is one of the few things Adam and Aaron actually like. They're kinda picky eaters."

"He's been okay?" she asks. "Adam, I mean? He's on north campus, so I don't see him much, but I heard he's back at school and seems to be better."

"Yeah. He's doing great." I smile and nod to the refrigerator. "Could you grab that pitcher of lemonade for me?"

"Sure." She walks to the fridge, grabs the pitcher, but doesn't move. "I just wanted to say . . ."

I brace for whatever criticism she has to level at me. Let's get this over with before Judah and his family arrive. We stare at each other, my own dark eyes blinking back at me from a face so much like mine, so much like my mother's, that my heart softens.

"What is it, baby?" I ask, setting the mac and cheese on the counter while I wait.

"I'm sorry I was such a jerk."

The wording makes me smile. "Is your sister making you apologize, by any chance?"

Her mouth loosens into a grin. "Lupe did threaten me with bodily harm if I screw things up for you tonight, yeah, but I was gonna apologize anyway. I just...I still miss Dad."

My smile disintegrates at the mention of Edward, but I stand in place to hear her out.

"I know what he did was wrong," she continues. "And I know Mr. Cross was just doing his job. I wish things were still the way they used to be, though."

I don't respond because I wouldn't choose the ease of that life with the lie Edward perpetrated to maintain it. I wouldn't want the empty facade he and I shared over the authentic love and respect and passion Judah and I have. I would not go back. I only want to move forward, and I won't pretend otherwise, even for my daughter I love so much.

"But I know things won't ever be the same," Inez says after a few seconds of silence. "I guess I just wanted you to know I'll be nice to Mr. Cross and his family."

I stretch my arms out and she rushes into them, burrowing into my neck. "Thank you, honey," I tell her, kissing her hair. "I love you, okay?"

"Love you too, Mom."

The doorbell startles me, and I jump, pressing my hand over my heart.

"Oh, my God!" Inez points to me and laughs. "You are so nervous."

"Shut it." I laugh, too, and swat at her shoulder. "Take that macaroni and cheese to the table and make sure everything's ready."

She walks back to the dining room, and I draw one last calming breath before I walk to the foyer and pull open the door. Judah, Aaron, Adam, Tremaine, and the man I presume is her husband, Kent, all stand on the porch.

"Hi!" I say, stretching my smile and hoping it still looks natural. "Please come in."

I step aside, and they file in one by one.

"So nice to see you again," I tell Tremaine, whose smooth skin and neatly coiffed two-strand twists render her in long lines of elegance. I'm in awe of Tremaine, all she's done and sacrificed for her boys. The badass lawyer, soon-to-be partner, and obviously such a great friend to Judah.

"Good to see you too," Tremaine replies, gesturing to the man who stands a few inches shorter than she does. "This is my husband, Kent."

"So nice to meet you." I extend my hand for a quick shake. "I've heard a lot about you."

"Same," Kent says. "Thank you for having us. I've seen what you can do in the kitchen online. Very much looking forward to tasting for myself."

"Oh, don't get your hopes up," I tell him. "It's nothing fancy."

"Don't believe her," Judah says. "Even her grilled cheese is fancy and delicious."

I roll my eyes but smile my gratitude. "Hi, Aaron. Hi, Adam."

"Hi," Adam says, giving a small smile.

Aaron smiles a little, making brief eye contact, and it feels like a reward to me, like it always does. Both boys carry backpacks, which I know hold their cubes, fidget toys, headphones, and anything else they might need if things get overwhelming.

"Well, everything's ready in here." I lead them to the dining room and ask them to take a seat. "I'm gonna grab the girls. Be right back."

I leave the dining room and am at the base of the stairs ready to call my daughters down when I'm grabbed from behind and kissed on the cheek.

"Oh, my God," I whisper, gasping and swatting Judah away. "Do not embarrass me."

His wicked smirk, uncharacteristic, tells me how happy he is this is happening and how much he doesn't care what our families think.

"Behave," I say, but I reach up to cup his face.

"Hey, Mr. Cross," Lupe says from above.

I step back, putting a few inches between Judah and me, my smile up at her a little stiff.

"Lu, can you make sure your sisters are on their way?" I ask.

"Here we are," Lottie says, coming to stand beside Lupe. Inez joins them, and seeing the three of them up there at the rail reminds me of Lola, Nayeli, and me, always stuck together. Whole hearts.

I can't delay *breaking* their hearts a little more for much longer. When I returned Brunson's call, he told me about Edward's upcoming early release. I wanted to let Edward tell the girls about his son with Amber, and though that is the easy way for me, it's probably not best for them. I don't trust him to navigate it carefully or honestly.

I've gotten used to doing the hard things Edward wasn't man enough to handle. I'll do it again to make sure my girls have the tools to process this latest of their father's transgressions.

We made it. There was so much that could have gone wrong. So much *did* go wrong after the night our whole world was torn asunder. None of it ruined us, though. Me and my daughters are still here, stronger, closer, and the knot of nerves that's been tangled in my belly all day dissolves. We have overcome so much, and we're still standing. I'm not only standing. I'm thriving. I'm in love...with myself, and with an amazing man who couldn't be more perfect for me. We'll be fine.

"Girls, this is Mr. Cross." I look up at Judah, whose face is set in its usual stern lines, but his mouth makes the tiniest concession of a smile.

"We've met," Inez says somewhat cheekily. "Remember?"

I widen my eyes at her, but she grins unrepentantly.

"We did." Judah offers a small smile. "Good to see you again. Nice to meet you, Lottie, Lupe."

"Nice to meet you too," Lupe says.

"You have two sons?" Lottie asks, starting down the steps.

"I do." Judah's smile grows. "Wanna meet them?"

It goes better than I could have hoped. Everyone devours the cabbage, chicken, and mac and cheese. Adam surprises me and picks at the chicken a little, and he has two servings of the macaroni.

I hold my breath when Aaron raises the first spoonful of mac and cheese up to his nose for an investigative sniff. After a few seconds, he takes a tiny bite. And then another and another. I have to suppress a squeal, and I can't take my eyes off him.

"He'll stop eating if you keep staring," Judah whispers beside me.

"Sorry." I avert my eyes but sneak another glance because my heart grows a size with every bite. "He likes it! He likes it!"

Judah's muffled laughter draws a playful kick from me under the table. When I look at him, for a few seconds the whole room disappears. The humor in his eyes melts into something soft and hot and affectionate. He leans down and presses a soft kiss into my hair. I don't even check to see who's watching. I don't care, but lean into it and squeeze his hand on my knee.

Lupe and Lottie have brought the Uno cards to the table because of course they have and are playing with Adam. Typically I wouldn't have that at my dining room table, but I make an exception because it's so amazing seeing our kids interacting. After one helping of macaroni, Aaron pulls out one of his cubes and starts shifting and sliding until it's finished in no time. He must have noticed Inez watching because he takes a cube from the backpack and offers it to her. Her face lights up and they start racing. Inez will never beat him, but she's giggling and struggling and doesn't seem bothered that he beats her every time. He really is exceptional. One of Aaron's teachers suggested entering him in some local cubing tournaments. Who knows what that could lead to?

"Well, this was delicious," Tremaine says, scraping her bowl of peace cobbler and vanilla ice cream. "We need to get home, though. Tomorrow's Saturday, but I have to pop into the office for a few hours."

"Boys, you ready?" Kent asks.

The dynamic Kent has with the boys is so natural, not authoritarian, just... involved. Tremaine and Judah are some of the most mature co-parents I've ever seen. There is obviously so much love and respect and friendship between them.

"It's still early," Judah says, reaching for my hand.

I look down at our joined hands and remind myself not to pull away. I know it's deliberate on his part, acclimating everyone to us being together, and he's right. I lean into him a little.

"It is," I agree. "Did you have something in mind?"

"A drive? The boys are headed to Tremaine's for the weekend, and I have a surprise outside to show you if that's okay?"

"We've got the dishes, Mom," Lupe says.

I didn't realize she was close enough to hear.

"Yeah, we got it, Mom," Inez says, looking from Judah to me, her grin small, but there. "Just don't break curfew."

"I won't keep her out long," Judah reassures her with a smile.

We laugh and say our final goodbyes to Tremaine, Kent, and the boys.

"Okay. I'll be back," I tell the girls, and grab my jacket from the mudroom. "Make sure that kitchen floor is—"

"Clean enough to eat off of," Lottie interrupts, rolling her eyes and gathering dishes from the dining room table. "We know."

"Thanks for having us over, ladies," Judah says to them. "And for letting me borrow your mom. I'll bring her right back."

"You can keep her for a while," Lupe says. "We could use the break."

"Very funny," I say, punching her arm lightly. "I'll be back."

We step out onto the porch and into the cool night. We are on the cusp of spring, and I draw in a lungful of crisp air and then blow out all the tension I carried preparing for tonight, hoping it would go even half as well as it did.

"We did it," I tell Judah. "We had dinner with our families and no blood was shed."

"Of course we did." He reaches for my hand again, guiding me down the porch steps. "I told you it would be fine."

"I know, but..."

I spot the motorcycle parked in my driveway, gleaming in the light from the streets and the moon. "Oh, my God, Judah!"

I turn to him and cover my mouth, beaming and meeting the pride and excitement in his eyes.

"Is that the—"

"1981 Honda CM400?" He steps behind me and slips his arms around my middle. "Yeah, now that you mention it, I think it is."

"Your Me List!"

"My dad and I finished the bike over Christmas, and I had it shipped here."

"It's purple." I twist to peer up at him over my shoulder. "But...I thought you said you couldn't pull off purple?"

"And I thought you said purple was your favorite color."

I'm momentarily stunned, not just by the act itself, that he painted the motorcycle purple, but that over and over he demonstrates how he listens and how he considers me.

"I have to be careful around you," I say faintly. "You pay attention to everything I say."

"Damn right I do." He kisses behind my ear, pulling me closer to his chest. "You up for a ride?"

"I've never been on a motorcycle before," I say, stifling the delight that tries to spill out all over the place.

"If you can hold on to me," he says, pulling me down the drive and toward the bike, "you'll be fine."

We stop in front of the motorcycle, moonlight reflecting off the purple and chrome.

"If holding on to you is all it takes," I say, wrapping my arms around him, tipping my head back to stare into his eyes, "then I'll be fine."

He lowers his forehead to mine, and I twine my fingers with his. Like always, just the touch of our hands sends a thrill through me, as if our hearts meet and beat between our palms. "I love you, Judah."

He dips to dust kisses along the curve of my throat.

"I adore you," he says, his breath at my ear raising an army of goose bumps, "Soledad *hermosa*."

At every turn this man demonstrates his care, his interest, his need to know and understand who I am. I'm seen in a way I've never been seen. After the neglect and disrespect of my marriage, Judah is a gift that's been fashioned especially for me.

"We better get going," Judah says, stepping away and nodding to the motorcycle. "Before your curfew hits and the girls come looking for us."

I laugh and, listening to his instructions, swing my leg over the bike and slip on the helmet he offers me. He pulls my hands around his waist and covers them with his own.

"Remember, you have to hold on tight."

"Don't go superfast," I squeak. "Have you driven one of these before?"

"Sol," he says, and I feel the vibration of his chuckle through his back, in my chest, "how do you think it got here?"

"I mean before tonight." I giggle, a girlish giddiness bursting like a cherry in my chest, oozing joy even though we haven't started moving yet.

"Yes, I used to ride all the time. Now be quiet before I make you purify yourself in Lake Minnetonka."

"Oh!" I lean forward and nip his ear. "Am I supposed to be your Apollonia?"

"I am definitely not your prince," he says dryly, stepping down on the kick-starter, coaxing a roar from the machine pulsing with restrained power beneath us.

"I disagree," I tell him, pressing my cheek to his back and squeezing him as hard as I possibly can. "You are my prince."

But there's nothing for him to save me from, because I've saved myself. He doesn't have to awaken me with a kiss. I'm wide awake, reborn, rebirthed through my own fire and pain and work and wisdom. He grips my arm around him but doesn't hold me back. I've never been held so tightly and still felt so free. With the wind rushing through my hair, the night sky overhead—an onyx quilt stitched with brilliant stars—and the bike devouring mile after mile as we ride though the city, emotion swells and overflows. Tears spill, but the cool night breeze licks them away before they have time to fall. I don't ask where we're headed, and I'm not sure he has a specific destination in mind. The ride is the point, and that we are on this road together.

EPILOGUE

SOLEDAD

About a Year Later

> "I fall in love with myself and I want someone to share it with me."
>
> —Eartha Kitt, iconic actress

It's not every day you wake up in Morocco with the man you love eating breakfast between your legs.

"Judah, Jesus." I blink dazedly up at the ceiling fan leisurely rotating overhead, my yawn swallowed by a moan as I push through layers of sleep. "Again? I can barely move after last night."

"Shhh." He doesn't bother lifting his head but slides his hands under my thighs and spreads them wider. "I'm trying to eat."

With deft fingers he peels me back, opening his mouth wide over me and sucking, licking, worshipping. My toes curl and pleasure crawls up my calves, kisses behind my knees, tightening my muscles like a tender vise. I dig my heels into the luxurious sheets, jerking, my back arching, one hand rifling through the short curls around my ears, the other cupping his head, pushing him deeper into me. He sends his fingers to skim up my torso, squeezing my breast, plucking my nipple.

"Not fair," I gasp. "You know what that does to me."

He chuckles, cool air misting the hot, wet place he's still giving his full attention. And then he shifts, flipping us with easy strength so that he's changed positions, him on his back and me on top. Grabbing my butt, he coaxes me up and up and up until my knees splay the width of his shoulders, and he urges me down onto his face.

This is my fantasy come to life. I glance over at the bedside table where his black-rimmed glasses rest, and it makes me even wetter, wilder. A whimper floats up from my throat, spilling into the room, which is quiet save for the sounds of my tortured pleasure and his greedy mouth feasting. I roll my hips over his face, all inhibitions gone, wafting on the Mediterranean breeze. Gripping the headboard with one hand, I squeeze my breast with the other, losing myself in leagues of rapture so deep, I gasp for breath. Judah's big hands tighten on my thighs, stretching me to my limit, his hunger voracious and consuming.

When I come, the orgasm wrests a strangled cry from me, and I sob, pressing my temple to the headboard, tears slicking my face, desire slicking my thighs. I'm a mess, disoriented even as he lifts me and flips me onto my back. Unhesitatingly, he hooks an elbow under my knee and plunges in raw, nothing between us. It's all the more intimate because of the trust that bare act requires, the trust that another broke before, fully restored with this man.

"Shit," he grunts, squeezing his eyes closed as, still orgasming, I clench around him. "So fucking tight, Sol. I love you."

"So much." I hook my ankles at the base of his spine, lifting to greet him, to meet him. I grip his neck and bring him down for a sloppy kiss that tastes like me and like him and like abandonment. It tastes like our devotion, and I lick the corners of it. I swipe my tongue into his mouth and leave nothing unloved. He braces one muscled arm over us, his palm flat to the wall as he pistons into me, shaking the bed, shaking my *foundations* until I crumble for him again, and he, with a hoarse cry, crumbles for me.

In the aftermath, we lie quiet, unmoving, like we're afraid to disrupt a sacred ritual. We stay joined, even as he lifts his head to find my gaze with his, love blazing there. Not looking away, he kisses me, trailing his lips down my jaw, over the curve of my shoulder, down to suck my breasts. He hardens inside me.

"Don't you dare," I croak, my voice shredded from last night's screams and this morning's shrieks. "You have to give me a minute, an hour. You're insatiable."

"For you," he whispers at my collarbone. "Okay. You've earned a break, but I'll be back."

He pulls out, stands, and rips the sheets away, exposing my body, naked and spent, to the cooler morning air.

"Shower," he declares, scooping me up in his arms and walking through the bathroom.

"I can walk," I tell him, my head lolling against his shoulder, but I'm not sure. My legs feel rubbery and my knees are Jell-O.

"I can carry." He drops a kiss in my hair, walking us past the sunken tub and massive shower out through the open door to the shower outside. He eases me down, my damp skin dragging over his, imprinting the love and passion of moments ago. My feet touch down and I lift my face to the Moroccan sun, smiling at the warm rays and the cool breeze. Our hotel villa is so secluded, privacy isn't a worry, and we've taken full advantage, open-air lovemaking every chance we get.

"This is perfect," I tell him.

"Perfect," he says, testing the weight of my breasts in his hands.

"Judah," I laugh, opening my eyes to meet the adoration in his stare. "Wash."

"Whatever my girl wants." He squeezes the soap into his hands and runs them over my hands and legs, my breasts and shoulders, taking special care between my legs. He doesn't miss the chance to stroke me, to invade me. My breath catches at the delicious punishment for denying him earlier. I repay the favor, clasping him with soapy hands, running up and down and up and down until his head tips back and with a groan he spurts over my fingers. I grin up at him, satisfied to have so easily undone him, marveling at the taut planes and corded muscles of his well-conditioned body. Every inch of him is a testament to his discipline, so controlled in every area of his life. Only I get to see that control bend and snap for me, to see it collapse at the altar our bodies build together.

He turns me around so my back is to him as he massages shampoo into the shorn waves and curls rioting around my ears and neck.

"You miss it?" I ask, twisting my head to peer up at him. "My hair?"

"You look beautiful either way." He kisses my nape. "And it was for a good cause."

I bend my head so he can rinse the suds from my hair and body.

"Lupe and Deja were so proud when we took our hair in to donate. Thank God Cora is in remission." I breathe out my relief. "It was touch and go there for a minute. I know better than anyone that it could have gone another way. So glad she pulled through. It made cutting our hair feel like such a moment of triumph."

"Wasn't that one of your most viewed posts when you shared it?"

"Yeah, and I loved that the girls really got to see the impact of it, to see how people all over the world responded to what they did. Those girls are amazing."

"You and Yasmen are amazing. You've raised great young women."

"Speaking of which," I say, reaching for the towels neatly folded nearby. "We need to call home today. I have a few things I need to do first."

He takes one of the towels and dries my hair with brisk swipes and strokes. "We're on vacation."

"Technically I'm working, babe," I remind him. "This hotel wants at least a little content in exchange for flying me here and putting me and my fine ass plus one up in this luxurious villa."

"I know. Proud of you. This is impressive. They only brought huge creators for this campaign. Really cool you're one of them."

"And will you let me include a few shots of you?" I tip up onto my toes. "Please? My followers want to meet the amazing man who won my heart."

He rolls his eyes but nods reluctantly. He is not a guy who flaunts his private life, and I respect that, but I have a community that is a huge part of my career and life. These women walked with me, as I walked with so many of them, through my #datingmyselfchallenge journey.

The response to seeing me find someone has been overwhelmingly positive. They've seen cropped shots of Judah and me holding hands on our first real date when I wore *the* black dress for him. They've seen carefully curated footage that provided glimpses of him and are constantly asking for a boyfriend "reveal."

Once we're both dry and in our robes, we order breakfast, planning the day as we dig into the fried eggs with olives and soft cheese. I scoop up honey and butter and oil with the *msemen* bread. We pluck grapes and pomegranate from the selection of fruit.

"You want to call the girls?" he asks, glancing at his watch. "It's early afternoon."

"I think I'll wait a little. They've been working at the bookstore during the day while they're staying with Lola. Best summer job ever."

"I bet they're having the time of their lives."

"They are." I stretch my legs out and wriggle my toes, still feeling languid from exhaustion, little sleep, and multiple orgasms. "They love Olive, of course."

"Things getting serious with her and Lola?"

My grin is wide and immediate. Seeing my sister get her happily ever after is as rewarding as getting my own. "They are. I wouldn't be surprised if we hear wedding bells soon. They've known each other forever, and starting the business together in Austin has only made them closer."

My good humor sours as I recall the last conversation with my sister.

"Lola told me she overheard the girls talking about Edward." I bite my lip and run an impatient hand through my hair. "Ever since I told them about the baby and Amber, something's shifted."

"What do you mean?" Judah plucks a grape from the bowl and sips his orange juice.

"For Lupe, I think it was like the last straw. She's the oldest, so she understands the most and had a lot less tolerance for her dad's bullshit. Inez and Lottie had some hero worship left, though it was really damaged. Knowing he was cheating was bad enough, but having a baby with another woman?"

I tug on my bottom lip, the worry creeping in over how my girls are processing the latest revelations about their trifling father.

"Sol, there's something I need to tell you," Judah says, leaning forward.

The sudden solemnity of his voice, in his eyes, snares my full attention.

"What?" I ask, gripping the collar of my robe at my neck. "It's about the girls?"

"No." He holds out his arms. "Come here."

I stand, my heart in my throat as I wait to know what put that look on his face. He pulls me down to his lap and sits back, releasing an extended exhalation. I lean into his chest, curling my legs under me on his knees, and tip my head back to study his face. "Just tell me."

"Edward is gone."

The news punches me in the chest, and shock paralyzes me for a second before a slew of questions flood my mind and spew from my mouth.

"Gone? What do you mean, gone? Gone where? How can he—"

"Left the country." Judah angles a careful look at me from under straight, dark brows. "After you told me your suspicions there might be more money we hadn't found, I dug some and did uncover another trail. I've been keeping very tight tabs on him. If he sneezed, I knew about it."

"And he sneezed?"

"He didn't check in with his probation officer, and he hasn't been seen or heard from in over a week. I had some surveillance on Amber. She and the baby are gone too. Probably with whatever money we never found to some place that doesn't have an extradition treaty with the US."

For a moment rage, the kind that only Edward has ever inspired, falls over my eyes like a red haze, and I want to feel the weight of my machete, find something he holds dear to destroy. My breath labors and my face is awash with heat because this is one more mess he's left for me to explain and navigate for the girls. One more trauma he's thoughtlessly inflicted and then run off after to pursue his own interests and pleasure. But then another emotion intrudes, overtakes.

Relief.

I'm rid of him. Like venom sucked from a bite and spat out. If he truly won't come back for fear of arrest, then maybe I'll never have to see his lying face again. Tears spring to my eyes. That son of a bitch has made me cry so many times, but these are cleansing tears, cathartic tears. I bury my face in the soft cotton of Judah's robe and let them flow, curling into him, holding on to him while he rubs my back and kisses my hair.

"I'm sorry," he says, once I'm spent and lying against his chest with tear-wet cheeks. "I know this is a lot to process."

I pull back to look at him, searching his face. "You know I'm happy he's gone, right?"

He lets his head fall back to the soft cushion of the lounge chair. "I hoped you would be, but I know this is complicated, especially for the girls."

"Did you tell CalPot about the new accounts you found?"

He hesitates, scraping his teeth over his bottom lip before shaking his head. "No."

"Did you...confront Edward?" I ask, confused because it's strange for Judah not to follow a trail to its resolution.

"No."

"Why not? You could have—"

"I wanted him out of your life more than I wanted to catch him," Judah says, his voice going curt, steely. "I wanted him out of your daughters' lives. He's not a good man and he never will be. The longer he's around, the more he'll fail them and make things harder for you."

Fresh tears sting my eyes because I'm so grateful, not just for this one act he has done but for *him*. Nothing in my mother's diaries, nothing I read in bell hooks's musings, could have prepared me for this man. For this astonishment of care and joy and grace.

Our lives are complicated. I have a few more years before I'm an empty nester, and in some ways, Judah may never be. Aaron may live in alternate housing, or maybe in an apartment over Judah's garage, depending on how much independence he wants and can handle. Adam may go off to college but is more likely to attend one really close to home. They may marry. May find life partners. Who knows how the boys' paths, their lives will change throughout the years.

Maybe one day I'll want to marry again. Or Judah and I may live together once the girls strike out on their own. I don't know the shape our relationship will take through every stage as the years go by, but I do know we'll be together. That commitment is so solid I feel it every time Judah holds my hand, a promise pressed between our palms like an oath our souls make. A vow our hearts confess.

"I love you, Judah Cross," I tell him, cupping his jaw and kissing that stern mouth until it gentles as it always does for me.

"I love you, Soledad Charles." He squeezes me, his eyes brimming with respect and adoration. "I'm so damn proud of you, sweetheart."

I know a goofy grin blooms on my face. This is what Hendrix calls my "resting joy face," and she says it's how I look when I talk about Judah. I can't help it. As hard as I try, I'm *not* the cool mom. I'm not the cool anything. I'm the girl who has always loved too hard and offered too much, sometimes to those who didn't deserve it. I always felt so distant from this feeling that burns between Judah and me. Like I watched it from afar in others. It was evident between Yasmen and Josiah even when they were divorced. Mami and Dad had their own version of it. It always crackled beneath the surface of Mami and Bray's every interaction until they could no longer ignore it and had to run back for this feeling. The sense that after being on your own—sometimes lonely and sometimes contentedly alone—you look down to find a dangling thread in your hands. One end of infinity, and across years and circumstances, he stands there holding the other. The ends of forever reunited and tied together.

It has been a long road to finding this feeling because I had to find myself first. Had to know and honor myself first. I now realize you can risk loving completely when you completely love yourself. Even if your heart is broken, it doesn't mean *you* will break. I've never been more sure of Judah and of me. This moment, this lifetime with him, no matter what shape it takes, is all I could have hoped for. It's what I prayed for but wasn't sure could be. I wasn't sure *we* could be. I suffered a betrayal so devastating it could have hardened me, could have taught me to withhold my heart. Instead, I have learned to *save* my heart for one worthy of it.

We exchange kisses and breaths and heartbeats, completely content in each other's arms and under a sun that belongs to only us.

Your skin is summer night and your kiss is all I want.

It's a silent whisper in my head as I hold him. He's a miracle in my arms, and I tremble with wonder and awe. I don't say the words aloud, but leave them a conversation with my heart—the sentiment an heirloom Mami passed down to me, like so many other secrets pressed between pages. That she was indeed a hornet, not a butterfly. That the plain of her heart stretched vast enough to love two men so completely, love her children so purely, love her mother and her friends and the world around her with such quiet fervor... because first she loved herself.

DON'T MISS HENDRIX'S STORY,
COMING IN SPRING 2025

READING GROUP GUIDE

DISCUSSION QUESTIONS

1. When the book opens, Judah and Tremaine are meeting with a social worker to determine living arrangements for their boys as part of the "collaborative divorce." What were your initial impressions of them as a couple? As parents?

2. Soledad's marriage is obviously in trouble. She knows something is amiss and has suspicions, but can never "catch" Edward. Have you ever found yourself in a relationship, romantic or otherwise, when you knew something was off but had no proof? If so, how did you handle it?

3. The attraction between Soledad and Judah at the Christmas party is instant. What were your thoughts about Soledad as a married woman, albeit in a troubled marriage, feeling that pull to another man?

4. At one point, Hendrix mentions being surprised someone as driven as Soledad never wanted a career. Soledad pushes back a little, saying she never wanted to work outside her home, and articulates the vocational validity of being a homemaker. How does that viewpoint challenge cultural ideas about women and ambition?

5. Once everything is revealed about Edward's embezzlement scheme, Soledad has to figure out a new path for herself and her girls, including how she'll leverage her skills to earn a living. Have you ever had to make a major life pivot? If so, how did you handle having to call on new skills or chart new territory?

6. Judah and Soledad are both devoted parents who have always put their children first and made sacrifices so they could have the best, but both acknowledge the value of children having parents who are happy. There have been times when they have forgone or delayed something they wanted for the sake of their children. How is this philosophy beneficial/noble? How could it be dangerous or harmful?

7. One of the most complex characters of the story doesn't have one scene. Catelaya, Soledad's mother, is a quiet study in contrasts and conflicts. Her story raises the idea of a child seeing her mother as a fully dimensional woman, beyond the maternal role. What were your impressions of Soledad's mother? How would you think about your mother or other parental figure beyond a caregiver role?

8. At one point, Soledad says, "There aren't enough sonnets for friendship." With this statement, Soledad seems to be saying we sometimes esteem friendship less than romantic love. Do you agree? Hendrix and Yasmen support Soledad, not only emotionally but financially at times, during this tough season of her life. Have you ever had or been that kind of friend during difficult times?

9. Inez is definitely the "daddy's girl" of the bunch. Did you sympathize at all with her perspective? Did you find yourself frustrated with her persistent desire to have a relationship with Edward even once she knew what he'd done? Is that realistic? Complicated? What are your thoughts?

10. One of the most poignant scenes occurs in the game store when Aaron has a meltdown. In this sequence and throughout the story, what do we learn about Judah as a father? About the two boys and how they depend on each other?

11. As part of her recovery after the divorce, Soledad self-partners and "dates herself," a process of self-discovery and contentment creation. What does she learn about herself? Did you think it was necessary? Have you ever had a similar season of life?

12. Do you have a favorite or least favorite character in the story, or one with whom you most identify? If so, why do they make you love and/or dislike them?

13. Was there a scene you enjoyed most? If so, what did you enjoy about it? Was there a scene that made you uncomfortable? If so, why?

14. Once Soledad and Judah pursue the attraction between them, it's a very passionate physical relationship. Did you consider this a "slow burn"? How would you characterize their physical and emotional intimacy as the story progresses?

15. Both are parents just entering their forties. So often, romance features younger heroines. Is there value in seeing a woman in or approaching middle age being this sexual? Why do you think we don't see it more?

16. If you read *Before I Let Go* and met Soledad in that book, did anything surprise you about her as you got to know her in her own story?

17. Soledad isn't sure she'll ever want to marry again. Josiah is more concerned about the quality of their relationship—that it's passionate, honest, supportive—than its legal standing. There are a lot of variables about their future, including the needs of Judah's boys, that could affect the shape their relationship takes. The vast majority of romance novels end with marriage and children. Judah and Sol have already experienced those things, and their HEA looks different. How did you feel about this somewhat unconventional happily ever after?

PLAYLIST

Scan here for the *This Could Be Us* playlist.

RECIPES

Picadillo

Ingredients

- 2 tablespoons olive oil
- 1 potato, diced
- 1 cup *sofrito* (You can buy this at the grocery store, but it's so easy to make. Check out *Diasporican: A Puerto Rican Cookbook* by Illyanna Maisonet for a great, simple recipe.)
- ½ cup yellow onion, chopped
- ⅓ cup green bell pepper, chopped
- ⅓ cup red bell pepper, chopped
- ⅓ cup yellow bell pepper, chopped
- 3 cloves garlic, minced
- 1 pound ground beef (or turkey or a meatless substitute for Lupe ☺)
- 1 teaspoon ground cumin
- Salt and pepper, to taste
- 2 tablespoons *sazón*
- 1 cup tomato sauce
- ¼ cup olives with pimiento, diced
- White rice, for serving

Preparation

Add the olive oil to a medium-sized pan/skillet over medium-to-high heat. Add the diced potato. Sauté the sofrito for 2 to 3 minutes, turning the heat down to low-medium once it's slightly brown. Add the yellow onion, bell peppers, and minced garlic. Stir for 2 to 3 minutes.

Add the ground beef, cumin, salt and pepper, and sazón. Stir and cook for 2 minutes.

Add the tomato sauce and sliced olives. Stir all the ingredients until they're evenly mixed. Increase the heat to medium until the meat is browned, uncovering occasionally to stir.

Turn the heat down and cook to desired consistency.

Serve over white rice.

Ooey-Gooey Brownies

Ingredients

- 1 cup semisweet chocolate chips (I recommend Ghirardelli Bittersweet 60% Cacao Baking Chips)
- 1 cup (2 sticks) butter, softened
- 1¼ cups confectioners' sugar
- 1 cup brown sugar
- 1 tablespoon vanilla extract
- 3 large eggs
- 1¼ cups flour
- ½ teaspoon salt
- ½ cup unsweetened cocoa powder
- ½ cup milk chocolate chips

Preparation

Preheat the oven to 350°F. Line a 9 × 9-inch pan with nonstick foil or parchment paper.

Melt the semisweet chocolate chips for about 1 minute in a microwave-safe bowl/container. Let sit for a minute and then stir to a smooth texture.

Add the butter, both sugars, vanilla, and eggs. Mix well. Whisk in the flour, salt, and cocoa powder.

Stir in the milk chocolate chips.

Transfer the batter to the pan and bake for 35 to 40 minutes (until a toothpick or fork comes out with just a few crumbs attached). Cooking a little less makes it gooier!

Allow to cool and cut into squares to serve.

Strawberry-Lemon Prosecco Sangria

Ingredients

- 1 lemon, thinly sliced
- 2 tablespoons sugar
- ¼ cup strawberries (stems off, sliced)
- 750-milliliter bottle chilled prosecco

Preparation

Lay the lemons in the bottom of a pitcher or punch bowl.

Sprinkle the sugar on top and smash the sugar into the lemons with the back of a spoon or a muddler.

Add the sliced strawberries.

Smash the strawberries in with the sugar and lemon slices.

Add the prosecco to the pitcher or bowl.

Serve right away or store in the refrigerator until ready to serve.

Pour sangria over ice and serve in glasses.

Peace Cobbler

Ingredients

- 4 tablespoons butter
- ¾ cup sugar, plus 1 tablespoon, for sprinkling
- ¾ cup all-purpose flour
- ¼ teaspoon salt
- 1 teaspoon baking powder
- ¾ cup milk (or do you! Use whatever dairy sub floats your lactose intolerance)
- 2 cups sliced fresh (or canned—no judgment!) peaches, or whole blueberries, strawberries, raspberries, blackberries, or a combination of fruits (or substitute a 12-ounce package of frozen berries). Get creative and fruity!
- Whipped cream or ice cream, for serving (optional)

Preparation

Preheat the oven to 350°F.

Use the 4 tablespoons butter to grease an 8 × 8-inch square or 9-inch round pan.

Place the pan in the oven until the butter is melted. Remove the pan from the oven and set aside.

Whisk together the ¾ cup sugar, flour, salt, and baking powder in a bowl. Whisk in the milk. A smooth batter should form.

Pour the batter into the pan you set aside.

Toss the fruit over the batter and sprinkle with 1 tablespoon sugar.

Bake for about an hour, until the top is lightly browned and the fruit bubbles.

Adding a dollop of whipped cream or ice cream would be a good idea!

Aunt Evelyn's Pear Preserves

Ingredients

- 8 half-pint jars
- 12 fresh pears, peeled, cored, and sliced
- 2 cups sugar
- 1½ cups water
- 2 tablespoons lemon juice

Jar Preparation

Wash the jars, lids, and bands in hot, soapy water. Rinse and drain. Fill a canner with water and place the jars on the rack. If you don't have a canner, you can use a pot deep enough to hold water and the jars. You can also boil the bands and lids in the pot, too, if you like. Bring the water to a medium heat. Turn the heat down, but keep the jars hot until it's time to fill them with the mixture.

Preparation

Combine the pears, sugar, water, and lemon juice in a stockpot.

Cook uncovered for 1 to 1½ hours. The mixture will thicken. Remove the pot from the heat. With canning tongs or some equivalent, remove the jars (the lids and bands) from the canner/pot. Scoop the mixture into 8 hot half-pint jars. Leave about ¼ inch of headspace in each jar. Slide a plastic knife or nonmetallic spatula around in the mixture to remove air bubbles. Center the lids on the jars. Screw the bands down until tight. Put the jars back into the canner/pot in hot water. You want about 1 inch of water over the jars. Let the jars boil on the rack in the canner for 7 to 10 minutes. Turn off the heat and let the jars stand for

5 minutes. Remove the jars from the water and set aside to cool. Don't disturb the jars at all while cooling.

Refrigerate any unsealed jars and use within a few days of processing. Store the sealed jars of preserves in a cool, dark place until ready for use.

ACKNOWLEDGMENTS

This Could Be Us is one of the most deeply personal books I've written in many ways. At the same time, there are so many things beyond and outside my lived experience that made this story so fascinating to write. I especially want to thank the Puerto Rican women who held extensive conversations with me about the heritage and traditions that I hope enrich Soledad's story. Your insight and care as you read early iterations of this novel made it something I hope will prove richly resonant for many readers.

To the actually autistic foks and loved ones of those on the spectrum who so generously shared your experiences, thank you! There is no one way to be autistic. There is no one expression or presentation of it, but you shared the myriad, personal, unique ways you've lived it, and this story is richer and, I hope, more representative for your involvement. And last, but so not least, I want to thank my boys. You are the only ones. The only ones who truly know what the last twenty years have been negotiating our family's autism journey. This book is for my son, who has taught me more about unconditional love than any single person on the planet. Who showed my heart what it was truly capable of. I had no idea it could expand this way, but you did it, kid.

To my husband, who has been whatever this life required of him. Provider. Stay-at-home dad. Partner and lifetime friend. I know that you saw some of your own fierce love in the way Judah loves his boys. I'll never forget sharing "that" scene with you before the book was done. You read it and got emotional, whispering, "It's us."

Yes, my love. It's us, and this one is for you.

ABOUT THE AUTHOR

USA Today bestselling author and Audie® Award winner **Kennedy Ryan** writes for women from all walks of life, empowering them and placing them firmly at the center of each story and in charge of their own destinies. Kennedy and her writings have been featured in NPR, *Entertainment Weekly, USA Today, Glamour, Cosmo, Ebony, TIME,* and many others. The co-founder of LIFT 4 Autism, an annual charitable book auction, she has a passion for raising autism awareness. She is a wife to her lifetime lover and mother to an extraordinary son.

Find out more at:
  KennedyRyanWrites.com
  TikTok: Kennedyryanauthor
  Facebook.com/KennedyRyanAuthor
  X: @KennedyRWrites
  Instagram: @KennedyRyan1